this book ma

Carol Mar_ting the

her job title. Thr_

she put writer. Then it asked what Carol did for relaxation and she put down the truth – writing. The third question asked for her hobbies. Well, not wanting to look obsessed she crossed the fingers on her hand and answered swimming but, given that the chlorine in the pool does terrible things to her highlights – I'm sure you can guess the real answer.

Married to the man she met at eighteen, **Susanne Hampton** is the mother of two adult daughters, Orianthi and Tina. Her varied career titles have included dental nurse, personal assistant, contract manager and now Medical Romance author. The family also extends to a maltese shih-tzu, a poodle, three ducks and four hens. Susanne has always read romance novels and says, 'I love a happy ever after so writing for Mills & Boon is a dream come true.'

Several years ago, **Josie Metcalfe** had a blood transfusion during an operation and went into anaphylactic shock. Afterwards, she discovered that she could no longer read. When her husband came home with a bag full of Mills & Boons it took a solid month of blood, sweat, and tears to finish reading the first one, but by the time she was fit to work again she had read them all and was hooked. Then her husband nudged her into action by daring her to write them, too! And the rest is history!

Twins

Twins:
Their Twin
Baby Surprise

CAROL MARINELLI

SUSANNE HAMPTON

JOSIE METCALFE

MILLS & BOON

First Published in Great Britain 2020
By Mills & Boon, an imprint of HarperCollins*Publishers*
1 London Bridge Street, London, SE1 9GF

TWINS: THEIR TWIN BABY SURPRISE
© 2020 Harlequin Books S.A.

Baby Twins to Bind Them © 2015 Carol Marinelli
Twin Surprise for the Single Doc © 2016 Susanne Panagaris
Miracle Times Two © 2011 Josie Metcalfe

ISBN: 978-0-263-29867-3

MIX
Paper from
responsible sources
FSC™ C007454

This book is produced from independently certified FSC™ paper to ensure responsible forest management.

For more information visit: www.harpercollins.co.uk/green

Printed and bound in Spain
by CPI, Barcelona

BABY TWINS TO BIND THEM

CAROL MARINELLI

CHAPTER ONE

Before

'YOU PAGED ME to see a patient.'

'No, I didn't.' Candy, holding an armful of sheets, smiled when it would have been far easier to stand there and gape. He was stunning—tall, slender, wearing a suit and a tie. His dark brown hair was cut short and his voice was so deep and commanding that it stopped Candy in her tracks. She met his chocolate-brown eyes fully and it took a moment to respond normally. 'Who are you here to see?'

'A Mr Thomas Heath.'

Candy walked over to the board. Emergency at the London Royal Hospital was quiet this afternoon but as she was in Resuscitation Candy didn't know which patients were in the cubicles. After a quick scan of the board, she located Mr Heath. 'He's in cubicle seven. Trevor's the nurse looking after him. He must be the one who paged you.'

'Thanks for that. By the way I'm Steele.'

'Steele?'

He watched as her very blue eyes moved to his name

badge. 'Well, Dr Guy Steele, if you'd prefer to be formal,' he said.

'Steele will do.' She must look like a dental commercial, Candy thought, for she simply couldn't stop smiling at him. He must be thirty or mid-thirties, which was a lot more than her twenty-four years, and he was also way older than anyone she had ever fancied, yet he had this impact, this presence, that had Candy's heart galloping in her chest.

'And you are?' he asked.

'Candy. Candy Anastasi.' She watched a smile twitch on his lips as she said her name. 'I know, I know, I should be tall, leggy and blonde to carry off a name like that!' Instead, she was short and a bit round with long black ringlets and piercing blue eyes. 'There's a story there.'

'I can't wait to hear it, Nurse Candy.'

He had the deepest voice that she'd ever heard. Like a headmaster, he was stern and bossy, yet it was all somehow softened by a very beautiful mouth that she could barely drag her eyes from. 'You'll never hear the story of my name,' Candy said.

'Oh, we'll have to see about that.'

Had they been flirting? Candy wondered as sexy-as-hell Steele walked off.

'Who's that?' Kelly said as they started to strip one of the resuscitation beds.

'Steele!' Candy said in a deep low voice, making Kelly laugh. She continued speaking gruffly while they bent over and tucked the sheet in. 'Or Dr Guy Steele if we want to be formal and, young lady, I'm going to make your eardrums reverberate with my deep—'

'Nurse Candy?'

Candy froze when she realised that Steele was behind her.

'Could I borrow your stethoscope?' he asked.

She laughed at being caught impersonating him and turned around and took her stethoscope from her neck and held it out to him, yet pulled back as he went to take it. 'You can,' she said, the stethoscope hovering. 'Just so long as you stop calling me Nurse Candy.'

He just took the stethoscope, smiled and walked off.

They made up all the beds and checked the crash trolleys and then gave up pretending to be busy, given that Lydia, the manager, was in her office. Instead, they took a jug of iced tea to the nurses' station, where Steele was tapping away on the computer. It was a lovely early summer day but the air-conditioning was struggling and it was nice to sit on the bench and gossip, though Steele had a couple of questions for her.

'How do you get into the pathology lab to check results?' he asked, not looking around.

'You've got your password?' Candy checked.

'I have and I've got into…' He tapped again. 'Got i

'Have you told your parents about Hawaii ye
Kelly asked Candy, resuming the conversation they'd been having in the kitchen as they'd made their drink.

'No.'

'You go in four weeks' time,' Kelly pointed out.

'They might not notice that I've gone,' Candy said hopefully, then let out a sigh. Her parents were Italian, strict and very prone to popping over to her flat unannounced. They also spoke every day on the phone. 'I know I'll have to tell them or I'll be listed on Interpol as a missing person.'

Candy had, on a whim, booked a holiday to Hawaii.

Well, it hadn't been purely on a whim—she had already been aware that she needed to get away when the infomercial had appeared on her screen with a very special offer for the first ten callers. She'd been tired, a bit jaded and upset over a stupid fling with Gerry, one of the head nurses here. Thankfully he was in Greece for a couple of months, which spared Candy her blushes, but when she'd reached for the phone and, lucky her, been amongst the first ten callers, she'd known she needed this break.

She couldn't wait for two weeks in which to lie on a beach and explore the stunning island at leisure while she attempted to sort out a few things that were on her mind.

'They're going to freak when I tell them,' Candy admitted. 'They know that I can't really afford it.'

'It's all paid for?' Kelly checked, and Candy nodded.

'All except for spending money, but I've just spoken to the hospital bank and I've got loads of shifts. Actually, I haven't got a single day off until I fly.'

'Where are your shifts?'

'In the geriatric unit.'

Kelly pulled a face. 'Yuk.'

Candy didn't mind. She had enjoyed working in the geriatric unit during her training and was really grateful for the extra work. Even if she was exhausted at the prospect of nearly four more weeks without so much as a day off.

As her parents would point out, when she finally got around to it and told them about her holiday, it was foolish to be working extra shifts because you were so tired that you needed a break—but Candy just wanted to get away for a while.

'When do you start working there?'

'The weekend. I'm working Friday night and then I've got a four-hour shift on Sunday morning, then back here Monday.'

'Okay.' Steele turned around. 'I want Mr Heath pulled over to Resus. He needs to be monitored while I start him on some medication. His bloodwork's dire.'

'Sure.' Candy jumped down from the bench and she and Trevor brought Mr Heath over.

Candy wrote his name on the whiteboard and turned to Steele. 'Sorry, what specialty is he under?'

'Geriatrics,' Steele said, then he gave her a thin smile. 'Yuk!'

Candy's cheeks went pink; she wanted to point out that she hadn't been the one who had said that.

'It's okay,' Steele relented when he saw her uncomfortable expression. 'You hit a nerve—I hear that sort of thing a lot.'

'So are you a new geriatric consultant?' Kelly asked, but Steele shook his head.

'No, I'm only here temporarily. I'm covering for six weeks while Kathy Jordan is on extended leave.'

'Just six weeks?' Kelly asked shamelessly.

'Yep,' Steele said, and walked off.

'Wow, talk about bringing the schmexy into geriatrics,' Kelly said. 'And you're going to be working there, you lucky thing. I bet you're not complaining now.'

She hadn't been complaining in the first place, Candy was tempted to point out.

They soon paid for the lull in patients because, not an hour later, the department had filled and she and Kelly were busy in Resus, Kelly with a very ill baby and Candy attempting to calm down Mr Heath. He was rather shaky from the medication and was getting increasingly distressed and trying to climb down from the resuscitation bed.

'The medicine makes your heart race, Mr Heath,' Candy tried to explain to the gentleman. 'It will settle down soon...' But he couldn't understand what she said and kept trying to climb off the bed so Candy tried speaking louder. 'The medicine—'

'You do it like this.' Steele saw that she was struggling and came over. 'Mr Heath!' he boomed.

The people in the Waiting Room surely heard him, Candy thought as he gave the same explanation to Mr Heath that she had been trying to give. The gentleman nodded weakly in relief and then lay back on the pillows. 'Good man,' Steele barked and smiled at Candy and, in a comparatively dulcet tone, added, 'I have the perfect voice for my job.'

'You do,' she agreed.

'So you're going to be doing a few shifts up on the geriatric unit?'

'Yep.'

'For a holiday that you can't really afford?'

'I know,' Candy groaned.

'Well, good for you,' Steele said, and Candy blinked in surprise. 'Okay, once Mr Heath's medication has finished I want him monitored for another hour down here. Then everything's sorted for him to be admitted. We're just waiting on a bed, which might be a couple of hours. I've spoken to the ward and they have said that they'll ring down when they're ready for him to come up.'

'Ha-ha,' Candy said, because there was no way that

the ward was likely to ring down. Instead, she would have to chase them and push for the bed to be readied.

Steele well understood her sarcastic comment. 'Well, I hope that they do ring down in a timely manner. I'm less than impressed with the waiting times for patients to get into a bed at the Royal.'

With that he stalked off, possibly to return to whatever fluffy white cloud he'd just drifted down from, Candy thought.

She'd never, ever been so instantly captivated by someone.

Candy left Kelly watching Mr Heath when she was told to go for her lunch break. She'd forgotten to bring lunch so she bought a bag of salt-and-vinegar crisps from the vending machine and put them between two slices of bread and butter. Sitting down in the staffroom, she smiled at Trevor, who was having his lunch too, and checked her phone. Yes, her parents had called, wondering why she hadn't been over.

She'd tell them about Hawaii tonight, Candy decided. Just get it over and done with and then maybe then she'd feel better. Yet she was incredibly tired and really just wanted to go home, have dinner and an early night.

'Here!'

That delicious voice tipped her out of introspection and she looked up at Steele, who was holding a stethoscope, which she took from him.

'Thank you,' Candy said, 'though you didn't have to rush to bring it back down. It's only a hospital-issue stethoscope.'

'Oh,' Steele said. 'I thought I'd pinched yours. Still, it doesn't matter, I was coming down anyway. I'm waiting for a patient to arrive—a direct admission from her GP, though she's refusing to go straight to the ward. She's just agreed to a chest X-ray and some blood tests, and then she thinks she's going home!'

'Thinks?' Candy asked as Steele sat down beside her and stretched out his long legs. It was nice that he sat down next to her when there were about twenty seats to choose from. She turned and smiled as he spoke on.

'Her GP is extremely concerned about her. He thinks there's far more going on than she's admitting to. Macey has had the same GP for thirty years and if he's worried about her then so am I. He thinks she's depressed.' He turned and looked right into her eyes and Candy felt her heart do a little flip-flop. 'It's a big problem with the elderly.'

'Really?'

Steele nodded and looked at what she was eating. 'That looks so bad it has to be good.'

'It's fantastic,' Candy said, and ripped off half her sandwich and gave it to him. 'The trick is lots of butter.'

'That's amazing!' Steele said, when he'd tasted it.

'I'm brilliant with bread,' Candy said. 'Toasted sandwiches, ice-cream sandwiches, beans on toast...'

'I thought a nice Italian girl like you would be brilliant in the kitchen.'

'Sadly, no,' Candy said. 'I'm a constant source of concern to my mother. Anyway, who said I'm nice?'

They smiled.

A smile that was just so deliciously inappropriate for a man you'd met only an hour or so ago. A smile she had never given to another man before and, really, she had no idea where it had come from.

Candy Anastasi! she scolded herself as she looked into those dark brown eyes.

Step away from the very young nurse, Steele told himself, but, hell, she was gorgeous.

Lydia came in then and they both looked away from each other. Lydia was waving a postcard of a delicious aqua ocean and Candy found that she was holding her breath in tension as Lydia read out the card. 'There's a postcard from Gerry. It reads, "Glad that none of you are here."'

Lydia gave a tight smile as she pinned it on the board and Candy just stared at the television.

Was that little dig from Gerry aimed at her?

'When is he back?' Trevor asked.

'End of July, I think.'

Lydia's voice was deliberately vague and Candy knew why. Gerry, the head nurse in Emergency, had been strongly advised to take extended leave.

Gerry was one of the reasons that Candy wanted a couple of weeks on a beach with no company.

Candy's parents had freaked when, at twenty-two, she had broken up with a man they considered suitable and had declared she was moving out. They had been so appalled, so devastated at the prospect of their only daughter leaving home that Candy had ended up staying for another year.

She'd simply had to leave in the end.

Her mother thought nothing of opening her post. She constantly asked whom Candy was talking to on the phone and when Candy pointed out she was entitled to privacy they would ask what it was she had to hide.

Last year she had moved out and, really, she had hardly let loose. She'd had a brief relationship with

Gerry when she'd first moved into her flat but that hadn't worked out and she had been happily single since then.

A couple of months ago, aware that Gerry was having some problems, she'd agreed to go out for a drink with him.

It had resulted in a one-night stand that had left Candy feeling regretful. Gerry had been annoyed to find out that their brief relationship hadn't been resumed.

It was all a bit of a mess, an avoidable one, though. Candy was just grateful that no one at work knew about that regrettable night and Candy wanted it left far behind.

'You'll be sending postcards soon,' Steele said, but Candy shook her head.

'I won't be thinking about this place for a moment.'

That wasn't quite true, though. She would be thinking about work—Candy was seriously thinking of leaving Emergency.

CHAPTER TWO

Just as she returned from lunch she was informed that Steele's patient was here but refusing to come inside the department and had requested, loudly, that the ambulance take her home.

'I'll come out and have a word with her,' Candy said as Steele was taking a phone call. She headed out to the ambulance and was met by a teary woman who introduced herself as Catherine, Macey Anderson's niece.

'I knew that she was going to do this,' Catherine said. 'It's taken two days to persuade her to come in. She used to be a matron on one of the wards here, and still thinks she is one.' Catherine gave a tired smile. 'She was in a few months ago and she was just about running the place by the time she was discharged.'

'I want to go home,' Macey shouted as Candy came into the back of the ambulance.

Macey was a very tall, very handsome woman, with wiry grey, curly hair, a flushed face and very angry dark green eyes. She had all her stuff with her, a huge suitcase, a walking frame and several other bags.

'Mrs Anderson—' Candy started, but already she was wrong.

'It's Miss Anderson!'

'I'm sorry, Miss Anderson. I'm Candy Anastasi, one of the nurses in Emergency, and I'm going to be looking after you today.'

'But, as I've told everyone, many times, I don't *want* to be looked after,' Macey retorted. 'I want to be taken home.'

It was all pretty hopeless. The more they tried to persuade her to come into the department the more upset Macey became. The last thing Candy wanted to do was wheel her through when she was distressed and crying and so, instead, she tried another tack, wondering if, given that Macey had once been a matron, she might not want to get another nurse in trouble.

'Dr Steele is already here to see you,' Candy said. 'He's been waiting for you to arrive. Am I to go in and tell him that I can't get you to come into the hospital?'

Macey looked at her for a long moment and then she looked beyond Candy's shoulder and Candy knew, she simply knew, that it was Steele who had just stepped into the ambulance.

'Is there a problem, Nurse? Only I've been waiting for quite some time.' His low voice sounded just a touch ominous and Candy met Macey's eyes for a brief moment.

'No,' Macey answered for Candy. 'They were just about to bring me in.'

'Good,' Steele said. 'Then I'll come and see you shortly, Miss Anderson.'

As he headed back into the department the paramedics lowered the stretcher to the ground and Candy found out perhaps why it was that Steele was so sharply dressed. 'At least he's not twelve and wearing jeans,' Macey muttered.

Candy smiled—yes, Steele's appearance and authoritarian tone had appeased Macey.

They took Macey into cubicle seven, aligned the stretcher with the trolley, and Candy positioned the sliding board that would help to move the patient over easily. 'We'll get you onto the trolley, Miss Anderson.'

'I can manage,' the elderly lady snapped, 'and it's Macey.'

'That actually means she likes you,' her niece said, and gestured with her head for Candy to follow her outside.

'I've got this,' Matthew, a very patient paramedic, said, and Candy went outside to speak with Catherine.

'It's taken two days for her GP to persuade her to come in,' Catherine said. 'Honestly, I'm just so relieved she's finally here. She's got a temperature and she's hardly eating or drinking anything. She doesn't take her tablets or if she does she gets them all wrong…'

'We'll go through all of that.' Candy did her best to reassure Macey's niece.

'She's so cantankerous and rude,' Catherine said, 'that she puts everyone offside, but she's such a lovely lady too. She's always been on her own, she's never had a boyfriend, let alone married, she's so completely set in her ways and loathes getting undressed in front of anyone. You're going to have a battle there…'

'Let us take care of her,' Candy said, 'and please don't worry about her saying something offensive. Believe me, we'll have heard far worse.'

'Thanks.' Catherine gave a worried smile and they went back inside. The cubicle was pretty full, with Macey's huge bag and walking frame, and Candy had a little tidy up. 'Why don't we first get you into a gown and then—'

'Get me into a gown?' Macey shouted loudly. 'You haven't even introduced yourself and you're asking me to take my clothes off.' Candy said nothing as Steele came into the cubicle. She had, in fact, introduced herself in the ambulance. 'You're not a nurse's bootlace,' Macey said to Candy just as Steele came in.

'Hello, Miss Anderson,' he said. 'I didn't introduce myself properly back there in the ambulance. I'm Steele, or Dr Steele, if you prefer to be formal.'

Candy smothered a little smile as he repeated a similar introduction to the one he had given her. He must have to say it fifty times a day.

He ran through a few questions with Macey as a very anxious Catherine hovered.

'You had a heart attack three months ago?' Steele checked. 'And you were admitted here for a week.'

'All they did was pump me with drugs,' Macey huffed. 'Where were you then?'

'I believe I was in Newcastle,' Steele said.

'So how long have you worked here?'

'Two days,' Steele answered easily.

'You'll be gone tomorrow.' Macey huffed. 'You're a locum.'

'I am, though I happen to be a very good one,' Steele said, completely unfazed. 'And I'm here for six weeks, which gives us plenty of time to sort all this out.'

They went through her medical history. Apart from the heart attack it would seem that Macey was very well indeed. She had never smoked, never drunk, and at eighty still did all her own housework and cooking, with a little help from her nieces, Catherine and

Linda. Macey had until a couple of days ago walked to the shops every day.

'It's quite a distance,' Catherine said. 'I offered to do her shopping weekly at the supermarket for her but Aunt Macey wouldn't hear of it.'

'I like to walk,' Macey snapped.

'It's good that you do—exercise is good for you,' Steele said. 'Do you have stairs at home?'

'Yes, and I manage them just fine,' Macey retorted. 'You won't see me with bungalow legs!'

'Right, Miss Anderson,' Steele said. 'I'm going to ask Candy to help you into a gown and do some obs and put an IV and draw some blood. Then I'll come and examine you.' He looked at two blue ice-cream containers that were filled with various bottles and blister packets of medication. 'I'll take these and look through them.'

As Steele went to go Macey called him back. 'I'm not having a nurse take my blood. That's a doctor's job.'

'Oh, I can assure you that you're better off with Candy than you are with me,' Steele said. 'I get the shakes this side of six p.m.'

His quip caused a little smile to inch onto Macey's lips and, after Steele had gone, Candy helped her into a gown while doing her best to keep Macey covered as she did so. But the elderly lady fought her over every piece, right down to her stockings.

'Leave my stockings on,' Macey said.

'Oh, I'll leave them for Steele to take off, shall I?' Candy challenged.

Macey huffed and lifted her bottom but as Candy rolled the stockings down she found out why Macey was so reluctant to get fully undressed—there was a bandage on her leg and around that the skin was very red and inflamed.

'I'll take this off so Steele can take a look,' Candy said. She went and washed her hands and opened up a dressing pack and then put on some gloves.

'Careful,' Macey warned.

'Is it very painful?' Candy asked, and Macey nodded.

'Okay, I'll just put some saline on,' Candy said, 'and we'll soak it off. Has your GP seen this?'

'I don't need a doctor to tell me how to do a dressing.'

Candy soaked the dressing in saline and then covered Macey with a blanket and checked her obs, before heading out to Steele. He was sitting at the nurses' station, going through all Macey's medications. He had a pill counter and was tipping one of the bottles out when Candy came over.

'She's got a nasty leg wound,' Candy said.

'How bad?'

'I haven't seen it,' Candy said. 'I'm just soaking the dressing but her shin is all red and I think it's very painful.'

'Okay.' He started to tip the tablets back into the jar. 'I don't want her left on her own,' Steele said.

'Sorry?'

'I don't like what I'm seeing with these tablets,' Steele said. 'I don't trust her not to do something stupid.'

'Oh!'

'I'll come in and see her now.'

They both returned to the cubicle and Steele examined Macey. He listened for a long time to her chest and felt her stomach, keeping her as covered as he could while he did so, and then they got to her leg.

Steele put on some gloves and took off the dressing and Macey winced in pain. 'Sorry, Miss Anderson,' Steele said. 'How long have you had this?'

'A couple of weeks.'

Steele looked up at Macey. 'That's very concerning. This has developed over two weeks?'

Candy could hear the note of sarcasm in Steele's voice and watched as Macey stared back at him and then backed down.

'I knocked my leg when I came out of hospital. It's just not healed and it's been getting worse.'

'That sounds far more plausible.' Steele smiled at her. 'Well, that accounts for your temperature!' He took a swab and though he was very gentle the cotton tip must have felt like a red-hot poker because Macey let out a yelp of pain. 'Very sorry, Macey,' Steele said. He put a light dressing over it. 'We'll give you something decent for pain before we dress it properly.' He spoke then to Candy. 'Can you take Macey round for a chest X-ray?'

Just as Candy had finished drawing some blood the porter arrived and Candy went to X-Ray with Macey and Catherine. They were seen relatively quickly but Macey was clearly less than impressed at what she considered a long wait.

Having looked at her X-ray, Steele came into the cubicle and then turned to Catherine. 'Why don't you go and get a drink?' he suggested. 'I'm going to be with your aunt for the next twenty minutes or so—you might as well take the chance for a break now.'

'Thank you,' Catherine said in relief.

'I just wanted to check a couple of things,' Steele said once Catherine had left the cubicle.

'And then I can go home?'

'You're not well enough,' Steele said. 'Now, while Catherine isn't here, I want you to tell me how many you smoke a day?'

'I don't smoke.'

'Miss Anderson, do you want me to bring in your chest X-ray and we can go over it together?'

'Two.' She gave a tight shrug. 'Maybe three a day.'

'We'll say ten, then, shall we?' Steele said, and Candy blinked when Macey didn't correct him. 'I'll write you up for a nicotine patch. How much do you drink a day?'

'I've told you already, I don't.'

'Six broken ribs of varying ages.' Steele smiled at the old girl. 'Come on, Macey. So am I to worry that you're falling down for no reason?'

'I slipped on some ice,' Macey said, 'and I've got a cat that gets under my feet.'

'Fair enough.' Steele nodded. 'So you don't want me to write you down for a couple of shots of sherry at night?' he checked. 'You can have either your own stuff, or the hospital's cheap disgusting stuff. We just need the bottle if you want to drink your own.'

Macey took in a deep breath before saying anything. 'It's in my bag.'

'Good, we'll make sure it's handed over to nursing staff out of sight of your niece.'

Candy stood there feeling a bit stunned but she hadn't seen anything yet. Steele had brought back in the two ice-cream containers that Macey had brought in with her and he started to go through them.

'Macey, you haven't been taking these regularly.' He held up a pill bottle. 'Yet you're not.'

'There's so many. I can't keep up.'

Steele picked up another bottle that had just a couple of tablets in it. 'And these were only dispensed two days ago,' Steele said, 'and there are only two left.'

'I didn't take them,' Macey said in a scoffing voice.

'I know that you didn't or we wouldn't even be having this conversation. So where are they now?'

'I don't know. My niece puts them into a pill box...'

'Macey?'

'I tipped them down the toilet. I don't trust the drug companies.'

'Are you depressed, Macey?'

'Oh, you're going to put me on antidepressants now. You're in cahoots with the drug companies.'

'Are you confused and mixing up your medication or are you ignoring your health?' Steele asked, and Candy stood there, watching him stare right into Macey's eyes. 'Are you depressed, Macey?'

There was a long stretch of silence before Macey answered.

'I'm not confused,' she said. 'Well, sometimes I am with dates and things.'

'But you're not confused where your medication's concerned?' Steele checked.

'No,' Macey said, and Candy frowned at the serious note to Steele's voice.

'Okay.'

'Could you just leave me, please?' Macey asked.

'Not happening,' Steele said, and he took down the edge of the trolley she was lying on. His legs were long enough that he sat there easily. She would need a ladder to do that, Candy thought, and then she stopped thinking idle thoughts as she started to realise the seriousness of this conversation.

'Why did you tip the tablets in the toilet?' Steele challenged gently, and Candy felt the back of her nose stinging as he pushed on. 'Were you scared that you might take them all?'

Macey's face started to crumple and Steele took her hand. 'Look at me, Macey. Are you having suicidal thoughts?' Steele asked bluntly, and after a moment she nodded and then started to cry.

'Well done for throwing them away,' Steele said. 'Well done for coming into hospital and speaking with me.' Candy watched as he wrapped his arms around the proud lady as she started to really sob. 'It's okay.' His voice was very deep but so gentle. 'We're going to look after you…'

CHAPTER THREE

CANDY SLEPT FOR a few hours on Friday afternoon before her first night shift on the geriatric ward and then she got ready and took the Underground into work.

She was actually rather nervous about her night shift. She was so used to working in Emergency that she wasn't too sure how she would go on the ward. She also had a short four-hour shift there on Sunday morning.

It will be worth it, Candy told herself as she stepped into the geriatric unit.

Hawaii, here I come!

The handover lasted much longer than it did in Emergency and the day staff went into far more detail about the patients than she had grown used to. Candy sat as the staff discussed in depth the patients' moods and their ADLs: activities of daily living. Steele was sitting at a desk in the room with his back to everyone but didn't leave as the handover started; he just carried on with whatever he was doing on the computer and offered comment or clarification at times.

Candy knew that she was far, far too aware of him.

The staff clearly liked him. If there was a question

they would toss it over to him and he would answer as he typed away.

Elaine, a student nurse, was giving her handover to the night staff, watched over by her mentor, Gloria. Elaine was very bossy and seemed to think she was the only one in the room who knew what she was doing. She had given a sigh of exasperation when Candy had introduced herself and said that she was from the hospital bank. 'Another one!' Elaine had said.

As Elaine gave her handover there were a few times when Candy caught Abigail's eye—Abigail was the senior nurse she would be working with tonight, and they both smothered a smile.

Mr Heath, who had been so unwell the other day in Emergency, was doing a lot better and Candy was allocated to look after him for the night.

She was also given Toby Worthington, a terminal patient who was on a lot of morphine for pain control and, Elaine said, liked to have his radio on till eleven at night and then turned on again at six.

'Then we have Macey Anderson.' Elaine moved on to the next patient.

'I know Macey,' Candy said. 'I was in Emergency when she was admitted.'

'Could you have her tonight as well, then?' Abigail checked and Candy nodded. They went through her history, which was pretty much what Candy already knew. How Macey had been since admission had changed rapidly, though. 'Since she's come to the ward she's been very withdrawn,' Elaine said. 'She doesn't want to eat, or wash. She's on an IV regime but if she continues to refuse meals and drinks she'll need an NG tube. Steele has taken her off a lot of her medications and has also started her on a low dose of antidepressants…' Elaine went through her medications. 'Make sure she takes them and she's not hiding them,' Elaine warned, and Candy nodded. But that wasn't enough for Elaine. 'You have to ask her to lift her tongue.'

'I shall,' Candy said, trying to keep the edge from her voice. Elaine was a funny little thing, with a very long, wide mouth that opened often.

She reminded Candy of a puppet.

'Why does she have to lift her tongue, Elaine?' Steele asked from the computer, and Candy felt her lips stretch into a smile because clearly he had Elaine worked out too.

'To make sure that she's not hiding any under there,' Elaine said, and looked at Candy to make sure that she understood the instruction.

'Thanks,' Candy said. 'I'll make sure that she takes them.'

As Elaine left the room Abigail winked. 'Matron Elaine!'

'Her heart's in the right place, though,' Gloria, the sister in charge of the day shift, said. 'But, oh my, she's hard work. Elaine insists on calling everything by its technical name. The patients haven't a clue what she's asking. Just this evening she asked Mr Heath if she could check for scrotal oedema.' Gloria smiled as she recalled it. 'He said, "Do you mean my balls, dear?" It was too funny.'

They were all very nice and after handover Elaine gave Candy a quick tour of the ward before she headed for home.

Actually, it wasn't that quick—Elaine was incredibly thorough, going through everything in detail when really Candy wanted to get started.

'I think that covers everything,' Candy said. 'Thanks for the tour.'

'I'll just show you where the torches and things are kept,' Elaine said, but Candy looked at the clock and it was already nearly ten. 'Go.' Candy smiled. 'It's Friday night. Enjoy it!'

Elaine gave a little nod and finally headed for home and then Candy went to check on her patients for the night.

Mr Heath was indeed looking better.

'Hello, Candy.' He smiled when she came over and he put down the book that he was reading.

'You remember me?' Candy asked in surprise, because Mr Heath had been so distressed in Resus that he hadn't seemed very aware of his surroundings or able to hear what anybody except Steele was saying.

'Of course I do.'

'Well, it's lovely to see you looking so much better,' Candy said. She then did his obs and gave him his medications for the night and, as she did so, they chatted for a while.

'I'm hoping to go home on Monday,' Mr Heath said. 'My granddaughter gets married next week.'

'How exciting,' Candy said. 'Is it a big wedding?'

'Huge!' Mr Heath nodded. 'She's marrying an Ital…' His voice trailed off.

'Don't stop on my account.' Candy grinned. 'I know what Italian weddings can be like. I must be the only girl in the world who's dreaded her wedding day since she was little rather than dreamt of it.'

Mr Heath laughed. 'Will it be big?'

'You have no idea,' Candy said. 'I have four older brothers, all married, and my mother is itching for it to be my turn. She buys sheets and towels for me when she shops—oh, and washing baskets and the like. I'm all set up!' Candy smiled. 'Apart from the groom.'

It was, in fact, a very friendly ward and the staff didn't mind that Candy had a few questions every now and then. But as she went to do Macey's medications, Candy frowned and looked around for Abigail, but she was in with Mrs Douglas, who was very sick indeed.

'Problem?' Steele had come onto the ward and was writing up some medication for a patient who wasn't Candy's.

'No, I just want to check something,' Candy said, taking the prescription chart over to him. 'Macey's written up for sherry, but she's on a lot of other medication.'

'No doubt she'll be having the sherry when she gets home,' Steele pointed out. 'Though I don't think you have to worry about it tonight—she's not having her sherry at the moment. She's not really having much of anything.'

He was right. Candy was shocked at the change in Macey. She'd been a fierce, proud woman when she had arrived in the emergency department but now she just lay on her side and stared into space. She didn't say anything when Candy introduced herself and her arm was listless when Candy checked her blood pressure.

'I've got your tablets for you, Macey,' Candy explained, and she helped her to sit up to take them. The old lady took her tablets without a word of protest and then tried to take the water Candy offered, but her hands were shaking terribly so Candy held the glass and helped her take a drink to wash them down. 'Sorry, Macey, but can you lift your tongue for me?'

She lifted her tongue and, yes, she had swallowed all the tablets rather than hiding them. Then she lay back down on the pillow.

'Can I get you anything else?' Candy offered. 'A drink?'

Macey gave a small shake of her head and Candy looked at the fluid balance and food charts. She was on an IV, and that was, apart from the water she took with her medicines, practically all that Macey was having at the moment.

'Macey,' Candy suggested as she put another blanket on and turned her pillows, 'why don't I get you some milk?'

Her lethargy was troubling. Candy would far prefer her to be shouting at her and telling her that she wasn't a nurse's bootlace.

'Some warm milk,' Candy elaborated. 'I know your hands are a bit shaky at the moment but I can help you to drink it. Will you have some milk?'

Macey didn't say yes but at least she didn't shake her head this time.

Steele looked over and saw Candy hovering, sorting out pillows and blankets on Macey's bed. He half expected Macey to shout for her to get off as she had done when she'd been with the other nurse that afternoon, but he was pleased to see that tonight Macey didn't seem to mind the small attention.

Steele liked Candy, which had certainly come as a surprise to him.

The attraction had been instant, yet Candy was nothing like the women Steele usually dated.

Oh, he dated.

A lot.

Steele went for sophisticated women. He liked women who understood right from the start that this could only ever be a fleeting thing for he was never anywhere long. Six months here, two years there and now just six weeks here.

Steele glanced at the date. He had been here almost a week, so make that five weeks he had left at the Royal.

And Candy was away for the final two of them.

Steele had already done the marriage-and-settle-down thing and it hadn't worked.

Or rather, it had worked, possibly more than he had realised, because ten years on his ex-wife, completely out of the blue, had rung him. Her second marriage had failed and she had suggested that they give it another go. Even before Steele could answer her and say he had never heard a more ridiculous suggestion in his life she had added her little postscript—there was one proviso to them getting back together.

There had been a lot of advances in technology after all.

Ten years on the hurt was there and she had just hit it with a sledgehammer again. His one raw nerve, the one chink in his confident persona, had been exposed again. Steele had promptly hung up on her without response because otherwise he might well have exploded and told her exactly the words that were in his head.

They weren't pretty.

For Steele, finding out that he was infertile had been a huge blow. His wife's response to the news had been devastating.

He made sure now he was never in a position to

reveal that part of himself again. He kept things light; he kept things intimate sexually rather than emotionally.

Then he moved on.

Candy walked past just then, carrying a feeding cup, and she went over and helped Macey to sit up.

Candy didn't say anything; she just gave Macey a smile as the elderly lady took sips of the milky drink. That was all Macey wanted for now: no conversation, just a warm drink and the comfort of companionable silence.

Candy was fine with that—she was used to it, in fact.

When she'd been ten, her *nonna* had come to live with them. Candy's job in the morning had been to make sure Nonna got her *biscotti* and milky coffee and then to see her to the bathroom and make up her bed. Candy had loved the mornings—the chatty ones when Nonna had told her all about the village that she had grown up in. The reminiscent ones when Nonna had spoken about falling in love and the parties and dancing. The sad ones—leaving Italy and the death of her husband, Candy's *nonno*. Candy had been comfortable too with the silent mornings, when Nonna had just eaten quietly, lost in a world of her own, as Macey was now.

'Do you want a bedpan?' Candy offered Macey when the milk was gone.

'I'll go…' Macey sighed and pulled back the bed covers.

Glad to see that she was making the effort to get out of bed, Candy helped her with her slippers and got Macey her walking frame and they walked over to the bathroom.

Candy waited outside and when Macey came to wash her hands Candy sorted the taps and squeezed the soap for her. Macey washed her hands very thoroughly. Her nail varnish was chipped and Candy watched her examine her nails for a moment, clearly less than impressed with the state of her hands.

'I'll sort your nails out for you on Sunday,' Candy offered, and then took Macey back to her bedside, where she asked her to sit for a moment. 'Sit there and let me make it up all nice and fresh for you to get into.'

Candy made the bed so nicely that she wanted to climb in it herself. 'You'd better get in quickly or I will.'

'You look tired,' Macey said, and Candy smiled at the first invitation to conversation.

'I am, though I shouldn't be,' Candy said. 'I slept all afternoon.'

She got the older woman into bed, put up the bed rails and tied the call bell to the side. 'Press it if you need anything,' Candy said. 'I hope you have a lovely sleep.'

Candy sorted out her other patients and, by one a.m., when Abigail asked if she'd mind taking the first break, Candy was more than ready for an hour to rest. It would seem she wasn't the only one who needed a doze, because when she walked into the break room there was Steele, asleep on a sofa with the television on in the background.

'Aloha,' he said sleepily, when Candy disturbed him as she took a seat.

'Aloha.' Candy smiled. 'How come you're still here?'

'I'm waiting for some relatives to come in for Mrs Douglas.'

Candy remembered from handover that Mrs Douglas wasn't expected to make it through the night.

'How long is it now till your holiday?' Steele asked.

'Three weeks,' Candy said, and set her phone alarm for an hour's time. She saw the date and that it was now Saturday morning. 'Actually, just under three weeks. I fly on a Friday night.'

'Are you working right up till then?'

Candy nodded and then yawned at the very thought. 'I almost go from here to the airport.'

'Is it just you going?'

'Yep.'

'I thought Hawaii was more a couples' destination,' Steele said, fishing shamelessly.

'I think you may be right but I saw an advert and I couldn't resist,' Candy admitted and nodded to the television, where an infomercial for knives was showing. 'It was a limited offer, with a huge discount for the first ten to call… I fall for it every time'

'Yep.' Steele nodded. 'And me. I bought the juicer, the chopper and some blender thing until I finally worked out that nothing is going to make me like vegetables.'

'It's one of the perils of working nights,' Candy agreed. 'What looks appealing at two a.m. seems stupid when the parcel arrives. Anyway, I saw the advert for the holiday when I was feeling particularly miserable. It looked absolutely beautiful and I really needed to get away…'

'How come?'

'Lots of things really.'

'Such as?'

Candy hesitated. She hadn't really spoken to anyone about the fact she was considering leaving. She glanced at Steele and realised that by the time she got back from Hawaii he'd be gone, so it really made no difference. 'I'm not sure if I still want to work in Emergency.'

'It must be a pretty stressful job.'

'It is at times.' Candy nodded. 'Though it's not just that. I made a mistake couple of months back.' She didn't elaborate; instead, she lay down on the sofa, determined to squeeze in some sleep during her break.

'A professional mistake?' Steele probed, and Candy let out a small laugh at his very direct question.

'No, it was a personal one.'

'Do tell.'

'No way.'

'So there are two things I have to find out about you now,' Steele teased. 'The story behind your name and the mistake that Nurse Candy made.'

'You can try, but it won't get you anywhere,' Candy said, and closed her eyes. 'I'm going to have a little rest.'

'Hopefully you talk in your sleep.'

She smiled with her eyes closed and was mildly surprised when after a moment or so Steele continued to speak.

'We all make mistakes, Candy,' he said. His lovely deep voice was soothing and broke into her semi-doze. 'If I've learnt one thing in this job, it's that everyone makes so-called mistakes and also that everyone wastes way too much time regretting them.'

She opened her eyes and looked at him. 'You really

do like your job,' Candy said, and it wasn't a question, more an observation, and Steele nodded.

'I really do.'

Yes, she should sleep and her aching body might regret it later but she chose to forgo the full hour of sleep just to find out a little more about him. She lay there and peeked over to Steele, who was still looking at her.

'Did you always want to work in geriatrics?'

'Not really,' Steele said. 'It sort of found me, I guess. I was pretty much raised by my grandmother…'

'Are your parents…?' Her voice trailed off and Steele grinned.

'They're not dead.'

'Good.'

'My parents are both doctors and were very serious about their careers. I was a late accident. I don't think they ever really wanted to have children. My mother was a top thoracic surgeon—which means she had balls.'

Candy laughed.

'My grandmother looked after me till I went to boarding school and in the holidays I stayed with her.' He saw her frown. 'My parents are good people. They were just very, very focused. Anyway, when I went to my grandmother's for Easter one year, she was very confused. Just completely off the wall. I rang my mother and she pretty much would have had her shipped off to a nursing home that day.'

'Really?' Candy said.

'Really!' Steele nodded. 'But the GP came and it turned out all she had was a urine infection. He explained the confusion it could cause in the elderly. Anyway, two days later she was completely back to herself. It just stayed with me, I guess.'

'My *nonna* lived with us.' Candy yawned. 'I think my mother thinks she'll be living with me…'

'Did your mother work?' Steele asked, and Candy shook her head. 'You do, though. You have a career.'

Candy looked at him. Right there, right then, she felt as if he knew the wrestle in her heart because though she loved her parents they clashed a lot as Candy struggled to be independent when they didn't want her to be. 'I do have a career,' Candy said, 'and I had to fight to have one.'

'Have your rest.' He smiled and Candy nodded.

She'd had to fight to simply be here, Candy thought as she closed her eyes. Her parents had wanted her to marry Franco, and for her to work in the family business. They hadn't understood that she'd wanted to study to become a nurse.

Candy fell asleep but it felt about twenty seconds later that her phone bleeped and told her that her hour was up and it was time to go back to work. The staff-room was empty and when she went round to the ward Steele wasn't there either.

She liked him.

Candy knew it properly then because she preferred the feel on the ward when he was around.

The rest of the night flew past quickly. Candy helped out with Mrs Douglas while Abigail took her break and then it was time to start her morning routine. At seven-thirty, after handover, Candy said goodbye to her patients and told Macey that she would be in to-morrow morning and, if Macey liked and Candy had time, then she would do her nails.

Macey said nothing.

As Candy walked along the main entrance corridor she saw Steele on his way into work. His hair was damp from his morning shower and he was wearing a dark grey suit and fresh shirt, though he hadn't yet done up his tie. He was standing looking at one of the pictures that lined the corridor, images of the hospital and the changes over the years. Renovations were taking place throughout the Royal.

'What are you looking at?' she asked.

'Come and see,' Steele invited, and as she stood beside him he started to do up his tie. 'Do you recognise anyone?'

Candy peered at the image that he had been focused on. It was a group of nurses and doctors standing in the gardens at the rear of the hospital. It looked like a presentation had just taken place as some of the nurses were sporting medals. Candy smiled when she saw the long dresses and aprons that the nurses were wearing as well as their hats and capes. Then she saw just who it was that Steele was looking at. 'Oh, my goodness, it's Macey.'

'It is indeed.'

She had the same wild curly hair, though it was tamed by a frilly white cap. Her cheekbones were high and her lips, though smiling, looked a touch strained. Her cape was around her shoulders and Candy smiled at the red cross that it made on her chest.

She looked incredibly young but certainly it was Macey.

'Do you think she'll come out of her depression?' Candy asked.

'Now I do.'

'What do you mean?'

But Steele didn't answer her directly. 'You were very good with her last night. I'm glad she had a drink and got up to the bathroom. How was she this morning?'

'Still very quiet, but she had another drink and I made her *biscotti*, which she ate.'

'Biscotti?'

'Biscuits in warm milk, all mashed in.' Candy smiled and then groaned as her stomach rumbled just at the thought. 'Now I've gone and made myself hungry, I'll have to have some when I get home.'

'Did you feed her?'

'I did.' Candy nodded. 'She's very shaky.'

'It's all the new medications,' Steele said, 'and a lack of sherry, but it should soon start to settle down.'

'How did you know that she was drinking?'

'Because drinking is incredibly common in the elderly. Far more than people realise. It's not all bad.' Steele smiled. 'Macey can't ask her niece to get her four bottles of sherry a week, or however much it is that she actually drinks. At least it keeps her walking to the shops each day. I admit that I worry what will happen when my oldies all discover online shopping.'

Candy realised she was doing her dental commercial smile at him again.

He made her smile.

'I'm going home.' Candy hitched up her bag. 'I'll say goodnight because it's night-time to me.'

'Have a good sleep,' Steele said, 'and don't talk too much.'

'I *don't* talk in my sleep.' She smiled back at him. 'At least, I don't think I do.'

As she walked off his deep voice caused her shoulders to stiffen.

'Make that three things that I have to find out about you.'

Oh, my God, Candy realised.

They *were* flirting.

More than that, she was considering revising her recently put in place rule—to never again get involved with someone at work.

He was *that* good.

CHAPTER FOUR

'CAN I HAVE a hand to turn Mr Worthington, please?'
Candy asked Elaine the following morning.

She had slept all of Saturday and had then got up for
dinner and gone out for a couple of hours with Kelly,
only to be in bed by ten and asleep again in a matter
of moments.

And she was *still* tired.

Elaine was very brusque and efficient and they soon
had Mr Worthington turned. 'Why isn't his radio on?'
Elaine asked, turning it on. 'Toby likes to have his
radio on, especially on a Sunday morning. I wrote it
down in his care plan.'

'Sorry,' Candy muttered as Elaine marched out.

As bossy as she was, though, Elaine's heart really
was in the right place because Toby started humming
a little as Candy shaved him and all too soon she found
herself singing along to the Sunday morning hymns.
It made Toby smile and his eyes encouraged her and
he even started singing along to some of the choruses,
which only made Candy sing louder.

'Mr Worthington!' Gloria popped her head in.
'Your family are here to see you.' She smiled at Candy.

'They'll be pleased to see him looking so cheerful. Steele was just having a word with them.'

Candy quickly tidied up the room and moved the trolley out of the way as Toby's family thanked Steele and then smiled at Candy as they made their way in.

'Did you enjoy your little singalong?' Steele asked when she came out.

'Actually, I did,' she said, 'although I'm not sure quite what Toby would have to say about it if he was able to talk.'

'Oh, I'm sure that, with the amount of morphine he's on, your voice sounded pretty fantastic.'

'Are you telling me that I'm tone deaf?'

'Ooh, just a touch,' Steele teased, but it didn't faze Candy.

'I'm going to sing louder next time.'

They would have chatted for longer but Matron Elaine was back and ready to move things along. 'Come on, Candy, we're falling behind. I'll help you with Macey.'

Candy would really prefer that she didn't.

'Have fun!' Steele said as Candy rolled her eyes.

The strangest thing was, though, that Candy did enjoy herself.

In fact, she had more fun then she'd had in a long time and so did Macey!

'Good morning, Macey.' Candy smiled as she pulled the curtains around the bed. 'Would you like to have a shower?'

Macey gave a slow shake of her head.

'Well, Elaine and I will give you a wash in bed, if that's okay, and we'll give you some nice fresh sheets and things. Then I'll do your leg dressing.'

'I'll do Macey's leg dressing,' Elaine said. 'I need to practice my aseptic technique.'

'Sure,' Candy agreed, and then spoke to Macey. 'Would you like me to wash your hair? We can do it in bed. I just need to take the bedhead off. It might make you feel a little bit better,' Candy pushed gently, but again Macey shook her head.

Elaine had everything set up on the trolley to wash Macey and she was busy collecting sheets and pillowcases for the bed change as Candy washed Macey's face. She then offered her the cloth to wash her hands but Macey didn't take it so Candy washed Macey's hands in the bowl. 'I'll take that nail varnish off in a little while and do your nails.'

'There isn't time to do nails,' Elaine said as she returned.

'I'll do it on my coffee break,' Candy said as they turned Macey and washed her back. Elaine was starting to seriously get on her nerves. 'I like painting nails.'

Delightfully, though, as Macey was turned back from her side she caught Candy's eye and gave her a tiny wink. This showed Candy she was coming back to the world and that Macey understood how difficult Elaine might be to work with.

She returned the wink and soaped up the cloth again.

'Would you like to wash yourself down there?' Candy offered, so that Macey could wash her private parts herself, but both Candy and Macey blinked at the same time when a loud voice interrupted them.

'No!' Elaine said. 'We do not speak down to our patients. You are to call it by its proper name.'

Candy shared a brief *yikes* look with Macey.

'I apologise, Macey,' she said, looking into Macey's eyes as they both tried to fathom what it was that she was supposed to say.

'Would you like to wash your private parts?' Candy offered and saw Macey's lips start to twitch into a smile, especially when Elaine chimed up again.

'No!' she said. 'You're to call it by its proper name.'

Given that Candy was the qualified nurse, she could have told Elaine to simply be quiet, but there was a glimmer in Macey's eyes that hadn't been there for a long time and, Candy guessed as they shared a smile, she was more than happy for the exchange to continue.

Macey presumably had a nurse's sense of humour after all.

'I'm sorry, Macey,' Candy said again as she stretched her brain as to what she should say. She rinsed out the cloth again and then mouthed to Macey, 'What do I say?'

Macey offered a tiny shrug.

Was she supposed to ask if she wanted to wash her vagina? 'Macey,' Candy said, and cleared her throat. They stared seriously at each other, though they were both laughing on the inside. Each knew the other's thoughts. 'Would you like to wash your genitals?'

'No!' Elaine, clearly incensed by Candy's apparent ineptitude, took the cloth from Candy. 'This is how you do it,' Elaine said, and soaped up the cloth again. 'Macey,' she said, holding out the cloth, 'would you like to wash your muffy?'

Macey and Candy cried from laughing.

Not in front of Elaine, of course, but as Elaine went to set up for the leg dressing Candy had to wipe the tears from Macey's eyes as they tried to keep their laughter quiet.

They clearly didn't succeed because Steele popped his head in.

'Did Elaine do her muffy thing again?' he asked.

'She did.' Candy grinned. 'Has she done it before, then?'

Steele nodded. 'Somebody has to tell her that that's not the technical name for it.' Steele grinned. 'Please, God, it's not me.'

'She'll be a wonderful nurse,' Macey said, still smiling. 'At least she's thorough.'

Candy was told to go for her coffee break and so she made a mug of coffee and put it beside Macey's bed, ready to set to work on her nails.

'Have your break,' Macey said.

'I honestly like painting nails,' Candy said. 'I do my mum's every week and I just wish I had four sisters instead of four brothers. It really does relax me.'

She held up a bottle of coral nail polish. 'Is that colour okay?'

Macey gave a small nod.

Macey sat quietly as Candy set to work. Candy didn't chat very much because she really was concentrating. There was something so soothing about painting nails that she truly did enjoy doing it. The immediate improvement was instantly gratifying and having nice nails was also a very easy lift to the sprits.

'Four brothers?' Macey said suddenly.

'And then came a daughter.' Candy gave a wry smile.

'Are they very strict?'

'They are but they're also very lovely. I know that

I really have nothing to complain about, but…' Candy shook her head. 'I'm still plucking up the courage to tell them that I've booked a holiday to Hawaii. They're not going to be pleased.'

'Why?' Macey asked. 'Because you're going with your boyfriend?'

'I don't have a boyfriend,' Candy said, taking Macey's other hand and starting to work on those nails. 'That won't appease them, though…me in America on my own…'

Macey looked across the ward and saw that Steele was looking towards them, or rather at Candy. When he realised that she was watching him he gave her a very brief smile and then looked away.

She might not say much but Macey knew everything that went on in the ward.

'There,' Candy said, finishing off and admiring her handiwork. 'Let them dry for a little while before you do anything.'

'No washing my muffy for the next half-hour, then,' Macey joked and smiled at Candy as she rested her head back on the pillow. 'Thank you, my dear.'

As she went to take her mug through to the kitchen Candy passed Steele. 'What time do you finish?' he asked.

'Eleven-thirty,' Candy said.

'Do you want to get lunch?'

He'd completely sideswiped her but, then, Candy thought, he had been doing that since the moment she'd clapped eyes on him. 'The canteen?' she suggested.

'If you like but I think we can do better than the canteen.'

Oh!

Did she want to have lunch with the sexiest man she had ever met? There really wasn't an awful lot to think about.

'Yes,' Candy said, 'that sounds great.'

'Good.'

'But aren't you on call?'

'My registrar can earn his keep for a couple of hours,' Steele said.

Wow.

There really was no messing with Steele; she had never really known anyone as direct as him before.

'Anyway,' Steele added, 'I've got a few questions that I'd like to know the answers to.'

'Question one,' Steele said as they sat in a very nice café that was just a short drive from the hospital. 'I want to know about your name—Candy?'

'You'll never know,' Candy said as she looked through the menu. 'It's the reason I'm never getting married. It's the reason I'm going on holiday alone. No one is allowed to see my passport!'

'I'm determined to find out.'

'You can be as determined as you like.' She smiled. 'It doesn't mean that you'll get anywhere, though.'

'What do you want to eat?' Steele asked.

'I would like…' She looked through the menu. What would she like? 'I fancy a roast.'

'Have a roast, then.'

'I shall.' Candy nodded. 'A Sunday roast is exotic to me. It was pasta and pasta and more pasta when I was growing up.'

'Well, I'll have the pasta, then.' He smiled, glad to

be out with someone who seemed to enjoy their food. 'That's exotic to me.'

'Please.' Candy rolled her eyes.

'Okay, second question—what was the mistake?'

Candy let out a breath; if this was leading anywhere, and it felt as if it was, then possibly she ought to tell him. Or possibly not, given that Steele would be long since gone by the time Gerry returned from Greece.

It wasn't just a question of that, though. She liked Steele's eyes, she liked his smile, she liked that she felt she could be honest with him. It would be such a relief to share what had been eating her up for these past couple of months.

'Have you ever slept with an ex?' Candy asked, quite sure, as she did so, that she was blushing from the roots of her hair to the tips of her toes.

'Doesn't everyone sleep with their exes?' Steele checked. He was so at ease with it all that she let out a breath that she felt as though she'd been holding in since it had happened.

'Well, I've only had two exes, and I only made that mistake with one of them.'

'Actually,' Steele added, 'I've never slept with my ex-wife. I knew from the day we broke up that we were done.'

He saw her swallow. And swallow Candy did—she had certainly thought him worldlier than her and that he had been married and divorced confirmed it.

'You sound bitter,' she said, and was somewhat surprised when he didn't deny that he was.

'I am a bit when I think about it, which I don't often do.' He smiled. 'She rang a few weeks ago and asked if we might consider getting back together. I long ago decided that I would never settle down with anyone again.'

He didn't reveal the initial reason for their break-up. There was no point. There was no need for in-depth explanations about his infertility, given that he wasn't going to be hanging around in any one place or in anyone's space for too long.

Though perhaps he needed to make that a little clearer to Candy, he realised. She was seriously gorgeous. The attraction had been instant for both of them, of that there was no doubt, but she was several years younger than him and a lot less jaded and he did not want to cause hurt.

'So you slept with your ex?' Steele checked, and she gave a glum nod.

'Do you know Gerry?' Candy asked. 'One of the head nurses in the emergency department.'

'I've never met him,' Steele said. 'But I heard a bit about him when I was looking into the waiting times in Emergency. He's an arrogant jerk apparently.'

'That's Gerry!' Candy rolled her eyes. 'He didn't used to be. He got beaten up by two patients a few months ago and it seems to have changed him.'

'He's the one currently in Greece?' Steele checked. 'The one who wrote "Glad you're not here" on his postcard?'

'That's the one.' Candy nodded. 'When I first moved out of home last year we went out, though not for very long.'

'You only moved out last year?'

'Believe me, twenty-four years of age is way too early in my family, unless it's to get married. I should only have moved out to marry the boyfriend they had sort of pressed onto me… Instead, I dumped him and rented a flat.'

'That would have been tough,' Steele commented.

'Yes, it caused a lot of arguments with my parents and I mean a *lot*, but in the end it was far easier to do that than marry someone just because my parents considered him suitable. Anyway, Gerry helped me a bit with the move, given that my parents were sulking. We went out for a while, like I said, but pretty quickly I ended it. That was last year but he's been having a few problems of late. He asked if we could go out for a drink a couple of months ago…' Candy gave an uncomfortable shrug.

'One thing led to another?' Steele checked, and she nodded.

'It was a complete mistake on my part—he thought that signalled we were back together and he wasn't best pleased to find out we're not. Since then he's been making things difficult for me at work. No one knows that we slept together again, thank God.' She looked at Steele, surprised she could meet his eyes after her big revelation. 'It should serve as a reminder—never get involved with anyone from work.'

'Too late,' Steele said. 'I think we both know we're heading for bed—guilt free.'

He liked it that she blushed and he liked it even more that she didn't disagree with him. Now was the time to make it clear that, though this could be incredibly pleasant, there was no question of it lasting for very long.

'I can assure you that I won't turn into a monster when we're over,' Steele said, not very gently spelling it out for her. 'I have very many exes who will tell you the same.'

Candy sat there as a delectable plate of roast beef, with all the trimmings, was placed in front of her. She was glad of the chance to think over his words rather than react immediately to them as she smiled and thanked the waitress. Steele was sitting there basically telling her that he was a playboy and warning her that before they started they had a use-by date hanging over them.

The strange thing for Candy was that she didn't mind. His openness was, in fact, refreshing. She was tired of games, tired of pretending she was enjoying herself. Tired of simply going along for the sake of going along. Gerry had got way too serious too soon, and Franco had been happy to marry her before they'd had so much as a coffee. She had been brought up with the expectation that any man she dated was a potential husband and had to somehow be a suitable provider. It drove Candy insane. She wanted to be twenty-four, she wanted to have fun, and with Steele she could. With him it was different—there were no games, just pleasure to be had with no expectation or end aim. There was something so unique about him, something that said she *deserved* to have sex with him at least once in her lifetime.

'What are you smiling at?'

'My thoughts,' Candy said. 'And they're not for sharing.'

'Would your parents be disappointed in you if they knew what they were?'

'Very.' She smiled.

'Good.'

'So you're here for six weeks?' Candy checked.

'Five now,' Steele said, 'and the last two of them without you, given that you'll be off on your holiday.'

Getting over you, she thought.

But, oh, at least she'd get to be under him.

That was the only sex Candy knew.

'Then where will you be living?' she asked.

'Kent,' Steele said. 'It's an amazing opportunity. I'm overseeing a complete overhaul of their geriatric department. I'm implementing an acute geriatric unit, where all medical patients will be admitted first.'

He had such energy for his job. Candy could hear it in every word he spoke. They had the loveliest lunch, chatting about work, about them, oh, about lots of things, but then Steele said he had to get back.

'I'm speaking with Macey's nieces at two. I'll give you a lift home…'

'I don't need a lift,' Candy said. 'I'm only two stops away.'

'You're sure?'

'Very.'

'So how will I know where you live when I come over to take you out tonight?'

'Where are you taking me?' Candy smiled.

'I haven't decided.' Out on the street he took her wrist and turned her to face him. 'Where would you like to go?'

Bed, she wanted to answer, when she had never felt or given that answer before. 'I'll leave it up to you. Though I warn you, I'm pretty wrecked. Night duty hasn't left me at my most sparkling.' She told him her address and he tapped it into his phone. 'I'll see you tonight about seven?'

'Sounds good.'

It was the middle of the day, there were people everywhere and yet when he took her in his arms it could have been the end of the most romantic night.

'Thanks for coming to lunch.'

'Thanks for asking me.'

It was a very new thing to her, to be somewhere simply because she wanted to be. It should be wrong, except it felt completely right. He was older, wiser and sexier than she had ever dealt with and she was more turned on than she had ever been in her life, and he hadn't even kissed her.

That was about to be corrected, though. Her heart was galloping even more than it had the first day they'd met. Right now it was almost leaping out of her throat in anticipation. An anticipation she had never known because when their lips met it seemed to set off a chain reaction. *This is what a mouth should feel like*, Candy thought, and *This is what a tongue was surely designed for*, she decided as his stroked hers.

Yes, there was a building anticipation because when first his body melded with hers Candy couldn't help but wonder what it would feel like if his hand moved a little higher, or how it would be if she moved in a little closer. Each question was answered—the sound of the traffic dimmed as their kiss intensified. She had never been kissed expertly before and his hand moved just a little higher than her waist to the edge of her rib cage and she ached for it to move higher still. His mouth, the pressure of his lips, the constant beckon of his tongue made her move in closer and she felt breathless.

Both rested their foreheads on the other's for a moment. Trust time to make things complicated, because if it had been nearly two a.m. they would be racing home right about now.

It was daylight, people were talking, a lazy Sunday afternoon was going on all around as they pulled back and met each other's eyes.

'Tonight' was the unspoken word between them.

Candy had never really looked forward to the night in that way before.

'I'm going to be late for my meeting,' Steele said as she got back to his mouth.

'You can be two minutes late,' she said.

She just needed one more taste.

CHAPTER FIVE

THANK GOD THAT she'd just had her period.

It had used to be Candy's excuse not to have sex, but as she had a lovely long bath and shaved and plucked and buffed her body into suitable Steele shape, she was grateful for that fact.

Yes, her Catholic guilt was hovering there in the background but she told it to please be quiet as she took her Pill.

She still hid them in her handbag. It was a matter of habit and her mother would freak, just completely freak, if she knew that Candy was on it. She'd come off it last year but, given what had happened with Gerry, she had gone back on it. She and Gerry had used condoms but what had happened had been such a surprise that she did not want to take any risks.

She hadn't gone home after lunch with Steele; instead, she'd dashed to the shops and bought fabulous underwear that she was now tearing the labels off. There was a silver-grey bra that gave her the best cleavage ever and silver panties that made her dimply bottom look fantastic. In fact, she was so impressed with them that Candy had bought a set in purple also.

She'd always felt fat, but she felt curvy now.

I'll regret it later, she promised her conscience as she looked in the mirror.

Just not yet!

With no idea where they were going Candy decided on a pale shift dress that would look casual with ballet pumps or fab with heels.

It didn't work with her new bra, though.

Second go.

A grey wraparound dress worked better, though showed a little more cleavage than her parents would consider suitable.

Perfect!

Not big on make-up, Candy put on some mascara and a slick of lipstick and when there was a knock at the door she was nervous, but nicely so.

'You're no help,' Candy said as she let him in and he handed her a bottle of wine. Steele was wearing black jeans and a black shirt. He looked incredibly handsome and had that air about him that meant he was suitably dressed for any venue.

'Meaning?' Steele asked.

'I was trying to decide whether to wear flats or heels given that I don't know where we're going.'

'We're going to the movies,' Steele said. 'I figured it might be nice if you're tired—though we shan't be making out in the back row. I like watching a film properly.'

'What are we going to see?' she asked. The movies was possibly the nicest place he could take her if they *had* to go out. It would be nice to turn her brain off for a couple of hours.

'Two choices,' he said. 'One is very dark, apparently funny in part. One is very sad… See what mood you're in.'

'I don't mind,' she said as she led him through her lounge and put the wine down on the bench of a very small kitchen.

'So this is what all the arguments with your parents were about?' Steele said, looking around the living room of her small but cosy flat. The front door opened to the living room. Off that was a small kitchen and to the side a hall that led to the bathroom and bedroom. 'It's nice.'

'I love it,' Candy said. 'It's a ten-minute walk to the Underground, a five-minute walk to my favourite Indian restaurant.

'We can eat before or after…' Steele said.

The thought of Indian before sounded too good to pass up, but then other senses were calling, the attraction wafting between them as potent as any delicious aroma from food.

Candy knew she was eons behind him sexually. She wanted to have slept with him, in part to have jumped that hurdle without knocking it over, in part just to dive onto the track…

And Candy usually hated even the thought of sport, but, oh, he was handsome.

And he was here.

'Do you want a glass of wine?' she offered, even though he'd brought it, but Steele shook his head.

'Not for me,' he said. 'I'm driving. You have one, though…' He went to open the bottle he'd brought but she stopped him.

'Not for me.' Candy shook her head. 'I don't really

drink and anyway I'm on early tomorrow. I'll just get my shoes.'

She went to her bedroom and put on flats but as she came out Steele frowned.

'What happened to the heels?'

'For the movies?'

'For me.'

She smiled and went and put on said heels, with Steele watching her from the doorway.

He made her shiver. If Gerry had stood watching her she'd have found it invasive, but with Steele she just wanted to strip off her dress, pull back the covers on the bed and climb in.

She could feel his eyes on her calf muscles and then on her bum and she turned and it was nice to feel provocative. It was something she had never felt before. He made her feel like this.

And he made her want to kiss him.

It was as simple as that, as natural as breathing to stand in the doorway of her bedroom and wrap her hands behind his neck and share a kiss for no other reason than they both wanted to. She didn't feel naïve or inexperienced with him. There wasn't enough space in her mind for those sorts of thoughts because it was filled instead with pleasurable ones as they got back to where they'd been on the street in record time.

Steele's hand did move higher than the base of her rib cage this time. He was stroking the underside of her breast as they kissed, and her nipples hardened and ached for his fingers to attend to them. She had one hand at the back of his head, just to feel his silky hair, not for pressure for there was plenty of that from Steele, and she had the other on his bum. His buttocks were taut and she checked again. Yes, they were still taut and it was that hand that demanded he press into her.

His moan to her mouth as he did so, his hand at the tie of her dress, told Candy there was no way they would be making the movie.

It was evening, not even semi-dark, and that was seriously uncharted territory for her. End-of-evening sex was all she was used to.

But this wasn't, oh, okay, then, it had been a week after all. This was, let me get this shirt open and this zipper down because I need you to take me now.

Her dress was open, his shirt too, and his fingers were at the back of her bra, ready to undo it, and Candy could barely breathe at the thought of their naked chests pressed together and his hot hands roaming her. She'd never had sex standing, never considered it, because she wasn't the tall, leggy version that a good Candy should be. She was a shorter, chunkier one, who any second now was going to scale Steele's body with the grace of a feline. It was that essential, that natural, that…

'Ignore it…' Steele said as there was a loud rap on the door.

'No…' She could barely breathe now but for a different reason. It was her father's very loud knock and she froze for a second.

'It's my parents.'

'Just ignore it,' he said again.

'They'll let themselves in.'

That her parents had a key came a close second to a bucket of water—actually, it beat the bucket of water because Steele was dressing her and himself with his hands as Candy stood there.

Then he chose to concentrate solely on her for now.

He did up her dress, a little loosely, and wiped off some lipstick and wished the flush on her cheeks would fade by the time she got to the front door. She looked as if she'd just come, or had just been about to. Her nipples were like the dials on his washing machine. Even her lips were swollen.

'Breathe,' Steele said.

'If they find you here…' Candy shivered as he knelt down and changed her heels to flats as there was another knock on the door.

'Will they have us married?'

'You have no idea.'

'Where do you want me?' Steele smiled.

'On my bed.'

'That's what I like to hear,' Steele said, then stopped joking. 'Are they likely to come in here?'

'I hope not.' Candy let out a breath. 'Probably not.'

'Relax,' he said as she closed the bedroom door on him and went to greet her parents. He checked under her bed and he could possibly fit there but first he smiled as he saw the scissors and labels from her brand-new underwear.

She was seriously gorgeous, Steele thought as he did up his shirt and wiped lipstick off. He was unused to thinking *seriously* anything about his dates yet she was so lovely, so focused on fighting for her independence and living her life and yet so kind.

Actually, right now, as Candy opened the front door all she was was stressed!

There were her parents buckling under the weight of jars filled with home-made tomato sauce.

'I said I'd pick them up next week,' she said.

'Why are you all dressed up?' her mother asked, instantly accusing.

'Because I'm just about to go out,'

'You need to wear a top under that dress!' Her mother warned.

They walked through and put the jars of tomato sauce on the bench and Candy got out the coffee machine. There was no such thing as her parents coming over and them not having a coffee, though her father's eyes lit up like a Christmas tree when he saw the bottle of wine on the bench and Candy poured him a glass.

'Where are you going tonight?' her father asked.

'To the movies with a friend.'

'What friend?' her mother checked.

'Kelly.' Candy glanced at the clock. 'Ma, I really do need to get going soon.'

'We've barely seen you these last few weeks.'

They chatted in Italian for twenty minutes or so. Candy had promised herself that the next time she saw them she'd tell them about her trip to Hawaii, but with Steele hiding in the bedroom she chose not to. It was not a conversation that would take twenty minutes—it would be an entire evening of tears and threats and shouting.

Her dad's wineglass was empty, her mum's coffee was gone and though they looked settled in for the evening and her father would no doubt love another glass of wine, Candy stood. 'I'm already late for Kelly,' she said. 'I really am going to have to get ready.'

She felt guilty kicking them out, and then cross that she'd had to. Couldn't they simply ring before they dropped around?

They'd be offended if she asked them to.

Talk about kill the mood, she thought once they had gone and she headed to her bedroom. Steele was lying on her bed, his legs crossed and reading her book.

'I'm so sorry about that,' she said.

'Why?' Steele shrugged. 'Your parents dropped around. It's no big deal.' He smiled at her as she came and sat on the bed beside him. 'I understand, though, that it would be a big deal if they found me here.'

'Thanks.' Candy smiled.

'Do they drop around a lot?'

'They do,' she said. 'They don't drive and, as a sweetener, when I moved out I said I was only moving nearby, which was a big mistake.' She let out a long sigh. 'Another one. I seem to be making rather a lot of them lately. Have I made us late for the movies?'

'I haven't even got the tickets,' he said. 'I didn't know if you'd like the idea.'

'I do,' Candy said, 'I haven't been in ages.'

'I go all the time,' he said. 'Well, not all the time, but I guess going to the movies, for me, is like reading a book is to you. I usually go on my own,' Steele said. It had surprised him that he'd considered taking Candy along. He really did prefer his own company when watching a film.

'How come you go alone?' she asked, gently poking him in the ribs as he lay there. 'Don't you have any friends?'

'I have a lot of friends but not any I'd want to go to the movies with. You should try going by yourself,' he said. 'I loathe trying to concentrate while getting the *What the hell did you bring me to this for?* vibe coming from my right or left.'

Candy started to laugh. 'I get that with my friend

Kelly.' She told him about the time she'd suggested to Kelly that they see what Candy had thought was a romance and he laughed as she described Kelly's reaction as she'd sat beside her, watching someone being tied to the bed.

'She said I was never allowed to choose the movie again,' Candy said, and then she looked down and saw that her hands were now on his chest and fiddling with his buttons and that his hands were playing with her hair. It was as if their bodies were having a little conversation of their own as they carried on talking.

His hand pressed the back of her head a little and she started to kiss him. Her heart was still hammering a bit from her parents' unexpected visit, and a long, slow kiss did nothing to calm it down, but slowly the turmoil of the sudden invasion by her family was fading.

His shirt was open again and beneath her hands were lovely flat nipples that she could not stop stroking, and her dress was open again and how she wished she had a front-opening bra, because she did not want to move her hands from his skin to get naked.

Steele peeled off her dress as she sat over him.

Till this point, till this evening, she had always felt that brief moment of judgment as she undressed. She felt only adoration now; she didn't even try to define what was going on in her head as her dress slid off. She did not care what he thought, safe in the knowledge he thought only good things.

He did think only good things. More used to slenderness, he adored her generous curves and her ripe breasts spilling as he undid her bra, but more giddying and satisfying was the mutual eagerness, as if they had somehow known this was where they were leading.

'I've got something I ought to tell you…' Steele said, pulling back.

'What?' she breathed. 'What do you have to tell me?'

He smiled at the dart of concern in her eyes.

'I'm not sleeping with you till I hear about your name.' His hand stroked one generous breast. 'Tell me,' Steele said.

'No.'

He pulled her onto him and then flipped her onto her back and she lay looking up at him, aching for his kiss. She had already kicked off her ballet pumps. All she had on were her panties and it was he who looked down at her now.

'I'm never going to tell you,' Candy said.

He stood and picked up his shirt.

'Come on,' he said. 'Get dressed.

'That's bribery.'

'Yep.'

Well, two could play at that game. 'Fine,' she said, half-heartedly sitting up, putting her legs over the bed and reaching for her clothes. 'Let's go and get something to eat…'

She picked up her bra and Steele took it from her hands.

He placed it beneath her breasts and did it up at the back and while he did so she could feel his breath on her shoulder and she was more than a little aware of his erection through his trousers. He took one of her breasts and gently stuffed it into the fabric but his hand stayed in there, stroking her, teasing her, and she sat still as his lips started to nuzzle the other one, licking and sucking at her nipple, stretching it with his lips as her hands moved to his head and urged him for more contact. But then he stopped. She looked down as he went to tuck her wet, very aroused breast back into her bra, and she decided he was cruel, so cruel that she knew if she didn't relent they would be sitting eating a curry or watching a movie about half an hour from now.

'Okay.' Her voice was all husky and she didn't really recognise it as hers. She cleared her throat, but it still sounded the same.

'As you know, my parents are Italian,' Candy said, and her head was on his shoulder as he unhooked her bra again.

'Okay.'

'Strict,' she said. His hands were now on her hips and she lifted her bottom to allow for him to take her panties down.

'Go on,' Steele said, which was contrary to his words because he was kneeling with his mouth on hers as she spoke.

'And they chose the most beautiful name that means pure and innocent...' she said, and she felt the stretch of his lips on hers as he smiled as she told him what she had sworn she wouldn't. 'And then when I hit my teenage years I noticed that people started to snicker and...'

'What is it?' Steele asked.

'What's the medical term for thrush?'

He pulled back and smiled. 'Candida.'

'Which is why I became Candy. Sadly, not to my parents. They still insist on calling me by my full name.'

'Were you teased?' he said to her mouth as his hand parted her thighs and his fingers slipped inside her.

Mercilessly.

'Poor baby...' Steele said.

'Oh...' Candy moaned, her thighs quivering.

He felt her thighs clamp around his hand and her head rest on his shoulder and there was that blissful choice whether to feel her come now or dive in for the pleasure.

Greed won.

He removed his hand and she let out a small sob of frustration combined with bliss as he stood and she sat naked, a breath away from him as he slid down his zipper and undressed. He handed her a condom and she shook her head.

'You do it.'

'You.'

Okay, she was bad at this part, except his erection was at her cheeks and she was licking her lips as she undid the foil. She had never seen something so lovely, so fierce, so tempting, and the quicker she did this and the quicker she came were very good incentives to get it on.

She played for a moment, loving the feel of him naked in her hands, teasing him with hot breaths to the head, cupping him in her hand.

'Candy.'

His voice was deeper, if at all possible, impatient and deliciously stern, and she would have loved to find out what might happen if she teased him further, dragged this out a little longer. Instead, she briefly looked up at chocolate-brown eyes that made her feel as sexy as hell.

'Put it on,' he said.

She did as she was told, unravelling it along his

lovely thick length and deliberately taking her time, loving the sound of his sharp breathing and then the impatient way he pushed her hands away when the job was done.

He pushed her shoulder lightly and it was like dominoes falling, because she toppled back on the bed and he lifted her legs abruptly for daring to keep him waiting. She was compliant, wonderfully so. *Talk about boys to men*, Candy thought as he seared inside her and then she wrapped her legs around him. It was like comparing apples to oranges. He knew exactly what to do as he moved deep inside her. His erection was so strong and fierce that each thrust took her to a place she had never been before.

'I'm going to come,' she said almost in apology, watching, feeling, arching to the bliss of him searing inside.

'I think that's the point,' he said, trying to hold on, revelling in the tight grip of her muscles and the tension of her as she came. It was so deep, so heavy, so intense that Candy briefly wondered if she'd even had an orgasm before.

He kept making love to her through it. She wanted to catch her breath, but then she didn't, for she loved the feel of him taking her as she came. Then she lost her head a little, stopped thinking about anything other than a very small bedroom and a whole lot of pleasure. Steele was looking down at her and then he stilled and she sobbed in pleasure as he started thrusting faster and released into her. To not come again would have proved impossible, to feel his tension release, to see this beautiful man above her and feel him come deep inside shot her into orbit again, her hand pushing at his chest, at the delicious hurt of a sensitive orgasm.

No regrets, never, she swore as, still inside, he collapsed onto her and they breathed their way back to consciousness.

He lay there, inhaling the scent of her hair, feeling her legs loosen and lower to the floor, and he knew this was different. Never had he been more perfectly matched in the bedroom. Her inexperience counted more than she knew for she melded to him, moulded to him. It was all he could do not to gather her things and carry her home.

And then normal service returned to his brain and he kissed her instead of saying the thoughts in his mind.

They ate at her favourite takeaway. A Formica table and cheap plates yet they fell on their food like savages, rather aware that sustenance might be needed later in this night, and then they headed for the movies.

'Sad or dark?' Steele offered.

'Dark,' Candy said.

They went to the blackest, grimmest, yet funniest film. He did watch it intently, yet the only reason he couldn't concentrate fully wasn't the *What the hell did you bring me here for?* vibe.

It was the *I really have to touch you* vibe that was coming from him.

'Stop it,' Candy said as his hand moved up her warm thigh and his mouth went for her neck. 'Concentrate.'

Futile words.

They were like teenagers, and that had been a long time ago for Steele and never for Candy. Those years she'd been keeping Franco at arm's length, not dropping her popcorn on the floor and necking.

'I'm going to have to come and see this alone.'

'So am I.' She smiled and got back to kissing him.

This was heading for morning, Steele knew.

This was heading to tomorrow evening and tomorrow night and the next morning too.

He had this vision of her parents arriving on the doorstep as her legs were behind her ears.

'Come back to mine tonight,' he said between kisses.

'Yes, please,' she agreed.

They weren't ready to be apart any time soon.

CHAPTER SIX

'HOW ARE YOU, Miss Anderson?' Steele asked the following Monday morning as he did his rounds.

'Macey.'

'How are you feeling, Macey?'

'A bit better.'

'That's very nice to hear,' he said as he examined her.

'How was your weekend?' Macey asked him.

'It was very nice,' he said, and she gave a soft smile.

He and Candy had been with each other for a week now. It had been the most intense week of either of their lives. Every available moment they had was spent together. Perhaps, aware how limited their time was, they were determined to make every moment count and were completely into each other. They were both exhausted but in the nicest of ways—between work and sex and eating, and dancing and drives at night just so Candy could find out what it was like to do it in a car, they were sleep deprived and loving it.

'Is Candy on this morning?' Macey asked, oh, so casually.

Steele answered a beat too late. 'I'm not sure what nurses are working this morning.'

'Well, I hope that she is. I haven't seen her for a few days.'

'I think she works in Emergency as well,' Steele said. 'From memory.'

'Does that mean that I won't get to see her again?' Macey fretted, or rather pretended to fret.

Steele knew when he was being played and he didn't mind a bit; he liked it that Macey was starting to notice things that were going on around her. 'I think Candy might be on duty later in the week.'

'Oh, that's good to know.' Macey smiled.

He had, on admission and again last week, interviewed Macey extensively and she had revealed nothing more but Steele pushed on. He knew where they were heading.

'I saw your picture in the corridor,' he said. 'They're putting up pictures of the history of the hospital as a part of the renovations. Emergency is getting a makeover at the moment and so too is the entrance corridor.'

Macey said nothing at first. She didn't want to hear about the changes to the hospital she had loved. It had been such a huge part of her life. 'I don't like hearing about renovations,' she said finally. 'I like remembering it as it was.'

'Things change,' Steele said. 'Not all things, though. Anyway, I saw you in one of the photographs. It looked as if you were getting a medal or a badge in the gardens…'

Macey's eyes filled with tears as she remembered those days.

'Can you talk to me?'

She shook her head.

'I want to see if I can help.'

'Well, you can't.'

'Okay.' He knew not to push her. Macey was starting to come out of her emotional collapse a little. The medicines were starting to help and she was engaging with the nursing staff and the occupational therapist.

He knew there was more, though, and that night he told Candy as he cooked them a stir-fry.

'Macey's holding out on me.'

'Maybe not,' Candy said.

'Oh, I'm pretty certain that she is.'

'How do you know?'

'I just know.' He smiled. 'Can you pass me the oyster sauce?'

She jumped down and went to the cupboard and got it for him.

'I hate this kitchen,' Steele said. 'It's really badly thought out.'

'I hate kitchens, full stop,' she said. 'You like cooking?'

'Not really,' he said, 'but I like eating.'

'Did you…?' Candy stopped. She'd been about to ask if he'd done the cooking when he'd been married. It was, she guessed, a no-go area, so she swiftly changed what she had been about to say. 'So why did you buy it if you hate it so much?

'It's just a serviced apartment.' Steele answered her question while knowing what she'd been about to say. He was used to avoiding such subjects with women he dated but Candy, or rather his feelings for her, was unlike any he had known and he was starting to come to grips with answering the tricky questions for her. For now, though, he was glad she had changed what she'd been about to say. 'All my stuff is in storage. Which is why I have to work out things like the coffee machine.'

'Oh! I thought you just need glasses. Well, I guess that accounts for the terrible pictures on the walls.'

'I was about to say all my stuff is in storage apart from the pictures,' he said, and then grinned at her pained expression. 'Joke.'

'Thank goodness.'

She opened the bottle as he stirred in the beef. The smell was incredibly strong, and she headed to the sink for a drink and took a few breaths, not wanting to show how the smell had affected her.

Tiny spots were dancing in her eyes and she was sure that if she said anything then Steele would simply tell her, as her parents had, to cut down on the extra shifts that she was working.

'Are you okay?' he asked.

'Fine,' she said as she ran a glass under the tap. 'I'm just thirsty.'

'You're wrecked,' Steele said. He turned off the wok and came over and turned her to face him. 'You need an early night.'

She smiled up at him. 'Our early nights are possibly the reason that I'm so tired.'

'I'm serious,' he said. He looked at her pale features and felt a touch guilty that she had been burning the candle at both ends. 'Why don't you go to bed?' he suggested. 'To sleep—a decent sleep.'

'It's seven o'clock.'

'Go to bed,' Steele said, 'and I mean to sleep. You need it.'

'I think I might.'

Because they could, because they were both tired,

for no other reason than they wanted to, when Steele had served up their meals they headed to the bedroom, stripped off, Steele closed the curtains and they ate dinner in bed while watching the news. Candy felt very spoiled and very lazy as he took their empty plates through to the kitchen.

'I don't think I've been to bed at this time since I was seven years old,' she said as Steele climbed back into bed. 'I used to beg to stay up then!'

'Do you want to watch a movie or just go to sleep?' he asked, and they shared a very nice kiss.

'I just want to sleep.' She sighed, wriggling down in the covers and getting comfortable with him.

'Then do.'

She lay on his chest, delighted with their early night, feeling the lovely crinkly hair on his stomach and wondering if she'd ever been happier. 'I love your stomach,' Candy said.

'If you want to sleep you'd better stop playing with it, then.'

She didn't.

She thought back to what she'd been about to ask in the kitchen. Whether Steele had done the cooking or if his wife had was irrelevant, she knew. There was other stuff she'd like to know, though. 'Can I ask you something?'

'You can,' he said, staring into the semi-dark and sort of knowing what was coming and wondering how he'd answer it.

'Why did your marriage break up?

'We just didn't work out,' Steele said. Then he went to add his spiel about they'd been too young, or they'd just grown apart, yet he and Candy had always been honest with each other. They were *so* honest with each other that it sometimes took his breath away. Which meant he didn't want to be evasive now, yet he had never told anyone the reason for the break-up. He'd never told anyone apart from his ex-wife that he was infertile.

And when he had told Annie, she hadn't taken the news well.

'I haven't really talked about it before,' Steele admitted.

'Were you a wife basher?' Candy whispered.

'No.' He laughed.

'Then it doesn't matter,' Candy said, and gave him a light kiss on the chest. 'You don't have to answer.'

He wanted to, though.

'Annie and I got married when I was twenty-three and she was twenty-six. We'd been going out for years,' Steele said. 'We bought the house, the dog, all good...'

Candy didn't like that.

It was funny but she felt the little stiffening of her body as he gave his past a name and an age but then she breathed out through her nostrils and lay there, waiting for him to continue. 'Then Annie decided, or rather we both decided, to start a family.'

'She decided or both?' Candy checked.

'I thought we should wait but Annie really wanted children so we went for it but nothing happened,' Steele said. 'And then nothing kept on happening. I went and had a test—they usually check for issues with the guy first as it's far less invasive—and so we found out, pretty much straight away, that the problem was me.

I'm infertile.' He waited for her to stiffen again, or some sign of tension, or what, he didn't know, but instead she looked up at him through the darkness. '*That's* why you broke up?'

'Pretty much. Annie was devastated. I mean, the news completely sent her into a spin.'

'You broke up just because of that?' Candy asked. She really didn't understand.

'It causes a big strain in a marriage. Then there was all her family and how they dealt with the news.' Steele let out a sigh. 'Can you imagine your family's reaction if you told them that your husband was infertile?'

Candy thought for a moment and she could and so she answered him honestly. 'One, I'm not very keen on getting married...'

'Come on.'

'Seriously, I'm not,' she said. 'Two, I wouldn't tell them—it's none of their business. I might tell them that *we* were having problems if they nagged enough.' She thought about it some more. 'Steele, I do everything I can not to discuss sex and such with them—I still hide my Pills in my handbag.'

'I guess.' He smiled. 'After all, you hid me in the bedroom.'

Candy nodded to his chest. 'So I certainly wouldn't be discussing my partner's sperm count with them.'

Steele gave a low laugh.

'You said that she'd been back in touch?' she ventured.

'Yep, her second marriage has broken up and she asked if I would consider giving us another go, though with one proviso—there have been a lot of advances in technology apparently...'

'What a cow!'

He smiled. 'My thoughts at the time—well, a little less politely put in my head. I just hung up on her.'

'You didn't consider it.'

'I don't love her any more,' he said. 'I haven't for a long time.'

He looked a little more closely into the timeline of his marriage and divorce, something he rarely did. 'When I found out that I probably couldn't be a father and Annie had wrapped her head around the news, she lined us up for this battery of tests and investigations. She started to talk about donor sperm and, to be completely honest...' Steele hesitated; it hurt to be honest at times. 'I think I knew then that we had more problems than my infertility.'

'Like?'

He had never really examined it. He'd just shoved that into the too-hard basket, but lying there, her fingers on his stomach and her breath on his chest, he felt able to go further. 'Well, I'd always planned on being the complete opposite to my parents with my children. I didn't want boarding school or that sort of thing. I wanted to be a real hands-on father. When we first started trying to have a baby, though I thought we were maybe jumping in rather too soon, I was also looking forward to it. I think we all assume, or at least I did, that I'd be a parent one day. When I got the results I suddenly lost all that. I told Annie and she sobbed and she cried and then she had to go to her family and wail with them. It went on for weeks, and do you know what, Candy?'

She heard the bitterness in his voice and now she could understand it. 'What?'

'I was feeling pretty awful at the time. Seriously awful. I wanted some time to get my head around it. I wanted to process the knowledge that I couldn't have children. In hindsight we'd had it really good till that point. We'd never had to deal with anything major. And when we did, I found out that I didn't like the way Annie dealt with the difficult things that life flings at us at times. She made it all about her, not even about us. It was all about Annie. I tried to understand where she was coming from, yet she never did that for me. I think I fell out of love. If I was ever properly in love in the first place…' he mused. 'So, yes, while I've always thought that it was infertility that broke us up, I don't think it's that neat.'

He loved it that she was still there. She hadn't even jolted when he'd told her. Maybe because they were temporary, Steele pondered. Maybe because she wasn't worried about his ability to make babies, but it was nice to have said it and to have got such a calm reaction.

'Was she blonde?' Candy asked, and it made him smile.

'No.'

'Tall and leggy?'

'Go to sleep.' He was really smiling now as he kissed the top of her head.

'Can I ask another thing?' she said sleepily.

'You can.'

'Why are we using condoms?'

'Because I always have.'

'So have I.' She gave him a little nudge and Steele lay there smiling at the potential reward for his little confession. 'Well, they do say that every cloud has a silver lining.'

Candy didn't answer.

She was fast asleep.

CHAPTER SEVEN

CANDY HAD NEVER slept better than she did when Steele was beside her. His breathing, his heartbeat, the way he held her through the night were like a delicious white noise that blocked out everything else other than them. They wrapped themselves around each other, then unwrapped themselves when they got too hot and then when they got too cold found the other again. It was a seamless dance that lasted a full ten hours and had them on a slow sultry simmer that, by morning, started to rise to boiling point.

Candy awoke slowly, face down on the pillow and with her arms over her head. Steele's arm lay over her waist. The scent in her nostrils was Steele and as she started to wake up she remembered what they had been talking about before she'd fallen asleep. She knew it wasn't something that he'd discussed with others and the privilege of him confiding in her gave her a warm feeling. She loved it that he'd told her. She loved lying in bed next to him and feeling him start to wake up. She loved every minute of her time with him.

She felt his hand roam her spine. Steele's slow, lazy explorations made her melt into the mattress. It was as if each vertebra, right down to the lowest, was an individual treasure worth examining. His hand moved up her back and then to the exposed flesh on her side. Her rib cage received a significantly slower perusal, and his fingers found the softness of her flattened breast. She wanted to lift herself up to let his hand in but he rolled heavily onto her. His mouth buried beneath her hair, reaching for her neck, and then kissed his way to her ear.

'You do talk in your sleep.' His lovely voice greeted her ear and was just as effective in turning her on as his hands.

'Don't believe a word I say.' Candy smiled as he whispered to her the rude things that she *hadn't* said.

'How are you feeling now?' he asked, because it had been a very long sleep after all.

'Better than I ever have,' she admitted. 'I never want to move.'

'Then don't.'

There was a thrill low in her belly and Candy, who had never, till Steele, had morning sex, was fast becoming a fan as, still face down on the pillow, she felt Steele's delicious weight come fully on top of her.

Temptation beckoned as she parted her legs just a little, closing her eyes as his fingers checked that she was ready, which of course she was. Clearly last night's conversation was still on his mind because there was no pause in proceedings to reach for a condom and put it on. Instead, she felt his naked warmth nudging her.

He entered her slowly and Candy let out a moan and so too did Steele, because to feel her wet warmth along his length was intimate, way more intimate than he had been in a very long time.

His mouth was at her ear. 'Cross your ankles,' he said.

Candy did so and she thought she might collapse with the pleasure as together they started to rock—she could feel every long generous inch of him, hear his ragged breathing. Her face was red and sweaty in the pillow, and Steele took her hand and placed it between her legs and got to work on her breasts.

Oh!

She'd feel guilty later, Candy decided, but he didn't seem to mind a bit that she touched herself. They were barely moving, just rocking, his mouth was at her ear, his fingers stretching her nipples, and then his fingers slid down and took over from hers.

'You're bad for my conscience,' she said.

'No conscience needed,' he said.

He could go for ever like this.

Usually.

Her buttocks were so soft and ripe and they started to lift and press into his groin, and the soft muffled moans of pleasure had Steele tip just as she did and it was bliss to feel him come unsheathed inside her.

'Oh…' Candy lay feeling his weight on her and never wanting him gone. Even the alarm clock that was going off seemed a mile away.

'Can you wake me up like that tomorrow?' she said.

'I can.'

He rolled off and they lay, Candy still on her stomach, facing each other, and sharing a smile.

'I'm going to try and swap so I can get this weekend off,' Steele said, because she flew out the following Friday. 'It's not long now till you go.'

She didn't want to go.

Well, she did, because she was probably going to spend the entire first week of her holiday in bed. With all these extra shifts and sex marathons she was looking forward to sleeping round the clock.

She just wished that her holiday was scheduled for after he'd gone.

Then she stared into his eyes and wondered who she was kidding because she knew that she was going to spend her entire holiday sobbing. Despite starting off with the best of intentions to keep things light, to simply enjoy, Candy knew she was in way over her head. Her feelings for this man were so intense, so instinctively right that she simply could not imagine how she was possibly going to begin to get over him.

'Steele…' She took a breath. She wasn't sure if what she was about to say would sound too pushy, but she'd never held back from the truth with him and she chose not to now. 'Why don't you come for a few days?'

'To Hawaii?'

'Yes.' Candy nodded.

'I don't want to intrude on your holiday…'

'It wouldn't be intruding. It would be nice if you came in the middle. You've got a long weekend coming up.'

'It would be nice,' Steele said. 'I'd be pretty wrecked, though.'

'Well, I'll have slept for a week by the time you get there,' Candy said. 'I'll have enough energy for both of us. Think about it,' she offered, and then she climbed out of bed and grimaced when she saw the time. 'I'm going to be late. I'll have a quick shower and then I need to stop by my flat.'

'I'll drive you in,' Steele said. To keep things well away from work Candy was still taking the Underground and he watched the little flash of worry flare in her eyes.

'We might be seen,' she said. 'Steele, you've no idea how gossip spreads at that place.'

'I'm sure I do.' He smiled. 'It doesn't bother me if we're seen, unless of course it's a problem for you.'

She thought about it for a moment. 'Actually, no.'

'I can have broken your heart and put you off seeing anyone for ages after I've gone.' Steele grinned, giving her an excuse to give to Gerry if he pushed her to go out with him when he returned from Greece. But then Steele met her eyes and his tone changed slightly and she, though late for work, stood there in the bedroom and felt her heartbeat quicken. 'You could even say you were still seeing me,' he said, and they just looked at each other.

'I guess he wouldn't know either way,' Candy said, though something told her this conversation had little to do with excuses to give to Gerry.

There were two, possibly three, conversations going on.

That Steele would be gone and that Candy could say what she liked about them if it made things easier for her with Gerry.

That he would be gone, Steele thought, and he was saying that possibly this might last longer.

That he would be gone, Candy thought, and she didn't want him to be.

'Get ready,' he said.

They stopped at her flat and Candy quickly changed into jeans, which was what she usually wore for arriving at work, and rubbed some serum into her hair as she chatted to Steele.

'We came back here for this?'

'I can't leave home without it,' Candy said, trying to tame her long wild curls. 'I should buy another bottle and leave it at yours.'

'Why don't you just pack some things now and put them in my car?' Steele said, and she hesitated because she'd been thinking exactly the same thing. 'It would save us dashing back and forth all the time.'

She packed a case and they loaded it into his car and drove to work. It was all so new, so exciting that neither could help smiling.

As they pulled into the staff car park, Louise, a midwife who had done a stint in Emergency last year, was walking past. She and Candy had got on well. Louise was blonde and gorgeous and rather pregnant and she waved to Candy and gave a little wink.

'We're public knowledge now.' Candy smiled as she waved back, because Louise was a terrible gossip, which was surprising, considering that she was married to Anton, an obstetrician whose middle name was discretion.

'I'm fine with that,' Steele said.

He had long ago stopped playing games and this felt nothing like a game with Candy.

'We'll keep it discreet on the ward, though,' Candy said, because she was working on the geriatric unit today till lunchtime.

'Yes,' Steele said. 'I just don't want to be dropping you at another entrance and things. Come back to mine after work. I've got a meeting at six, though,' he continued, 'so I won't be back till about eight.'

'I'll have bread waiting in the toaster for you,' Candy said as he peeled off a key, which he had never done before. She snapped it onto her key ring as if it was no big deal.

It was a big deal. Both knew it. It was way too soon, but in other ways it was not soon enough.

Neither knew where this had come from or fully what it was.

They were planning holidays, her suitcase was in his boot, his key was now in her bag and they were kissing in the front seat as if one of them had just stepped off a plane after a year's absence. When she pulled back from his kiss, she returned to her question from before she'd fallen asleep. Candy was curious about his ex-wife and that spoke volumes in itself.

'*Was* she tall and leggy?' Candy smiled, watching him cringe just a little as he shook his head.

'Gamine?' Candy ventured. 'Please say no.'

'Not gamine *exactly*...' Steele said, and she groaned.

'Careful, Steele,' she warned. 'You may live to regret your next choice of words.'

He just smiled as they got out of the car.

There was nothing about their time together to regret.

Just that it was running out.

CHAPTER EIGHT

'I'M GOING TO take off your dressing, Macey,' Candy said. 'Steele wants to have a look at it.'

'Are you working tomorrow?' Macey asked, because Candy only had a four-hour shift and finished at lunchtime.

'I am, but I'm working down in Emergency.'

Macey was improving. Her medications were starting to kick in and she was engaging with the staff and other patients. She was also taking her meals unaided but she was still far from the feisty woman who had arrived in Emergency.

Steele came in just as Candy had got the dressing off. It was clearing up but it was very sloughy and still a bit smelly and as she saw it, Candy blew out.

'I'm just going to get the phone,' she said, even though it wasn't ringing, but she felt a bit sick. 'I won't be long.'

'I was like that,' Macey said to Steele, 'when I was…' Macey quickly changed what she had been about to say mid-sentence. 'When I was nursing.'

'No, you weren't,' Steele said. 'You weren't some young pup who couldn't stomach a bit of pus.'

Macey looked at him.

He knew. She was sure of it.

Steele did know because he had seen the cape carefully held to hide Macey's stomach in the photo in the entrance hall. He'd also done a little delving and it would seem that Matron Macey Anderson had gone to Bournemouth to recover from polio, though she'd made no reference to it when Steele had asked her for her medical history.

Tell me, his eyes said as Macey's own eyes filled with tears. Steele sat on the bed and took her hand. 'Talk to me, Macey.'

'When I was *carrying*, I was like that.' She started to cry as a fifty-five-year-old secret was finally released and Steele let her cry. He passed her tissues from her locker, not saying a word as Macey wept.

As Candy came in to do the dressing he briefly looked up to her. 'I've got this, thanks,' he said.

Candy saw that Macey was upset and left them.

When Macey stopped crying, he didn't press her for more information; instead, he did the dressing on her leg and afterwards he sorted out the covers. 'Do you want a cup of tea?' he asked.

'I'd like a sherry.'

'I bet you would,' he said. 'I'll be back in a moment.'

He took away the trolley, leaving Macey alone for a little while to gather herself. He left the curtains closed around her.

Candy was having a glass of water at the desk and he asked her for the keys to the cupboard where the sherry and things were kept and poured Macey a glass.

'Is she okay?' Candy asked.

'She will be. I'm going back in to talk to her,' Steele said. 'Macey saw you get a bit dizzy and has got you down as pregnant. I told her you're not and that they don't build nurses as strong these days.' He gave her a grim smile and then explained what was happening. 'As it turns out, she had a baby.'

'Oh…'

'Macey has never told anyone until now so it's a huge deal to her. I'm just giving her a few moments to gather herself,' Steele said, 'and then I'm going to go in and speak with her. Would you tell Gloria to make sure that we're not disturbed?'

'Sure.'

'If she has any visitors…'

'I'll say that the doctor's in with her.'

'Thanks.'

He walked back behind the curtains. Macey had stopped crying and she gave Steele a watery smile.

'Sorry about that,' she said.

'Why should you be sorry?' Steele asked, handing her the glass of sherry. 'I'm glad that you told me. Would you like to talk about it?' he offered.

'I don't know how to,' Macey admitted. 'It's been a secret for so long.'

'Not any more,' Steele said. 'It might help to talk about it.'

'I got pregnant when I was twenty-seven,' Macey said. 'He was married. I was never much of a looker and I suppose I was flattered. Anyway, my parents would have been horrified. They would have said that I was old enough to know better. We're never old enough to know better when it comes to matters of the heart, though. Instead of telling them, I confided in one of the matrons here. I thought she'd be shocked but she was more than used to it and took care of things. I was sent down to Bournemouth to have him. Everyone thought that I had polio and that was the reason I was away so long. Instead, I had my son and he was handed over for adoption.'

'I'm sorry, Macey,' Steele said. 'That must have been so painful.'

'It still is.' She nodded. 'I was very sick when he was delivered. I did everything I could not to push because I knew that as soon as he was born he would be taken away. I passed out when he was delivered and I never got to hold him and I never even got to see him. When I came around the next day I asked if I could have just one cuddle but I was told it was better that way. It wasn't.'

'Have you ever tried to look him up or make contact?'

'Never,' she said. 'I've thought about it many times but I didn't want to mess up his life if he didn't know he was adopted. I was told that he had gone to a very good family and that I was to get on with my life. I came back to work and threw myself into my career, but I've thought about him every single day since.'

'And his father?'

'I had nothing to do with him after that,' Macey said. 'We worked alongside each other for a few years afterwards. I think at first he thought he could carry on with me as before but I soon put him right. I told him to concentrate on his marriage. I'm very ashamed that I had an affair with a married man.'

'Try not to be ashamed,' Steele suggested. 'Perhaps it would be better to view that time with remorse but do your best to leave the shame out of it.

'I know you must have felt very alone at the time

but I can tell you from all my years doing this job that what happened to you happened to a lot of women from your generation.'

'He was married, though.'

'You weren't the first and you certainly won't be the last person to have an affair with a married man. My guess is you've more than paid the price.'

'I have.'

'Forgive yourself, then,' Steele said. 'Have you thought about discussing what happened with your nieces?'

'Sometimes,' Macey said. 'I wake up some nights, imagining them finding out what happened after I'm gone and not being able to speak about it with me.'

'Maybe consider speaking with them again,' Steele suggested. 'And if you want help telling them, or if you want me to do it for you, let me know.' He watched as Macey frowned, though it wasn't a dismissive frown. He could see that she was thinking about it. 'And if you never want to discuss it again, then that's fine too.'

'I might think again about telling them...' she said. 'There's just so much guilt. Sometimes when I'm enjoying myself I feel that I don't deserve to.'

'Let the guilt go, Macey,' Steele said. 'You are allowed to be happy.'

Candy sat at the nurses' station, staring at Macey's curtains, but, though usually she'd be curious, right now she wasn't wondering what was going on behind closed curtains.

Steele's throwaway comment about Macey thinking that Candy was pregnant had immediately been disregarded but now a small nagging voice was starting to make itself known.

She felt *so* tired.

Seriously tired.

There were many reasons that could account for that but the usually energetic Candy could barely walk past a bed without wanting to climb into it.

And she *had* felt sick a couple of times.

Actually, she'd had a bout of stomach flu a few weeks ago. Or she'd assumed it was stomach flu.

But she'd had her period, though it had been light, but she was sure that was because she had gone back on the Pill.

God, was it that fabulous bra that had given her such cleavage?

Stop it, Candy told herself.

Except she couldn't stop it.

'How is she?' she asked, when Steele came out from behind Macey's curtains.

'She's having a cry so keep them closed.' He told her a little about it. 'She doesn't want her nieces to know at this stage but at least she seems to be thinking about telling them.' He frowned at Candy's distraction. 'Are you okay?'

'I'm fine,' she said.

She wasn't, though.

Macey's words had seriously unsettled her.

Candy did her best not to let them.

She headed for home and looked around her flat. She opened the fridge to sort out the milk and things but let out a moan when she saw that it had already been done.

Her parents had been around.

Candy looked at a letter on her kitchen bench and saw that it had been opened.

It was her bank statement.

And there were flashing lights on her answering machine that Candy knew would be messages from her parents—they were really the only people who called her on her landline.

Candy took a breath and called her mum. She sat for five minutes wondering why it had to be like this as her mum demanded to know where she'd been and what she'd been doing.

'I've been really busy with work,' she said, loathing that she had to lie and then deciding not to. 'I've been doing a lot of extra shifts,' she explained, and took a deep breath. 'I've booked a holiday. It was a last-minute thing.'

'Where?'

'Hawaii. I go next Friday for two weeks.' Candy closed her eyes and tried to answer in calm tones as the questions started.

'I'm going by myself,' Candy said. 'I just felt that I needed to get away.'

No, she couldn't afford it and as she was told that Candy thought of the first day she had met Steele, who had simply said, 'Good for you.'

'Mum,' Candy interrupted. 'I'm going on holiday, I want to go and I'm not going to argue about it with you.'

'You listen—'

'No,' she said. 'I love you very much, you know that I do, but I'm not going to run everything that I do by you.'

It hurt to have this discussion but she knew it was way overdue. She knew they loved and cared for her and that they expected to be involved in every facet of her life. It just wasn't the way Candy wanted to live any more.

'Ma, I'm not arguing,' she said. She took a breath, wanting to tell them to please ring in the future before dropping around. She wanted to ask for the return of her keys but baby steps, Candy decided, so she dealt with that morning's events. 'Mum, I don't want you opening my mail and I've told you over and over that I don't want you coming around and letting yourself in when I'm not here.'

She meant it. So much so that when her mother pointed out she was just trying to help and, anyway, she'd need someone to take care of the flat while she was in Hawaii, Candy snapped in frustration. 'It's not a stately home that needs taking care of. It's a one-bedroom flat!'

It didn't go well.

Candy knew her requests would be, as always, simply ignored so after she put down the phone she did what she didn't want to but felt she had to.

She made a trip to the hardware store, but not just for locks. She also bought a drill.

Then she had to go back to the hardware store a second time because after numerous attempts her shiny new drill wouldn't screw in a nail but a very nice guy explained what a drill bit was for!

She loathed that she'd done it.

She loathed more than that that she'd had to, but she had realised that despite the move she hadn't really left home. Her parents saw her flat as a bedroom with a slightly longer hall to walk down. Candy thought of Steele hiding in her room that night and knew that was the reason they stayed at his place.

No, Candy thought as she turned the new lock on her door and then headed for Steele's, it was her life.

It was a long day for Steele.

A very long day.

He stopped by Macey's bed at the end of his shift and she asked if he would speak with her niece when she visited tomorrow.

'Of course I will,' Steele said.

Then he had a meeting to sit through, which really had nothing to do with him, given that he'd be gone in a few weeks. Not that it stopped him putting his point across about the lengthy waits in Emergency. Oh, and a few other things too.

By nine he should be more than ready for home but for once Steele was tentative.

There was no bread waiting for him in the toaster.

Steele walked through his apartment and put Candy's case, which he had bought in from the car, down in the hallway. He knew she was here and he knew where she probably was.

He walked through to the bedroom and, sure enough, there was Candy, fast asleep in bed with the light still on. He looked at her black curls all splayed out on the pillow and he looked at the dark circles under her eyes and he stood there for a full two minutes, watching her sleep deeply.

Steele made his own toast and then had a shower and tried to watch a film. It was a film that he had been meaning to watch for ages but, unusually for him, he couldn't concentrate.

There was something else, far deeper, on his mind.

He turned off the television and lights and got into bed next to Candy, and she rolled into him.

'Sorry,' she said sleepily. 'I saw the bed and couldn't resist. When did you get back?'

'Just now,' he said, though it had been a good hour.

'I changed the lock on my front door.' Her voice was groggy with sleep.

'Good for you,' Steele said. 'Go back to sleep.'

She did.

He didn't.

Instead, he lay staring at the ceiling.

Yes, there was a lot on his mind.

Macey's words had now seriously rattled him too.

CHAPTER NINE

After

CANDY WOKE IN Steele's arms and listened to the sound of his breathing.

She wanted him to wake and roll over and make love to her. She wanted the pregnancy thought in her head to be obliterated by his kiss.

Then she didn't want his kiss because she felt sick.

Candy's mind flicked over the past few weeks.

Yes, she'd been sick last month, but it had been one of those bugs.

Surely?

She really felt sick now and she crept to the bathroom and tried to throw up as quietly as she could.

It was exhaustion, Candy told herself, brushing her teeth and then showering, but when she glanced in the mirror she could see the fear in her eyes.

Steele lay there listening to Candy flush the toilet to drown out her gags and he blew out a breath.

'Morning,' he said a few moments later, when he came in and she was already in the shower.

'Morning.' Candy smiled but she couldn't quite meet his eyes.

There was an elephant in the room that they both chose to ignore and they dashed around, getting dressed, finding keys, exclaiming they were running late when really they were actually doing quite well for time.

There was the first uncomfortable silence between them as Steele drove Candy and the massive elephant in the car to work.

There was no frantic kissing and they walked through the car park in silence, Candy making the decision to do a pregnancy test as soon as she got there, Steele wondering what the hell he should say.

If anything.

The sound of an ambulance siren had her look up and she saw Lydia standing in the forecourt, frantically gesturing for her to run. Clearly there was something big coming in.

'I've got to go,' she said.

'Go!' Steele said, and he watched her run through the car park and to the forecourt, where not one but three flashing-light ambulances were now pulling up. Kelly ran past him too and as Steele walked up the corridor the anaesthetists and trauma teams were running down it towards Emergency.

Candy, Steele thought, was in for one helluva morning.

She was.

She raced into the changing rooms and stripped off her jeans and T-shirt and got into scrubs as Kelly did the same.

'What is it?' Kelly asked.

'Multi-traumas.' Candy passed on the little Lydia had told her as she'd dashed past. 'Four of them.'

'Four are coming here?'

It was rare to get four all at once but apparently there were several more critically injured patients going to different emergency departments. A high-speed collision, involving several vehicles, meant there would be nothing to think about other than the patients any time soon.

It was on this morning that Candy fell back in love with Emergency.

Yes, it was busy and stressful but it was what she loved to do. Helping out with a little girl who had looked dire when she'd first arrived but who was now coughing as Rory, the anaesthetist, extubated her was an amazing feeling indeed.

'It's okay, Bethany,' Candy said as the girl opened her eyes and started to cry. 'I'm Candy. You're in hospital but you're going to be okay.'

Thank God! She looked up at Rory, who gave her a wide-eyed look back because it had been touch and go. Bethany had had a chest tube inserted as her lung had collapsed in the accident and her heart hadn't been beating when she'd arrived in the department.

To see her coughing and crying and alive, Candy knew why she'd fought so hard to do a job she loved.

Rory and the thoracic surgeon started talking about sedation and getting Bethany up to ICU, and it all happened seamlessly.

'Busy morning?' Patrick, the head nurse in ICU, smiled when Candy came up with her patient.

'Just a bit.'

'You look exhausted,' Patrick commented. 'So this is Bethany?' He looked down at the little girl, who was sedated but breathing on her own. He nudged Candy away for a moment. 'I'm going to put her in a side room. I thought about putting her next to Mum but I think it's going to scare her more for now.'

'How is her mum doing?' Candy asked, because she had been so busy working on Bethany that she didn't really know what was going on with the rest of her family.

'Won't know for a while,' Patrick said. 'They'll keep her in an induced coma for at least forty-eight hours. Is it settling down in Emergency now?'

'I don't know,' she admitted. 'I haven't looked up yet.'

'Go and grab a drink,' Patrick said.

He was nice like that and Candy headed round to the little staffroom and had a quick drink from the fridge, pinched a few biscuits and then headed back to the unit.

It was quiet. One elderly man was being wheeled in on a stretcher and Candy rolled her eyes at Kelly as she walked into Resus to start the massive tidy up.

It was going to be a big job.

'Let's get one bed completely stocked and done,' Kelly said, 'just in case something comes in, then we can deal with the rest.'

They got one area cleared and restocked and were just about to commence with the rest when Lydia came in.

'I've asked if everyone can come through to the staffroom.'

'Now?' Candy checked, because there was still an awful lot to do.

'Just make sure that one crash bed is fully stocked,' Lydia said, 'and then come straight through. I need to speak to everyone.'

* * *

Steele's morning flew by too.

He had a video meeting with some of his new colleagues in Kent and arranged to go there next Thursday as he wanted to see how the extension was coming along. He also had a house lined up with a real estate agent and wanted to take a second look.

Mr Worthington passed away just after eleven, his radio on, his family beside him. Steele spent a good hour with the family afterwards in his office at the end of the ward.

As they left, instead of heading back out, he sat and thought about Candy. He didn't know how he felt and he didn't know what to do.

He looked up when there was a knock at the door and he called for whoever it was to come in then remembered that he'd asked Gloria to send Macey's niece in once the Worthington family had gone home.

'Hello, Dr Steele.' Catherine smiled. 'Gloria said that you wanted to talk to me.'

'I do,' he said. 'Come in.'

'Aunt Macey has just gone for an occupational therapy assessment,' Catherine said. 'It's nice to see her walking again.' She took a seat and then looked at Steele. 'It's bad news, isn't it…?' she said, and her eyes filled up with tears.

'No, no.' Immediately Steele put her at ease. 'I haven't called you in to break bad news about your aunt's health.' He watched her let out a huge breath of relief. 'Her physical health anyway,' Steele amended. 'But as you know, Macey's been depressed.'

'She seems to be getting better, though,' Catherine said. 'The tablets seem to be starting to work.'

'They are,' Steele said. 'She's talking a bit more and engaging with the staff. The thing is,' he said, 'it isn't just medication that your aunt needs at the moment. She's asked that I speak with you. There's something that's upsetting her greatly and it's been pressing on her mind.'

'I don't know what you mean.'

'Your aunt has something she wishes to discuss with you, a secret that she has kept for many, many years, and it's one she doesn't want you to find out about after her death...' He told her that Macey had had a baby more than fifty years ago and that he'd been given up for adoption at birth, but Catherine kept shaking her head, unable to take in the news. 'We'd have known.'

'Very few people knew,' Steele said. 'That's what it was like in those days.'

'But my aunt's not like that...' Catherine said, and then caught herself. 'When I say that, I mean she's so incredibly strict—she's always saying that women should save themselves and...' She stopped talking and simply sat there as she took the news in. 'Poor Aunt Macey. How can we help?'

'I think speak with Linda and then perhaps you can both come in together. Talk it over with Macey, maybe ask if she wants to look for her son, or if she simply wants it left. Her fear is that you'll find out after her death, whenever that may be, and you might judge her.'

'Never.'

'I know it's a shock,' he said.

'It is.' Catherine smiled. 'My mother would have had a fit if she knew. Is that why she's been depressed?'

'I think it's a big part of it,' Steele said. 'Maybe

when she's got it off her chest and spoken with her family, things can really start to improve.'

He was about to head down to Emergency to check to see if his new admission had arrived, but before he left he quickly checked some lab results and then scrolled through his emails. Then he checked the intramail as they were hounding him to go and get another security shot for his lanyard. He saw an alert that the Emergency Department had been placed on bypass and let out a sigh of frustration, because he really didn't want his patient ending up in another hospital.

He clicked on the intramail and, for a man who dealt with death extremely regularly, for a man who usually knew what to do in any given situation, Steele simply didn't have a clue how to handle this.

We are greatly saddened to inform staff of the sudden death of Gerard (Gerry) O'Connor, a senior nurse in the Emergency Department.

Gerry passed away after sustaining a head injury in Greece. Currently the Emergency Department has been placed on bypass as his close colleagues process the news.

He blinked when his pager bleeped and saw that his patient had, in fact, arrived in Emergency.

Steele considered paging Donald, his registrar, to take it. He wanted some time to get his head around things.

Yet he wanted to see how Candy was.

Steele walked into the war zone of Emergency. Resus was in shambles, though some staff, called down from the wards, were trying to tidy it up.

There were just a few staff around and he was surprised when, after checking the board, he walked into the cubicle where his patient was, to see Candy checking Mr Elber's observations.

'I'm Steele,' he said to his patient.

'Dr Steele, if you want to be formal.' Candy smiled at the elderly man as she checked his blood pressure. She was trying to keep her voice light but Steele could hear the shaken notes to it.

'I thought the place was on bypass,' he said to her as she pulled off her stethoscope.

'Mr Elber arrived just before we closed.'

'Can I have a brief word?' he said, and he watched her eyes screw up at the sides a fraction but she nodded and followed him outside.

'I'm so sorry,' Steele said, but Candy shook her head.

'Please, don't.'

'Candy—'

'Please, don't. I can't talk about it. I think I'm going to go home,' she said. 'Lydia offered.' She thought about it for a moment. 'I think I just want to go home.'

'Come round tonight,' Steele said, 'or I'll come over to you.'

'I don't want you to,' Candy said. 'I don't want to sit and cry over my ex with you. It's too weird.'

'It's not,' he said, but he didn't push it. 'Call me if you change your mind.'

'Thanks.'

Candy headed off and spoke with Lydia and said that, yes, on second thoughts, she was going to go home.

The news had come completely out of the blue. All

the staff were stunned. Candy had headed straight back out to the department, not really knowing what to do, when she'd seen that Mr Elber was sitting on a trolley and had been pretty much left to himself.

Now the complete numb shock that had hit her after finding out that Gerry was dead was wearing off and she was very close to tears.

And very scared too.

She changed and as she headed out of the department she saw Louise walking in on her way to work.

'Candy.' Louise came straight over. 'I just heard about Gerry. It's such terrible news...'

Candy started to cry but as Louise wrapped her in a hug, feeling Louise's pregnant stomach nudging into her was just about the last straw.

'I know you had a bit of a thing going on last year,' Louise said. 'It must be so—'

'Louise,' Candy begged, 'it's not that that I'm crying about.' Well, it was, but she certainly wasn't about to tell Louise the entire truth either. 'I think that I might be pregnant and I don't know what to do...'

'Come on,' Louise said, and led her to the canteen. There were groups sitting and talking, some from Emergency and in tears, so it didn't look out of place that Candy was crying.

Louise went and got them both drinks and then came over.

'How late are you?' Louise asked, knowing full well that Candy was seeing Steele—she'd seen them in the car after all.

'I'm not late,' Candy said. 'But I've been feeling sick and I'm so tired...' She knew it didn't sound much to go on. The awful thing was that she *knew* that she was. 'I simply can't be pregnant,'

. 'It will be okay,' Louise said. As a midwife she was extremely used to a woman's shocked tears when they first came to the realisation that they were pregnant.

'I don't think it can be,' Candy sobbed, 'and I can't tell you why.'

Louise sat and thought for a moment. If Steele was only here for a few more weeks, which was what she'd heard, then it wasn't any wonder that Candy was upset.

'I don't know who to talk to,' Candy said, and then blew her nose and told herself to get it together.

'Can you talk to me?' Louise offered. 'Do you want to do a pregnancy test? I'll come with you.' When Candy said nothing Louise pushed on. 'Could you talk about it with Anton?' Louise asked. Anton was Louise's husband and one of the most sought-after obstetricians in London. 'I was just on my way to have lunch with him so I know that he's got time to see you.'

Candy nodded.

It was time to find out for sure.

Louise took out her phone and sent a text and a few moments later she got a response. 'He says to come to the antenatal clinic and he'll see you. I'll take you over there now.'

'People will wonder what I'm doing in the antenatal clinic.'

'People will think we're just two friends catching up for lunch,' Louise said. 'Don't be so paranoid.'

As they arrived at the clinic Candy felt a moment's reprieve as she looked around at the pregnant women all sitting waiting for their turn to be seen.

She was overreacting, she told herself.

This world didn't apply to her.

'You might as well come in,' Candy said to Louise as they arrived at a door that had a sign with Anton Rossi written on it. 'He'll only tell you what's happening anyway.'

'God, no.' Louise rolled her eyes. 'Unfortunately for me Anton's all ethical like that. If you tell him not to tell me, then wild horses wouldn't drag it from him! You don't have to worry about that.' Louise gave her a lovely smile. 'But if you do want to tell me then I'm dying to know!' She gave Candy a cuddle just before she went in. 'You'll be fine.'

Candy really hadn't had anything to do with Anton before this. She just knew him by reputation and had seen him occasionally when he'd come down to Emergency to review a patient there.

'I'm sorry to interrupt your lunch break,' she said. 'Thank you for seeing me so quickly.'

'Louise said that you were very upset.'

Candy nodded. 'I know that everything is confidential but the thing is, this is terribly delicate and—'

'First of all,' Anton interrupted, 'you are right—everything you tell me is completely confidential. I never gossip.'

'Thank you.'

'I'm not even taking notes. Do you want to tell me what's happening?'

'I think I might be pregnant,' Candy said. 'The thing is, my partner...' She didn't even know if Steele was that but she pushed on. 'It can't be his.'

'Because?'

'He's infertile.'

'Have you been seeing someone else?' Anton asked

gently—he was used to that being the case—but Candy shook her head.

'I've only been with my current partner for a couple of weeks. We weren't supposed to be serious, but…' It sounded so terrible put like that but Anton's eyes were sympathetic rather than judgmental. 'I had a one-night stand with my ex a couple of months ago.' She thought back. 'Three months, maybe. We used condoms.'

'Nothing is fail-safe,' Anton said.

'I went on the Pill afterwards,' Candy said. 'I wasn't expecting anything to happen again but I just decided I wasn't coming off it. I have had my period.'

'A normal period?' Anton checked.

'It's been light but I thought that was because the day I got it I started the Pill.'

'The first thing we need to do—' Anton was very calm '—is to find out if you are indeed pregnant.'

He gave her a jar and a few minutes later she sat in his office and she knew, she simply knew that she was. A few moments later Anton confirmed it.

'Candy, you are pregnant.'

He let it sink in for a moment.

'How do you think your partner will react?' Anton asked.

'I don't think I'm going to find out,' Candy said, and she just stared at the wall. 'There's really no point telling him. We both agreed from the start—'

'What about the father?'

Oh, that's right. Candy's brain was moving like gridlocked traffic. It was like telling a joke and forgetting the punch line, because she hadn't told Anton the good part yet. 'You know Gerry, the head of nursing in Emergency…'

'Oh, Candy.' Immediately he took her hand. Anton didn't gossip—in fact, he had been in this office all morning—but he had seen the email twenty minutes or so ago informing everyone that Gerry had passed away while on holiday in Greece and that Emergency was on bypass.

'I don't know what to do.'

'Of course you don't know what to do at the moment,' he said. 'This is all too much of a shock. How long have you been worried that you might be pregnant?'

'Since yesterday,' Candy said, 'A patient said something. I know I'm a bit overweight, it just…'

'Hit home?'

Candy nodded.

'I knew you were pregnant before I did the test,' Anton said, which concerned him a little as it did not seem to fit with her dates. 'We could do an ultrasound now, here, and see exactly where we are,' he suggested. 'Are you ready to do that?'

She nodded.

'Go to the examination table and undo your jeans. He came over and had a feel of her stomach but said nothing—though he was starting to think that Candy would soon be in for another shock.

He squeezed some gel on and turned the machine away from her. 'Can you turn the sound off, please?' Candy said, because she didn't want to hear its heartbeat.

'Of course I can.'

He took a few moments, running the probe over her stomach and pushing it in over and over.

'I really am sorry to interrupt your lunch break,'

Candy said, more for something to say because she was dreading the next conversation.

'My wife would have been nagging me to do an ultrasound on her anyway.' He smiled and then he looked across at Candy. 'I shan't be discussing this with her.'

'Thank you.'

He had finished.

'Stay there,' Anton said as she went to sit up. 'You are close to thirteen weeks pregnant, which means conception was eleven weeks ago.'

'I've had my period, though.'

'Breakthrough bleeding,' Anton said. 'Nothing to worry about. All looks well on the ultrasound. Obviously your hormones are everywhere right now.'

'Would the Pill have harmed it?'

'No. Many, many women I have seen have taken the Pill while not knowing that they are pregnant. You've had no symptoms?' Anton checked.

'Not really.' Candy shook her head and then lay and thought back over the past few weeks. 'I had what I thought was a bug and I've felt sick a couple of times and been a bit dizzy, but I never really gave it much thought.' She looked up at Anton. 'I've been so tired, though. I mean *seriously* tired. I actually booked a holiday because I was feeling so flat.'

'Candy,' Anton said gently, 'I'm not surprised that you have been feeling exhausted—it's a twin pregnancy.'

It was just as well that he had kept her lying down.

Candy lay there, stunned, trying and failing to see herself as a mother of twins. Finally she sat up and when she took a seat at the desk Anton gave her a drink of water.

'I don't know what to do.'

'As of now,' he said, 'I would expect that your mind is extremely scattered. Is there anybody that you can talk to about this?'

'Not really. My parents will freak,' Candy said, panicking just at the thought of telling them. 'I can't tell anyone at work or it will be everywhere.'

He nodded in understanding but he was practical too. 'You are going to start showing very soon—in fact, you are already,' Anton said. 'I could feel that you were pregnant before I did the ultrasound. Your uterus is out of the pelvis and you will show far more quickly with twins.'

'I can't have it, Anton,' Candy said, but then she started to cry because it wasn't an it. It was a *them*.

'Candy, you do need a little time to process this news but you also need to come and see me next week. You don't have much time to make a decision. I do want you to take the time to think very carefully about this.'

She didn't need the time. In that moment, she had already made her choice.

'I can't…' Candy said, and then took a deep breath. 'I'm not having an abortion.'

'Well, you have a difficult road coming up,' Anton said, 'but I can tell you this much—I will be there for you and in six months from now you will have your babies and today will be just a confusing memory.'

'Thank you.'

They chatted some more and Candy told him that she was booked to go to Hawaii next week. 'Can I still go?'

'Absolutely!' he said. 'It will be the best thing for you. Let your insurance company know. Put me down as your obstetrician. I do still want to see you next week, though. You need to have some blood tests and I want to go through things more thoroughly with you. Right now, it's time for the news to sink in.'

Poor thing, Anton thought as she left his office. He had looked after many women whose partner and even ex-partner had died and knew that it was a very confusing time.

He smiled as there was a knock at the door and Louise came in. 'How was she?'

'She's fine,' Anton said, and then rolled his eyes as Louise picked up the gel. 'Step away from the ultrasound machine, Louise.'

'Please,' Louise said. 'It's wide awake. I can feel it kicking.

'Because it probably knows its lunchtime,' Anton said. 'Come on, I would actually like to get some lunch.'

'Is Candy okay?' Louise shamelessly fished as they walked down to the canteen. Anton absolutely trusted his wife but part of what he adored about her was that she could not keep a secret and so, to be safe, he said nothing.

'She's on with him...' Louise nudged.

'Who?' Anton frowned.

'The sexy new geriatrician that just walked past,' Louise explained. 'Candy is on with him.'

He loathed gossip, he truly did, but, unusually for Anton, he turned his head.

He felt sorry for her new partner too and tried to imagine how he would feel if his gorgeous wife had already been pregnant when they'd met.

Anton was man enough to admit that he didn't know.

* * *

Candy stepped into her flat and put down her handbag and she didn't know where to start with her thoughts.

Just after seven there was a knock at the door and Candy opened it to the angry questions and accusations of her parents.

'Where were you?' her mother asked, and demanded to know where Candy had been last night and the night before that.

'We came over and you were not home.'

'Please, not now,' Candy said.

Yes, now.

'For the last two weeks you are hardly home. We call around and the lights are off. We telephone and you don't pick up.'

'I'm twenty-four years old, Mum,' Candy said. 'I don't have to account for my time…'

She might as well have thrown petrol on the fire because all the anger that had been held in by her parents since Candy had moved into her flat came out then.

She was heading for trouble, her mother warned.

They didn't raise her to stay out all night.

Who was she going to Hawaii with?

Candy thought of Steele then and stood there, remembering the beginning of tentative plans.

How much simpler life had seemed then.

'I'm not discussing this,' Candy said. 'I'm very tired. It's been an extremely long day.'

She simply refused to row.

When they finally left she stood in the hall.

No one understood. Her friends at work thought she was ridiculous to worry about what her parents might think, but she did. Candy loved them. She just didn't know how to be both herself and the daughter they demanded that she be.

Imagine telling them that the she was pregnant.

She simply could not imagine it.

Not just pregnant, but pregnant with twins and the father was dead.

Candy dealt with things then as any rational, capable adult would.

She undressed, climbed into bed and pulled the covers over her head.

CHAPTER TEN

'Hi.'

Steele could hear the tension in her voice when Candy called him on Saturday, though she was trying to keep her voice light.

'Hi, Candy.'

'Is it okay if we give it a miss tonight?' she asked. They had planned to go to a stand-up comedy and the tickets had been hard to come by.

'Of course it is,' he said. 'I doubt you're in the mood for laughing out loud. Do you want me to come over?'

'I'd really just like a night on my own,' she said.

Another one.

And then another.

And then another.

On Tuesday, four days before she flew, Steele saw her briefly in the admin corridor. She was coming down from Admin, where she had been trying to sort out her salary for her annual leave when she bumped into him.

'How are you doing?' he asked.

'I'm fine,' she said. 'I actually can't stop and speak. Lydia has messed up my annual leave pay and I've been trying to sort it out.'

He walked in the direction of Emergency with her. 'How's the mood in Emergency?'

'Pretty flat,' Candy said. 'His funeral is being held in Sunderland, where he's from, but the hospital is holding a memorial service for him. They're naming the new resuscitation area after him,' She gave a tight smile. 'Thankfully I'll be in Hawaii when it's held.'

'Thankfully?'

She shook her head. She really didn't want to discuss how mixed up she was feeling right now, especially with Steele. She had considered changing her holiday so she could attend the memorial service but the thought of facing his parents there was too much for Candy. While she knew she had to tell them, she wanted to get her own head around it first. As for them naming Resuscitation after him! Well, the thought of wheeling patients in and out of Gerry's Wing, day in and day out, had her stomach in knots.

Then she turned and looked at the man she was quite sure she loved with all her heart and she wanted to break down and tell him. She wanted the pregnancy to go away and to be back to where they had once been, but it certainly wasn't Steele's problem so she gave him a very tight smile. 'I do have to go.'

He nodded and watched her dash off.

Leave it, the sensible part of his mind said as he headed back to the geriatric unit and went and hid in his office.

He was certain now that Candy was pregnant. In a matter of days her body had changed and she was completely unable to meet his eyes.

He was roused from his introspection by a tap at the door and he called for whoever it was to come in.

'Sorry to trouble you.'

'No trouble at all.' Steele smiled at Catherine, Macey's niece and another woman.

'This is my sister, Linda.'

'Good afternoon, Linda.' He expected Linda had some questions, that they perhaps wanted to know how best to broach things with Macey. But, as Steele found out every day in his job, there were always surprises to be had.

'When Aunt Macey had her heart attack,' Catherine started, 'Linda took care of her home, fed the cat, that sort of thing…'

'I see.'

Linda spoke then. 'A letter came while she was in hospital. I was doing her mail and paying her bills so she didn't have to worry about being cut off. I opened this letter and it was from a charity that deals with adopted children. It explained that Macey's son wanted to make contact. I didn't know if it would make things worse. She was so sick…'

'Of course you didn't know what to do,' he said.

'I didn't even tell Catherine,' Linda said. 'I just didn't know what to do with the news. I spoke to my husband and he suggested that we wait till Aunt Macey was feeling better. Really, though, she's been slowly going downhill for so long…'

'Do you have the letter with you?' Steele asked, and she nodded and handed it to him.

'He wants to make contact,' Linda said. 'I feel bad for not telling her.'

'Don't feel bad,' Steele said. 'It could have been an

awful shock for her, though now I think it will be very welcome news. Why don't you go in now and speak with her? Facing it will be hard and I'll be around if she gets upset but, to be honest, I think it will be a relief.'

He did hang around, but all seemed calm with Macey. He sat at the desk next to Elaine. He could see Macey and her nieces talking earnestly and at one point Macey actually laughed.

'It's good to see her laughing,' Steele said, and turned and smiled at Elaine.

'Sorry?'

'Macey,' Steele explained, then he saw Elaine's swollen eyes. 'Are you all right, Elaine?'

'I am.' She gave a small shake of her head. 'I'm worried about my assessment.'

Steele frowned. 'Elaine, you're doing really well. I know I'm not a nurse, but I do know how well you look after the patients.'

'Even if I get my words wrong at times,' Elaine said, because Abigail had had a small word with her about the muffy thing.

'Even if you get your words wrong.' He smiled, and was pleased to see that she did too. 'Is there anything else on your mind?'

'No.' She shook her head and stood up and left him sitting alone.

Steele looked over again at Macey and her nieces and knew it was time for him to take his own medicine.

It was time for him to face things.

When he arrived in Emergency he saw the smudges beneath Candy's eyes and she was still refusing to meet his gaze.

Direct as ever, Steele asked the question. 'Are you avoiding me?'

She stood there and went to lie to him, to say of course not, or whatever, but his beautiful eyes demanded the truth so she nodded. 'Yes.'

'Can I ask why?'

There was no point in telling him about the pregnancy so she made up an excuse. An excuse that was partly true. 'I've been a bit mixed up about Gerry and I had a big argument with my parents. They've realised that I've been staying out at night...'

'Really?' He looked at her for a long moment. He knew she was lying, knew how she'd fought for her independence and knew too that she wouldn't give in to them.

'I think we should just leave things,' Candy said. 'I don't want to upset them.'

'I don't believe you,' he said. 'While I understand you might need a bit of space after what's happened to Gerry, I don't believe that's it.' When Candy didn't respond he pressed on. 'Do you know, one thing that I've really enjoyed about our time together is how honest we have always been. It's fine if you want to end things, but at least tell me the reason why.'

'Can we go somewhere private?' she asked.

'Sure,' he said, his voice clipped. 'My office?'

They walked through the hospital in silence and then onto the geriatric unit and it felt to both of them as if they were walking to the gallows—which they were, for this killed them.

Through the ward they went and to his office at the end, and Macey watched their strained faces as they passed by.

Candy stepped into his office and didn't take a seat. She had a feeling she wouldn't be here for very long.

'Do you want to tell me what's going on?' he invited.

'Not really,' she said.

'Okay. *Are* you going to tell me what's going on?'

'I'm pregnant,' Candy said.

For Steele it was the strangest sensation. Ten years ago he had wondered how he might react when the woman he was crazy about told him such news.

Now, ten years on, the woman he was seriously crazy about was telling him such news.

'With twins,' she added.

He hadn't been aware that she'd brought a cricket bat with her when she'd come into the office. Of course Candy hadn't but it felt like that as she added her little postscript and he was left with one thought, one regretful, sad thought.

They're not mine.

'They're not yours,' she added, like an echo to his brain, and Steele snapped his response, in his gruff, low voice.

'I think I'd already established that, thank you.'

Yes, he actually felt as if he'd been knocked on the back of the head because his reactions, his words did not belong to the man he knew he was, yet, concussed by the impact of her news, he continued to speak. 'What do you want me to say here, Candy?'

'I don't know,' she admitted.

He honestly did not know how to react. Was he supposed to step in and say, *That's fine, darling, I'll raise his babies*? Or, *How convenient, Candy*, he should perhaps say with a smile, *given that I shoot blanks*. Or was he supposed to say that it was no big deal?

It was a massive deal.

He should, Steele knew on some level, take her in his arms and tell her that things would work out, that she could get through this.

His arms couldn't move, though, and his mouth was clamped closed so that no words could come out.

'I'm going to go,' she said.

'Wait.'

'Why?' Candy answered. 'Steele, we agreed to three weeks. We managed two. I was hoping to get through this week without telling you.'

'But you have.'

'Because you're right—we *have* always been honest. Yes, I've been avoiding you. I didn't want to spoil what we had.'

'Have you told your parents?'

Candy shook her head.

'Have you told anyone?'

'I have now,' she said, and she looked straight through his eyes and to his heart. 'I've got the hardest part out of the way now.'

And telling Steele *was* the hardest part. Her parents, Gerry's parents, all of that she would deal with in time, but this part hurt the most.

'I'm going to go,' she said again. 'If you could drop my case off that would be brilliant. Just leave it at the door.'

She walked out then and he sort of came to and opened his office door and stepped onto the ward. There was Candy, walking out quickly, and he closed his eyes in regret for his lack of response. Then he turned and saw that Macey was watching him.

No, Steele did not smile.

Instead, he walked up to the nurses' desk. 'I'm going home,' he said to Gloria. 'Page Donald if you need anything.'

CHAPTER ELEVEN

IT WAS A long lonely night for both of them.

Candy woke in her flat and was more tempted than she had ever been in her life to ring in sick this morning. She had a shift on the geriatric ward, her last one. She was desperate to avoid Steele yet she wanted somehow to see him. And to see Macey too and say goodbye.

Then she had two more shifts in Emergency and then she flew to Hawaii.

Alone.

Or rather not alone—she ran a hand over her stomach and felt the edge of her uterus.

She had no idea how she felt about being pregnant.

No idea how to tell her parents or friends or anyone.

Right now, none of it even seemed to matter.

She loved Steele.

It wasn't like the crushes she'd had on other men, which Candy was rather more used to.

It felt so much deeper than that, like an actual concrete thing that now resided within.

Except the twins resided within also.

Twins?

As he did up his shirt that morning Steele was thinking about them too.

He was also thinking about her words—how telling him had been the hardest part.

He knew how impossible her parents were and he knew telling Gerry's parents would be supremely difficult.

Yet telling him…

As he did up his tie, he found himself closer to tears than he had been at his marriage break-up. Closer to tears than he had been at his grandmother's funeral.

In fact, Steele wasn't even close to tears—he was sitting on the edge of the bath in a serviced apartment, bawling his eyes out, for the fact they were over and the grief that her babies were not his. He'd never cried. Even when he'd found out that he couldn't have children, Steele hadn't broken down. He'd been too busy mopping up Annie's tears. Now, ten years later, he let out what had long been held in. He cried alone.

He was as nice to himself as he had been to Macey.

At seven a.m. it was a bit early for sherry but he made a strong mug of tea and put in extra sugar and then sat and thought what best to do.

He could avoid Candy, Steele knew. He could call in sick today. He had a day off tomorrow and then it was just her final shift in Emergency on Friday—he could send Donald to deal with anything that came up in Emergency, and he would never have to see Candy again.

He couldn't do that, though.

'Morning,' he said as he came into the kitchen on the geriatric ward, and there was Candy, making a mug of tea.

'Morning,' she said, though she brushed past him pretty quickly and headed off for handover.

Steele headed into his office and checked his emails.

Oh, joy.

There was Gerry.

His smiling face was surrounded by flowers, and Steele, along with the entire hospital—as long as cover could be arranged, of course—was invited to attend the memorial service next Tuesday and the naming of the resuscitation area as Gerry's Wing.

Candy was trying to get her head around that terrible name too.

Lydia, who had been on the edge of taking disciplinary action against Gerry, was now talking about him as if he'd been an angel—an angel with one wing—a wing named after him that Candy would work in, walk through, deal with day in and day out...

As Candy helped Macey shower, she was wondering how the hell she could continue to work there. Kelly had given her an odd look in the changing room yesterday and a little huddle at the nurses' station had suddenly gone very quiet when she had approached.

No one had had the nerve to outright ask her. Candy was quite plump and they were clearly trying to work out if she'd been hitting the doughnuts or if indeed she was pregnant.

Imagine them knowing she was pregnant by Gerry.

'You're very quiet this morning,' Macey said as Candy turned off the taps and helped her to get dried and dressed.

'I'm sorry, Macey, I was miles away.'

'Dreaming of Hawaii, no doubt,' Macey said. 'Are you looking forward to your holiday?'

'I am,' Candy said. 'I fly on Friday night.'

'It's Wednesday today.' Macey smiled. 'I think for the first time in years I actually know what day it is.'

'You're so much better,' Candy commented, as Macey dressed herself with just a little help. When they got back to the bed, Candy would remove Macey's dressing for Steele to have a look at her leg ulcer, which was doing much better. After lunch, Macey would lie on the bed for a couple of hours' sleep, but apart from that she sat in the chair or walked to the day room. It was wonderful to see the improvement in her.

'Steele says I should be able to go home next week.'

'How do you feel about that?' Candy asked as she walked with Macey back to her bed.

'I'm looking forward to it very much,' Macey said. 'I'm having some modifications done to the bathroom and kitchen, which my niece Linda is sorting out for me. Things will be a lot easier now.'

'Your nieces seem very nice.'

'Oh, they're wonderful women.' Macey nodded, taking a seat by the bed and putting her leg up on a footstool. She watched as Candy made up the bed. 'You've earned your holiday,' Macey said. 'I wish I could be here to see the postcard.'

'I'll send you one, Macey.' Candy smiled, despite her earlier declaration about not sending any. 'If you're okay with that?'

'Oh, yes, please! It would make my day! Is it just you going?'

Candy nodded.

'Hawaii would be a beautiful place to go with the right man...'

'It would,' Candy agreed, her heart twisting as she thought how close she had come to sharing a part of her holiday with Steele.

'You don't have a boyfriend, though,' Macey continued. 'If I remember rightly.'

'No.'

'And you're carrying?' Macey said gently, and Candy's eyes filled with tears as she nodded.

'I'm having twins.'

'Congratulations, my dear.'

Macey was the first person to offer congratulations and she said it so nicely that Candy started to cry.

'Pull the curtains,' Macey said.

'No, no.' Candy sniffed. 'I'll go to the staffroom.'

'You'll pull the curtains and sit with me for a while.' Macey's orders were clear and Candy did as she was told.

'Have you told...?' Macey hesitated. She had been about to ask if Candy had told Steele, if that was what the argument the other day had been about, but her sharp mind was returning. Macey sat quietly for a moment, remembering when she had been admitted and had snapped at Steele for being a locum. It had only been his second day here, Macey recalled.

Certainly there had been a romance between Candy and Steele. She had seen it unfold in front of her own eyes.

'Have you told the baby's father?' she asked instead.

'Macey...'

She saw Candy swallow and reached out to take

the hands of the younger woman to encourage her to speak on.

'I made a mistake a few months ago, so please don't feel sad for me when I say this—I'm not a grieving widow. The baby's father died a week ago.'

'Gerry?' Macey said, and watched Candy's eyes widen in surprise. 'I hear all the gossip.'

'Yes.' Candy gave a watery smile. 'It was him.'

'That's very sad.'

'It is,' Candy said. 'I don't know how he'd have felt about it,' she went on. 'We wouldn't have got back together but I'm sure we'd have sorted something out.'

'What about Steele?' Macey asked, and she watched the tears spill down Candy's cheeks, though she neither confirmed nor denied there was anything going on.

'You have your holiday to look forward to,' she said, and Candy nodded. 'It's a good job you booked it before you knew.'

'Oh, yes,' Candy said, because it would be her first and last overseas adventure alone. 'I don't think I'll be lounging around on the beach next time I go. It will be buckets and spades…' She shook her head. 'I can't see how I'll manage,' she admitted.

'You know, I can remember being alone and pregnant,' Macey said. 'I expect it's still a very scary place even fifty years on, even with all the choices you girls have these days. I still remember how scared I felt when I got pregnant but I'll tell you this much—by the end of my pregnancy I wasn't scared about having a baby. I wanted him so much and I know you'll feel the same way about your two.'

Candy nodded. She knew Macey was right. 'I'm sorry for what happened to you, Macey.'

'I know you are but don't be sorry. My nieces are getting into contact with him. If I can see him just once I'll be happy…' Her voice trailed off and she looked up and Candy followed her gaze and saw that Steele had popped his head in.

'Sorry,' Candy said, standing up from the bed. She was supposed to have removed Macey's dressing and she was embarrassed at him seeing her cry.

'It's fine,' Steele said. 'I'll come back later.'

He left them to it. He was glad that Candy was having a chat and a cry with Macey and when she came out a little while later and told him Macey's dressing was down, instead of ignoring what he'd seen he addressed it.

'Do you feel better after speaking with Macey?'

'I do,' she said. 'I'm going to miss her.'

And I miss you, Candy thought, but she could not say that without starting to cry again.

'Could we go somewhere after work?' he said. 'Just to talk.'

She didn't really want to say goodbye to him here, not like this, so she nodded.

They returned to the café he had first taken her to, yet it felt so different now—the innocence and fun of before had left them.

'What would you like to eat?' he asked.

'I'll just have a cup of tea,' she said. 'I'm meeting my parents tonight.'

'Have you told them?'

Candy shook her head 'I'll tell them about the twins when I get back.'

'They'll know very soon.' He'd tried not to notice

her bump but now that he had he couldn't not see it. 'I'm not a very good doctor, am I?'

He somehow made her smile.

'I think it popped out about ten seconds after I found out...' Candy said. 'I'll just wear a big baggy top to-night. They're not talking to me anyway, because I changed the locks and I'm going to Hawaii, so I doubt I'll be there for very long.'

'Yet you still go.'

'I love them. I don't agree with them a lot of the time but I still love them very much and I know when I do tell them I'll break their hearts.'

'For a little while,' Steele said.

He took a breath. He could do this type of thing so easily for his patients but when it came to matters of a very private heart, things were very different, but he forced himself to step up.

'Would you like me to tell your parents for you?'

Candy frowned. 'Why would you do that?'

'Because I'm used to breaking news to difficult, stubborn, immutable people. I do it every day,' he said, and then made her smile. 'I promise to leave out the part that we've been at it like rabbits. I'll just say I'm a colleague. A doctor...'

Candy smiled. She really understood why he wore a suit and tie for work—the older people liked it. And he was right, her parents would respond very differently to Steele from the way they would to her. If not at first then fairly soon, they would calm down for the *dottore*.

'I need to do this myself, Steele. It's really nice of you to offer and I admit I'm tempted to pass it over, but...no. Thank you, though.'

'Is there anything I can do to help?'

'It's not your problem, Steele.' Then she looked over to him. 'Actually, this has helped and talking to Macey too. It makes it feel a bit more real.'

'Keep talking, then,' he said, but she shook her head.

'I can't really. I mean, I'm upset about Gerry too and I'm trying to work out how to tell his family and I don't think getting upset about Gerry is fair to you,' Candy said. 'I know I felt jealous when you spoke about your wife. I got an Annie burn.'

He loved her openness and he smiled when she admitted to having felt jealous. 'Candy, you *can* talk to me about that.' Ten years older, there were some things he did know. 'Two days before I turned thirty I found out that a woman who I had gone out with for close to six months, just after my divorce, had died. Now, she wasn't *the* love of my life. She was one of possibly too many *loves* of my life...' He saw her pale smile. 'And it hurt. I was stunned and devastated. I was all of the things that you probably are now.'

'It doesn't make you feel jealous when I talk about him?' Candy checked.

'I don't know how it makes me feel,' he admitted, touched that even with all that was going on in her world she could be concerned in that way for him. 'But that's my stuff to deal with. Right now you've got enough of your own.'

'Oh, I do!'

'You know there is one teeny positive,' Steele said.

'Tell me.'

'Well, there was one thing about you that was starting to get on my nerves, a potential deal-breaker, in fact,' Steele said. 'Confirmed bachelors are very picky and selfish, you understand...'

Candy smiled. 'Tell me.'

'Your ability to fall asleep. God, I knew you were tired, we both were, but I was starting to wonder if you had narcolepsy or something.'

She laughed but it changed in the middle and she fought from letting out a sob because he'd just reminded her how very good it had been between them.

'Candy...' He took her hand but she pulled hers away.

'Please, don't, Steele,' she said. They had always been honest and she was never more so than now. 'Please, don't confuse me now. I miss you very much. I think we both know that it was turning into a bit more than a fling. I think we both know that feelings were starting to run deep.' Which was milder than the complete truth but now was not the time to admit to love. She pointed out the impossibility of it.

'You like the single life.'

'I did,' he said, 'but I very much liked being with you.'

'You've geared your life around not having children.'

'I have,' he said.

'You start your dream job in a couple of weeks.'

'I do.'

'And I'm pregnant with another man's babies.'

It dawned on him then that he had only ever known Candy pregnant. That, really, nothing had changed between them, except that they both now knew and he told her so.

'Candy, since the moment we met you've been pregnant with another man's babies. I think we—'

'Steele,' she interrupted. 'I have to work a few things

out myself. I've been raised to share everything, to discuss every decision. I don't want to do that now. I want to think. I want to know that I can do this on my own. I have to know that I can do this on my own...'

'I get that.'

'And please don't pretend this isn't difficult for you.'

He thought back to that morning, sitting on the edge of the bath and crying in a way he never had before, but he felt better for it, clearer for it. He looked at Candy and knew she was right. She didn't need his thoughts now. She needed her holiday, she needed space, she needed to get used to the idea that she was going to be a mother.

'I need to go,' she said. She was on the edge of tears—just one touch of his hand and she wanted more, she wanted his arms, she wanted the comfort of him. She felt as if she had just got off a merry-go-round as they stepped outside. She had felt like that since the news about Gerry's death had hit, since she'd sat in Anton's office, since...

The world seemed to be spinning too fast of late, and Candy took a big breath and tried to steady herself, but big breaths seemed to be working less and less these days. Steele must have seen she was struggling. He wrapped her in his arms, as he had wanted to yesterday but hadn't known how. The shield of him, the feel of him, the tender strength of him brought the first glimpse of peace she had craved, just a tiny glimpse of tranquillity as solo she halted navigated stormy seas.

'You're going to be okay,' he said, and his voice was like the deep bass of a guitar coming up through the floorboards, a rhythm she recognised and understood, and she clung to the delicious familiarity of him and wished it could last. 'I know it's going to be hard, telling your parents, but when you do just remind them that this is their grandchildren they are discussing and that in few months they'll be here…'

'Right now I'm actually not worried about them,' she said. Right now she was wondering how she might ever get over this broken heart, but she daren't be that honest and so, for the first time, she lied to him. 'Right now I'm worried about stretch marks and my boobs reaching the moon and getting fatter…' *And losing you.* 'I'm going to go.'

Still he held her. 'I'll drive you home.'

Still she clung to him. 'I don't want you to.'

'I can drop off your case.'

She hated that he had it in his car.

Steele hated that it was in his car too. He wanted it in his apartment unpacked, he wanted her in his bed, yet he was terribly aware that he must not push her, not confuse her when she was already in such turmoil.

Maybe there was something he could do.

'Do you fancy a day pass?' he said to her ear.

'A day pass?'

'I'm going to Kent tomorrow to look at the new unit and also to look at a few houses that I'm thinking of buying…'

'You're buying a house?'

'I always buy houses or flats wherever I work and I renovate them in my spare time and sell them or rent them out.'

'I'm working in Emergency tomorrow.'

'Oh, if anyone deserves to ring in sick, I think it might be you. Why don't we just have a nice drive, a lazy day…?'

'And no talk about pregnancy.'

'You don't have to pretend you're not pregnant, Candy.'

'I want a day away from it,' she admitted. 'I just want a whole day when I don't even have to think about it.'

'Then that's the day you shall have,' he said, and saw her to the Underground. 'I'll pick you up at eight.'

Candy sat on the tube, looking at all the people, and she saw an elderly woman look at her stomach and then her hand. She glanced up and saw that Candy had seen her and the old lady gave her a very nice smile.

Yes, times had changed.

She didn't feel quite so alone now.

It really was time to deal with what was.

Instead of heading home, she went to her parents'.

They were still sulking about Hawaii.

'Do you remember Gerry, who I work with?' Candy said. 'The one who helped me when I moved?'

'What about him?' Her father frowned. 'Is he going to Hawaii with you?'

'He died last week,' Candy said.

There were all the *How terribles* and Candy took a deep breath. She knew there was no easy way to say it.

It just needed to be said.

'I've just found out that I'm pregnant with twins,' Candy said. 'They're his.'

There were sobs and wails from her parents; her mother actually fell to the floor. As if that was going to change anything!

She had never understood Steele more than she did then. She understood fully how his love for Annie might have died as she watched her parents carry on.

This was about her, this was the hardest part of her life to date, and yet they made it all about them.

She had known they'd be upset but, as Steele would say, that was their stuff. How Candy wished they could give some teeny shred of comfort as she tried to deal with hers.

Candy sat there as her father declared he'd like to kill the man who had taken his daughter's honour and then she stood up.

'Lui è già morto,' Candy said, reminding her father that Gerry was already dead, and then she remembered Steele's words.

'These are your grandchildren we're discussing.' Her voice was incredibly clear and strong. 'And these are my babies and I refuse to listen to you calling them a mistake or talking about shame. In a few months they'll be here and you know as well as I do that you're going to love them. So why do this to me now? I'm going to go and I don't want to hear from you till you've calmed down.' She went to the door. 'And if you want to come to my flat, then you're to telephone before you do. Clearly I have a life you don't know about, and if you still don't want to know about it, then you're to telephone first before you come around!'

She left her parents and she could perhaps have headed for home but instead she did as Steele had once suggested she try.

She bought a single ticket for a movie—the one they hadn't seen that night. It was a real tear-jerker from start to end and she sat there, tears pouring down her face and not trying to hide them.

It was nice, a tiny press of the pause button as she

cried over the couple on the screen instead of dwelling on herself.

On Steele.

On what could surely never be.

CHAPTER TWELVE

HER JEANS JUST did up.

Nervous and a little excited, just as she had been the first time he'd come to her door, she opened it the next morning with a smile.

'I'm ready,' she said, 'or did you want a drink first?'

'No, thanks,' Steele said. 'It's probably better that we get going. I've got a lot to get on with today.' He couldn't not comment. 'You've been crying.'

'I had a rather big argument with my parents last night.'

'You told them?'

'I did.' She blew out a breath. 'And I told them a few other things too. Anyway, we're not talking about all that stuff today. I really do want a day off from it.'

'Fair enough.' He smiled. 'But can I just say that I'm really proud of you for telling them.'

'Thank you.'

'You'll enjoy your holiday far more without that hanging over you.'

'I shall.'

They went out to his car and were soon on the motorway. 'First up,' Steele explained, 'I'm going to look at the new wing of the hospital, which might bore the hell out of you. You can go for a walk or to the shops if you like.'

'No, I'd love to see it,' Candy said, 'unless explaining me makes things awkward for you.'

'I never feel the need to explain myself,' he said, and then he amended that slightly. 'Actually, I did cancel dinner with my parents tonight, you would have taken some explaining.'

'Oh, sorry,' Candy said, 'I didn't want you to change your plans for me.'

'I was more than happy to change them. I'm moving closer to them in a few weeks.' He turned and smiled again. 'Though not quite close as you are to yours, but they'll be seeing more of me than they do now.'

'What are they like now?'

'They've mellowed,' Steele said. 'They're much nicer as old people. Though I have to admit that when they start asking questions about my life, my love life, I'm often tempted to tell them to back off, given that they showed little interest in me when I was growing up.' He gave a roll of his eyes. 'I wouldn't do that to them, though.'

Candy knew that he wouldn't. He was too nice.

'You like old people.'

'I do,' he said. 'I don't like *all* old people. It's not a free pass to being a good person but I like how they've let go of the stuff that's not important. I like how they say what they think and share what they know. I like it even when my patients drive me mad with their stubbornness. I learn something every day, every single day, from how to put a brass doorknob on a house I'm renovating to how to face death.'

They arrived at the hospital and Steele shook hands

and introduced her to Reece, a consultant who'd clearly had a lot of input into the new wing.

'Any chance of you starting sooner?' Reece joked. 'Emergency is full.'

'No chance.' Steele smiled. 'I don't need you to show me around if you're busy.'

'You're sure?'

'Of course.'

'I'll see you at the meeting, then.' Reece nodded. 'Make sure you put a hard hat on.'

'I feel like a builder,' Candy said as she put hers on.

'Come on, Bob,' Steele said, and he took her through the building. It was near complete in parts and the roof was going on in others. 'This is going to be the acute geriatric unit,' he explained as he showed her a huge area where the wiring was going in. 'Very high-tech computer system,' he said. 'It has its own occupational therapy assessment area.' He took her in. There were two kitchens and various sets of stairs being built, as well as showers and baths of various heights so that patients could be assessed on how they would manage at home. 'I'm aiming for a forty-eight-hour admission time. Either home afterwards with support or admitted to the correct ward, but most of my patients will first come through here—well, that's the plan.'

'Forty-eight hours isn't very long.'

'Best time frame,' Steele said. 'It gives us enough time to put proper support in place for when they return to their homes.'

Steele showed her the other wards—a palliative care ward and also the acute medical unit—and then he opened a door and they stood in a huge empty space.

'This is the dream,' he said. 'It's not happening yet.

We're facing lots of obstacles and red tape, insurance issues and things, but I'm hoping this space will be a gym.' He smiled. 'Actually, I'm not allowed to call it that. I'm hoping this space will be utilised for healthy living…'

'Sorry?'

'Well, I always feel a bit of a bastard when I know someone's lonely and that a cream cake at three in the afternoon means not only a cream cake but a walk to the shops and some conversation too. Instead of asking them to give it up, I'm hoping that they can come here and have a chat with friends and maybe a bit of exercise. I'm hoping for a slimming or exercise club or something like that. It's all a bit of a pipe dream at the moment, but at least we have the space earmarked for it, if we ever do get to go ahead.'

'How long's your contract for?' Candy asked.

'Two years,' he said. 'They wanted five but I wouldn't agree to it.'

'Because?'

'Because I've never stayed anywhere for more than two years. I like fresh starts. I like putting everything into it and building things up…'

Or rather he had.

They drove to a pub and had a lovely lazy lunch overlooking a huge village green.

'Gorgeous, isn't it?' Candy said, and he nodded.

'Even if we don't get the go-ahead for the gym, I'll probably start a walking club over there.'

'You're going to go start a geriatric walking club!'

'Yep, I walk with my dog every morning that I can. Why not have company?'

'You have a dog?'

'I do.' Steele smiled. 'You have me pegged as a loner—no friends to go to the movies with, no pets. I have a dog, I have nice furniture and I have, when I'm not sleeping with Nurse Candy, a very busy social life.'

'Where's your dog now?'

'At my parents',' he said. 'He's a chocolate Labrador called Newman.'

'Newman?'

'You'll…' Steele stopped. He had been about to say she would see why when she met him but that wasn't what today was about. *No pressure*, he reminded himself. Today was doing her good, he could see that already. Her cheeks were pink and she seemed more relaxed than she had since…well, since Macey had opened her mouth and knocked their worlds off their axes, but they were starting to spin again, tentatively, though. 'He's got blue eyes,' Steele said instead. 'And he's the love of my life and he knows it.'

'Does he sleep on your bed, Steele?'

Steele shook his head. 'He sleeps on his bed for about seventeen hours a day and graciously lets me share it at night.'

After lunch they walked across the green and Candy laughed as she looked at it through what she imagined were Steele's eyes. 'I have this vision of all these old people doing Tai Chi…'

'So do I.'

She stopped walking. 'And then you'll leave.'

'That was the plan,' he said. 'Though this is a huge project…' He looked around. Since his divorce he had never been able to imagine staying in one place for very long. Here, though, he was close, though not too close to his parents; here was the job he had been working towards his entire career. He looked over as a car pulled up and a man got out and gave them a wave as they walked over to him.

'That's the estate agent,' Steele explained.

'Oh.'

'And that's the renovator's delight I'm hoping to buy, but I'm not telling him that.'

It was a huge rambling house with a small wooden gate, overlooking the green.

'Are you going to come and take a look?' he said.

'I think I might just take another walk,' she said. She didn't want to see his future home, so she walked on the green as Steele inspected the house.

He looked at the cornices and the hanging-off doors; the windows would all need to be taken out.

Don't start on the electrics, he thought as he flicked lights on and off.

And as for the plumbing! The estate agent tried to distract him from turning on taps but Steele was not easily distracted and when he turned on the taps the whole house seemed to rattle. Steele grinned as, in his head, he knocked another five grand off the asking price.

It was magnificent, though.

'Could you give me a moment?' he said to the agent. 'I'd like to walk through it again on my own for a minute.'

The estate agent agreed and Steele took way more than a minute.

The last time he had looked at a home this size had been with his ex-wife. The natural assumption at that time had been that the bedrooms would soon be filled.

The natural assumption as he walked around now was that the bedrooms would be filled too.

It was more than an assumption. It was a feeling it was how it should be. He looked out of a window and could see Candy idly walking around. He wanted to go and fetch her, bring her in, ask her her thoughts, yet her thoughts were cluttered enough now.

His weren't.

He thanked the estate agent and said that he'd be in touch then he walked over and joined her.

'Maybe I can explain you after all,' he said.

'Sorry?'

'I could just say to my parents that you're a friend from work who needed a day out. You can meet Newman.'

'No, thanks,' she said.

'Candy, can we talk—'

'Please, not now,' she said. 'I just need this day. I just need a day of not dealing with it and then I need my holiday to start dealing with it on my own.'

Steele nodded. It was what they had agreed to after all.

They drove back to his flat to collect her case, which was no longer in the car, and Candy needed it as she flew tomorrow.

Candy, of course, fell asleep in the car but now it just made him smile.

She awoke to his lovely deep voice and the sight of his flat and then she turned and there he was.

'I'll go and grab your case,' he said.

'Can I borrow your loo?' Candy said, because, as she was starting to find out, this was something she would be saying rather a lot in the weeks and months ahead.

She went to the loo and remembered the last time she'd been here—when her pregnancy had just started to become a possibility. As she looked in the mirror while washing her hands, she remembered the fear that had been in her eyes then.

The fear was gone now.

Yes, she was confused and exhausted and nervous about how she would provide for two children, but the terror was leaving and, after such a wonderful day's reprieve, she was starting to feel a little more like herself.

'Thank you for a lovely day,' she said.

'Do you want a cup of tea?' he offered, and she nodded.

'Make yourself comfortable.'

'Ha-ha,' she said, and stood and watched him make the tea instead.

Meaning...

She lifted her top and showed him the straining zipper that had simply refused to go all the way back up.

Only Steele didn't really see that. He saw pink lace and a teeny flash of jet hair and the stomach that his mouth had kissed over and over.

And as she put down her top Candy looked at the teabag he was squeezing the hell out of with his spoon and, yikes, there was a sort of gravelly note to his voice as he asked her how many sugars she had in her tea.

'The same as last time,' Candy said.

'Sorry, I'm a bit distracted.' Steele smiled. 'Two?'

'Two.'

'Do you really want tea?' he checked.

'No.'

'Because I don't,' Steele said. 'I want a glass of wine but I'm driving.'

'Poor Steele.' She smiled. 'It really is a problem.' Candy thought for a moment. 'I know!' she said brightly.

'Do tell.'

'Why don't you have a glass of wine and drive me home later?'

He turned and faced her. 'That's so clever, but you're stuck in those uncomfortable jeans. I insist you take them off...'

They started to kiss, the best kiss ever, because she'd got so lost in babies and feeling massive and unsexy but his tongue swiftly took care of that.

It hadn't really entered her head that he might want her again in that way. Now his fingers were at her zipper and somehow she felt back to the woman she had been.

Out of her jeans, she moaned in relief.

'Nice?'

'Nice,' she said to his mouth.

'That bra looks a bit tight too.'

He unhooked it and took it out through her arms and it was lovely to be all loose and floppy and to rest a moment in his arms.

'Feels so good,' she said.

'It does,' he said. There would be no rushing. He loved feeling her all relaxed against him.

'Get your wine.'

They headed over to the sofa and it was nice to be back there. Steele sat and Candy lay down as he drank his wine and played with her hair. It was good not to talk. She remembered the mornings with Macey and her *nonna*, and the bliss of hush when words could only serve to make you sad.

'Are you all packed for Hawaii?' he said finally.

'Nope.' Candy sighed. 'We're here to get my case, remember?'

This time tomorrow she'd be at Heathrow.

'Can I paint your toenails?' she asked.

'Er, why?'

'It relaxes me and my mum's still sulking at me so I haven't been able to do hers.'

'Do you have some nail varnish with you?'

'In my bag.'

He was so laid back and yet so austere. It was a lovely mixture that made her stomach curl and also gave her a peace that she could be herself.

And she was.

He lay down and she sat on his calves and started on his right foot. 'I like men's nails,' Candy explained, 'because they're bigger.'

'Have you painted a lot of men's nails?' he asked, and then let out a moan of surprise. 'Oh!'

'What?' She smiled as she painted his big toenail.

'I have nail-painting jealousy issues,' Steele said. 'I just felt it burn. I'm looking at your bum and enjoying the view when I suddenly got the Annie burn that you had.'

'I've never painted another man's toenails from this angle.' Candy smiled again.

'Take your knickers off, then.'

She did as told and then got back to painting the toenails on his left foot but she made a terrible mess of his long second toe because she heard his zipper slide down.

'I'm making a bit of a mess here, Steele,' she said.

'I forgive you,' he said.

'Steele.' She was arguably the most turned on she had ever been. She had never thought she'd feel sexy again, had never thought sex would ever be fun again, and yet here they were and it was bliss. 'Can I turn around?'

'You'll finish what you started,' Steele warned.

She gritted her teeth and did the last three toes really quickly. 'Done.' She turned around on his calves to the delicious sight of him and she moved up to sit on his thighs and lowered her head and they shared a long, deep kiss. Her breasts flattened against his chest and she could feel his erection pressing against her stomach.

She brought the kiss to a giddy halt and stared at him. He looked right back at her in a way that had her almost feverish. She started placing small kisses over his cheeks as his hands moved to her breasts, working her nipples.

'Candy…' Steele nearly said something he shouldn't. Today wasn't a day for confusing her, today wasn't a day for declarations, it was about keeping it light and he felt her sudden tension at the tender tone to his voice. 'Time for your hula lesson,' he said, and got the reward of her laugh in his ear.

She lowered herself onto him and he held her hips and had her sway a little and circle, and then Candy could not play any longer and she started moving of her own accord. His hands exploring her breasts had her greedy for more and she leant forward, lowering her breasts to his mouth, dizzy with the sensation of his hands now on her hips, grinding her down a little harder as his mouth worked her tender nipples.

'Steele…' There was almost panic in her voice, a delicious panic because her body wasn't hers any more but was moving into a rhythm of its own.

His mouth left her breast and she looked down at him. His lips were slightly parted and there was tension in his expression, just as there was in hers.

Steele adjusted the angle of his thrust just a fraction and she let out a sob. It was an actual sob as Steele started to come.

And then another sob and it was one of relief as somehow, some way, as she came to him, all she was at that moment was Candy.

Not pregnant, not scared, not worried at all.

The world felt a lot better when she was in Steele's arms.

CHAPTER THIRTEEN

STEELE STARED AT the morning light as she lay in his arms.

It was the last morning they would share in this room.

'Excited?'

'Very.' Candy nodded.

Despite her misgivings at times, now she was looking forward again to going on holiday. There was so much more to sort out now and Candy truly wanted to get on with it.

Right now, though, here was where she wanted to be, and she lay stroking the crinkly hair on his stomach that she loved so.

'What date do you get back?' Steele asked.

It was the first day of his new job.

'Do you want me to see if I can get away this evening and take you to the airport?'

'No, because then we'll have to say goodbye again.' She looked up at him. He'd been so lovely to her. Her time with Steele had been the most wonderful time of her life but she wasn't foolish. Two weeks away from each other, him starting a new job, very soon he might look at things in a very different light. She didn't want to find out a few weeks or months from now that, despite best intentions, they hadn't worked out... A very big part of Candy wanted it left at this. She wanted it to end while they were crazy about each other, while it was fun and sex and romance—before it all got too hard.

They got out of bed and got ready and he picked up her case and when they got to her flat he carried it in and he laughed when he saw the lock she'd put on.

'How many holes did you put in the door?'

'I'm very proud of my work,' Candy said.

'I'm not sure your landlord will be,' Steele said, and smiled as Candy went a bit pink. 'Did you ask permission?'

'No.'

'Do you want me to fix it up?'

'No,' she said. 'I want to fix it myself.'

'I know you do.'

They had a cuddle in the hall, a quiet one, just stood there and held each other and the moment was theirs.

He drove her to work and as they went to say goodbye it was too hard to do. 'I'll pop in and see Macey and if you're on the ward...'

'Sure.'

He gave her a kiss and they both did their very best to get on with their day.

'Candy...' Kelly said as she came into the changing room. 'How are things?'

'Sorry?'

'You were off sick yesterday,' Kelly fished.

'I wasn't sick, though.' Candy smiled. 'It was a mental health day.'

'So everything is okay?' Kelly checked.

'It will be about ten hours from now when my plane takes off.' She knew Kelly was fishing—everyone was.

And at midday Candy broke her news as they dealt with a multi-trauma.

'I'm stepping out,' she said as they went to do the X-rays. She always wore a heavy lead gown and so she knew it would not have affected the twins, but she just chose to let people know then. 'I'm pregnant, so I'd rather not take the chance…'

She left the room and let out a breath. Steele was right, she'd enjoy her holiday much more without that hanging over her.

And she dealt with the second question on everyone's minds as she stepped back in.

'I'm not comfortable yet discussing who the father is, but you'll all be very excited to know I'm expecting twins.'

There were smiles and congratulations and even a bottle of iced lemonade to toast her at the end of her shift.

'Have fun!' Lydia said. 'Lots of it.'

'Oh, I shall.'

She headed up to the geriatric unit and said goodbye to a couple of patients before she got to her very favourite one.

'Enjoy yourself,' Macey said. 'You deserve to be happy. A rather clever doctor told me that.'

Candy nodded. She had every intention of being happy, but as she gave Macey a cuddle and said goodbye she asked a question, desperate for the older woman's sage thoughts.

'Macey,' Candy said carefully. 'I want to be happy but what if you're not certain that the other person truly is? What if they might be there only out of a sense of duty?'

'Duty?' Macey thought for a long moment and Candy realised she was holding her breath as she awaited her answer, but Macey clearly didn't quite understand her question. 'Duty to who?' Macey asked.

'It doesn't matter,' Candy said, and gave her a smile. 'Stay well and I shall send you a postcard.'

As she left Macey she saw Steele going into his office and she went and knocked at the door.

'Are you off?'

'I am,' Candy said. 'Well, I've just got to see the obstetrician, buy a bikini, pack, take the Underground…'

'You're sure you don't want me to take you?'

'I'm very sure,' she said, and he took her in his arms. 'Thank you,' Candy said. 'I know we only had a short time and I know it was a bit fraught but you really helped and I just…' She couldn't really finish saying what she wanted to say without crying. 'I might write to you,' she said. 'Or call you. I really don't know…'

'You stop worrying about me and just go and have a wonderful time,' he said. 'Do what you have to do. Oh, one thing…' He took out his wallet and peeled off some US dollars.

'Stop!' Candy said. 'I don't need a sugar daddy.'

'I'm not old enough to be your sugar daddy.' He laughed. 'Seriously, I've had these for about five years, since my last trip to the States. Have fun with it.'

'Thank you!' Candy smiled.

'Go,' he said.

'But—'

'Go,' he said again, and she was glad that he did

because she wanted to say goodbye smiling and if she stayed a moment longer she might possibly cry.

Then it was time for her official appointment with Anton.

'I told you that you were about to start showing,' he said with a smile as she walked in. 'Have people started noticing?'

'Yes, though no one had the nerve to ask if I was pregnant just yet, though a patient told me that I was before I even knew. I've just announced it. I also said that I'm not comfortable with telling them who the father is.'

'Well done.' Anton smiled again.

He checked her blood pressure and all was well then Candy climbed up onto the examination table and he spoke to her about twin pregnancies. He said her babies would probably be born at around thirty-seven weeks and that he would see her more regularly than he would for a singleton pregnancy.

'Have you told your parents?'

Candy nodded. 'They didn't take it very well at all.'

'They'll come around.'

'I know,' she said. 'I told them to contact me when they do. I think I'm going to tell Gerry's parents when I return from my holiday. I think that it is only fair to them to know.'

'What about your new partner?'

'He's not really my partner, I don't think,' Candy said as Anton helped her to sit up. 'It was supposed to be just a casual thing. He starts a new job soon and is moving. He'll be gone by the time I get back from my holiday. I don't know what will happen then, if anything.' She smiled at Anton. 'My bad for falling in love.'

'You have told the insurance companies that you're pregnant?'

'I have.'

'Go and have and amazing holiday. Grieve, cry, smile and heal.'

'Thank you.'

They sounded like pretty straightforward instructions and as she packed the last few pieces into her suitcase she called for a taxi to take her to the Underground.

Usually her parents would go with her to the airport to wave her off as if she were going on an expedition for a year but they were clearly not over the news yet so Candy took the Underground and battled with evening commuters and her suitcase.

She caught sight of a pregnant woman's reflection in the window and it took a second before she realised that it was her own.

We'll get there, she said in her mind to her small bump. She loved them already. The numb shock had worn off. The fear had gone. Already Candy knew she'd cope.

They would get through this.

As she checked in at Heathrow and watched her case shoot away she turned and saw her parents.

'Ma...' Candy ran over and hugged them.

'We love you.'

'I know you do.'

'We'll help.'

'I know you will,' Candy said, and they kissed and made up with much relief.

'You move from that flat and come home,' her mother said. 'We can help you to raise them—'

'We'll talk when I get home,' Candy said. 'Thank you so much for coming to the airport. It means an awful lot to me.'

It had but as she sat on the plane she knew she was moving from her flat but not to her parents' home.

She thought of Steele raised by his grandmother. No, she didn't want that for the twins. She wanted to raise her children herself, her way, and not her parents' way.

There was so much to sort out, so very much, but as she disembarked from the plane nearly a day later and a lei was placed around her neck Candy was the happiest tourist on the planet and knew Hawaii was the right place to be.

'Aloha,' a gorgeous woman said.

Yes, she was happy, yet that evening as she walked along the beach, how she wished Steele was here beside her—dipping his red toenails in the Pacific, making her laugh, making her smile, letting her be who she was.

Candy loved the way he accepted her just as she was.

CHAPTER FOURTEEN

'ARE YOU GOING to a funeral?' Macey checked, seeing Steele's dark suit and tie the following Tuesday morning. 'Wait till you get to my age. I go to one a month.'

'It's a memorial service,' he said. He really liked speaking with Macey. She was so blunt about everything.

'Oh, is it for that nurse in Emergency?' she asked. 'The one Elaine's crying over?'

'Elaine?' Steele glanced across the ward and sure enough a very flat Elaine, very un-bossy of late Elaine, was sitting at the desk when she'd normally be bustling about. 'He got off with her at a Christmas party,' Macey said, 'from what I can make out. Then he had nothing to do with her the next day. I would say he wasn't a good caretaker of lovely young hearts.'

'Oh, he's St Gerry now.' Steele rolled his eyes.

'And I shall be St Macey for a while after I die and then people will start to remember what a cantankerous old thing I really was.'

He laughed and looked into her wise eyes. 'You don't miss anything, do you?'

'Not with the new medication.' She smiled. 'I'm back.'

'God help us, then.' Steele smiled.

'You wouldn't have met him, though,' Macey said, and the smile was wiped off his face at her perception.

'Sorry?'

'He was in Greece, had been there a couple of months when it happened, well, according to the porter who took me for my X-ray... That's what he said to the radiographer anyway.'

'I believe so.'

'So why are you going to his memorial service if you never met?'

Steele said nothing, just gave Macey a small nod and walked off.

He sat at the desk and tried to write notes, but he ached. He actually ached sitting there.

He missed Candy, more than he had ever missed anyone.

He'd never missed anybody really, apart from his grandmother when she'd died.

It felt like grief. It really did.

It was grief because he missed her. He even missed the bump of her twins, or was he just imagining that?

He pulled up his emails and looked at the image of Gerry and it wasn't jealousy he was feeling. Steele understood that now.

It was guilt.

Guilt because this young man had died. Guilt that he might be swooping in and raising his babies because he couldn't have any of his own.

Steele let out a breath and then jumped slightly as a voice startled him.

'I'm here to see Macey Anderson...' Steele glanced

up and saw a good-looking middle-aged man wearing a suit and tie and carrying a huge bunch of flowers.

He was nervous, he was anxious and he was hers, Steele knew.

'I'll take you over.' He stood and as they walked to the bed he would never forget the small cry of recognition that escaped Macey as she looked down the ward and for the first time saw her son.

He ran to her.

Those last two steps he actually ran and Steele pulled the curtains around them as Macey held her fifty-five-year-old baby for the very first time.

Some things were private but Steele knew he'd just witnessed love.

Steele checked in on Macey a couple of hours later. She had gone to bed for a lie down, but he found her sitting up, smiling, with a huge bunch of flowers beside her bed and a photo album that her son had brought for her.

'I'm a grandmother,' she said, showing Steele a photo. 'And in two weeks I'll be a great-grandmother. He was a bit worried about telling me that.' Macey gave a delighted smile. 'His daughter, Samantha, is only eighteen. They're coming to visit me when I'm home.'

'You're going to be busy, Macey,' Steele said.

'I shall be. I'd say I'm going to have to hang around for a while yet.' She looked at him. 'Do you know, I always worried what sort of home he'd gone to, more than I worried about what he thought of me. He was raised beautifully. They loved him from the moment they got him and still do… It's a huge weight off my mind.'

'I'm very glad,' he said, and then he moved to go because she was cutting a bit close to the bone.

'I wondered if they'd love him as their own,' Macey said. 'I wondered if he'd resent them if he found out he wasn't biologically theirs, but they were just so open about it...'

'I'm very pleased to hear that,' Steele responded. 'Now, if you'll excuse me, I have to go.'

As he went to do that Macey's words stopped him.

'So she's in Hawaii...'

'Sorry?' he said, and turned.

Macey gave him an odd look. 'Are we going to pretend that you don't know who I'm talking about?'

'I don't,' Steele said.

'Do you think you stop being a matron? I used to know everything that went on in my department. Do you really think I just lie here?'

Steele had never had anyone meddle in his love life, or lack of a love life, and he wasn't going to start now. 'I have to go, Macey.'

'You just interrupted me, Doctor. Why is she in Hawaii and you're here?'

'I don't discuss my private life...'

'But you're fine with me discussing mine?'

'You're my job,' Steele said to her, but she just smiled at him.

'And you're hard work!' she said. 'You're certainly not so chipper these days.'

'I apologise,' he said. 'I shouldn't bring my problems to work with me.'

'How are *you*, Steele?' she said. 'And that's Matron asking.'

Steele remembered Candy sitting here, crying, on this very bed. It had been Macey who had told them both that Candy was pregnant after all. He sat on the bed and this time he was there for himself rather than Macey and he told her how he felt.

'Sad.'

'I'm sorry.'

'I miss her.'

'You don't have to miss her, though.'

'She needs this break.'

'Perhaps, but she'll come back and you'll be gone, living miles away, immersed in your new job. That's not the start that you two need.'

'She needs time to think.'

'Of course she does,' Macey said, 'but you can have too much time and get yourself into a space that it's very hard to get out of.'

She was right. Steele knew that. Of course, Candy's parents would soon come round. From the little he knew about them, he knew that they loved their daughter. They would want to help. They would probably suggest that she move back in with them. He thought about trying to forge a relationship with her parents as gatekeepers.

They didn't need to forge anything, Steele realised.

He didn't need to question himself about his motives towards the pregnancy.

He loved her.

It was that easy.

Macey watched the smile that spread on his face and, yes, some things were private but she knew too that she'd just witnessed the realisation of love.

Steele sat through the long memorial service and heard what an amazing man St Gerry had been, but it didn't hurt him now.

Indeed, he could laugh at a few of his antics.

By all accounts he had been a bit wild, a bit bold, and now, as the shock of his death started to recede, the real Gerry started to appear.

They all stood as his parents cut a ribbon for the new resuscitation ward and everybody headed up towards Admin for drinks and nibbles and more talk about Gerry, but Steele chose not to go there.

'Steele!' Hugh, a surgeon he had asked to consult on a patient, came over and shook his hand. 'Have you met Rory?'

'I have.' He shook Rory's hand.

'And this is Gina. She's also an anaesthetist here,' Hugh introduced, but Steele couldn't place her.

'I *used* to be an anaesthetist here,' Gina said.

'It's lovely to meet you,' he said, and then watched Gina's features tighten as a man made his way over.

'This is Anton,' Hugh said, and Steele shook Anton's hand as Hugh introduced them. 'Anton's an obstetrician.'

'Well,' Steele said, 'that would explain why we haven't met. We don't have much call for obstetricians on the geriatric unit.'

'I'm also a reproductive specialist,' Anton said. 'Though I guess you don't have much call up there for them either.' He turned to Hugh. 'Are you going up to Admin for drinks?'

'No.' Hugh shook his head. 'I've got to get back to Theatre. Anyway, I've done my duty and put in an appearance but, frankly, he was an arrogant piece of work and I had more arguments with him than anyone else at the Royal.'

Anton watched as Steele gave a wry smile.

'Well, I certainly don't need to be around booze,' Gina said. 'I'm heading for home. I might see you around.' She smiled at Steele. 'I've got an interview next week.'

'Good luck,' Steele said.

Anton, he noticed, made no comment.

Gina walked off and there was an uncomfortable silence for a moment.

'How is she?' Hugh asked Rory.

'How would I know?' Rory said. 'We're not really talking any more.'

The two men walked off, leaving just Steele and Anton.

'Undercurrents?' Steele checked, because around Gina things had seemed incredibly tense.

'Hell, yes,' Anton said, but didn't elaborate. 'I think I might give the drinks in Admin a miss too, although I could use a drink. Do you want to go over to Imelda's?' he offered. Imelda's was a bar across from the hospital and Steele nodded.

'Sure.'

'Have you worked here long?' Steele asked as they gave their orders a few minutes later.

'Just over a year,' Anton said. 'You?'

'I'm only here for a few more weeks. I move to Kent the week after next.'

'My first intention was to be here for a couple of years and then return to Milan, but my wife works here and she's pregnant. I can't see me leaving here any time soon.'

'You said that you worked in fertility?'

'That's right.'

'Is it hard to do both?' Steele asked.

'I set firm boundaries,' Anton explained. 'I first did obstetrics then moved into fertility. I missed it, though, and so when I moved to England I changed back to obstetrics. I still keep my hand in when I can. I would love somehow to do both but they are both very consuming.'

'There are a lot of changes, I guess?' Steele could not believe he was pushing this conversation.

Anton could. 'There are constant changes.'

'What about for men?' Steele asked. 'I mean, you hear all the advancements for women…' He could not believe he was discussing this. He actually wanted to stop because if there wasn't hope then perhaps it would be better not to know.

'Things are different for men also. There is a procedure called ICSE now. Basically, if you can get one healthy sperm an egg can be fertilised. Even if the sperm count comes back as negative, you can go into the vas deferens…'

Steele pulled a face at the thought of a needle in his balls.

'Under local.' Anton smiled.

He'd do it.

And there was the difference, Steele realised. He'd had a lot of loves in his life but never till now 'the one'.

One that meant two hours after taking his first sip of a very welcome Scotch and a whole lot of talking with Anton, he was standing in a room, pants around his ankles, filling a specimen jar.

'That was quick,' Anton teased as Steele came into his office and he took the jar. 'You might want to work on that.' Then he was serious as he prepared the sample. 'You know that if I find nothing in the specimen I can still go into the vas deferens. I might want to do that sober, though.'

'Just tell me.'

CHAPTER FIFTEEN

CANDY CRIED OVER GERRY.

And on days two and three Candy cried quite a bit about finding herself twenty-four years old and pregnant with twins.

Day three she had explored the island and on day four the dam broke and Candy sobbed at the unfairness of it all, that the man she knew she loved had arrived in her life at a time when all the odds were stacked against them.

By day five she gave up on crying and took Steele's money, which she had in a separate purse, and bought a fabulous, seriously fabulous sea-green sarong.

As she handed over the money it felt crinkly and new and she glanced at it and she started laughing.

Liar, liar.

These were far newer notes than Steele had said they were.

He had been to the bank after all!

She loved him.

A lot more relaxed and a little bit sunburnt, in the late afternoon Candy put on her sarong and set off. She sat on a hill, looking out at the ocean, and tried to finally sort her list out.

She dealt with the easiest first.

Job.

She chewed her pen for a full two minutes before deciding that she did love Emergency. No, she didn't want them all finding out that the twins were Gerry's but, of course, they would.

And she'd deal with it.

The Gerry's Wing thing was a bit *ouch*, but she'd just have to suck it up.

She needed the maternity leave.

Which brought her onto the next thing that was worrying her—money. She didn't write that down. Candy didn't even have to think about that. She wrote 'Ha-ha-ha' instead and then moved on to the next one.

Gerry's parents.

Okay, she would telephone them when she returned and tell them the news and, if they wanted to or when they'd calmed down, she would offer to go and speak with them.

Next.

Her parents.

Candy had already decided she was moving, far away so that they couldn't just drop in. Even if it would be easier to have them nearer.

She took a breath. The harder matters were approaching.

Gerry.

'I should have gone to the memorial service.'

Candy didn't know what else to write. She didn't know how to write that she didn't love him but she hated that he was dead and that not only would the world move on without him, but he would have children and not know.

They would know about him though, Candy promised.

'I will tell the twins about you and keep in touch with your family.'

And then she got to the top of the list but she'd left it till last because it was the one that left her so, so confused.

Steele.

She could write to him perhaps. Maybe it would be better in a letter. But telling someone you loved them when you were pregnant with someone else's children came at a huge disadvantage and it was an impossible letter to write.

She never wanted him to think that she wanted him simply as a father for her children.

The natural order of falling in love had for the most part been denied them.

She tried to keep it light, wondering through her words that if it was all too much to deal with for him, maybe they could somehow be friends with benefits. Then she screwed up that piece of paper because given how much her stomach had grown in the past few days she doubted if very soon she would appeal to him.

And so she wrote him a postcard—one she had swiped from the villa and had meant to use for Macey.

Steele,
I wish...how I wish...that you were here now.
Candy xxx

List sorted, she decided.

Now she had to get on with relaxing.

As she walked back she thought she was seeing

things because there, sitting on the little chair outside her villa, was Steele. He was wearing dark jeans and a black T-shirt and was very unshaven but very welcome to her eyes.

'I didn't know I had a genie.' She met him with a smile.

This was how he remembered her, Steele thought as she approached. This was how she'd been before it had all happened—here she was smiling, laughing, intuitive and sexy. She handed him the postcard she had written and he read it with a smile.

'That explains what happened, then,' Steele said. 'One minute I was sitting chatting to Macey and the next, *puff*, here I was in Hawaii…' He looked at her and took in the changes, and not just to her body.

She had been right to come alone, he conceded, because it had served her well—she looked relaxed and healthy and happy.

It was very nice to see.

'I've been making lists,' Candy said. 'I'm all sorted now.'

'Can I see?' he asked, and then shook his head. 'Sorry, stupid thing to ask.'

'Go for it,' she said.

'Let's go for a walk,' he said, and he dropped his bag in the villa and took her hand. They headed to the beach and sat there.

She could hear the wind through the palm trees and was all knotted on the inside but in a very nice way.

Steele was here.

'Why are you here?' she asked.

'Because I had this vision of trying to date you from

Kent while you were living with your parents,' Steele said as he read through her list.

'I'd already addressed that,' she said, and pointed to her decision on the list she had written.

So she had.

'I feel like the teacher is reading my homework,' she admitted. 'Do I get marked?'

'Verbal comments,' Steele said. 'I didn't bring my red pen.

'Okay, I think moving away from your parents is very brave and very sensible.'

'Thank you.'

'And I think telling Gerry's parents is very brave and very right too,' Steele said, and carried on reading through her list.

'Work…' Steele said, and his hand wavered in the air. 'That's a tough one.'

'I like what I do.'

'I know.

'What's "Ha-ha-ha" for?'

'Money,' Candy said, and he laughed.

He was serious when they got to Gerry. 'As for the memorial service…'

'I feel bad that I didn't go.'

'I went,' Steele said.

'Were there a lot of people?'

'It was packed,' he said. He decided not to mention Elaine and her tears. He had spoken to her the next day and had hopefully helped by listening a bit.

'I met Rory, and Gina…'

'Gina!' Candy's eyes were wide. 'She's been on extended leave. I think she's been in rehab.'

'Well, it looks as if she's coming back,' Steele said.

'Oh, and I met Anton. We went for a drink afterwards.' He watched as she blushed. 'Is he the doctor oversee-ing your pregnancy?'

'Yes.'

'Did you happen to mention my infertility?'

'I did.'

'It's fine that you told him. I don't have any issue with that at all. You must have been in the most con-fused space.'

'So how did you guess that he was my doctor?'

'Heathrow to Hawaii gives you quite a lot of think-ing time.' He told her all the questions he'd had for Anton and then he told her why. 'I'm here because I love you, but I never wanted you to think I wanted you for the babies. Does that make sense?'

'Sort of.'

'Anyway, I'm not. I want the babies very much but if it hadn't happened, it helps to know that you very probably can have a baby with me. Not naturally, but the choice and the chance is there.'

She turned and smiled at him. 'Did you do it into a jar for me?'

'I did,' he said. 'And, had it been necessary, I would have undergone a procedure that would involve a lot of local anaesthetic on a very delicate area but, thank-fully, Anton seems to think I've got enough swimmers to work with.'

'You asked Anton all those embarrassing questions for me?'

'Yes.' Steele sighed. 'I did. I had no idea at the time that Anton had practically led me to ask them—you've got a lot of fans, you know.'

'Who?'

'Anton, Macey...'

'How is Macey?'

'Meddling. She practically told me to get on a plane.'

Then he got to the hard part. 'Gerry's parents and brother and sister were at the service and they told a few tales.'

'How did they seem.'

'Lost,' Steele said. 'Confused. I think the news of the twins is going to mean an awful lot to them.'

'Why did you go to the service, Steele?' she asked.

'Because I wanted to know more about the man whose children I want to raise and perhaps if they have questions I might be able to answer some,' he said. 'And I'm here because I love you,'

Candy looked at him and her eyes filled with tears. She realised then what Macey had meant when she'd asked her about duty.

Steele had no duty to her babies unless he wanted them.

They had been together for just two weeks when the news had hit.

He had every reason to walk away, to be gone, for things to fade out quietly, and yet he was here, sitting beside her and loving her with his eyes.

'I'm sorry they're—'

'You're going to say that once,' Steele broke in. 'Now. Then it's done.'

He was the most direct person she had ever met.

'You're sorry they're not mine?' he checked.

Tears shot out of her eyes without a sob. They just spilled out with such force that they splashed on her sarong.

'We have to be honest now,' he said. 'We have to

have the most honest conversation of our lives and I'm ringing in sick even if it take six months to sort this out because we're staying here till it's done.'

'We've only got five months left till they're here.'

'So we need to talk, right here, right now, and nothing, *nothing* gets left unsaid. My first thought, when you found out you were pregnant, was just that…I wanted them to be mine,' Steele said. 'Then I asked myself what would have happened if the twins weren't already here? My guess is that we'd have made it, because I was already coming to Hawaii and I don't go on holiday with women yet I was about to with you…'

She thought back. Things had been so easy then.

'And if we had made it, would you have wanted a baby at some stage?' he asked.

'I don't know. I think I would want children but if we couldn't…' She looked at Steele.

Did his infertility change how she felt about him?

Never.

Could she love him less?

Not a chance.

'If we couldn't have children we'd have gone for treatment,' Steele checked, and she nodded.

'Or adoption.'

'Okay,' he said. 'Had we adopted, would you have loved them less?'

'No!'

'Would you, in an argument, say that they weren't biologically mine?'

'No!'

'So what's the difference?'

'I don't know.'

'If we had to use donated sperm, would it change how we feel about them?'

'Of course not.'

'I'm going to be there for the pregnancy, the birth, the nappies. The twins will be mine,' Steele said. 'They will know about Gerry and when they turn into feral teenagers and say that I'm not their real father, I won't be hurt, not for a second. Instead, you and I will laugh in their moody, acne-laden faces when they say that, because we know we dealt with all that in Hawaii many, many years ago.'

Candy let out a breath.

'It's not just you that has concerns about getting married,' he said. 'I made a list of my own.' He took out his boarding pass and she read it.

Movies.
Football.
Cricket.

'It's a lot less complicated than mine,' she said.

'Oh, no, it isn't. I like my life very much and there are certain…er…requirements that I swore I would not forgo…'

She looked at him.

'The movies,' Steele explained. 'I like to go on my own sometimes. I just do. I don't want you saying, "But you used to take me"…'

Candy smiled.

'And I know it's horrible and selfish to take myself off when you'll have been stuck indoors with screaming twins, so perhaps you might like to take yourself off now and then to wherever ladies take themselves off to...'

'Like a spa day?' she said.

'I think so.'

'And you'd never say, "Oh, Candy, why do you have so many spa days? Why don't I come with you this time?"'

'Never,' he promised.

'Deal.'

'The football and cricket are one and the same...' He looked a bit worried and so too was Candy as she hated sport—it made her sweat and feel shaky and that was just watching it. 'I don't do romantic holidays,' he said. 'I shall, of course, and I'll do family ones too, but I have a group of friends and we like some big-ticket stuff.'

'Such as?'

'You remember how well we negotiated the movie issue?' Steele checked, because was he really going to land a perfect woman who didn't mind what he was about to suggest?

'I do.' Candy was very curious. She loved their discussions. 'What sort of big-ticket stuff?'

'International cricket events. World Cup...'

'Oh.'

'We don't always all go to everything.'

Candy said nothing at first. It really was a bit awkward. 'Would I be expected to go?'

'Well...' he said. 'There's a lot of drinking and singing...' He waited for her to say that no way would she ever want to go. Yes, this was awkward. 'Might be a bit of bad language, which wouldn't be great for the twins.' Still Candy said nothing and so he told her the real deal. 'There's also a very strict no-girlfriends-or-wives agreement, which I have, over the years, enforced on my friends several times. I'd never be able to live it down if I asked to bring you.'

He watched a little smile play on her lips.

'However,' he said quickly, 'I would think, given I'd be going away with friends for a couple of weeks now and then and leaving you, that you might need to escape with your girlfriends for a holiday every now and then, and I'd look after the twins and however many others we have...'

'Oh, I think I could agree to that.' Candy smiled and she looked at him, a man so happy in himself he wasn't looking for the other half. It had just turned out that she happened to be it. 'I love you, even without the twins, you do know that.'

'Why isn't there anything written about me on your list, then?' Steele asked, loving the way she blushed.

'I tried to write a letter.'

'Show me.'

'That's so unfair.'

'I need to know you love me, Candy,' he teased, and held out his hand.

It was so embarrassing as he sat there and read how crazy she was about him and then he started to laugh.

'"Friends with benefits." I'm sorry, Candy, this might be insensitive but if I'm having a friend with benefits then I want the blonde, leggy Candy. Not the heavily pregnant with twins one—that's husband stuff.' He looked at her. 'Marry me?'

'Honestly?'

'Honestly,' he said, his heart thumping in his chest.

'I want to be with you but I've never wanted to get

married,' Candy admitted. 'I just don't want the big white wedding that my parents would insist on. I don't want to be standing there in a fluffy white dress pregnant with twins…'

'And you'd have to say your name out loud in a packed church,' he pointed out. 'And I'm a divorced heathen…' Then he smiled. 'We're in Hawaii, Candy. We can be married tomorrow, if that's what you want. I know it will upset your parents but I think they will be pleased as well.'

She started to smile.

'Is that a yes?' he checked. 'I'm starting to get worried here.'

'It's a very big yes,' she said. 'But won't your parents be disappointed to miss it?' Candy asked. After all, he was their only child.

'Yes,' he said, 'and I'll be tempted to point out that they missed most of my milestone events growing up, but I shan't do that, of course. They'll soon get over it, especially when they hear about the twins.'

They were back at the villa, all their lists checked and sorted. She loved their honesty, how they just spoke and worked it all out. 'We dealt with that very maturely.' Candy grinned in delight as she congratulated them.

'Oh, I can assure you that I don't feel very mature today,' Steele said. 'In fact, I want to do something very immature.'

He handed her the phone with a text from Annie, asking him if he'd had a think about her suggestion.

'This came through when I landed,' Steele explained. 'Can I?'

'Go on.' She smiled and watched as he started to type out a text.

There's nothing to think about or discuss. I am in Hawaii with Candy and we're about to get married. She's pregnant with twins, which means that she's very moody and volatile at the moment, so it's probably better that you don't text again. Regards, Steele.

He hit 'send' and with that he let go of the past and moved into the glorious future.

'You lied to me, though,' she said as they stepped into the villa and he took her in his arms.

'Never.'

'Yes, you did,' Candy said, and wrapped her hands around his neck. 'You said that the money you gave me had been lying around for five years, but it was only printed two years ago.'

Steele merely smiled at being caught. 'That's because I didn't want you worrying about taking food from your babies' mouths as you looked at that fantastic, sexy sarong.' He stroked her thick nipples through the fabric, and then he ran a tender hand over her stomach and his hand told her how sexy the changes were to him.

His kiss told her that too.

Her fabulous sarong dropped to the floor and Steele undressed with rapid ease.

The only thing missing from her perfect holiday had been her perfect man and now here he was, making love to her.

The doubts, the hesitation about whether or not he should intrude on her time here, were put to rest as he entered her. She wrapped herself around him, moved her body with his and held nothing back.

'I love you so much,' Candy said as she started to come.

No question, no hesitation, they both knew how precious the love they had was. Steele felt the roundness of her stomach press into his and he wanted to say he loved her back but she dragged him in so deep that all he could do was moan.

'I love you too,' he said afterwards as they lay there.

'You've still got red toenails.' She smiled as she looked at his feet next to hers.

'I was too embarrassed to buy nail-varnish remover,' he said. 'We'll need it if we're getting married on the beach.'

'Or not.'

'Oh, no.' Steele shook his head. 'We're getting it filmed for our families and a photo for Macey. I don't want everyone wondering if I'm secretly wearing your underwear.'

'Are we going to live in Kent?' Candy asked.

'We are,' Steele said. 'My offer's been accepted for that house. I wanted to ask you to marry me there,' he said. 'My plan was to do that when we looked through the house, except you chose not to come in.'

'You were going to ask me then?'

'Yes,' he said. 'But I didn't want to rush you.'

'So you gave me an extra five days?'

'I couldn't wait any longer,' Steele said, and then kissed the top of her head. 'So let's go and get the licence and get married so that the honeymoon can begin.'

It already had.

EPILOGUE

IT WAS, FOR CANDY, who had never wanted her own wedding, the perfect one.

It was, for Steele, who had sworn he would never marry again, the best wedding ever too.

Steele opted for sunset, though he didn't tell her why.

They walked to the beach together and stood, their bare feet caressed by the silky sand, Candy nervous, excited and all the things he made her feel as she faced him.

'Aloha,' he said, and she smiled. It was very hard to believe, after all their little teases about her holiday, that he was here with her and that this was their wedding.

'Aloha,' Candy said, grateful when he took her shaking hands.

The air smelt of coconut and frangipani. She was wearing a single flower in her hair. The breeze whipped her hair from her face and moulded Candy's dress to her soft curves. She had chosen a pale blue chiffon that was very simple and tied beneath her bust. He wore a linen suit, which was the colour of damp sand, and a white shirt and no nail varnish. He took her breath away and made her smile just as he had the moment they'd met.

She could hear the roar of the waves as they crashed onto the shore and then hissed back out to sea, leaving the sand as smooth, clean and pristine as their beckoning future.

As the huge crimson sun sank slowly into the sea the service started. They had decided on traditional vows—timeless and classic. She looked right at him as he placed the simple gold band they had chosen on her finger and Candy felt a soft shiver run through her as she heard the gorgeous, deep voice that had come into her life less than a month ago now vow to be with her for ever. 'With this ring I thee wed. With my body I thee worship.'

Then it was Candy's turn and her voice was very clear when she promised the same.

The sun had set, bamboo tiki torches lit the beach and the celebrant told them they were husband and wife.

'You may kiss your bride.'

Steele did and his kiss was long and lingering and then he moved his mouth to her ear. 'I'm the happiest I've ever been,' he said.

To hear those heartfelt words from Steele meant everything to Candy.

'I'm the happiest I've ever been too,' she agreed.

That was how they made each other feel.

With the service over and the documents signed, they walked hand in hand along the beach towards their villa with the waves lapping at their toes.

It was done, she was married and it was exactly as she'd wanted it to be, but as she saw the photographer taking down his equipment, even though they'd had the service filmed Candy felt a niggle of guilt that she had denied her parents this day.

Back in their suite she was determined to push the thought aside, but having again kissed his bride he pulled back and asked for her parents' number. 'You'll feel better when you've told them,' he said. 'You know you will.'

'They'll freak,' Candy said. 'I don't want to spoil today…' But she gave him the number and lay there with her eyes closed as a deep calm voice, one that was very used to dealing with upset, stubborn, set-in-their-ways people, introduced himself and told her father that he was a doctor who worked alongside Candy.

'No, there's nothing wrong with Candy or the babies,' Steele said, and then he told them how he had fallen in love with her, how he was going to take care of her, how he was completely fine about the twins and that they would be his. 'However,' Steele said, 'Gerry's parents will know…' He looked over at Candy. 'Candy and I have discussed it and we both agree that a baby can never have too many grandparents to love them.'

He spoke and listened and then said that he and Candy had got married today. Candy could hear her mother come onto the phone and the rise of drama that she'd dreaded ensued. She'd have to talk to them and deal with their recriminations and the guilt. She held her hand out for the phone but Steele simply listened to her mother and then spoke in that calm way of his and slowly the tension in her uncoiled.

'Candy didn't feel it appropriate, given that the pregnancy is already showing, to get married in a church, but we might renew our vows there.'

He dealt with the drama and examined his thumbnail at one point as they droned on and on and then, finally, he smiled. 'Perhaps you'd like to tell your daughter that.' He handed her the phone. 'Your parents want to speak with you.'

She took the phone and braced herself for whatever her mother would fling at her and closed her eyes.

'Complimente...' her mother said, and it was so unexpected, so far from what she'd anticipated, that Candy burst into happy tears as her mother continued to speak. 'He sounds a nice man...'

'A very nice man,' Candy said.

A very nice man who was playing with her breasts and kissing her neck and was ready to get on with his honeymoon.

'Better?' Steele said as she hung up the phone.

'Is that why you wanted an evening wedding?'

'Yep. I didn't want to scare them calling late at night,' he said, 'and I knew you'd be worried.' He gave her a smile. 'Come here, Steele.'

'Steele?' Candy said, and then realised that was her surname now.

'Well, "Mrs Candida Steele", if you want to be formal.'

She was back to her dental commercial and smiling as he took her in his arms.

They were back to *before*.

* * * * *

TWIN SURPRISE FOR
THE SINGLE DOC

SUSANNE HAMPTON

To everyone who thought they had closed their hearts to love…only to be proved wrong by a love stronger than the heartache they had survived.

And to Alli and Gilda and all of my amazing friends who constantly provide inspiration for my books.

CHAPTER ONE

'CONGRATULATIONS, CLAUDIA. You're having twins!'

Claudia Monticello's deep brown eyes, inherited from her Italian father, widened like dollhouse-sized plates against her alabaster skin, a present from her Irish mother. In a rush of panic and disbelief, her gaze darted from the gel-covered bump of her stomach to the grainy black-and-white images on the screen, then to the *pleased as punch* radiologist's face before finally looking up to the ceiling to where she imagined heaven might be. Not that she thought her parents would be smiling down at her after what she had done.

Suddenly the room became very hot and she struggled a little to breathe. The clammy fingers of one hand reached for the sides of the examination table to steady herself. *Two babies*. Her mouth had dropped open slightly, but her lips had not curved to anything close to a smile. In denial, she shook her head from side to side and nervously chewed on the nails of the other hand. There had to be a mistake. The radiologist, still smiling at the screen and apparently unaware of the panic blanketing her patient, gently moved the hand piece over Claudia's stomach to capture additional images.

She must have zoomed in too quickly, Claudia mused.

Double imaged.

Misread the data.

Be new at her job.

But Claudia knew without doubt, as she slowly and purposefully focused on the screen, there was no mistake. There were two tiny babies with two distinct heartbeats. The radiologist was using her finger to point to them. Her excitement was palpable. A reaction juxtaposed to Claudia's. At twenty-nine years of age, Claudia Monticello was anything but excited to be the single mother of twins. For many reasons... The first was her living five thousand miles from home... and the second was the fact her children would never meet their father.

Twenty weeks had passed since Claudia discovered she was to be the mother of two and, as she dropped her chin and looked down at her ample midsection while waiting for the elevator, she was pleased to see they were healthy-sized babies. Her waist was somewhere hidden underneath her forty-five-inch circumference and she hadn't seen her ankles for weeks. Her mood was one of anticipation as she waited for the doors to open on her floor. Her final obstetric visit was imminent and she was thinking about little else than her flight home to London the next day. It couldn't come quickly enough for her. She couldn't wait to farewell Los Angeles.

And turn her back on the disappointment and heartache the city had brought.

Or, more correctly, that she had invited into her life.

The day was warm and she was wearing a sleeveless floral maternity dress, one of three she'd picked up on the sale rack in Macy's when she rapidly outgrew all her other clothes, flat white sandals and her oversized camel-coloured handbag that she took everywhere. Her deep chocolate curls were short and framed her pretty face, but her eyes were filled with sadness. She pictured her suitcases, packed and waiting just inside the door of her apartment. She was finally leaving the place she had called home for almost a year. The fully furnished apartment was in a prime high-rise gated community on Wilshire Boulevard and in demand. The home would have new tenants within days. It had only been temporary, like so much in that town, and she wondered who would be sleeping in the king-sized bed later that week and what the future held for them. She hoped for their sake they hadn't rushed into something they would live to regret.

The way she had.

Patrick Spencer waited inside the elevator for the doors to open. It had only managed to travel down one floor and was already stopping. A sigh escaped from his lips. He prayed it wouldn't stop on every floor on the way to street level. His patience was already tested. He was having another one of those days. A day when he felt frustrated with life and struggled with a cocktail of resentment mixed with equal parts of doubt and disappointment and a dash of boredom with his new reality. Not that his reality was devoid of life's luxuries, but it was missing the passion he'd once felt. It was another day when he felt cheated out of what he had planned and wanted for his future, even though he was the one who'd walked away from everything. A day when he almost didn't give a damn. And whenever he had those days he always put on his sunglasses and tried to block out the world in which he lived. He had been cornered into this new life. That was how he saw it.

If things had not gone so terribly wrong, he would be living in London instead of calling Los Angeles home.

With melancholy colouring her mood, Claudia paid little attention to the tall, darkly dressed figure when she stepped into the elevator. But she noticed the affected way he was wearing wraparound sunglasses with his suit. It was more of the same pretentious LA behaviour.

Sunglasses inside an elevator? In Claudia's sadly tainted opinion, all men were hiding something; perhaps this one was nursing a hangover. She rolled her eyes, confident in the fact he couldn't see anything from behind the dark lenses and even more sure he wouldn't be looking in her direction anyway. Probably obsessed with his own thoughts and problems. Just like so many in this town. A town full of actors, many with an inflated sense of self-worth and a complete lack of morals. Perhaps this man filled that same bill, she surmised. She felt sick to her stomach even thinking about the man who had wooed her with lies and then walked out of her life as shamelessly as he had walked into it.

She patted her stomach protectively and, not caring a damn what he thought, she whispered, 'You may have been a surprise, boys, but I love you both to the moon and back already.' Then she silently added, *And I will make sure you don't run away from your responsibilities...or wear sunglasses in a lift!*

'They're very lucky little boys.' Patrick said it matter-of-factly. It surprised even him that he had made a comment but hearing the woman speak so genuinely to her unborn children in an accent once so familiar struck a chord with him. In a town so devoid of anything genuine, Patrick felt compelled to comment.

Claudia thought for a fleeting moment his words had been delivered with genuine sentiment. But her body stiffened as she reminded herself there was little or no sentiment in that town. Maternal hormones, she assumed, had temporarily dressed her vision with rose-coloured glasses. His English accent, for some reason, made her drop her guard just a little. Against her better judgement, she looked over to see the man remove his sunglasses. His lips were curved slightly. Not to a full smile, not even a half smile, but she could see his teeth just a little. They were almost perfect but not veneer flawless.

He was tall, six foot one or two, she guessed, as she was five foot nine in bare feet or the flat shoes she was wearing that day. He was broad-shouldered and, she imagined from the way his shirt fell, buff, but he wasn't overly tanned. His hair was short and light brown in colour and it was matched with a light covering of stubble on his face. His grooming was impeccable but, aside from the stubble, quite conservative. While his looks, she conceded, were worthy of a billboard, his styling was more professional than the usual LA playboy slash actor type. Or, in his case, an English ex-pat playing the LA field.

'I'm sorry?' she finally said after her assessment.

She was hoping he would shrug his shoulders, put his sunglasses back on and return to thoughts of himself or his most recent conquest.

But he didn't.

'I said that your babies are very fortunate that you care for them so much even before they enter the world. I hope they make you proud.'

Patrick had not said anything like that in twelve years. They were words he used to say every day as a matter of routine, but never so routine that they were not sincere. But something about this woman and the palpable love he could see in her eyes and hear in her voice made it impossible not to make comment. She appeared different from the women he knew.

And a very long way from the women he bedded. She was cute and beautiful, not unlike a china doll. His women were not fragile like that.

And her love for her unborn children was special. It was something Patrick very much appreciated.

Claudia felt her stance stiffen again and her expression become quite strained. His accent was cultured and, with her own English upbringing and resultant class-consciousness, she suspected he had more than likely experienced a privileged boarding school education. His clothes were high end designer. She knew he must have an ulterior motive. All men did. There were a handful of people she had met in the year since she'd left London to make Hollywood her home who had shown a level of genuine kindness but she doubted this man would join those ranks. In fact, she doubted that any man would ever again join that group. Her desired demeanour was defensive and with little effort she reached it. No man was going to get within a mile of her or, more particularly, her children with any line. She had told herself that she had finished with men and all of their agendas. And she decided to prove it to herself.

Her first step would be keeping this man, albeit a very attractive man, at arm's length. Perhaps even offside.

'You really should refrain from eavesdropping; it's rude,' she said before turning her attention back to the blank gunmetal doors. *There—it was done!* She had stood up for herself and it brought her a sense of empowerment.

It had been a long time coming and she conceded her ire was directed towards the wrong man but she had finally felt strong enough to say something. And it felt good. As if she was claiming her power back.

But the elevator didn't feel good or seem to have any power. It seemed to be slowing and, for want of a better word in her head, since she didn't particularly like confined spaces, it seemed to be *struggling* in its descent. She wished it would pick up speed and get her out of the awkward situation. Deep down inside, she knew her response had been overly dramatic and cutting but she was still proud she had found the strength to do it. There were only another fifteen floors and she hoped the elevator would reach the ground before he handed her a business card and she discovered the reason he'd struck up the conversation. Insurance, investment or even real estate. There had to be something behind the smile. Since she was so heavily pregnant, she felt very confident it was not going to segue into a pick-up line.

With her chin lifted slightly, she felt the colour ris-

ing in her cheeks; she played with her small pearl earrings the way she always did when she was nervous.

Patrick considered her in silence for a moment as
he watched her fidget with the small pearl studs. He
had made an uncharacteristic effort to acknowledge
her pregnancy and he was taken back at her disparaging remark. He hadn't expected it as she had appeared
at first glance to be very sweet. Her pretty face was
framed with dark curls and he thought she had an innocence about her. He hadn't foreseen her reaction and
to his mind he definitely did not deserve the harsh re-
tort. He wasn't going to take it on the chin.

Without making eye contact as he stared at the same
gunmetal door, he decided to answer her abrupt reply
with one equally insensitive. 'I think you're the rude
one here. You enter a lift, or should I say elevator, due
to our location, with only one other person, that being
me, and begin a conversation with your unborn children, for which I did not judge you to be mad, but in
fact complimented you, and then you remark that I'm
rude for making a comment.'

Claudia was surprised by his formal and acerbic re-
buttal. His response had been articulate and he had not
raised his voice but she wasn't in the mood to eat humble pie. Men, or rather one man, had just let her down
very badly and she wasn't going to break her promise
to herself. They were all the same if they were given
the opportunity. And she had no intention of ever giving a man such an opportunity with her again.

With her eyes facing straight ahead at their shared
focal point, she was about to reply when she was
stopped by a twinge in her stomach. Her body stiff-

ened with the pain and she hunched a little, almost protectively.

She knew it couldn't be a contraction. It was too early. One hand instinctively reached for her babies and her stomach suddenly felt hard to her touch. She was grateful the stranger was looking away as she leant a little on the elevator wall. She told herself it must be the Braxton Hicks contractions that her obstetrician had mentioned but it seemed to be quite intense and more than a little painful.

It passed quite quickly and finally, after catching her breath, she replied, 'I think it was obvious I was having a private conversation. And clearly you *are* judging me, by implying that I'm mad. That's hardly a nice thing to say to someone you don't know.'

'You're right,' he responded and turned to face her. 'I concede it was less than polite but you have to agree that you most definitely left your manners back up on the thirty-fourth floor.' He looked away as he finished his tersely delivered response and checked for mobile phone reception.

By his abrupt tone and the fact he had noticed which floor she lived on, Claudia looked out of the corner of her eyes at him and wondered for a moment if he was a lawyer. Lawyers always paid attention to details that the general public ignored. Of course, she thought, she would have the slowest ride to the ground with an overbearing man with a legal background. She dropped her chin a little but not to admire her middle; instead she looked tentatively across the elevator to where the man stood. He was wearing highly polished shoes. Slightly raising her chin, she noted his perfectly pressed charcoal-grey slacks and finally, with her head turned a little more in his direction as she gave in to her curiosity, she saw his crisp white shirt and jacket. She had thought initially that he was wearing a suit but on closer, but not too obvious, inspection, she could see flecked threads in the weave. And then there was his expensive Swiss watch. Not forgetting the fact he was already in the elevator when she'd entered, which meant he either lived, or had a client, on the only floor above her. The penthouse on the thirty-fifth floor.

Suddenly she felt another twinge. She wanted to get out of the lift and get to her obstetric appointment immediately. She didn't want to be dragged into a conversation.

'I apologise—I'm sorry,' she returned sharply and without emotion as she once again faced the elevator doors. She rubbed the hollow of her back that was beginning to ache. The niggling pain was spreading and becoming increasingly uncomfortable. She just wanted the short time in the relatively tiny space to be uneventful, so she took the easy option and hoped the conversation would end there.

But it didn't.

'Frankly, I think I'm a little past caring for your less than genuine apology.'

'I beg your pardon?' Claudia knew the handsome stranger had called the situation correctly; she just didn't want to admit it.

'I think you're just giving me lip service,' he continued. 'Forget I said anything nice at all. To be honest, I'm sorry I did, so let's just go back to an awkward silence that comes with sharing an elevator with a stranger and hope the thing picks up speed for both of our sakes.'

Claudia felt a little tug at her heart. The stranger really had been trying to make pleasant conversation and compliment her in the process and she had shot him down.

'Gosh, I did sound awfully rude, didn't I?' she asked, as much to herself as him. Wishing she had not been as dismissive and had put some meaning behind the words, she offered a more contrite apology. 'I really am sorry. I do mean it.'

'Perhaps.'

Her eyes met his and she could see they were not warm and forgiving but neither were they icy. They were sad. They were filled with a look close to disappointment and she felt her heart sink a little further. She had never been quite so rude to a stranger before. Heaven knew what day he had endured and she had behaved abominably.

Circumstance had made her distrust the male population. She had not even thought how her behaviour would affect the handsome stranger sharing the slowest elevator on the west coast of North America, until he'd pointed it out. But she was surprised by his reaction. She assumed most men would have shrugged it off but he seemed genuinely disappointed, almost as if he was directing the disappointment inward for some reason.

With a humble and heartfelt expression she replied, 'I really do apologise. I'm very sorry and there's really no excuse for my behaviour.' Taking a deep breath, she outstretched her hand like an olive branch. 'I'm Claudia Monticello, slightly hormonal mother-to-be and having a very bad day. I could add that I'm perhaps a little stressed right now as I'm flying back to the UK tomorrow and I have so much still to do. I have to see my obstetrician and finish packing. There's so many things I have to remember…' And so much she wanted to forget. But she had no intention of telling the handsome stranger that.

'Well, perhaps you do have a reason to be a little on edge,' he said, looking into her eyes, almost piercing her soul. 'Apology accepted. Patrick Spencer, doctor, not eavesdropper.'

Claudia smiled. She had picked the wrong profession too. As she kept staring into his eyes, she noticed they were a deep blue with flecks of grey. Like storm clouds swirling over the deepest part of the ocean. She felt herself wondering why he hid such stunning eyes behind dark sunglasses. They were too captivating a shade to be hidden. She shook herself. His eye colour was not something she needed to busy her mind with at that time. Nothing about him was her concern, she told herself as she noticed there was only a short trip of eight floors until they reached street level and she would never see the man again.

But it did feel strangely reassuring to be in the elevator with a man with a medical background after the fleeting contraction she'd experienced. She knew they were commonplace nearing the latter part of pregnancy and it appeared to have been a once-off but his nearness made her feel a little safer.

No, *very* safe and she didn't know why.

Out of a sense of awkwardness in the silence that were now sharing, she glanced up again to check how many floors they had travelled. The elevator had not picked up any speed. She was glad they weren't in the Burj Khalifa in Dubai or the boys would be ready for pre-school at the rate they were travelling.

With her mind brought to travel, Claudia was excited to be heading home. Once her obstetrician signed her flight clearance she would be on her way back to London. Her contract with the television studio had finally ended, leaving her free to return home. Instinctively, she patted the recent ultrasound scans tucked safely in her bag. She had no swelling in her legs and her blood pressure had been fine at the last visit. Her pregnancy had been uneventful until the twinge, something which was at complete odds with her disastrous personal life. But she was grateful she had something positive upon which to focus.

As they passed the fourth floor and the elevator seemed to almost pause, suddenly she felt another more intense contraction. Claudia tried to smile through it but suspected it was closer to a grimace. Braxton Hicks contractions were a lot different to what she had expected. She had been told that a woman could experience up to four in an hour but she hadn't thought they would be so close together.

Patrick eyed her with concern but, just as he opened his mouth, the stalling elevator came to a jarring halt. Claudia grabbed the railing to steady herself and they both looked up to see the floor light flickering and waited for the doors to open. But they didn't. Instead the lift dropped what she imagined to be another floor and stopped. Patrick had already taken two purposeful steps towards Claudia and she felt his strong arms wrap around her to prevent her from falling. His touch should have worried her but instead a wave of relief washed over her. She was not alone.

'Let's get you on the floor. It will be safer.' Hastily

he pulled off his jacket and dropped it to the elevator floor before gently lowering Claudia onto it.

'Your jacket—it will be ruined.'

'At this moment, a ruined jacket is not my concern. You are,' he said matter-of-factly but with an unmistakable warmth in his voice and one Claudia didn't believe she truly deserved after her behaviour. 'When are the babies due?'

'The twins aren't due for another six and a half weeks and I'm fine, really I am,' she insisted as she tried to sit gently and not move and crease the jacket underneath her. 'I'm flying out tomorrow with the doctor's approval; it's the last possible day that the airline will allow me to travel.'

'You're cutting it fine with the whole long haul at almost thirty-four weeks,' he replied with his brows knitted. He added, 'You seemed to be in pain a moment ago.' It was a question he framed as a statement. He didn't want to appear overbearing but he was concerned. He was also doubtful whether she should be travelling at such a late stage of pregnancy. Even with a clean bill of health, it seemed risky for her to take a long haul flight so close to delivering.

'Yes, just one of these Braxton Hicks contractions.'

'You're sure?' His frown had not lifted as he spoke.

This time it was a question and she sensed genuine concern. It heightened hers.

'Absolutely,' she said, followed by a nod. It wasn't the truth. The truth was that she had never been quite so scared in her life but she had to push that reality from her mind and remain positive. The worst-case scenario was too overwhelmingly frightening to consider without collapsing into a heap. She had been holding everything together tenuously for so many months her nerves were threadbare.

'If you say so,' he told her, doubt about her response evident in his tone. 'Just stay seated till we reach the ground.' He retrieved his mobile phone from his trouser pocket, but Claudia assumed there was no reception through the heavy elevator walls as he turned and reached for the emergency telephone.

He didn't take his eyes away from Claudia, even when the standard response finished and he cut in. 'This is Dr Patrick Spencer, I'm in Terrace Park Towers, Wilshire Boulevard, not far from Highland. We're somewhere between the fourth floor and street level and the elevator's come to a halt. I have a female resident with me. Approximately thirty-four weeks pregnant.' He paused. 'No, no, there's no immediate medical emergency. I have the resident seated and there's no obvious physical injuries but I want a crew to get us out stat. And after the jolt it would be wise to send an ambulance. The patient may need to head to the hospital for a routine obstetric examination.'

With that he hung up and turned his full attention back to Claudia.

Her resolve to remain calm had deserted her, despite attempts to tell herself she was overreacting. She wasn't overreacting. Her eyes darted to the steel doors, willing them to open, and then back to Patrick, unsure what she was willing him to do.

'We'll be out of here before you know it,' he said and very gently wiped the wisps of hair from her brow, now covered in tiny beads of perspiration. 'They're on their way.'

'Yes, they are...I'm afraid.'

'There's nothing to fear. Just stay calm and the crew will have us out of here very quickly. And there'll be an ambulance on hand if we need one.'

'It's not the crew I'm talking about…it's the babies. I'm afraid my twins are on their way… This isn't Braxton Hicks, Patrick. I'm in labour.'

CHAPTER TWO

CLAUDIA'S WATER BROKE only moments later, confirming she was very much in labour and going to deliver her babies in an elevator unless a miracle happened. As she wriggled uncomfortably on the hard elevator floor with only Patrick's now soaking wet jacket beneath her, she stared at nowhere in particular and prayed with all of her might that it was a bad dream. One from which she would wake to find herself giving birth in a pretty delivery room in a London hospital surrounded by smiling nurses…nurses just like her sister, Harriet. She always allayed Claudia's medical concerns with sensible and thoughtful answers delivered in a calm manner, just like the way their mother had always spoken to them.

How she wished more than anything that Harriet was with her. She would know what to do. She always did…but, as Claudia looked at her surroundings from her new vantage point on the floor, she knew it was pointless to wish for her sister to be there. Or for a birthing suite. She would have neither. Harriet was in Argentina to do something selfless and wonderful and she was paying for her own irresponsible behaviour by being trapped in a Los Angeles elevator in the first stage of labour.

Giving birth to the babies of a man who didn't give a damn.

With the help of another she didn't know.

The next painful wave of contractions broke through her thoughts. Labour had not come on slowly or gently. And there was no point worrying about dust soiling Patrick's jacket; the piece of clothing was now past being saved.

The jacket was of no concern to Patrick, who was kneeling beside Claudia. At that moment he would give a dozen of his finest jackets to make this woman he barely knew comfortable if only he could. But he had nothing close to a dozen of anything to make what lay ahead easier. The situation was dire. There was no way around that fact but Patrick intended to do everything to ensure Claudia remained calm and focused. All the while he fought his own battle with a past that was rushing back at him. Fine perspiration began lining his brow but he had to push through. He heard Claudia's heavy breathing turn to panting and knew he couldn't give in to his thoughts. Not for even a minute. He had to stay with Claudia.

For the time being at least.

'There's no cell reception but if I can get through on the elevator phone, who can I call? Your husband, boyfriend...your family?'

Claudia shook her head, a little embarrassed by the answer even before she delivered it. Harriet was on and off the communication grid for almost two days while she travelled and even if she could contact her it would be unfair to worry her. And she knew there was no point reaching out to the babies' father. He wouldn't care.

'No, there's no one to call.'

Patrick's eyes met hers in silence. He was surprised and saddened to hear her answer. While she clearly had her defences up initially, Patrick had not suspected for even a moment that a woman like Claudia would be alone in the world.

Unexpectedly, he felt himself being pulled towards her. He was never pulled towards anyone. Not any more. Not for years. He had locked away the need to feel anything. To need anyone...or to be needed. But suddenly a tenuous and unforeseen bond was forming. And he suspected it was not due just to the confines of the elevator.

Claudia wriggled some more and looked down at the jacket. 'I'm so sorry...'

'Claudia—' he cut in as he looked intently into her eyes, not shifting his gaze for even a moment, not allowing himself to betray, to any degree, the very real risks that he knew lay ahead '—you're in labour and you think I'm worried about a jacket.'

'But it's ruined.'

'The only thing I care about now is finding something clean for the babies. Do you have anything in your bag? Anything I can wrap them in?'

Claudia shook her head. While her bag was the fashionably oversized style, it held very little, other than her wallet, apartment keys, her phone, a thin, flimsy scarf, a small cosmetic purse and a bottle of water. And her ultrasound films.

Patrick couldn't wait any longer. There would be two babies arriving and they needed to have something clean to rest upon while he tended to their mother. He was not going to put them on the floor of the elevator. Without hesitating, he began to unbutton his white linen shirt and, slipping it from his very toned and lightly tanned body, he spread it out.

Claudia knew she was staring. She was helpless to pull her gaze away. The man about to deliver her babies had stripped bare to the waist. It was overwhelming and almost too much for her to process. The whole situation was quickly morphing from a bad dream into a nightmare. She was about to give birth to the sons of a man who didn't love her and they would be delivered by a half-naked stranger in a broken elevator. Tears began welling in her eyes as the waves of another contraction came. This one was more powerful than the last and she struggled to hide the level of pain.

Patrick reached for her hand. 'I want you to squeeze my hand when the contractions happen.'

'I'll be fine,' she told him as the contraction passed and she felt uncomfortable getting any closer to the semi-naked stranger than she already was. His arms looked lean but powerful. And she could smell the light tones of his musky cologne.

'I know you'll be fine but if you squeeze my hand each time you have a contraction I'll know how close together they are.'

'I think you will be able to tell without me squeezing your hand.'

Patrick nodded. 'Have it your way, but my hand is here if you need it.'

Still feeling wary, Claudia eyed him suspiciously, wondering who this man was, this man who was so willing to come to her aid. Only a few minutes before, they had exchanged less than friendly words. Now the man she had initially assumed to be a lawyer hiding a hangover behind dark glasses was in fact a doctor literally on bended knees helping her.

'The contractions seem to be evenly spaced at the moment,' he said, breaking through her thoughts.

'But they're awfully close and awfully painful. Does that mean the babies will be here soon?'

'It could but it's impossible to tell.' Patrick hoped that it would be a prolonged labour. Prolonged enough to allow the technical team to open the elevator doors and bring in help.

'Do you think there's any chance they will get us out before my babies arrive?'

'They're doing their best.'

Ten minutes passed with no news from outside and two more contractions. Claudia caught her breath and leant back against the cold walls of the elevator. It was soothing on her now clammy skin. The air was starting to warm up, and she imagined it would be stifling in a short time if the doors were not opened soon. But they would be. She had to hold on to the belief that any minute paramedics would burst through the steel barriers and transport her to hospital.

Patrick stretched his long legs out in front of him and rested against the adjacent cool wall. 'So which London hospital had you planned on having the boys?' he asked as he looked up at the ceiling for no particular reason. All sense of reason had left the elevator when Claudia began labour.

'I thought the Wright Street Women's and Children's Hospital. I checked in online a few months back and it has a lovely birthing centre with floral wallpaper and midwives and everything my babies and I would need. I've booked an appointment with a midwife there next week.'

'Well, you won't be needing that appointment. Not for this delivery anyway, but perhaps you could book in for your next baby.'

'I'm not sure there will be a next,' she replied quickly with raised eyebrows, still not forgetting the pain of the contraction that had barely passed.

'Perhaps you will change your mind and have more but these children will definitely be born in LA. With any luck, the paramedics will have us out soon and they'll be born at the Mercy Hospital.'

Claudia felt her pulse race a little. 'What if that doesn't happen?'

Patrick turned to her and took her hand in his. Suddenly the sensation of her warm skin on his made him feel something more than he had felt in many years. It made him feel close to being alive. He swallowed and pushed away the feeling. That sort of intimacy had no place in his life. For the last decade, whenever he felt a woman's body against his, there was nothing more than mutual pleasure. It didn't mean anything to either of them. They served a purpose to each other and walked away. Feeling anything more was not worth the risk.

He couldn't get attached to a woman he didn't know who was about to give birth to the children of another man. The idea was ridiculous.

'Let's not go there, Claudia. The medical team will be here soon.'

'But they may not...' she argued.

'Then we'll bring two healthy boys into the world

on our own.' He said it instinctively but as the words escaped his mouth he prayed it would not come to that.

Claudia took another deep breath. There was a chance they weren't going to be rescued. And she had to prepare herself for the imminent wave of the next contraction and then worse. She closed her eyes.

Patrick studied her. 'Now don't go closing your beautiful eyes on me,' he told her. 'I need you to listen to me and work with me. You will get through this but you have to stay strong. You have your children to think of.'

Slowly she forced her lids open and found herself looking into the warmest eyes she had ever seen. Her stomach did a little somersault and it wasn't a contraction.

'That's better,' he told her with a smile filled with so much warmth she thought her heart would melt. Everything he was making her feel was unexpected. And the feelings seemed so real. Was it just the intense situation they were facing or was there something about the man that was very different from anyone she had ever met?

She wasn't sure.

But his nearness was affecting her. She doubted he was trying to affect—he just was.

'What about you—do you have any children? Did your family move here to LA too?' She rattled off successive questions, trying to deflect the blush she suddenly feared he had brought to her cheeks. She could see there was no wedding band on his hand but, as she knew first-hand, the lack of a ring on a man's finger did not bring any certainty there was no wife. It was out of character for her to be so direct but nothing about the situation was normal.

'No, I'm not married, Claudia, and the rest of my family…well, they're back in the UK…' Patrick's words trailed off. He wasn't about to tell Claudia about his life, his past or his loss. After twelve years it was still raw at times but now focusing on Claudia removed his desire to give any consideration to his own pain. He had to be in the moment for the woman who needed him. He couldn't think about what had happened all those years ago or the price he still paid every day.

He had to let something go.

And that had to be the past—for the time being. But he knew that it would come back to him. It always did.

'Do you want children one day? I guess if you've done this before, bringing them into the world would make you want a brood or run the other way,' she cut in again. As she felt the warmth in her face subside she was slightly relieved on that front but the need for the banter continued. Any distraction would do.

He felt a muscle in his jaw twitch. She was unwittingly making it very hard to stay in the moment. 'No,' he said, not wanting to go into any detail. The answer was not that he didn't like children; in fact it ran far deeper than that. Children meant family and he never planned on being part of a family again. The pain still lingered, twelve years after he had been forced to walk away from his own.

'So am I right—you don't want to take your job home?'

'You're full of questions, aren't you?'

Claudia didn't answer. She felt the next contraction building and as it rolled in she couldn't say anything. She dropped her head to her chest and took in shallow breaths.

Without prompting, Patrick's hands gently massaged her back. Instinctively, he knew what was happening and he kept up the physical therapy until it passed. And then a few moments longer.

She felt his hands linger, then shook herself back to reality. He was a doctor doing his job. Nothing more.

'Why did you move to LA?' she piped up, then bit her lip as she realised it was none of her business and she had no clue what had driven her to ask him such personal questions. She felt as if the pain had taken over her mind. She was acting like a different person, someone who suddenly wanted to know everything about Patrick. Perhaps it was to distract herself. Perhaps not. But she knew the moment the words fell from her mouth that she had overstepped the boundaries of polite conversation. 'Please forget I asked. Blame it on the stress. I really am exhibiting the worst manners today. I've asked the most improper questions and ruined your jacket…'

'Forgiven for both.' Patrick hesitated. 'I guess I'm just a private person, Claudia. I'm happy to answer any medical questions, anything at all, but I'd prefer to leave the rest alone. Suffice to say, my family and I didn't see eye to eye about something that happened and this opportunity came up. So I left London and headed here.'

'Oh, I'm sorry.' Claudia suddenly felt even more embarrassed that she had asked but she also felt a little sad for him. She barely knew the man but, with the way he was taking care of her, she suddenly felt that she wanted to be on *his side* in a situation she knew nothing about.

Patrick knew it sounded as if they had parted ways

on something insignificant. He thought it was best to leave it at that. There was no need to mention that he'd made the opportunity to allow him to move to the US. It was something he'd had to do to help everyone with their grief. To not be there, reminding them every day of what had happened.

It was not the time or place to tell a woman he had just met that his sister had died.

And he had taken the blame for her death.

An unspoken agreement not to revisit the conversation about his family was made in the awkward silence by both of them.

'I'll need to examine you in a few minutes and assess whether you have begun to dilate and, if you have, if the first baby is visible,' he told her as he pulled himself from the past back to where he belonged.

Suddenly the elevator lights began to flicker. Claudia bit her lip nervously. She felt her chin begin to quiver but was powerless to stop it. All questions disappeared. She didn't want anything from Patrick other than reassurance that her babies would survive.

Patrick drew a deep breath but managed to keep his body language in check. If they lost the lights, then he could not convince himself there would be a good outcome but he would never let Claudia know that. He even refused to admit it to himself.

'I need to do the exam while we still have some lights to work with; if we lose them it will be challenging as I'll have to work by feel alone. But, whatever happens, I'm here for you and your babies, Claudia, and together we'll all get throughout this,' Patrick told her with a firmness and urgency that did not disguise the seriousness of the situation, but he also managed to make her feel secure in the knowledge that he was with her all the way. He filled his lungs with the warm air that surrounded them, determined he would do his damnedest to make his prayers a reality.

She nodded her consent as the contraction began to subside, along with her uncontrollable need to push.

'Breathe slowly and deeply,' he said while he stroked her arm and waited for the contraction to pass before he began his examination. Twins made the birth so much more complicated, along with his lack of equipment and the risk of losing the lights.

'Have you delivered many babies?'

'Yes, I've delivered many babies, Claudia, but never in an elevator and not for...'

The elevator phone rang and stopped Patrick from explaining how long it had been since his last delivery. Instinctively, he answered the phone. 'Yes?'

'This is the utilities manager. We're working to have you out as soon as possible but it may be another twenty minutes to half an hour. Our only rostered technician is across town. How's the young woman?'

'She's in labour.'

'Hell... Okay, that's gonna be brutal on her.' The man's knee-jerk reaction was loud. 'I'll put the tech to get here ASAP or get an off-duty one over there stat. We've already got an ambulance en route.'

'That would be advisable,' Patrick responded in an even tone, not wanting to add to Claudia's building distress. 'I'm about to assess her progress but you need to ensure there are two ambulances waiting when your technician gets us out. We're dealing with the birth of two premature infants so ensure the paramedics are despatched with humidicribs and you have an obstetrician standing by with a birthing kit including cord clamps and Syntocinon.' Then he lowered his voice and added, 'And instruct them to bring plasma. There's always the slight risk of a postpartum haemorrhage.' With that he hung up the phone to let the team outside do their best to get medical help to them as soon as possible.

He immediately turned his attention back to Claudia, who lay against the elevator wall with small beads of perspiration building on her brow and the very palpable fear of what lay ahead written on her face.

'I don't want my babies to die.'

'Claudia, you need to listen to me,' he began with gentleness in his voice along with a reassuring firmness. 'We *are* going to get through this. Your babies will be fine but you need to help me.'

Claudia couldn't look at him. She couldn't lift her gaze from her stomach and the babies inside of her. Fear surged through her veins. It was real. They weren't getting out of the elevator. No one was coming to rescue them. No one was going to take her to the hospital. The harsh reality hit her. Her babies would be born inside the metal walls that surrounded them.

And they might not survive.

'I am going to have to cut your underwear free. I don't want to try and lift you and remove it.'

Claudia felt her heart race and her mind spin. She was losing control and the fear was not just physical. Deep inside, she knew the odds were stacked against her and her boys but she appreciated that Patrick hadn't voiced that. The man with the sunglasses wasn't anything close to what she'd thought. He was about to bring her sons into the world.

And she suddenly had no choice but to trust him.

Her hand ran across her mouth and tugged at her lips nervously. 'Fine, just do it,' she managed to say as she steeled herself for what was about to happen to her, her boys and Patrick as the urge to push and the pain began to overtake her senses once again.

Patrick ripped off the gloves that had handled the elevator telephone, covered his hands in antibacterial solution and slipped on another pair of gloves. Carefully using sterile scissors, he gently cut her underwear from her and checked the progress of her labour.

'You are fully dilated and your first son's head is visible,' he told her. 'Labour is moving fast and you're doing great. Just keeping breathing slowly...'

His words were cut short by the cry she gave with the next painful contraction. More painful than the previous one.

'I can't do this. I can't.'

'Yes, you can.'

'Should I be as scared to death as I am right now?'

'No,' he said, leaning in towards her. 'Just remember, Claudia, you're not alone. We'll get through this together. You and I will bring your babies into the world.'

He prayed, as every word slipped from his now dry mouth, that he could do what he promised. He had the expertise, he reminded himself. But he also knew that was not always enough. There were some situations that no skills could fight.

Steeling himself, he knew he was prepared to fight for Claudia and her boys.

She closed her eyes and swallowed.

'I need you to try and get onto your hands and knees...'

'Why?' Her eyes opened wide. 'I thought you have babies lying on your back. Is there something wrong?' Panic showed on her face as she stared into Patrick's eyes, searching for reassurance but frightened of what he might tell her.

'It will be easier on you and your babies if you're on all fours,' he told her. 'It opens up the birth canal and, even though it may seem uncomfortable, believe me, it will be far better than being on your back. Just try it. Here, I'll help you.'

He reached for her and she felt the warmth and strength in his hold as his hands guided her into the position he needed to best deliver the babies. He made sure her hands and knees were still resting on the damp jacket, not the bare floor.

'I'd like to put a cool compress on you. It's getting warm in here but I'm running out of clothing to give you.'

Even in pain, Claudia smiled at his remark. It was true. He had given his jacket and his shirt. 'There's a clean scarf in my bag but it's very small. You could wet that.'

Patrick reached for her large tan leather bag and dragged it unceremoniously across the metal flooring. He emptied the contents onto the floor, found the small patterned scarf and then noticed the films.

'Are those films for your obstetrician?'

She turned her head slightly. 'Yes, he was going to check them and then sign the papers to allow me to fly home to London.'

He pushed the envelope to the side and took her bottle of water and sparingly dampened the scarf. Gently lifting the sweat-dampened curls on the nape of her neck, he rested the tiny compress on her hot skin. There was nothing he could do about whatever showed on the films now. They wouldn't change anything in the confines of the elevator. He had no idea what the next few minutes would hold but he would be beside her and do whatever he could to keep Claudia and her babies alive.

Feeling his hand on her skin felt so calming and re-assuring and Claudia wondered if it was the touch of his skin against hers as much as the makeshift compress. But neither gave relief when the next powerful contraction came and she cried out with the pain.

Her cries tugged at Patrick's heart. He hated the fact there was nothing he could do. But he needed to focus on delivering both babies or risk losing them all. He wouldn't let that happen.

Suddenly the first baby began to enter the world. A mass of thick black hair curled like a halo around his perfect tiny face.

'Just push slowly and think about your breathing,' he instructed her. 'We need that to control the baby's arrival. We don't want to rush him. You can tear your skin and I want to avoid that.'

The urge to give a giant push was overwhelming but Claudia knew she had to let her breathing slow the pace. She thought of Patrick's handsome face and tried to follow his instructions. There were a few more contractions and finally Claudia's first baby was born into Patrick's waiting hands. He let out a tiny cry as Patrick quickly cleared his mouth of mucous and quickly checked his vital signs.

The baby was small but not so small as to put him in immediate danger by not having access to a humidicrib. Patrick had feared he might have been tinier considering the gestational age and the fact he was a twin. He clamped the cord with a sterile surgical tie before he laid him on the shirt. The baby had endured a harsh entry into the world and the shirt was a far cry from a soft landing but, until his brother was born, there was little Patrick could do for the new arrival. He could not put the child to Claudia's breast as she needed to remain on all fours until the second baby was delivered.

Another contraction began and the second baby was quickly on its way. Patrick hoped that he would not be faced with a foot. That would mean a breech birth and complications he did not want to contemplate.

That next painful contraction came and Claudia cried out loudly but managed with each following breath to push her second baby head first into the world. And once again into Patrick's arms, where the baby took his first breath and cried for the first time. Patrick checked the second baby's vital signs and again was relieved that the delivery had no complications. It had progressed far better than Patrick had imagined.

With beads of perspiration now covering her entire body, Claudia looked over at her two sons and felt a love greater than she'd thought possible.

And a closeness to the man who had delivered them. He was like her knight in shining armour. And she would be indebted to him forever.

Quite apart from being an amazing doctor, Patrick was a wonderful man.

Through the fog of her emotionally drained state, Claudia suddenly suspected her feelings for Patrick ran deeper than simply gratitude for saving them all.

* * *

Patrick remained quiet. There were still two afterbirths and Claudia to consider. Despite the peaceful and contented look she wore, he knew they were not out of the woods yet.

Gently he placed the second baby next to his tiny brother and wrapped the shirt around them both before he carefully helped Claudia from her knees onto her back again. He grabbed her leather bag and made a makeshift pillow for her head. Claudia was past caring about the bag or her own comfort as she watched her tiny sons lying so close to her.

Patrick reached for them. 'I'm going to rest the babies on you while we wait for the afterbirth.'

While the delivery had been relatively straightforward, Patrick was aware that Claudia's double birth put her at increased risk of haemorrhage. Gently he placed the two tiny boys into their mother's arms and he watched as her beautiful face lit up further as she cradled them. Her beauty seemed to be magnified with the boys now securely with her and, with her genes, they would no doubt be very handsome young men.

Within minutes, part of the placenta was delivered but as Patrick examined it he was concerned that it was not intact. Claudia would require a curette in hospital if the remaining placenta wasn't expelled. But, that aside and despite the surroundings, Claudia had delivered two seemingly healthy boys. Patrick took a deep breath and filled his lungs as he looked at Claudia with a sense of pride for the strength shown by a woman he barely knew.

Then he noticed her face had become a little pale.

'I sort of feel a little cold now,' she said softly, as her

body began to shiver. 'It feels odd; I was so hot before. There's no pain but…'

Patrick noticed her eyes were becoming glassy and she was losing her grip on the boys. There was something very wrong. Quickly he scooped them from her weakening hold and placed them together beside her, still wrapped in his shirt. He felt for her pulse. It was becoming fainter. He looked down to see blood pouring from Claudia and pooling on the jacket underneath her.

It was his worst nightmare—a postpartum haemorrhage.

Claudia had fifty percent more blood in her body because of the pregnancy, which would help, but, with the amount of blood she had already lost on the floor, it would still only buy them a small amount of time. He needed to encourage her uterus to contract, shutting off the open blood vessels. Immediately he began to massage her belly through to her uterus but after a minute he could see there was no difference. She was barely lucid and he needed to administer a synthetic form of the hormone that would naturally assist, but that was on the other side of the closed elevator doors with the paramedics. It wasn't something he carried in his medical bag. Not now anyway. Once he would have had everything he now needed to save Claudia—but that was a lifetime ago.

'Claudia—' he ceased the massage momentarily and patted her hand '—I need you to try to feed one of the boys. It will help to stimulate a hormone that will lessen the bleeding. Do you understand?'

'Uh-huh,' she muttered while trying to keep her eyes from closing. 'I feel so light-headed.'

'That's the blood loss. I'm going to do everything

I can to stop it until help arrives, but again we need to work together. You'll be on your way to hospital very soon.'

He reached down and gently unwrapped the babies and, picking up the larger of the twins, he lifted Claudia's tank top and bra and placed him onto her breast. Instinctively the baby latched onto his mother and began to suckle while Patrick continued the massaging.

'Do you have any names for the boys?' he asked, trying to keep Claudia focused as he dealt with the medical emergency that was unfolding before his eyes.

She tried to think but the names weren't there. They were special names and they should have spilled out without any effort but she was befuddled, which wasn't her. 'I think…' She paused momentarily as the names she had chosen now seemed strangely out of reach. She blinked to bring herself back on track. 'Thomas…and Luca…after each of their great-grandpas.'

'I think they are strong names for two little fighters. Is this baby Thomas or Luca?'

Claudia smiled down at her son, still attached to her breast but not really sucking successfully. 'Thomas… but I think he's tired already and a bit too small.'

'I think you're right on both counts.'

'I'm feeling quite dizzy again.' She paused as she felt herself wavering and her vision was starting to blur. Fear was mounting again inside her. 'Am I going to die?'

'No, you're going to pull through and raise your two sons until they are grown men.'

Claudia felt weaker by the minute. She knew there was something very serious happening, even though she couldn't see the blood. 'If I don't make it…'

'You will,' he argued as he reached for Thomas, who was unable to suckle, and placed him safely on the floor beside his brother, Luca.

She closed her eyes for a moment. She felt too weak to fight. 'You need to contact my sister, Harriet. Her details are in my phone. She needs to be there for my boys if I can't be.'

'Claudia, listen to me. You're going to make it, but I'm going to have to do something very uncomfortable for you.'

'What?' she asked in a worried whisper.

'I'm going to compress your uterus with my hands. It will further slow the bleeding.'

She nodded but she felt as if she was close to drifting off to sleep. 'If you have to, then do it.'

'Try to stay awake,' he pleaded with her as he attempted to manually compress the uterus with the firm pressure of his hands.

Minutes passed but still the blood was flowing over his hands to the floor beneath her. Claudia needed to be in a hospital and she needed to be there now. This was something more serious than the usual postpartum blood loss.

She was dangerously close to losing consciousness as he gently removed his hands. The manual pressure could not stop the bleeding. Claudia needed surgical intervention if she was to survive. He reached for the films and ripped open the envelope. The films scattered on the floor but, as he grabbed the report, his worst fears were confirmed. Claudia's placenta had invaded the walls of her uterus. Every part of his body shuddered. It was déjà vu. The prognosis was identical to what he had faced all those years ago. There was no way her obstetrician would have allowed her to board a plane with the condition. Claudia would have delivered her sons in America, whether it had been this day or another.

With a heavy heart, he dropped his gloves and the report to the floor and pulled a barely conscious Claudia into his arms, where he held her while he stroked the faces of the little boys lying on the floor beside them. If help didn't arrive within a few minutes he would lose Claudia.

And her two tiny babies would never know their beautiful, brave mother.

CHAPTER THREE

As Claudia's body suddenly fell limp in Patrick's arms, he heard the doors open behind him and instantly felt a firm grip on his bare shoulder.

'We've got it from here,' the deep voice said.

Patrick turned his head to see a full medical team rushing towards them. He had never been happier in his life than he was at that moment and, with adrenaline surging through his veins, he immediately began firing instructions at lightning speed. The miracle Claudia needed had arrived at the moment he had run out of options.

'We're dealing with a postpartum haemorrhage—she needs Syntocinon immediately and a catheter inserted so that the uterus has a better chance of contracting with an empty bladder. If she doesn't stabilise she'll be looking at a transfusion. Forget cross-matching as there may not be time; just start plasma now and have O negative waiting in OR.'

Patrick moved away as the medical team stepped in to begin the treatment he had ordered. Immediately they inserted an IV line, began a plasma transfusion then administered some pain relief and Syntocinon in an attempt to stop Claudia's bleeding while another two paramedics collected the baby boys and left the elevator with them securely inside portable humidicribs.

'Any idea why she's still bleeding?' the attending doctor asked.

'Placenta accreta,' Patrick said as he reached for the films lying on the floor. He kept his voice low so he would not alarm Claudia. 'I checked the report on the ultrasound films. Only a very small amount of the placenta was delivered and the rest is still firmly entrenched in the uterus wall. If the report is correct, she may be looking at a surgery but a complete hysterectomy should be the surgeon's last option. I doubt she's more than late twenties, if that, so she might like to keep her womb.'

'I'm sure they'll proceed conservatively if they can.'

Patrick nodded. He had no idea what the future would hold for Claudia and he wanted her to have every choice possible. 'The boys appear fine but they'll need a thorough examination with the paediatrician,' Patrick continued, not taking his eyes from Claudia. 'One is a little smaller than the other but let's hope there's no underlying issues with their premature arrival.'

'You did a remarkable job, all things considered,' the paramedics told Patrick as they watched the barely conscious Claudia being lifted onto the gurney and then securely but gently strapped in.

Keeping his attention on Claudia, who was beginning to show signs of being lucid, the doctor added, 'And you, young lady, are very lucky this man was sharing the elevator. It would not have been this outcome without him, that's for certain. You and your boys all owe your lives to him.'

Claudia smiled a meek smile and held out her hand

in an effort to show her gratitude. Patrick cupped it gently in his own strong hands and smiled back at her then he turned to the attending doctor. 'I'll be travelling side-saddle to the hospital if there's room.'

'There's definitely room.'

For a little over three hours, Patrick divided his time between pacing the corridors outside Recovery and visiting the Neonatal Intensive Care Unit to check on Luca and Thomas. They had given him a consulting coat to cover his bare chest upon arrival at the hospital. Claudia's dark-haired boys, one with sparkling blue eyes and the other with deep brown like their mother, were doing very well and he felt a deep and very unexpected bond with them. A bond that he hadn't felt towards anyone, let alone tiny people, for more years than he cared to remember.

But these boys were special, perhaps because he'd delivered them in a crisis, or perhaps because their mother was clearly a very special woman. Perhaps it was both but, whatever was driving him to stay, he knew the three of them were bringing out protective feelings in him. A sense that he was needed and almost as if he belonged there. He should have felt unnerved and wanted to run but he didn't. That need to protect himself from being hurt was overridden by the need to protect Claudia, Thomas and Luca.

Both boys weighed a little over four pounds, which was a relief. They were still in their humidicribs and being monitored closely but both had passed all the paediatrician's initial tests and were being gavage fed by the neonatal nurses when Patrick left the nursery and headed back to check on their mother. Her surgery had taken far longer than he had anticipated. He had for a moment contemplated scrubbing in to assist when they'd arrived in Emergency and were rushed around to the OR but he'd immediately thought better of it. A reality check reminded him that his last obstetric surgery had ended his career.

Patrick wanted her to be spared the additional stress and long-term repercussions of the hysterectomy if possible and voiced that again upon arrival. The surgical resident had reassured Patrick that Dr Sally Benton was well respected in the field of gynaecological surgery and that Claudia would be in expert hands. Patrick hoped that the option to give birth again one day in the pretty delivery room with floral wallpaper, midwives and pain relief was not taken away. But, three hours later, he knew the reality of her surgery taking so long meant she had probably undergone a hysterectomy. And she would have to give up on that dream.

'I'm Sally Benton.' She pulled her surgical cap free and outstretched her hand.

'Patrick Spencer,' he responded as he met her handshake. He looked at the woman before him. She was tall and thin, her short black hair with smatterings of grey framed her pretty face and he suspected she was in her early fifties.

'Dr Spencer, I assume.'

'Yes.'

'I wanted to personally thank you for the medical intervention you provided in the elevator. Miss Monticello is in Recovery now and she certainly wouldn't be if you hadn't done such an amazing job delivering her sons and keeping her alive. If you hadn't been with her today, there would most definitely have been a question mark over their survival.'

Patrick drew a deep breath and chose to ignore the compliment. 'Was it conservative surgery?'

'No, unfortunately, Miss Monticello underwent a full hysterectomy to stop the haemorrhaging. She retained her ovaries but her uterus has been removed,' Dr Benton continued as she took a seat in the corridor and indicated Patrick to do the same. 'The attending doctor briefed me on your diagnosis of suspected placenta accreta, but the depth of invasion was not first but second grade. I was faced with placenta increta as the chorionic villi had invaded the muscular layer of the uterine wall so I had no option but to remove her womb. She was lucky that it had not spread through the uterine wall to other organs such as the bladder. Let's just say I'm glad I didn't have to deal with that; as you would know, even in this day and age, there's still a six to seven percent mortality rate for that, due to the complications.'

Patrick knew the statistics for death only too well.

'Thank you, Dr Benton.'

'Don't thank me. As I said before, you did the hard work keeping her alive. And she has two wonderful little boys. Perhaps the loss of her womb will not be a complete tragedy.'

Patrick nodded. He wondered how Claudia would react to the need for a hysterectomy.

'And how are her sons doing?' the surgeon enquired.

'Very well,' Patrick said with a sense of pride that surprised him. 'They're handsome young men and a good weight for their gestational age.'

'Great. Now that's out of the way and we've spoken

about our mutual patients, I have a personal question for you,' Dr Benton continued. 'How do you know Miss Monticello?'

'We were just sharing the elevator.'

Her expression revealed her surprise. 'Well, that's serendipity for you. I don't think she could have asked for a better travelling companion. Where do you practice obstetrics?' Then, without waiting for an answer, she added, 'Am I right in assuming, with your accent, and because I haven't heard of you around LA, that your practice is out of state or perhaps abroad?'

Patrick hesitated. He didn't want to talk about himself but he knew the doctor sitting beside him had every right to enquire. 'No, I practice here in LA but I'm not in OBGYN.'

'Really?' Her brow wrinkled as she considered his response. 'What's your field then?'

'I'm a board certified cosmetic surgeon.'

Once again, she didn't hide her surprise. 'I'd never have picked that,' she said with a grin on her somewhat tired face as she stood up and again offered a handshake. 'Well, Dr Spencer, if you ever get tired of your current field, you should consider obstetrics. There's a shortage of experts in the field and you're very skilled. Your intervention was nothing short of amazing in the conditions you were forced to work in. As I said, Miss Monticello owes her life to you. She will be in her room in another two hours or so. She lost a lot of blood, as you know, so we'll be monitoring her in Recovery for a little longer than we normally would. But I'm sure she'd be pleased to see you.'

Patrick met her handshake and she smiled before she left him alone.

* * *

Patrick spent the next two hours with Luca and Thomas. He had called his practice and rearranged his schedule. While the boys were being monitored closely he still didn't want to leave. Not yet anyway. Thomas was in a humidicrib and Luca required additional oxygen to be provided through an oxy-hood so he was in an open bed warmer. The neonatologist felt certain that would only be a temporary measure as both appeared to be healthy and a satisfactory weight for their gestational age. Patrick was aware they had some basic milestones to achieve, both in weight and development, before they would be released; he doubted it would be more than three or four weeks before they would be allowed to leave hospital with their mother.

He went downstairs to the florist and picked the largest floral bouquet they had and two brown bears with blue bows. Claudia had told him she had no one she could reach out to and he knew how that felt only too well. He tried not to think of what he had lost when he'd walked away from his family.

Only now at least Claudia did have two little people to call her family. Still, he knew her room would be devoid of anything to brighten her day and lift her spirits and, after the day she had endured, she deserved a room filled with flowers. And something to remind her of the boys when she was resting and not able to be with them in the neonatal nursery. And when she had to face the reality of the hysterectomy she had undergone without her consent.

The nurse at the station arranged for the flowers to be placed near her bed.

Waiting outside the room twenty minutes later, he couldn't contain, nor fully understand, the smile that spread across his face and the warmth that surged through his body when he saw her hospital bed being wheeled down the corridor towards him. She was still pale but not as drained as when he had last seen her, and she hadn't noticed him. In the pit of his stomach he still remembered her limp body collapsing against his and he'd thought the boys had lost their mother.

Patiently he remained outside as she was settled into her room but, as the nurses exited, he tapped on the door that was ajar.

'Are you up to a visitor?'

'Patrick?'

'How did you guess?' he asked as he quietly entered her room. 'Perhaps it's the British accent—there are not a lot of us around these parts so I guess it's a giveaway.'

'In this city, it's a dead giveaway.' It was more than just his accent, but Claudia couldn't tell Patrick that it was also his reassuring tone that told her exactly who was at her door. It was the same strong voice that had kept her going when she'd wanted to give up. It was the voice of the man who had saved her and her sons.

'May I come in?'

'Of course,' she said, ushering him in with the arm that wasn't connected to the IV providing pain relief after her surgery. 'What are you still doing here?'

'Keeping an eye on…your handsome young sons.'

'They are gorgeous, aren't they? The nurses wheeled me on the bed into the nursery to see them a few minutes ago on the way back from Recovery. They were sleeping but they told me they're both doing very well.'

She paused and nervously chewed on the inside of her cheek to keep her emotions under control. 'Thanks to you.'

Patrick moved closer to her in the softly lit room. 'Not because of me; you did the hard work, Claudia. I just assisted.'

'Maybe the hard work, but you did the skilled work. Without you,' she began, then her chin quivered as she struggled again to keep her tears at bay, 'they could have...well, they might not have made it if you weren't there with me.'

He reached for her hand. It was instinctive and something he had not been driven to do in a very long time. 'Not a chance. They're as strong as their mother.'

Claudia looked down at his hand covering hers. After the trauma of the preceding hours, it made her feel secure. But she couldn't get used to that feeling of being safe. Not with anyone, no matter how kind. She knew that she and Patrick were bonded by what they had been through and it was a normal reaction to the traumatic experience they'd shared. But now, in the safety of the hospital, she had to accept it was nothing more. Although he had proven her initial assumption of him very wrong, she couldn't afford to get swept away by some romantic notion there was more to it. As if he'd appeared like her white knight, saved her and would steal her away to his castle. That wasn't the real world.

Knowing she needed to create some distance between them, she slipped her hand free and haphazardly ran her fingers through her messy curls that had been swept up in a surgical cap for hours.

The move was not lost on Patrick and he graciously accepted her subtle rebuff. He had overstepped the mark. And he never overstepped the mark with a woman. Perhaps it was because she looked so lost and vulnerable that he wanted to make her feel less alone, but clearly she was not looking to be saved again. And he needed to step away. He was grateful she'd reminded him subtly that he wasn't looking to become attached to anyone.

That time in his life had passed. Being alone was what he did best. *What had he been thinking?*

'So…how are you feeling?' he asked in a doctor-patient tone. 'Your body has been through a lot today, quite apart from bringing Thomas and Luca into the world.'

'You mean the…hysterectomy?'

He nodded then waited in silence to hear Claudia's response to the emergency life-changing surgery. She was a resilient woman but he knew this would certainly test any woman and he would not be surprised if she struggled to come to terms with it.

She dropped her gaze for a moment then, lifting her chin and her eyes almost in defiance at what the universe had dealt her, she nodded. 'I'll be okay. I'm alive and I have my sons. It would be stupid to mourn what I can't change and perhaps it would be selfish to ask for more than what I was given today. My life and the lives of my children is miracle enough.'

Patrick was already in awe of the strength that she had shown in the elevator but her reaction to the news almost brought him to his knees with respect for her courage and acceptance of what she couldn't change. She was a truly remarkable woman.

Her fingers nervously played with the woven blanket for a minute before she looked back at Patrick. 'When I think of how terribly wrong everything could have gone today, losing my womb is a small price to pay.'

While Claudia looked like a porcelain doll, Patrick had learned over the few hours since their lives collided that she was made of far tougher material. Still, it puzzled him that she was alone in the world. Had she pushed people from it? Or had they abandoned her? Had being alone made her that strong? He couldn't imagine anyone walking away from such an amazing woman.

Then he realised none of his questions mattered. She had been his unofficial patient for a few hours. Nothing more.

'That huge arrangement of flowers is stunning. I'm guessing it's from you,' she added as she looked around the room and spied the huge bouquet on a shelf near her. It was getting dark outside and she could see the lights of the Los Angeles skyline. But the flowers were more spectacular than any view.

Patrick nodded and tried to look at her with the doctor-patient filter but it was becoming a struggle with each passing moment. It had been an intense first meeting in the elevator but there was more pulling him to her than the fact he had delivered her babies under such conditions. They were not in the confines of that small space any more and she no longer needed his help but still he wanted to be there for the stunning brunette still dressed in a shapeless white surgical gown.

And he was confused as hell. He had unexpectedly become a passenger on a roller coaster of his own emotions. Before, he had always been the driver. He needed to gain control. Quickly. He needed to make it less personal.

'Have you noticed how drab the walls in these rooms are? I needed to brighten your room somehow. I thought flowers would do the trick.'

'The rooms are not that bad, young man,' a stern voice replied from the doorway. 'My name's Vanda, and it would do you well not to complain. I'll be tending to your wife tonight and, for your interest…'

'Oh…we're not married,' came their reply in unison.

There was a moment's uncomfortable silence as the three of them looked at each other in silence.

'Sorry if I presumed your marital status; it's just habit at my age,' the nurse, who Patrick imagined to be in her early fifties, with short auburn hair and twinkling blue eyes, said. She crossed the room, manoeuvring around Patrick to get access to her patient. 'I have two grandchildren and their parents aren't married either. *Haven't got time*, they say. Well, as long as they're happy, I'm happy.'

'No, we're not together,' Claudia began before the nurse wrapped the blood pressure monitor around her arm. 'He's my…' She paused, not knowing how to describe Patrick. *What was their relationship?* she wondered. They weren't friends, but nor were they connected as patient and doctor in a formal sense. Their relationship really couldn't be defined…not easily at least…except, perhaps, for *intense* and *sudden*.

'I'm her emergency elevator obstetrician…not the father of her babies.'

As Patrick said the words, he wondered, against his

better judgement, who was the father of her children. What sort of man was he? And why wasn't he rushing to Claudia's side? Patrick knew that if he was the father, no matter how forcefully the mother of his children tried to push him away, he would stand fast to the spot.

But he wasn't the father of Claudia's children or anyone's children. And he never would be.

'Oh, of course, you're the young woman who delivered in the elevator this afternoon,' Vanda answered. She confirmed that Claudia's vitals were stable, then unwrapped the arm wrap and packed it away before she turned back to Patrick. 'And you must be the doctor who was in the right place today and brought this young lady's twins into the world.'

Patrick nodded. His mind was still filled with questions about Thomas and Luca's father but he needed to block them out. It wasn't his business. Claudia was alive. And now he could walk away as he should, knowing they were safe.

'Well, I'll compliment you on your skill in the baby-delivering field, which was on the six o'clock news, if you didn't already know. But you'd still do well not to criticise the rooms.' With a tilt of her head that signalled she meant business, then a wink that left them both wondering if she was serious or joking, Vanda left the room and Patrick and Claudia found themselves staring at each other, both confused by her demeanour and a little surprised at her announcement of their prime-time notoriety.

'We were on the six o'clock news?' The inflection at the end turned Claudia's statement into a question.

'Apparently—let's hope they didn't manage to find out your identity so you're not bothered by reporters.'

'I hope not,' she said, slumping back into the pillows and nervously fidgeting with her pearl earrings. Her parents had given them to her for her sixteenth birthday, while Harriet had been given a pearl necklace.

'I'll let the nurses' station and the main admissions know you don't want any interviews or fuss made of you or the boys. I'll head them off at the pass.'

Claudia looked at Patrick and thought once again he was her knight in shining armour... Or, with his modern good looks, perhaps he could be riding in on his stallion, tipping his Stetson and saving her. She hadn't even needed to ask. He just kept rescuing her. But she had to stop him doing it. She needed to save herself and her boys. Patrick wouldn't be there for them going forward. It would only be the three of them until they got back to London and Harriet returned.

'Don't worry,' Claudia replied. 'I'll let Vanda know to tell them I'm not interested in speaking to anyone. You've already done too much. Honestly, I appreciate more than anything all that you have done but you don't have to do any more. I can take it from here.'

Patrick agreed with her. He had done all that was needed and now she would be taken care of in hospital. She would leave for the UK once she and her children got clearance so there was no point in forging any sort of relationship. Romantic or otherwise.

'Here's my number,' he said, putting his business card on the tray where Claudia's water jug was placed. 'If you need anything, call me. Otherwise, I wish you and Thomas and Luca a safe trip home to London in a few weeks.' He fought the desire to kiss her forehead and stroke the soft curls away from her face. With a deep and unexpected sense of regret that he would never see Claudia again, he turned heavily on his feet and headed to the door, pausing for the briefest moment to look at the beautiful woman who had captured more than his attention that day.

Claudia wasn't sure what was suddenly stirring in the pit of her stomach and surging through her veins, making her heart beat faster, but she knew she was torn about watching him walk away. The day had been so intense but something inside of her wasn't ready to let that happen.

She knew she had to be crazy but she had to call after him.

'Please...wait,' she said then, taking a deep heartfelt breath, she continued, 'I didn't mean to seem rude or ungrateful in any way. I just mean I've put you out and I know you're a doctor and you probably have patients and...'

'Claudia—' he turned back and stopped her speech '—it's fine, really; you're right. I'm sure you can take it from here. I'm glad that you and the boys are well and through the ordeal that was today. I couldn't ask for more and I just want all the very best for the future for all of you.'

Patrick smiled at Claudia before he left but he knew in his heart her first instincts to push him away were right. There was more to the way he felt about this woman than a simple doctor-patient relationship so he had to keep his distance.

The only relationships he had were one-night stands with no strings attached and no feelings involved. And he doubted with Claudia it would be anything like that. She was already stirring feelings he didn't want to have.

It had to be just the intense experience they had shared, he reminded himself. He needed to walk away and let her *take it from here*.

CHAPTER FOUR

'So what exactly are you saying is the issue with Miss Monticello's international health insurance?' Vanda demanded of the caller on the other end of the telephone. She was frowning and her cheeks were becoming flushed.

Patrick's ears tuned in to the conversation and, against his better judgement, he slowed his steps. Her serious tone caused him some concern, as did her expression as he neared the desk. The exchange of words confirmed it. He couldn't walk away and pretend he hadn't heard there was a problem. Something was driving him to want to protect the woman who he knew he should stay away from. A woman who had given him no information about herself, other than the fact she was returning to London with no explanation of why.

Questions were starting to mount in his tired mind. Was the father of her children in London, waiting for her? Or was he no longer in her life? He felt sure Claudia would have asked to call her husband or boyfriend, if she had one, even if he was away on business or fighting for his country. But she'd told him there was no one. Patrick knew he had no right to ask anything about her life that she had not willingly surrendered.

Wanting to know more, let alone feeling the way he did about a woman he had known less than twelve hours, was ridiculous.

It had to stop. He knew he wanted to protect Claudia but he had to be realistic about his feelings. She was alone and he felt sorry for her. That had to be the driving force of his desire to protect her. Perhaps coupled with the desire to see her and her children safely out of hospital. He didn't want to think that there could be setbacks with any of them.

He needed to know they were safe then his job was done.

How could it be anything more than that?

'Uh-huh…okay… All right, I'll will let her know in the morning that someone from Finance will have to come and see her and make arrangements. I know she told the nurse in Recovery she was worried about the bills but we don't want her to stress. Perhaps she can extend the policy.'

Patrick looked as Vanda's expression fell further and her brow furrowed at what she was hearing. 'Oh, I see, so the twins can't be covered… Well, that's a bit of a mess but I'm sure the hospital will work something out and she'll have to pay the debt over a period of time. Yes, I appreciate it's an international policy and there are restrictions but in my ward there are no restrictions to her care.' She paused for a moment, drumming her fingers on the desk. 'No, I do hear what you're saying but please listen to my concerns.'

She continued listening with anxiety showing clearly on her face while the other staff bustled around her with the change of shift and handover. Patrick kept his focus on the conversation. She was being very po-

lite but firm with the caller, despite her expression and
the colour in her cheeks. He doubted she was the type
to lose too many battles, but he couldn't help but notice she was struggling to hold her ground.

'I'd rather not. No, let it wait until the morning. Miss
Monticello needs her rest and if she's stressing about
hospital bills it won't help her sleep and, after what
she has been through today, sleep is what she needs,'
she said firmly then paused. 'I will be moving her to
a ward tomorrow but tonight she's in a private room
that was available. No, she doesn't have any next of kin
in California or anywhere in the United States on her
admission forms. She has a sister, and she appears to
be her only living family, but she resides in the UK.'

With that, Patrick learnt a little more about the mystery that was Claudia's life. She had no one else in the
world to call family other than her sister. Then why
didn't she call her? he wondered.

'Yes, I do understand the seriousness of the situation but we will handle it in the morning. I'm back on
at six,' Vanda said. She was becoming short. 'No, absolutely no. I won't budge on it. My patient comes first
so please do not send anyone up now because I won't
allow them in to her room.'

Patrick paused for a moment, wanting to offer assistance, but then thought better of taking over the
situation. He made a mental note to have his lawyer
contact the hospital administration the next day and
sort through the insurance issues. After bringing the
boys into the world, he wasn't about to stand by and
let their mother be stressed after the fact. He tried to
tell himself it was his gift to Thomas and Luca. But

he knew it was not the boys alone that he was thinking about.

'I'm hanging up now,' Vanda continued sternly. 'We'll continue this conversation in the morning. There are far more practical problems to solve, like sourcing some fresh pyjamas for my patient. She'll remain in a hospital gown tonight but she has no nightdress or toiletries, not even a toothbrush, poor thing, so I can't sit around chatting to you; I'll have to go and sort out something before I finish my shift or she'll look like Orphan Annie in the morning.'

Patrick continued walking and made his way outside to the cab rank and, as he did, he sent a text to his receptionist. He needed her to run an errand for him.

Claudia woke after an uncomfortable and restless sleep and wanted desperately to see her babies. The uncomfortable part of her night was due to post-operative constraints but the restlessness, she suspected, was a combination of anxiety for her sons and then a strange feeling of emptiness, knowing that she would never see Patrick again. She knew it was absurd to even have any sort of reaction to not seeing Patrick, let alone this feeling in the pit of her stomach. Less than twenty-four hours before, she hadn't known him and now she thought she would miss him. It was as if by meeting him she'd found a piece of the puzzle she hadn't known she had been looking for.

As she lay in bed thinking about the facts she realised how silly she was being. Fact one, she told herself, you are a single mother of twins so your life is already full. Fact two, you are a month away from being an illegal overstay in the US so you need to get back to the UK as soon as possible. Fact three, you don't trust men and never will again. Fact four, you know very little about the handsome man who delivered your babies except that he doesn't seem to want children and you have two of the most adorable children ever born. He was just checking you were all right when he visited last night, as any doctor would, she reminded herself. And he walked away. Said goodbye and good luck. That is as final and impersonal as it gets.

'Besides, it's ridiculous', she mumbled out loud. 'To even think you could miss someone you barely know.'

Her practical side forced her to push any thoughts of Patrick from her mind and blame the funny feeling in her stomach on her internal stitches or her reaction to the general anaesthetic. It had to be one or both making her stomach feel uneasy, she decided, as she pushed the nurse call button. She wanted to see Thomas and Luca as soon as possible. She wanted to hold them in her arms, if she was allowed. If not, she wanted to reach inside their humidicribs and stroke their soft warm skin and tell them that they were safe and she was there for them forever.

That they would never be apart. That she would protect them from life's harms in any way she could.

Just the way Patrick had protected them all the day before.

Her eyes were suddenly drawn across the room to the flowers. The beautiful blooms did just as Patrick wanted in brightening the borderline drab hospital room and she felt her mouth curving a little. The walls of her room were a light beige colour and the blinds a deeper shade of the same with the floor a mottled light grey. The night before she had not paid too much attention to the flowers other than thinking there was a pretty pop of colour in the room. In the morning light she could see cheerful yellow and white gerberas, a white daisy spray and blue chrysanthemums in a lovely white-blue vase, with a checked blue and white ribbon giving a pretty finishing touch. And the two small brown bears with blue bow ties. It was so thoughtful of him to have them in her room when she arrived. But then it seemed that everything he did was so considerate.

But why? she wondered. What was motivating him to be so kind to a stranger? He had already done more than could have been expected of anyone. Blinking furiously, she looked away from the floral arrangement. She had to put Patrick out of her mind. She couldn't allow herself to think of him that way. She had learnt her lesson the hard way not to trust anyone, not even herself.

The nurse, who introduced herself as Alli, arrived and unhooked the IV line. 'I'll leave the cannula in, but I'll tape it down,' Alli told her as she thoroughly flushed the tube and placed strong clear tape across Claudia's wrist where the small cannula had been placed. She was one of the youngest nurses on the ward and, Claudia would quickly come to learn, one of the cheekiest. 'Just in case you want IV pain relief during the day or tonight. Believe me, if they offer drugs, take them.'

Slowly, Alli helped her out of bed and assisted her to take small steps into the bathroom. Keeping the dressings dry, the nurse bathed Claudia while she sat on the shower chair.

'Do you have a clean nightdress?' she asked as she towel-dried her patient.

Claudia shook her head. She had no one to collect anything from her apartment and she only had over-sized T-shirts, nothing really suitable for hospital. She had packed a suitcase for her trip home and only left out a pair of comfortable leggings, sweater and coat with flat boots for the flight. The other small boxes of her belongings would have been collected and already be on their way with the shipping company back to London. She had planned on shopping for pretty nightdresses for her hospital stay when she returned to London.

While she had made a few acquaintances in Los Angeles, after she'd found out the truth about her relationship with Stone and then about her pregnancy, the obvious questions that would raise had made her keep everyone at arm's length. She didn't want to make friends and then have to hide the truth from them, so she'd chosen to be alone.

'Looks like you'll be in a stylish hospital gown again today,' Alli replied as she left to retrieve another gown. Moments later, she reappeared and helped Claudia to dress. 'At least it will be clean.'

'Thank you.'

'Since they have that revealing back opening, I'm going to give you a second one to wear the other way. Like a coat to complement your stunning runway ensemble.'

Claudia smiled. Although normally she did care how she was dressed and paid particular attention to her grooming, that morning she wouldn't have cared if the nurse had dressed her in a giant brown paper bag. She just wanted to get downstairs to the neonatal nursery.

'Not before you eat, Miss Monticello,' Vanda said, walking into her room and spying Claudia in the wheelchair, ready to go downstairs. 'You'll be no good to your sons without both rest and nutrition.'

'But I want to know they're all right,' Claudia argued as she sat upright. The anticipation was building and she wanted nothing more than to be with her little boys.

Vanda picked up the breakfast tray and put it on the bed near her impatient patient, handing Claudia a small plate with some buttered wholemeal toast. Standing directly in front of Claudia and not taking her eyes from her, she said firmly, 'Thomas and Luca are doing very well. I had a call from the resident paediatrician in the neo-natal ICU about an hour ago. They're expecting you but I won't let you visit unless you've had some toast and juice. I'm quite serious, Claudia. Your body suffered a huge shock yesterday and you need to take things slowly and not forget to eat and rest, just as your little boys are doing. I'm Italian and, by the sound of your surname, so are you, so you'll know that Italians take their food very seriously. You will not get away with skipping meals with one of your countrywomen on duty. Food first, before you head anywhere.'

Just then there was a knock at the door and another young nurse brought in a delivery box with the insignia of an exclusive store on Rodeo Drive; it was about a foot long and just as wide and tall. Vanda reached out and took the box.

'Well, what's this then? It's addressed to you. Have you been shopping online overnight, Miss Monticello?'

As Claudia took a bite of her toast, she shook her head. 'Are you sure it's for me? I couldn't afford to shop there in a mad fit.'

'Well, it definitely has your name on it, so someone's been shopping for you. I'll pop it on the bed and you can check it later.'

'P'raps it's a present from a handsome stranger because you were on TV last night,' Alli added before she left the room to continue her rounds.

'Oh, gosh, I hope not,' Claudia said as she put down the toast, as her already fragile appetite completely disappeared. 'I'm hoping no one knows my name or Thomas and Luca's.'

'With the proximity of the apartment complex and the fuss made on the evening news, viewers would probably assume you'd be here but neither your name nor your sons' were released and we've told the main admissions desk to refuse any media requests. It's our usual protocol,' Vanda replied. Then, spying the still uneaten toast on Claudia's plate, she continued, 'Would you like me to help you open the box and put you out of your misery?'

Claudia nodded as she tentatively sipped her orange juice.

'All right, here's the deal. I'll get some scissors from the nurses' station while you finish your breakfast but I won't open the box until you've had both pieces of toast and either your juice or a cup of tea.'

Claudia nodded begrudgingly.

Vanda stayed true to her word and when she returned with the oversized scissors she waited until Claudia had eaten and finished her juice before cutting through the packaging tape on the box. She opened it and handed it to Claudia.

Claudia lifted the tissue carefully. 'Oh, goodness, they're beautiful,' she exclaimed as she pulled the stunning jade-green silk pyjamas from the box.

'Very nice. Whoever arranged for those to be sent has great taste. Hold on a minute; now it makes sense...' Vanda paused for a moment, a strange look on her face.

'What is it? Do you know who sent this to me?'

'No idea, actually, but I had a conversation in handover this morning about a call one of the young nurses took from that store after I finished my shift last night. Apparently they had a phone order and wanted to check if they could deliver to a patient in our ward. They didn't say who and of course we would not have given your details even if they had asked.'

'How curious,' Claudia replied as she reached inside to find there was more. A short nightdress and a long one in varied tones of apricot and a matching floral wrap that picked up the colour palette of all of the other items and added some black trim for dramatic effect. There were also some jade satin slippers wrapped in more tissue at the bottom of the box, along with a toiletries bag. She unzipped the bag and it was filled with everything she would need.

'Was there a card?' Claudia asked, peering inside the box and then closing the lid and carefully checking the packaging. She couldn't see any sender other than the store—it had been a telephone order.

'No, it appears to be anonymous. As you said, very *curious* indeed,' Vanda replied.

Claudia put everything back into the box. 'I can't accept an anonymous gift.'

'I would—they look like silk and they're a whole lot better than your current outfit,' Alli argued as she stepped back into the room to collect the breakfast tray with a huge smile. 'I'll be back in ten minutes to take you to Neonatal Intensive Care so it gives you time to slip into one of those stunning pieces if you like.'

Claudia looked down at the shapeless white gown and came close to agreeing for a split second but then bit her lip and shook her head. 'No. I can't.'

Vanda took the box and put it on the bed again. 'You don't have to accept it; however, you are in need of everything that's in that box, so—' she paused to put her words together '—what if you accept the gift on the condition that you will repay your generous benefactor when you've been discharged from the hospital? I'm sure you can track them down through the store.'

'I don't feel comfortable with the idea and I'm not sure I could afford to anyway.'

'Do you feel comfortable with the idea of staying in your present outfit for a few days? You'll get a fresh one each day, of course, but still the same white number with the lovely back opening! Do you have anyone who could go shopping for you?'

Claudia nodded. 'No, there's no one I can call.'

'I thought as much. You'll be in the nursery a lot over the coming days and the pyjamas and gown would be most helpful. I did manage to find you some toothpaste and a toothbrush and a few other bits and pieces but they are pretty basic and I'm sure whatever has been sent to you would be a whole lot nicer.'

Claudia once again bit her lip as she tried to put everything into perspective. 'I know I need them, particularly the toiletries, but do you really think I will be able to find out who sent the gift and repay them?'

'All I can say is that we'll do our best.'

'I *will* find them and I *will* send them a cheque for the entire amount as soon as I can. I mean it.'

Vanda left the room and Claudia slowly and carefully changed without contorting too much. The softness of the pyjama fabric felt glorious on her skin. Feather-light and cool to wear. Her body felt as if it had done battle the day before and this was a little bit of pampering.

Claudia sat down again to rest. She wanted so much to see her sons. She couldn't wait to hold them and tell them how much she loved them. Alli had not arrived so she decided to call Harriet and give her the good news about Thomas and Luca. Her sister had no idea of what had transpired over the last twenty-four hours or that she was now the aunt of two wonderful little boys. It was eight o'clock in the morning and, knowing that Argentina was five hours ahead of LA, Claudia felt confident she wouldn't wake her sister.

Harriet answered the phone after only two rings.

'Hi, sis, how are you? I miss you so much and I have *soooo* much to tell you.' Her voice then dropped to a loud whisper. 'Oh, I'm so confused. My boring, predictable as mud life has turned completely topsy-turvy. I met this man, as close to Adonis as you would find, well, the Argentinian version of the Greek God anyway…I don't know if there is an Argentinian version, to be honest, but he is so ridiculously handsome as well as intelligent and we, well, sort of had a thing, just one night, actually, back in the UK, and I never thought I'd see him again. But now I'm here in his country. He looks even better under the Buenos Aires sun than he did in London—and he was already an eleven out of ten...'

Claudia was surprised to hear Harriet sound so nervous and clearly smitten by this man but, ecstatic as she was to hear that her sister had a love interest, she was aware that Alli would return to take her to the nursery so she blurted out her news. 'I had the babies, Harriet. You're an aunty!'

'What?'

'I had my babies.'

'So early, Clau? Are you and the babies okay?' She stopped in her tracks.

'Yes, I'm fine and Thomas and Luca are so handsome.'

'Thomas and Luca! You named them after both grandfathers?'

'I hope you don't mind that I took both names in one fell swoop. I didn't leave you a grandfather for when you have children.'

Harriet laughed. 'Phuh—me? No, I don't think I'll be having children anytime soon. I'm happy you used Nonno's and Papa's names. I still can't believe you had twins! So tell me about my nephews—are they happy and healthy little boys considering they were early?'

'They're doing well, particularly since they were born in a lift.'

'In a lift?'

'Yes, a lift, or maybe I should say an elevator since I'm here in LA.'

'LA? I'm confused. I thought you were heading back to London to have the babies?'

'I was but my water broke in the elevator and Patrick helped me to give birth. Actually, Patrick saved my life because I haemorrhaged and passed out and then paramedics rescued us all and I had an emergency hysterectomy.'

'How can you tell me you're okay with all of that going on? I need to get there now.' Harriet began pacing nervously.

'No, Harriet.' Claudia's voice was firm. As much as she wanted more than anything to have her sister with her, she refused to pull her away from the first adventure of her life. She was proud that her twin was finally jumping into something with both feet. Maybe they weren't so different after all, or maybe they were switching roles. For a while, at least. 'You can't do anything. For once you need to stick with your plans and stop trying to rescue your big sister. I'm fine, the surgery went well and I have two adorable little boys. We'll be heading home to London as soon as they're strong enough and you can meet them.'

'I need to hop on a plane and get to LA now.'

'Harriet, please listen to me. The orphanage needs you more than me. I'm well taken care of. Everything's fine here. I have a place to live until I leave for London.' Claudia had to lie or she would risk her sister doing what she always did—stepping in to save the day. Claudia had no idea where she would live. Her apartment was gone, she assumed her suitcase would have been taken down to the concierge's office, but she had barely any savings to her name and only a changeable ticket back to London. She would have to work things out quickly, but not at Harriet's expense. Her sister had finally found her dream job and perhaps even her dream man and Claudia was not taking either away from her.

'Is the ex keeping his distance? Does he know about the birth?'

'Yes, he's keeping his distance and no, he doesn't know I've had his sons. He wouldn't care. His lawyer told me he didn't want to be updated about the pregnancy. So I thought I would keep the news to myself. It would hardly have had him skipping with joy.' Claudia paused. 'His wife still has no idea that the boys or I even exist. Just as I had no idea she existed when I fell for his lines. It's amazing how he hid his marriage so well. I must be the most stupid woman in the world.'

'You're not stupid in any way,' Harriet countered softly. 'Just way too trusting for your own good. But you're better off without him, Clau.'

'I know,' she said then, thinking back to the tiny little boys waiting for her in the nursery, she smiled. 'But I have the most wonderful sons so my regrets about my relationship with that man are tempered. He gave me the greatest gifts, Thomas and Luca…and permission to *not* have him in my life. The papers arrived from his lawyer last week. He doesn't want his name on the birth certificates and waived any parental rights.'

'That's so cold!'

'He offered me a trust fund for the boys but I told him to keep his money.'

'Will you be all right without an income?'

'I'll be fine once I get back home in a few weeks. My life will be perfect…'

'I worry about you being alone.'

'I'm won't ever be alone. I have Thomas and Luca, and I'll always have you.'

'That's the truth,' Harriet agreed.

There was also someone else who had momentarily stepped into her life. Claudia was determined that in the future, when he would be just a memory, she would tell her sons as they grew up about the man who'd brought them into the world and also saved their mother's life. Even though they might never meet Patrick, they would always know about him. And how very special he was.

'I'd better say goodbye, though, as the nurse will be back to wheel me down to the nursery any minute.'

'Okay, but you call me if you need me. I can be on a plane and there with you in a few hours. I love you, sis,' Harriet told her.

'Love you too, Harriet,' Claudia replied then hung up before she had a chance to answer her sister's final question.

'Wait, who's Patrick...?'

CHAPTER FIVE

'MISS MONTICELLO, I'M Dr Wilson, the neonatologist here at Los Angeles Mercy Hospital. I need to speak with you in private for a moment.' The doctor leant down and held out his hand and Claudia tentatively met his handshake. She had only just arrived in Neonatal ICU and had not yet seen her sons. She had no idea why he wanted to speak with her but she felt her heart pick up speed as his tone seemed quite serious. She hadn't considered there could possibly be any bad news after yesterday. The boys both seemed perfect despite what they had all been through.

What had changed?

'Please call me Claudia,' she replied as she began to nervously play with her freshly scrubbed hands and continued observing the doctor suspiciously. She tried to contain her emotions and wait for the doctor to speak but questions driven by mounting fear came rushing out. 'Are my babies going to be all right? Is there something wrong? I thought everything was fine yesterday.' She wanted to jump from her wheelchair and find them. Her eyes darted around but she could not see the boys as their humidicribs were blocked by a tall beige partition.

'Claudia, they are both doing very well, all things considered,' he returned, clearly trying to calm her down.

'What do you mean—all things *considered*?'

'I mean their delivery in an elevator and the simple fact they are six weeks early. I was going to come to your room but the charge nurse said you were on your way down here so I thought I'd wait. You can see your boys the moment we've finished speaking. I didn't want you to be anxious in the elevator.' The neonatologist, in his late fifties, had a warm smile; his hair, which was grey around the temples, and his deep brown eyes reminded Claudia of her father. Although the doctor's very contained demeanour was not like her father's passionate, gregarious Italian personality. He was controlled and that was reassuring to Claudia but she was still scared.

'Tell me, is there something wrong?' Her eyes widened as she spoke. While he had said nothing dire nor even hinted at it, Claudia had a sense of foreboding but she was trying very hard not to fall to pieces.

'There's been a small setback with Luca and I would like to talk to you about his treatment.'

Claudia's chin began to quiver with the words coming so calmly from the neonatologist's mouth. She had just been wheeled from the scrub room where Alli had helped her to put on a disposable gown over her pyjamas and suddenly she was being ushered into a small consulting room. She had been so excited to see her boys. She hadn't thought for a moment she would hear bad news. She'd had enough, she felt sure, to last a lifetime.

'I can take Claudia from here if you'd like,' he told

Alli and reached for the handles of the wheelchair. 'I'll call the nurses' station when she's ready to go back to her room,'

'Certainly Dr Wilson; I'll come back whenever Claudia's ready,' Alli said gently and reassuringly patted Claudia's shoulder. 'You'll be fine, honey. Just breathe slowly and stay calm.'

Dr Wilson wheeled Claudia into the small office and sat opposite her. His expression was stern.

'How serious is it? I need to know.' Claudia felt her stomach tie in knots and it was nothing to do with her surgery.

'Luca had a few breathing problems yesterday and that is why he was in the open bed warmer so that we could provide oxygen through an oxy-hood, or head box as we often call it. It's a small perspex box that allows babies to breathe more easily, but Luca didn't improve overnight. In fact he seemed to be struggling so I suspected a condition called PDA. It's short for a longer medical term, and I can give you more information later. I ordered an echocardiogram an hour ago to confirm my diagnosis…'

'What's an echocardiogram? Did it hurt him?' Despite her resolve to remain in control, tears began to well in her eyes but the questions kept coming. 'Where is Luca?'

'Luca is fine at the moment, Claudia,' the doctor continued in a firm but calm tone. 'The echocardiogram didn't hurt because it's much like an X-ray. Luca and Thomas are over there, where they both were yesterday.' He motioned with his hand in the direction her sons. 'The humidicrib with Thomas is beside Luca's open bed warmer and they have one nurse looking after

them both. The setback at this time, Miss Monticello...
I'm sorry... Claudia,' he corrected himself, 'has been
confirmed by the echocardiogram and, while it's not
serious and more than likely just due to his premature
arrival, we need to keep an eye on Luca and you need
to be aware of his condition.'

'Will Thomas develop the condition too?'

'No. There's no sign of PDA with Thomas. We're
just monitoring Luca around this issue.'

'And what exactly is the problem, Dr Wilson?'

'He has an opening between two major blood vessels leading from his heart.'

'Oh, my God, no.' Claudia's hands instinctively covered her mouth. She didn't want to cry but the news
brought her to the brink.

It was all too much. She'd thought bringing her babies into the world under such harsh conditions was ter-
rifying but this was so much worse. She felt so helpless.

'Claudia, I know you must be very scared by what
I'm telling you but that is why I asked you in here to
talk,' the doctor continued in a very soothing tone. 'All
parents have that initial reaction—it's perfectly normal—but you need to understand a little more about
Luca's problem and the treatment options. The opening
between the blood vessels I'm discussing is a normal
part of a baby's circulatory system *before birth* but it
normally closes shortly after birth. While a baby is in
the mother's womb, only a small amount of his or her
blood needs to go to the lungs. This is because the baby
gets oxygen from the mother's bloodstream.'

'So why did Luca's not close?'

'It is probably due purely to his prematurity. You
see, after birth, the baby is no longer connected to

the mother's bloodstream and the baby's blood needs to go to his or her own lungs to get oxygen. When a baby is born on or around their due date the baby begins to breathe on his or her own and the pulmonary artery opens to allow blood into the lungs, and the other opening closes. But in premature infants it is not uncommon for it to remain open and a small PDA often doesn't cause problems.'

'Does Luca have a small PDA or a big one?'

'We don't know yet but if it's small then he may never need treatment.'

'But if it isn't small, what then?'

'A large PDA left untreated can allow poorly oxygenated blood to travel in the wrong direction, weakening the heart muscle and causing heart problems.'

Claudia's world just became a little darker and her own heart sank. 'Will he need surgery?' She felt increasingly powerless to do anything as she waited on tenterhooks for the answer.

'Not at this stage. His treatment for the time being will involve monitoring and medication.'

Her mind was spinning and her body reeling from the news about her baby boy. She felt so overwhelmed and unsure of where to turn. Then she realised there was nowhere to turn. She only had herself. And her little boys only had their mother. She drew a deep restorative breath and faced the doctor. She had to be strong for the three of them.

'What sort of medication?' she asked, shaking her head.

Before the doctor could respond, there was a knock at the door.

She looked over her shoulder to see Patrick standing

in the doorway with the same expression she remembered from the day before. The expression that told her she would get through whatever lay ahead when she had no idea how. Her brow was lined in confusion and a single tear of relief trickled down her cheek. Quickly she wiped it away with the back of her hand.

'Claudia, I came as soon as I could,' he began as he stepped inside the room. And closer to her.

'But I didn't call.'

'No, I asked the hospital to keep me posted about the boys as I was listed as the doctor who delivered them. It was professional courtesy for them to keep me updated. I called late last night and asked to be informed if there were any problems with either Thomas or Luca. I knew, with their premature births, there may be issues and I wanted to be here for them.'

What Patrick wanted to say was he wasn't just there for Thomas and Luca. He wanted to be there for her. But he couldn't bring himself to say it. He felt certain she wouldn't want to hear it and he didn't want to say it and believe it. Having feelings for someone—wanting to be a part of Claudia and the boy's lives—was so foreign to him.

He had collapsed onto his bed after a long hot shower the previous night. After returning from the hospital, he had tried to put Claudia out of his mind. He'd hoped as the steaming water engulfed his body he would come to his senses. But he didn't. Her gorgeous face, her feisty nature and her strength in the face of pain that would have crippled the strongest of men, kept pulling his thoughts back to her. And then there was her instant love for her boys. All of it made it impossible for Patrick to push her image away. He couldn't erase her from his thoughts. He had spent hours trying but failed and gave in to what he knew he wanted to do. Against his better judgement, he wanted to be there for them all if they needed him.

Claudia felt relieved to have Patrick so close but so torn at needing him. She was confused. She said nothing as she looked at him. There was nothing in her head that would have made any sense if she'd tried to speak.

Patrick turned his attention to the doctor. 'Dr Wilson, I'm Patrick Spencer. We spoke on the phone earlier.'

The doctor stood and extended his hand to greet Patrick and, in doing so, broke the tension between Claudia and Patrick.

'Nice to meet you in person. Please call me Geoffrey. And I must commend you in person for your medical intervention in the elevator. You wouldn't want to do all your deliveries that way, I'm sure.'

'No, an elevator delivery is not something I would've willingly opted for,' he responded with a lightness to his voice. He met the other doctor's handshake but gave away nothing more. Patrick's current medical specialty bore no relevance in the neonatal nursery. He had been honest with the obstetric surgeon when asked directly the day before, but offering up information not requested was pointless. His former medical knowledge was still very much intact, even if his career with babies was long gone.

Claudia watched the men's conversational banter with a blank expression on her face. Her emotions were a roller coaster but she still had questions about her boys that were clear-cut. Even if anything to do with her own heart and head was not close to straight-forward.

'You mention drugs, Dr Wilson. What drugs are you talking about for Luca? Do they have any side effects?'

The doctor immediately returned his focus to Claudia. 'Ibuprofen will be the drug that will be given to Luca. It's an anti-inflammatory that could help to block the hormone-like chemicals in Luca's body that are keeping the PDA open. Ibuprofen could very simply allow it to close in a very short space of time.'

'Is this condition common?' Her voice was steadier and she felt as if her co-pilot had returned and was standing beside her. Still hugely confused by her own feelings, she was slowly digesting the idea that together they would navigate a problem that only moments ago she'd found overwhelming.

'It occurs in about eight in every thousand prema-ture births but most correct themselves in a very short time frame and some in only a few hours.'

'So Luca will be all right?' she asked with her eyes still searching for reassurance, moving from Patrick to Dr Wilson and back again.

'I am fairly sure that over the next day or so the con-dition will correct itself,' Dr Wilson offered. 'But you still needed to be informed. I don't like to hide any-thing.' Claudia felt reassured to hear those words. She didn't want anything to be hidden from her ever again.

'And you agree, Patrick?'

He nodded. 'I do.'

Patrick's eyes met hers. The level of vulnerability in Claudia's eyes made him want to pull her into his arms and comfort her but he couldn't. He was provid-ing medical advice. He had to behave as a medical practitioner and refrain from doing what he wanted to do as a man.

'I don't think we should cross a bridge that hasn't presented itself,' he volunteered from his professional viewpoint. 'Luca has a high chance of avoiding any invasive treatment so let's not overthink the situation.'

'Then I won't worry any more.'

Patrick sensed from the doctor's curious expression that he was trying to read the relationship playing out before him; he opened his mouth to speak but Patrick cut in quickly. 'Have you visited with Thomas and Luca today, Claudia?'

'No.'

'Then, Dr Wilson, now Claudia is fully versed with Luca's condition, may I wheel her over to see her babies?'

'Certainly,' the older doctor replied before he could ask anything else. Together they left the small room, with Dr Wilson showing the way and Patrick pushing Claudia's wheelchair. Patrick glanced down to see Claudia still fidgeting with her fingers and suddenly felt very protective. She lifted her face and smiled at him and a warm feeling rushed through his body.

It was as if he was where he needed to be and where he belonged and he hadn't felt that way in a very long time.

He pulled Claudia's wheelchair between the humidicrib and the open bed and then sat down beside her. The neonatologist tended to some new arrivals to the nursery and left them with the neonatal nurse.

'They both look almost red, and I can see their veins... I didn't notice it yesterday.'

'You didn't notice because you were so happy to see

them alive and you were lucky to be alive yourself. I don't think you were up to focusing on the details.'

'But is it normal?'

'Yes, premature babies appear to be red as well as much smaller than you had imagined. You can see all the blood vessels through their skin because there hasn't been sufficient time to develop any fat underneath.'

'There are so many wires attached to them. Will I be able to hold them?' Claudia asked as the desire to have them both in her arms was stronger than any need she had ever felt before.

The nurse approached and shook her head. 'Not yet, but you can certainly stroke them both and that is important. They need to feel their mother's touch. While Thomas and Luca aren't the smallest babies in here, we still need to allow them to remain in temperatures stable enough to keep them both warm without needing to be wrapped up in blankets.'

'It also decreases the risk of an infection,' Patrick added as his eyes panned from one baby to the other. 'The humidity in the crib is controlled to help maintain the baby's hydration and prevent water loss. And Luca on his open bed is wearing a cap to help limit the heat loss.'

Claudia gently stroked Luca's tiny arm and prayed that Patrick was right and the problem with his heart would pass in time.

'Patrick,' she began, 'I know you said not to cross a bridge that isn't in front of me, but I can't put blinkers on and pretend there's no chance of something serious. I need to ask just one question and I want you to be completely honest with me.'

Patrick had a million questions for Claudia but he knew she might not stay in town long enough for all of them to be answered. He accepted the simple reality that whatever time they shared in the next few days might be all they would ever have.

Their lives had collided and they had both shared the most precious and intense experience. But it was not the real world and it would all end soon enough. And one burning question in particular still resonated in the back of his mind. *Where was the man who should be by Claudia's side?*

He pushed that thought away and took a deep breath. 'Certainly—what's your question?'

Claudia looked over at Thomas inside his glass humidicrib and then back to tiny Luca. The question erred on the side of the worst-case scenario, which she didn't want to think about. But she needed to know and, if she had to, she wanted to hear the worst from Patrick. 'Can they guarantee the ibuprofen will work?'

Patrick paused, wishing he could tell her there was a written in stone guarantee but there was no such guarantee. 'No, to be honest, the medications aren't one hundred percent effective and if Luca's condition is severe or causing complications surgery might be needed, but that is not something you have to consider now. Luca's doctor seems very hopeful that the drugs will work.'

'But if they don't?'

'Claudia,' he said, taking her hands in his instinctively and, against his better judgement, he looked at the tears welling in her eyes. She wasn't looking at him any more. She was lovingly watching her tiny son but he noticed she didn't flinch or pull away and left her hands in his. He hated admitting it but there were undeniable sparks as her skin touched his. She was lighting a fire inside him where he'd thought there were only cold embers incapable of feeling any warmth ever again. 'Like I told you before, let's not worry about something over which we have no control. If surgery is needed we'll deal with it then but now is about remaining positive and optimistic about your boys and getting yourself well too.'

Claudia turned her gaze back to Patrick and then to his hands protectively holding hers. Who was this man who kept saving her? she wondered. Should she let him get close to her? He appeared to be so upfront and honest and caring but she still needed to protect her herself from further disappointment. He'd only come into her life twenty-four hours before and she really knew very little about him. There were so many unasked questions. Maybe he wasn't hiding anything but he wasn't overly forthcoming either and that worried her.

She had been promised a life by the boys' father that was just a lie. How could she be sure that Patrick was any different?

She felt herself wanting to believe in him and everything he was saying and she was feeling, but she was scared. Was it just because of what they'd shared the day before that made her feel that she could trust him? Or was it more than that? Perhaps she felt indebted to him for saving her life and her babies. She knew she had never felt about a man the way she did at that moment.

It was as if she had known him for years.

Her head was spinning. Why could she imagine herself wrapped in the comfort of Patrick's strong arms, her body pressed against the warmth of his…and his lips reaching for hers…? She shook herself back to reality. She was in no place to be having those thoughts.

It wasn't right…but it was happening. And, try as she might, she couldn't pretend it wasn't.

She had feelings she didn't understand for a man she really didn't know.

It didn't make any sense, she thought, as she slipped her hands free.

She had to channel thoughts of Harriet: what her sister would do and how she would think. She would certainly be more realistic and practical. That was how she had to behave. It had to be about her sons from now on. There was barely enough of her left emotionally to give both sons the love and undivided attention they deserved. She had to consider them in every decision she made. She needed to keep it simple, despite the way she felt herself drawn to the handsome Englishman. To her knight in shining armour.

Perhaps they could be friends.

She threw away that idea as quickly as it had arrived. The electricity she felt surge through her body when Patrick was near made *friends* untenable. She just had to manage her feelings for the short time he was around and behave as the unofficial patient of a very handsome, charismatic doctor would. However difficult that would be.

'Is there something else on your mind?'

'No, my mind's still reeling from the news about Luca. You'll think I'm absurd if I keep asking questions…'

'Claudia, never apologise for asking questions. These are your babies and you have every right to have each and every question answered honestly and to ask it again and again if need be.'

Claudia drew breath and with a tremble in her voice continued, 'Why is only Luca affected?' As she spoke, she looked at Thomas and wondered if she had been told everything. Or if there was more she should know.

Patrick wanted so much to hold her close and comfort her. She was frightened and there was nothing as a professional he could do other than provide standard advice, albeit in an empathetic manner. For some inexplicable reason, he wanted to offer so much more but he couldn't. He had to veto the feelings that were stirring in him. And before he swept her into his arms and kissed her more passionately than he had ever kissed a woman before.

It wasn't going to be easy but he couldn't allow romantic thoughts to invade his mind and his heart. With his arms folded across his chest, he answered her. 'Dr Wilson isn't worried because Thomas doesn't have the condition now, so he can't ever have it. The opening between two major blood vessels leading from his heart closed naturally after birth. You need to understand that Thomas and Luca are fraternal twins so they are quite different developmentally in a number of ways. While they're twins, they're essentially just like any siblings so not all of their developmental conditions are going to be shared. Fortunately, this is one of them.'

Claudia was relieved to hear everything that Patrick was explaining and his calm bedside manner was alleviating her concerns. 'I have a non-identical twin sister,' she offered, as he watched her appear to relax a little. 'Harriet. She's the complete opposite of me. She's my rock. She's a nurse, quiet and sensible, always thinking about other people. We've been there for each other since our parents died nine years ago.'

'I'm sorry you lost your parents while you were still young.' Patrick had been an adult when he'd found himself alone so he could understand the overwhelming sadness that must have been Claudia's world when she lost her parents.

'It was just before our twentieth birthday, so we weren't that young, but we had been very protected, growing up in what was essentially a close-knit household. We grew up quickly. Harriet more so than me.'

'You're obviously close to her. Was there a reason that you didn't call her from the elevator yesterday?'

'She was on her way to Argentina. I wasn't sure if she was still in transit and I didn't want to worry her. I mean, there wasn't anything else she could have done except worry.'

'I suppose you're right. Have you spoken to her yet?' he asked as he sat back in his chair a little and glanced over at Thomas and Luca, both still sleeping soundly. 'Does she know she's an aunt?'

'Oh, yes, I just called before the nurse brought me down here.'

A smile crossed Claudia's face. It was the first full smile that he had witnessed. And it made her even more beautiful, if that was possible.

'Of course,' she continued, unaware of the effect she was having on Patrick. 'And, in typical Harriet style, she wanted to rush here to be with me. Drop her life to rescue her big sister. I was born first so I'm older by three minutes but she always behaves like the older, far wiser sister.'

Patrick smiled. 'So she's on her way here then?'

'Absolutely not,' she said with an expression that told him she thought he should have known better. 'I wouldn't allow her to. She's working in an orphanage and I'm not going to have her alter her plans. I'll see her at home when she finishes her work over there in a few months.'

'So you lived together back in London?' he asked and then curiosity got the better of him. 'Were you on holiday here or a work exchange of sorts?'

Claudia went a little quiet and Patrick wondered if he had asked too many questions. Perhaps he'd been too intrusive.

'You know what, forget I asked. It's none of my business. I'm here to help answer any questions you have about your boys, not interview you.'

She paused before she spoke although she hadn't intended on opening up about the details of her past. Looking at Patrick, she couldn't help but feel they had known each other for a long time. She had felt that way from the moment he'd taken off his sunglasses in the elevator and she had looked into his grey-blue eyes.

'My sister and I still share our family home. I came over here for work. I won an internship with a weekly drama series on a major network. It was a huge opportunity and I took it. Again, I jumped in with both feet like I always do,' she announced as she gently ran her finger over her tiny son's shoulder.

'I don't think jumping in is a bad idea. You experience all that life has to offer that way.'

'And some,' she muttered under her breath and felt a shiver of regret run down her body. 'Anyway, my contract is over so, as soon as the boys are strong enough, we will all head back to London. That's where I want to raise them,' she added, turning to look Patrick squarely in the eyes. 'And my leaving is something the boys' father does not object to… In fact, he is quite…' She stopped. There was no need for Patrick to know any more. 'Let's just say my leaving is not causing him any grief.'

'Well, then, we need to get them strong enough to travel.'

Patrick stayed with Claudia for another twenty minutes, then excused himself as he needed to get to his practice. He had an afternoon roster of new patients and a few post-operative.

'I'll leave you with your boys, but if you like I can call again over the next few days to check up on all of you.'

'I'd like that,' she said instinctively but the moment the words passed over her lips she knew she shouldn't have given him that answer. It was opening them both up to the inevitable.

She now had a date with a potentially sad farewell looming on the horizon.

Claudia had spent two days sitting beside Thomas and Luca, praying for them to reach the next tiny milestone and, despite the rush of hormones after the birth, she was feeling better emotionally but physically exhausted. She had stroked both boys between their gavage feeds and she chatted with the nurses and doctors. The doctor had reassured her that Luca's condition was already showing improvement and he believed that within days they might be able to stop the ibuprofen.

She had also received a call from Harriet. Her sister wanted an update on her nephews but she seemed distracted. She hadn't been disinterested at all but there seemed to be something on her mind. Claudia put it down to the tireless work she must be undertaking at the orphanage. She had nothing but admiration for her sister and could hardly wait for Thomas and Luca to meet her.

After she hung up, she suddenly felt tired and a little sore as they had ceased the IV pain relief and she was just having four hourly tablets. She decided after dinner to stay in her room and have an early night and get up early to spend the next day down in the nursery. To her surprise and relief, she had been able to stay in her private room.

She had missed seeing Patrick the previous evening and during the day and wondered if she would ever see him again. Perhaps he had done his heroic act and then disappeared into the night, she thought. Her eyes drifted to the night lights of Los Angeles that she could see from her bed and she wondered where he was. Was he thinking about her and the boys?

While he had every right to be enjoying dinner or drinks with another woman, a crazy part of her felt jealous. Was he dining at an elegant Beverley Hills restaurant or somewhere swank in downtown LA? Was his stunning date enjoying his company, laughing at his anecdotes or just mesmerised by his stunning eyes?

Was the thought of the woman who had ruined his jacket and shirt the furthest thing from his mind?

Hesitant to overstretch, she gently moved her body to the edge of the bed so she could put her teacup back on the bedside cabinet. Then she eased back into a comfortable position and plumped up her pillow before she nestled under the covers. Thinking about Patrick and actually spending any time caring what he was doing at that time of the evening was ridiculous, she berated herself. And having flashbacks to the moment he'd removed his shirt in the elevator was borderline torturous since she knew they would never have a future together.

She looked up at the ceiling, wishing suddenly that her parents were alive to meet their grandsons. They would stroke their tiny cheeks and kiss them from morning to night and the boys would have loved their grandparents. If only they'd had the chance to meet them.

And how would her parents have reacted to Patrick? They would most certainly thank him for bringing Thomas and Luca into the world. Her father would shake his hand and then pull him into his strong embrace with a hearty laugh. Her mother would be a little more reserved but still tell him how grateful she was for what he had done in saving their precious grandchildren.

She felt a tear slip from her eye and onto the pillow.

Her heart ached for what she had lost, now more than ever.

CHAPTER SIX

PATRICK STOOD OUTSIDE the door of Claudia's hospital room, trying to resist the temptation to knock. He wondered why he had returned. He had tried to stay away and had almost succeeded. But something drove him to see the gorgeous brunette.

Was there a man who still owned Claudia's heart? Despite alarm bells ringing, he knocked on the door. Why was he going against every rule he had followed for over a decade? Never get close to someone, never form a bond or risk his heart, never look for more than one night. His decision to become an island had been born of necessity and it had served him well. But that resolve had never been so tested as it was now. The idea of Claudia, Thomas and Luca featuring in his future was a recurring thought that haunted him.

His rejection of family and his family's rejection of him were combined in fighting his thoughts about Claudia and the boys. And Claudia and the boys were winning.

'I hope it's not too late. The nurse said you were still awake.'

It was a voice that the sensible part of Claudia's brain

didn't want to hear but one that made her hopeless heart do a little dance. She wiped her eyes with the back of her hand and tried to pull herself up in the bed as Patrick walked into the room. He was dressed in dark clothing and he cut a ridiculously attractive figure. His trousers were black and he had a charcoal polo top and black leather shoes. His clothing highlighted his sun-kissed brown hair and light tan and the stubble that she imagined would be soft to her touch.

His appearance was intoxicating. He wasn't fighting fair, she thought. How was she supposed to keep her thoughts to doctor-patient when he looked so damn good?

'You shouldn't have come; it's so late and you probably have far more important places to be than here.' Her voice was crisp and it belied how truly happy she was to see him. She didn't want to need him the way she did. She didn't want to repeat the mistake of thinking she knew everything about a man, only to have her heart broken by what he was hiding.

But something about Patrick made her think he wasn't hiding anything.

Was he an exception to the rule?

Patrick looked into her eyes in the dim light of the room and searched for something.

He didn't find it immediately but he persisted and moved closer to the bed.

He saw her full lips curve into a smile. And her eyes were smiling too. He found what he was looking for. Despite what she was telling him, there was a welcome on her beautiful face. Part of him didn't want to see any warmth there. He normally chose women who weren't looking for the picket fence and happily ever after because he couldn't provide it.

With one look he was reminded of just how different she was and how he didn't want to walk away without knowing more about her.

'I'm sorry I couldn't be here earlier today or last night. I had patients until late and a surgical roster today that finished about an hour ago.' There was more he wasn't saying. He had forced himself to stay away. Tried to push thoughts of her from his mind and pretend that she hadn't crept under his skin.

He had no choice but to give in to his desire to see her.

'You know there's no obligation to come. You're a busy doctor and I suppose there are lots of women having babies.' She fussed with her bedclothes and averted her gaze as she spoke. She didn't want to fall into the warmth of his eyes.

He looked at her for a moment in silence with a curious expression.

'What is it?' she asked, sensing she had said something silly but not understanding why.

'I'm a doctor, Claudia, but I don't spend my days delivering babies.'

She shot him a puzzled look. 'What do you mean— are you a children's doctor, not an obstetrician?'

While he had not articulated his specialty during labour, with the risk of raising her anxiety level, she had obviously not read his business card.

'Do you still have the card I left you in case you needed to reach me?'

'Yes, it's in the cabinet. Why?'

Patrick crossed to the cabinet with long purposeful steps. 'May I?' he asked as he reached for the drawer.

She nodded. There was nothing personal in there.

'Here it is,' he announced, the small white card in his hand. 'You haven't read it, have you?'

Claudia shook her head. 'I had no reason to. I haven't called you.'

She put her hand out and he passed the card to her. Squinting in the soft lighting, she searched the card for his details and read the words aloud.

'Dr Patrick Spencer…cosmetic surgeon?' She collapsed back into her pillow in horror. Her arms instinctively folded across herself in an attempt to feel less vulnerable. There had to be some mistake. 'You're a plastic surgeon? You're not an obstetrician? Why didn't you tell me?'

Patrick shook his head and drew in a deep breath but, before he could begin to answer Claudia's questions, she asked more.

'Then…how did you know what to do—are you even qualified to deliver my babies?' Her voice was a little raised and equally shaky. She felt physically sick that she'd put her life and the lives of her babies in the hands of a cosmetic surgeon.

'I knew what to do because I'm a doctor.'

Claudia frowned. She felt exposed. 'Why didn't you mention that you were a cosmetic surgeon?' she asked, looking directly at him. She was angry that he hadn't told her. His announcement brought reality home. She really knew very little about Patrick and, except for the few words they'd exchanged, which had come mostly from her, he was like any man she could have passed in the street.

Only something inside had made her want to believe that he would not wilfully hurt her. *Had she done it again? Had she trusted someone at face value?*

Patrick rubbed his neck slowly and in silence. 'You need to listen to me for a minute.'

'I'm listening. Go ahead—explain why you never shared your real medical specialty with me when you were cutting free my underwear and examining me!'

Not needing to give his reply any thought because it was the truth, he answered her quickly. 'Because telling you might have sent you into a panic. The situation wasn't desirable, you were understandably anxious and the last thing you needed to hear was the man about to deliver your babies hadn't done so in over a decade. I was confident I could do it as well as anyone but you wouldn't have known that.'

'So you have delivered babies then?'

'Yes, I delivered babies many years ago and, to be honest, in the situation we were in two days ago, anyone sharing that elevator with you would have been sufficiently qualified to help. You could not have done it alone.'

With the bedclothes tucked up firmly around her like a shield, she continued. 'So these babies you delivered, were they during your training then?'

Patrick didn't want to go into too much detail but knew Claudia deserved more of an explanation. The boys were safe now but she needed to know that they had been safe the entire time. 'I was an obstetrician in the UK. I worked in the field for a number of years so that's why you and your boys were, all things considered, in safe hands.'

It made sense and it was logical but it still unsettled her. 'Why didn't you just tell me that?'

'Because it had been almost twelve years and I knew that it still would have heightened your fear. You would have worried that I might not have been competent. I knew I could do it but I couldn't spend my energy re-assuring you of the fact.'

Claudia accepted his reasoning and even agreed in part but still…

Was there anything else he hadn't told her? Was there something else she should have known?

She fixed her eyes on him intently and decided to just ask. 'So why did you change profession? Why did you stop delivering babies?'

Patrick lowered his tall frame onto the chair beside her bed. He had never wanted to tell anyone anything about his past as much as he did Claudia at that moment. He wanted to be honest about what had transpired and the future that had been so unfairly taken from him, but he couldn't. It had been locked inside for too many years to bring it up. He had moved on and so had everyone else. He would have no idea even where to start and he was worried where it might end.

So telling Claudia made no sense, he thought. He shook his head. 'I needed a change of scenery and thought I would change my specialty at the same time.'

'So you just upped and moved countries so you could surgically create perfect noses and big…' She paused and looked down towards her breasts.

'Yes, I perform breast augmentations and facial en-hancements,' he admitted. He was proud of the work he performed but it had never been his dream. Bringing children into the world had always been what he had wanted to do until he'd had to walk away.

'You said it was over a decade but when exactly did you deliver the last baby before Thomas and Luca?'

Patrick felt his jaw tense. He had made his mind up not to relive that painful time in his life, so made his answer brief. 'Twelve years ago next month and it was back in the UK...'

'Why did you give up?' Claudia interrupted him as she sought to uncover a little more detail. She sensed Patrick was perhaps not telling her the entire story. His story about leaving obstetrics in England to pick up cosmetic surgery in Los Angeles seemed to be missing a piece. What was his motivation for the change? She was curious about the handsome man beside her, whose subtle woody cologne was suddenly penetrating her senses.

'Like I said, time for a sea-change and a challenge.' He felt cornered. It wasn't a lie but it wasn't the entire story either. 'You need to know that I wanted only what was best for you in that elevator. Maybe I should have told you, maybe I was right in not telling you. We'll never know now.'

'I guess we won't.'

'You're an incredibly brave woman; I hope you know that.'

'I had limited choices.' Her mood was still pensive and his compliment didn't sit well. She had been deceived by the father of her children and, while this situation was different, it felt horribly similar. She didn't like the truth being hidden from her, no matter what it was.

'You're an amazingly resilient woman. You made

a conscious choice to face adversity head-on,' he replied. In a perfect world he would open up to Claudia and let her into his past. But his world wasn't perfect. In a perfect world he would still be Dr Patrick Spencer, OBGYN in the Harley Street practice he had dreamt of opening. But if compensation for his years of disappointment came in the chance meeting with Claudia, and even if it only lasted a brief time, he felt at peace with that. She had a positivity and strength that he had never witnessed before and he felt in time he would be a better man just being around her.

Not that he would have much time.

Claudia had been let down once; he didn't want to be the second man to let her down. He wouldn't make any promises other than to enjoy the weeks until she left. To be someone she could depend on during those weeks.

A rock for her.

It all sounded so logical in his head but his body had different ideas and it took every ounce of willpower not to kiss her. Not to press his lips against hers and taste the sweetness he knew her mouth would hold.

Claudia Monticello was testing Patrick in a way he had never expected.

Claudia leant back against the pillows and felt her eyes becoming heavy.

Being close to him and reacting the way she did confused her. Looking at the curves of Patrick's handsome face in the soft lighting of her hospital room, she struggled with what she knew she had to do. What she wanted to do was to find any excuse to have him nearer to her. To feel the warmth of his breath on her face, smell the sweet muskiness of his cologne and wait expectantly for his mouth to claim hers.

But what she had to do was to push him away. She had to have learned something from her last disastrous relationship. She couldn't allow herself to develop feelings for Patrick, only to find herself disappointed again. This time she had her boys to consider. Becoming involved on any level with Patrick would be risky for everyone. Not to mention pointless. She was leaving soon anyway.

Patrick watched as Claudia seemed lost in thought. 'I should go.'

'I am a little tired,' she said, agreeing.

'Would you like me to call in to see you tomorrow?' he asked as he stood.

Claudia hesitated before she replied. She was torn. 'I'm not sure that's a good idea, Patrick,' she replied in a low voice.

'I really am sorry that I didn't tell you everything outright but there was nothing self-serving about what I did, I can assure you of that.'

'It's not that.'

'Then what is it?'

'There's no point to this…to…you and me…' She stumbled over her words, unsure of how to define a relationship she didn't understand. And one that scared her.

'To me visiting you when you have no one else in the country because your only family is the other side of the world?'

'It's not that, it's just that I don't really know you and…'

'We shared a life-changing experience and, quite

apart from that, I enjoy your company. It doesn't have to become complicated.' Patrick knew that wasn't entirely true. Just being near her was driving him to want more.

'I'll always be grateful for what you did, saving my boys and myself, but I'll be returning to London soon. And there's no need for you to keep me company when you have your own life.' She paused for a moment to cement the resolve in her mind. To make sure that she was doing the right thing. To remind herself that no good would come from stringing out the inevitable. Nor could she become involved on any level with a man who hid the truth, no matter how seemingly insignificant it might appear or whatever logical reason he could provide. It was a shaky point to hang her argument on, but it was all she had and she would use it.

She had to try to be more sensible like Harriet and less impetuous. And it had to start then and there. There was no time to rethink.

'You should find a nice young woman who lives in Los Angeles. Remember I have two little boys and you don't want children. You told me as much in the lift.'

'Whoa, slow down,' he said. 'You're thinking way too far ahead.'

Claudia smiled at his response. 'I have to, Patrick. I have my sons to consider.'

'And I would always consider your children. I helped bring them into the world and they are special little men. I couldn't forget about them.' It was the truth. Patrick's feelings for Claudia and her sons had grown very real. And his desire for her was equally real. 'Can you just let this play out and see what might happen?'

'No…' She drew a breath. Whilst it was lovely to

know how he felt, it didn't change what she had to do. She needed to look after her boys and forget about romance. It wouldn't be in the cards for her now or anytime in the near future and he was making her feel that it could be. And *should* be.

She had to cut him free and remove any risk of her becoming attached.

'I'm sorry, Patrick, but I think it's for the best if we say goodbye tonight…for good.'

CHAPTER SEVEN

PATRICK WALKED INTO his house, feeling more alone than before he'd met Claudia. He dropped his keys by the door and decided to take a shower and try to forget her. Put everything in perspective and move on.

As he lay in his bed, looking up at the ceiling in a room lit only by the moonlight, he wondered why he cared so much.

He didn't want a future. Or a family. She was being sensible and clearly he wasn't. For the first time in more years than he could remember, he had allowed his heart to lead him.

And his desire to kiss the woman whose face would not leave his mind that night.

He had so many questions he'd wanted to ask Claudia but he hadn't. Perhaps that was where he had gone wrong, he thought as he tossed again, throwing the bedclothes free of his body, dressed only in boxer shorts. If he knew more about Claudia he might better understand her need to push him away. She had obviously been hurt by someone.

He ran his fingers through his still damp hair and looked towards the bay window of his bedroom and the full moon suspended in the clear night sky and knew it had to have been Thomas and Luca's father who had broken her heart. She had put on a brave face when she had spoken of him having no interest in his sons but there had to be more to it. Walking away from the boys' father or watching him walk away surely wouldn't have been easy for a woman like Claudia. Her family values seemed so strong.

In that case, the man who'd fathered her children must have made her fearful of getting close to anyone. But why, he wondered, would any man treat a woman that way? It didn't make sense in the way he saw the world. A man should protect a woman, and particularly the mother of his children. He should lay his life down for her and his sons.

That was what Patrick knew in his heart he would do if he had been Thomas and Luca's father.

After a restless night and the acceptance that Claudia wanted to be alone, Patrick knew he had to keep a distance between them. But there was one last thing he intended to do. He would visit Thomas and Luca one final time to say goodbye. Even though they would never remember him, he would never forget them.

And he would always remember their mother too.

Claudia showered and changed into the silk nightdress and wrap. As the cool softness of the fabric fell against her skin, Claudia wondered who had been so kind yet secretive in gifting them to her. Could it even have been Patrick? She shook the thought from her mind. He couldn't have known she needed a nightdress and he'd had no time to go shopping as he had been spending all of his spare time with her. Running a soft brush through her hair, she looked in the mirror and thought it was definitely the prettiest nightdress she had ever seen, let alone worn.

And, as soon as she could, she would be contacting the store to find a way to repay them.

Claudia was feeling physically stronger by the day but emotionally drained. Insisting a man like Patrick leave her had been a choice she hoped not to regret but one she had an uneasy feeling that she just might. But she wasn't prepared to take the risk that she might be hurt again. Not any more.

The man made her feel butterflies in her stomach whenever he was near. Dropping the brush onto the bedside cabinet, she wondered what on earth had come over her. If she didn't know better, she would think that she had developed a crush on Patrick.

'Thank goodness, he's left your life,' she muttered to herself as she put the brush into her handbag and waited on the bed for her breakfast. She could hear the clanging of the metal plate covers as the trays were being delivered in the adjacent rooms.

'Here's yours, sweetie,' the food service worker said, bringing the tray into her room. He was an older man of African-American heritage, and he'd served her dinner the evening before. He'd been quite chatty then too.

'Thank you very much.'

'You're looking happy this morning. Any reason?' he asked, a curious smile on his time-weathered but cheerful face. 'I hope it's contagious 'cos there's some biddies on this floor that don't smile near enough for me. It's like they drink vinegar not tomato juice!' His smile wrinkled the skin around his warm brown eyes.

Claudia laughed at his words. 'I'm just looking forward to seeing my sons in the nursery as soon as I've had breakfast. The head nurse insists I eat before I'm allowed to travel downstairs so I'll eat quickly and get back down there.'

'They are very lucky little boys to have you as their mother,' he said before he left the room.

Claudia felt a lump form in her throat. That was exactly what Patrick had said when they'd met in the elevator. He had given her the same compliment and she had spat back at him something acerbic. She couldn't remember exactly but she knew it had been rude and uncalled for. She felt ashamed. Had she pushed him away unnecessarily? Had she overreacted yet again?

She also felt terribly confused. How could those few words from a friendly old man bring her emotions back to a level of chaos?

What was happening to her? Was Patrick already inside her heart and that was why the words hit home? She took the first bite of her toast and then dropped it on the plate and slumped back in her bed.

Patrick arrived at the hospital a little after eight. The heaviness in the warm morning air set the tone for the day. He had been gutted by Claudia's hasty and unexpected dismissal and had no choice but to accept he wouldn't see her again. But he would see the boys one last time.

The first patient at his private practice was scheduled for nine-thirty so he had plenty of time to visit Thomas and Luca and then head to his surgery near the corner of Rodeo Drive and Santa Monica Boulevard. He had been practicing in the ultra-modern office building for almost seven years and had no need to advertise as the post-operative faces and bodies willing to admit to having been his patients were testament to his skills. As were those people who wanted further freshening up over the years. However, he did set a limit and directed those who he suspected of addiction to cosmetic procedures to a therapist who was better placed to address their issues with body image.

The waiting list for a consultation and surgical procedures was growing but his passion for his work was not. He was dedicated and skilled but not excited. He missed that sense of excitement. The delivery in the elevator had been everything he missed about his former profession…and more.

Patrick strolled into the nursery and spoke with the attending neonatologist about the boys.

'So Luca has improved? How is the closure of PDA progressing?'

'It's looking good.' The doctor nodded as he continued to read Luca's notes on the computer screen. 'I think we'll be able to cease the medication in a day or so.'

Patrick's mouth curved to a smile as he looked at the tiny infant, dressed only in a nappy and pale blue booties that had been kindly knitted by the Mercy Hospital Women's Auxiliary.

'And Thomas? Is he still progressing?'

The doctor nodded again. 'Yes, no major problems with Thomas. There's a few milestones to reach yet, including weight gain for both of them, before they'll be discharged but they're going from strength to strength.'

'Great to hear.'

'I'll leave you to visit with them,' the doctor said and walked away to attend to another tiny patient.

Patrick stood watching over both boys. It had been

three days since their birth. Three days since he had met their wonderful mother. He wondered what their future would hold on the other side of the world and knew if things were different that he would ask if he could visit. Travel over to London and spend some time with them—and with Claudia. But that couldn't happen. He would never visit that city again.

He stayed longer than he had planned; being with them was a joy to him that was unexpected but welcome. Finally he stroked their tiny foreheads and turned to leave.

'What are you doing here?'

Patrick's gaze lifted to see Claudia staring at him. He couldn't read her expression.

'I came to say a final goodbye to the boys. You made it clear that you didn't want to see me again so I thought I'd call in and check up on them for one last time and leave. I didn't mean to stay as long as I did. I won't intrude again.'

Claudia looked closely at the man standing next to her sons. He had been watching them the way a father should look at his children. She knew their father would never do that. She had noticed the gentle way Patrick had stroked their little faces. They would never feel that love from the man who had requested she sign a confidentiality form and not mention his *involvement*.

Claudia wasn't sure if she was doing the logical thing but it suddenly felt right. At least it felt right for the next few weeks.

'Please, Patrick, you can sit a while longer if you like.'

Patrick did just that and then did it again every day for the next four days. Just after breakfast and before his day began, he travelled to the Mercy Hospital to sit with the boys and with Claudia. He still knew little about her past but whatever had happened had made her the woman she was and that was all he needed to know. Just being around her made him feel alive.

Could he possibly feel more? Could he take a chance of being a part of their little family? He wasn't convinced he would ever be ready but Claudia had made him want to believe it was possible. He tried to ignore the simple truth that his happiness would be short-lived, with her imminent return passage to London. Instead he enjoyed every moment he spent with her and refused to question the reality of what they shared and for how long it might last.

Claudia needed to stay until Thomas and Luca were discharged and that would give them even more time to get to know each other better. Perhaps if things went well she might extend her stay. He knew he was being hopeful but nothing about their meeting in the first place had been straightforward. Perhaps fate would intervene again.

Patrick smiled as he scrubbed and entered the nursery. Claudia was already with the boys and he couldn't help but let a grin spread wide across his face as he approached the three of them.

'How's my two favourite little men and their mother this morning?'

Claudia looked up at him from where she sat holding Thomas. 'We are all very well, thank you. In fact the doctor said the boys could be released before their due date. They might be ready to go home in four weeks.'

'That's great news,' Patrick said, feeling a little deflated that the three of them would potentially be leaving his life. Although he was thrilled to hear that Thomas and Luca were progressing so well, it also dashed his hopes that something might develop between Claudia and himself. All they had now were the next four weeks. He just had to make the most of every minute.

'I have a small confession,' he said one morning as they took a walk around the hospital gardens for fresh air after visiting Thomas and Luca in the nursery. Claudia was to be released the next day and he doubted they would see much of each other after that.

'What?' she asked, feeling very relaxed in his company and equally not wanting their time together to end.

'I'm very sorry that you gave birth in the lift and all that you and the boys have been through, but I'm not sorry that you shared *my* lift that day.'

Claudia felt her heart flutter but she knew she should fight her desire to make more of it than it was. Patrick lived in LA and she was heading back to London. She had to put their relationship in context. This feeling would not lead to more. No matter what her heart was trying to tell her head.

'I'm exceptionally glad I shared *your* lift,' she said lightly, patting his arm. 'If I'd shared a lift with a pizza delivery boy none of us might have survived…or at the very least the pizza boy would have been scarred for life.'

'Pizza boys do have to deliver under pressure, so that the pizza's still hot. He might have coped.'

'Now you're being silly,' she said.

Claudia turned to see the look in his eyes. His expression was serious. Almost a little brooding.

He took her hand to draw her in. 'I mean it, Claudia. I'm glad I was there. But not just because I could help deliver your sons. I'm very glad I met you.'

Claudia couldn't agree more but she couldn't tell him that. She felt her stomach fill with butterflies at the tone in his voice, the intensity in his eyes and the feeling of his hand against her skin. It was soft and warm and it pierced through all of her defences but she didn't want to give in to how she was feeling. She didn't want to get hurt again. She had to make him believe that she saw nothing between them when in fact she thought she was close to falling hopelessly in love with him.

They arrived back at the entry door to the nursery. They both stepped back as a nurse entered and collided softly with each other. Claudia felt the warmth of Patrick's firm body against hers. A tingling sensation overtook her entire body and it took a few seconds to calm herself. She closed her eyes for a moment, not trusting herself to turn and look up into his eyes so close. As she turned tentatively to face him, his lips hovered only inches from hers and she wanted nothing more than to lean in to him a little longer.

But she couldn't. She had to put a stop to any hint of her feelings. She was leaving the hospital. She had leased an apartment the other side of town and, while it had been wonderful with Patrick visiting every day and demystifying everything medical that was happening with the boys and being there when they'd both been transferred to the nursery on day six, she had to face the rest on her own.

She would be happy if Patrick continued visiting

her sons but she needed to stop fantasising about what might be between them. Nothing could become of them because she couldn't stay and explore that possibility. She belonged back in London with her only other family—her sister. She didn't want to be on the other side of the world in this city where—apart from with Patrick—she'd experienced little kindness. Her boys deserved a clean start in life and so did she. While Patrick seemed so very perfect, he was also perfectly settled in LA.

She couldn't tell all of that to Patrick. She would rather he didn't know the sordid story about Stone and hoped he would think of her fondly after she left. She had reminded herself of that every night as she lay alone in her hospital bed, wondering how it would feel with his strong arm around her. Or imagining the softness of his lips against hers when she woke in the middle of the night and all she could think of was him.

She waited until they were alone and Patrick had taken a seat beside the bed. 'There's something I need to say.'

'I'm all ears,' he told her as he stretched out his long legs and leant back in the chair.

'It's just that I'm leaving the hospital tomorrow so I guess this is the last morning we'll be spending together.'

He sat up, pulling his legs underneath the chair. 'You're leaving the hospital, not the country, Claudia. There's no need to make it sound so final.'

'It is final,' she replied. 'I've leased a place for a month…'

'You've found a place? I could have helped you out,' he said, cutting in, a little surprised that she had found somewhere to live without mentioning it before then. He'd planned on helping her to secure somewhere or even offering a room in his own home. It was far too big for one person and he would have been happy for her to take the guest room. But it was too late.

'I think you've been too gracious in offering help so I did this alone. I found a realtor and he secured a home for me. It's a little bit further out of town but it will be fine for the next few weeks.'

Patrick could sense her need for independence so he backed off.

'I'll more than likely be visiting the boys during the day and you'll be at your practice or operating so we might not bump into each other. That's all. But I'm happy for you to call in and see the boys if you like. They smile whenever you're around.'

'I don't think they recognise me quite yet; I think it's more likely wind but I'd like to continue to keep an eye on them.'

Claudia laughed. 'That means so much to me.'

'And you mean so much to me.' As soon as he'd said it, he knew it was too soon. But it felt natural and he didn't regret telling her.

'Please, don't. You don't know me. Not really.'

'I'd say, after what we shared, we know each other very well. We survived the most stressful situation. Surely we share a special bond.'

Claudia wished her world was different. But it wasn't.

'You're a good man, Patrick, but we can't be more than friends.'

Patrick reached for her hands and he wasn't deterred when she pulled away this time. He reached further until he had them firmly inside the warmth and protection of his own. 'We can be anything you want us to be while you are here.'

That was just it. It would only be while she was in LA. *Then what?* Claudia felt tears welling in her eyes and she couldn't blame it on hormones. Her heart was breaking just a little.

'I enjoy spending time with you,' he continued. 'There—I said it. I'm not promising anything, any more than you are. We are two expats on the other side of the world who happen to enjoy each other's company. Unless you don't enjoy my company?'

She took a deep breath. 'Of course I enjoy your company. I enjoy your company very much, but…'

'There are no buts from where I'm standing.'

'You're not making this easy.'

'No, I'm not. I think you're amazing and I think that it would be stupid to say goodbye tonight when you will be in the same city as me for the next four weeks, maybe more.'

'It seems a little pointless…'

'I disagree.' He paused over the words. 'I think we should continue to enjoy each other's company until you have to leave.'

Patrick knew that their relationship, whatever it might be, would have to end. He would never set foot back in the UK for reasons that he couldn't bring himself to share. His family were there and he couldn't see them again. Not after what had happened. In his mind it was better for everyone concerned for him to forget he'd once had a family.

'How are you getting to your new home tomorrow?'

'A cab,' she quickly replied.

'How about I take you? Absolutely no strings attached to my offer,' he continued with even greater speed. 'I'm operating in the afternoon. So I have the morning free to pick you up and settle you in. It's your choice, a smelly cab or chauffeur driven by me?'

Claudia felt her lips curving to a smile. He wasn't giving up. 'Not all LA cabs are smelly.'

'Not all…but why take the chance?'

She shook her head a little with frustration. Why did he have to be so handsome, so charming and so persistent? 'Okay…thank you.' There were a hundred things she could have said and each one would have been closer to how she was feeling but she couldn't allow herself that luxury.

'I'll see you back here in the morning,' he told her as he walked away.

Claudia offered him a smile as she wondered what she had let herself in for. And that thought played on her mind all through the night.

CHAPTER EIGHT

PATRICK ARRIVED MID-MORNING, just as he had promised. He knocked on her door.

'Anyone here needing a smelly cab?'

'Come in,' she replied, still feeling apprehensive about spending time together away from the hospital. It became a little more frightening to be in the real world with Patrick. 'I'm nearly ready. I spent a bit more time in the nursery with Thomas and Luca as I wasn't sure if I would be back again today until late.'

'No need to rush,' he told her. 'The meter's not running.'

She came out of her tiny bathroom with a few toiletries and, as always, her breath was taken away. He looked gorgeous and she felt sure his smile could melt an iceberg. She dropped the things into her oversized handbag and went back in to brush her hair.

'The address is on the bed,' she called out. 'I wrote it down on a scrap of paper.'

Patrick crossed to the end of the bed and picked up the paper. As soon as he read the address he shook his head. It was not a good part of town. In fact, it was straight out unsafe and, despite his resolve to respect her boundaries, he couldn't let her unknowingly put herself at risk. He decided not to say anything until she had seen it first-hand. It might not be as bad as he suspected. Her independence was akin to stubbornness, and he hoped once she had seen the location she would change her mind. He typed the address into his telephone so he could get the directions. He knew the general direction but it wasn't a part of town he frequented so he would need the GPS to find the street. He waited until she emerged in a pretty sky-blue sundress. It skimmed her knees and against her porcelain skin it looked, in his opinion, stunning.

'You look beautiful, as always.'

'Thank you,' she replied with a smile.

'Shall we go?' he asked as he picked up her bag and headed for the door.

'What about the account?' Claudia asked at Administration.

The young assistant flicked through the paperwork and then checked the computer screen. 'It's all been taken care of.'

'Are you sure?'

'Yes, your insurance company has covered you. Your sons' accounts will not be due until they leave the hospital in a few weeks' time, according to the notes.'

Claudia was relieved to hear that and Patrick was relieved she didn't ask any more questions about the insurance. His lawyer had contacted the international carrier and worked out an arrangement so that Claudia had no out of pocket expenses. But, with all the uncertainty between them, he didn't want her knowing he had stepped in to help.

They drove along with the top down on his sports car. The fresh air felt good after so long in the hospital air-conditioning. They talked about the boys and a little about Patrick's surgical roster for the afternoon and the time went quickly. As they drew closer to the street, Claudia began nervously chewing the inside of her cheek. The suburb was not what she had expected.

Finally they pulled up outside a run-down semi-detached house. It was worse than Patrick had thought it would be. He suspected a cab driver would have dropped her off without so much as a second thought so he was glad that he had insisted on taking her there. The two foot high wire fence was rusted and missing a gate and the front yard was devoid of any plants or lawn, save for the weeds that had made their way through the broken concrete. He looked over at Claudia and, while he could see her expression had dropped, she said nothing as she released her seat belt.

'You don't have to go in, you know that,' he told her.

'Don't be silly. I've given the realtor a deposit and I'm moving in today. The shell's a little worn, but I'm sure it's probably lovely inside. Besides, I'm not buying the property, I'm only renting it for a month.'

Patrick remained silent but he felt a chill run through him as they walked up the cracked pavement to the faded teal-blue house that looked as if it had not been loved in many years. Perhaps many decades. The wire screen on the security door was torn and would be useless in providing any level of security.

He watched as Claudia took the key she had been given by the realtor and, pulling back the screen door, unlocked the wooden front door and stepped inside. He followed closely, pausing for a moment to look over his shoulder at the neighbouring properties as he did. It was not a good part of town.

The house was quite dark inside for the time of day. Claudia reached for the light switch but nothing happened. They both looked up in the poor light to see the globe was missing from the hallway. An electrical cord was hanging down from the ceiling but there was no light fitting.

'I can get a new one,' she said as she made her way down to the brightest room at the end of the short corridor, which turned out to be the kitchen and was equally well worn. The floor was covered in pale green linoleum and it was almost bare, torn in more than a few places and lifting by the back door. There was a small table and two chairs but the wicker weaving was unravelling on one of the chairs, rendering it useless. The refrigerator motor was rattling and the back window looked out onto a car-wreckers' yard. There were no curtains or blinds and the hotplates on the stove were coated with years of burnt grime.

'It's only for a few weeks until the boys are ready to travel home. It's not as if I'd be bringing them here. It will just be me.'

Patrick remained silent, but he arched one eyebrow as he followed her into the bathroom. The shower was over a bath stained with rust where the water had been dripping from the tap and running down towards the drain. And the shower curtain was missing. The mirror on the cabinet above the basin was cracked and blackened in places by mildew. There was a small window of smoky glass for privacy but it too was cracked and Patrick suspected that with very little force the window would break completely.

'Let's see the bedroom,' Claudia announced, swallowing hard and trying to sound optimistic as she made her way into the larger of the two bedrooms. There was a double bed but no bedhead and a blue nylon bedspread with a faded floral pattern that couldn't mask the dip in the mattress. A free-standing oak stained wardrobe that had one door slightly ajar stood by the window. The dirty cream-coloured net curtains covering a stained blind sagged where they were missing hooks. Claudia crossed the dark brown shaggy-carpeted floor to close the wardrobe door and discovered that the handle was broken. 'I'll be living out of my suitcase anyway so the door doesn't matter. I'm not about to be picky,' she said.

'Claudia,' Patrick began in a serious tone, 'you can't be considering living here.'

'Of course I am. I backpacked around Europe in my late teens. It'll be an adventure just like that,' she replied as she walked towards the front door, noticing there were holes in the plasterboard that looked as if someone had put their foot through the wall. 'Shall we get my suitcase so I can settle in and you can get back to the hospital? I know you have surgery this afternoon.'

'So you're moving in?'

'Yes.'

'Then I'm moving in too; we'll be house mates. I backpacked around Europe in my late teens too, so I'll share the adventure with you,' he announced. 'Let's go take a peek at my room. I hope it's as nice as yours.'

'You're not living here; that's ridiculous.'

'And you don't think you living here is ridiculous?'

'No, that's different.'

'Not in my opinion. If you move in, then we'll do it together and both risk our lives and general wellbeing!'

Claudia shook her head and narrowed her eyes at him before she walked across the narrow passageway behind Patrick to the darkened room. Reaching for the light switch, Patrick discovered it didn't work so he used the light of his phone to see the room. It was smaller and there was a single bed and what looked like a grey chest of drawers. He walked across to the window and lifted the blind to allow them to see the room properly. It took him three attempts to lift the damaged blind but when he did he could see another short electrical cable hanging down from the ceiling. There was no light fitting and again the globe was missing.

'Looks like we both need light bulbs when we head to the store.' He patted the bed, not daring to think about how many years the faded orange bedspread had gone without washing. It was stained and frayed in places along the hemline. Then he noticed the chest of drawers was actually a filing cabinet and he walked over and pulled open the top drawer. 'Great, I can keep some of my patient files in here to work on in the evenings.'

'Don't be awful. You're teasing me now.'

'Not at all. If it's good enough for you, then it's good enough for me.'

'You're being stupid. You don't need to babysit me.'

'I'm not thinking of babysitting. In this part of town my role would be more bodyguard.'

Claudia put her hands on her hips and shook her head. 'It's not that bad. I used to drive through here on the way to the studio every day. I never saw anything untoward happen.'

'And what time was this exactly?'

'What do you mean?'

'I mean did you drive through this street after dark?'

Claudia thought back. 'Not dark but early evening and early morning.'

'Then you and I will spend one night here together and if everything is fine then we'll discuss it again but I think you'll find that after the sun goes down this isn't a nice place to live. There are gangs in adjacent areas.'

'I have an idea. Why don't I ask a neighbour, or the business out the back? They'll tell me what it's really like.'

Patrick ran his long fingers through his hair in exasperation. Claudia was as stubborn as she was beautiful and intelligent. 'Let's ask, but if you get the answer I expect then I hope you agree we should just leave.'

Claudia didn't agree to anything. She showed no emotion as they walked out of the house and along the sidewalk beside the fence to where they found the owner of the wrecking yard locking up for the day. He was pulling the tall wire fence closed and securing it with a heavy padlock. Claudia picked up speed so he didn't leave before she had a chance to speak with him.

'Excuse me,' she called out. 'I'm wondering if you could tell me a little about the area. I'm thinking about renting the house that backs onto your property.'

Patrick watched as the man's face fell.

'Listen, lady, do you see the two dogs over there?'

'Yes,' Claudia answered, looking at the two heavy-set black guard dogs that were chafing at the bit, waiting for their owner's signal to begin patrolling the yard.

'They're not here for their good looks. There's not enough money in the world to make me live in this neighbourhood.' He tapped his watch with his grubby fingernail. 'Three o'clock every day I'm outta here. I've got some clients that look after the yard, if you know what I mean. I work on their cars and they make sure that my yard and my dogs are still here in the morning.'

'Perhaps the dogs will look after me too. They'll scare away anyone who thought to break into my place.'

'Not a chance unless you want to live in my office. Sorry, miss, but you're on your own if you move into that house. You'd be dead crazy if you did.' He signalled to the dogs before he climbed into his utility and drove away. Immediately the dogs rushed towards the wire fence, gnashing their teeth and making Claudia jump back nervously.

'So do you think you need a second opinion or can we leave now and find you other accommodation? Unless you want to wait and ask a not so friendly gang member his opinion.'

'Okay, I get it. I suppose you may have a point,' she said with a decidedly sheepish look upon her face.

'May have?'

'Fine, the man confirmed your suspicions about the suburb. And I concede the house is not as nice as the realtor described on the phone. I can't believe he lied to me.'

Patrick didn't comment. There was nothing he needed to add except to ask her to get into his car while he locked up the house.

A few minutes later they were on the freeway and heading towards Beverly Hills. 'I'll only stop at your home long enough to make some calls and secure another short-term rental,' she told him. 'I can make a reservation in a hotel tonight if necessary.'

'Whatever you think is best, but my home is big enough for both of us.'

'Thank you, Patrick, but I won't get too comfortable. I'll be leaving in a few hours.'

It was only ten minutes on Freeway 405 and then three miles on Wilshire Boulevard before Patrick turned into a street lined with towering palms. The sweeping grounds of each of the palatial homes was perfectly manicured, and small gardeners' vans were dotted along the street with men in wide-brimmed hats busily planting and trimming the gardens. They drove a little way to a slight bend in the road and then slowed. Heavy black electric gates slowly opened and Patrick drove the car inside and the gates closed behind them.

He drove the car up the driveway to the front door of the double-storey white stucco mansion he had called home for two years. The property also boasted a tennis court, a heated swimming pool, spa and a four-car garage but Patrick didn't mention any of it. Cosmetic surgery had been kind to him, he admitted, but equally he had worked hard in his new field and had been recognised as one of the best by Hollywood's very particular clientele.

He helped Claudia out of the car and then opened the front door. 'Please go in; I'll get your bag.'

'I won't be staying,' she reminded him. 'Perhaps you should leave my things in the trunk.'

He smiled to himself. He wondered again if she had always been that fiercely independent or had circumstance made her that way? But, whatever the case, he understood she had every right to want to make her own decisions. He just hoped they didn't include another dubious choice of realtor.

'I'll get your belongings in case there's anything you need.'

Claudia spun on her heel to take in the magnificent surroundings. The foyer had a large atrium with a stone water feature. The sound of running water echoed in the large open space. Looking past that to outside, she could see more gently moving water. It was, she assumed, an endless pool and a panorama of the Hollywood Hills formed a backdrop.

'I will let you find your way around. The guest bedroom is on the ground floor, third door on the left, if you'd like to have a shower or a lie down. It might do you good to rest for a while. I can take you back to the hospital to visit the boys this evening.'

'You're being too kind. And too generous. It's unnecessary, honestly.'

'Claudia, it's a big house. I live here all alone and you're most welcome to stay here until you leave. I'd rather you were here than making *friends* in that neighbourhood! And, by the way, never recommend that realtor unless you really dislike someone,' he said with a wink before he closed the door and left her alone.

Claudia was more confused than she had ever been in her life.

The most handsome, kind, considerate man wanted her to live with him. She owed her life to him. And she wanted to be with him more than anything, but she couldn't. He had made it obvious he had feelings, not only by opening his home but also the way he kept reaching for her. But she wasn't ready to take that leap of faith and trust again. He was a kind man and as much as she wished he was the father of her sons, he wasn't. And she couldn't risk them all falling in love with Patrick. What if he walked out one day— the way that the boys' father had done? And turned her life upside down.

She had to be sensible and see the world the way Harriet would. Put a practical filter across her decisions and stop being led by her heart.

Certain and confused in equal amounts, she found her way to the guest bedroom and, kicking off her shoes, she sat on the bed. She suddenly felt a little tired and the bed felt very soft and comfortable so she thought she might just lie down for a moment. She told herself that she wouldn't fall asleep but just close her eyes for a moment, then she would call another realtor and find another short-term lease. And that night she would stay in a hotel.

Patrick came home to a darkened house but in the light from the porch he could see Claudia's suitcase still lying against the wall in the hallway. He turned on the lamp in the living room, unsure if she was at home or had caught a cab to the hospital. Quietly, he walked through his home and found her asleep on the bed. While it was still warm outside, the air-conditioning had kept the house cool and she was wearing a thin sundress so he pulled the throw rug up over her and closed the door. She was exhausted and he had no intention of waking her so he put a call through to the hospital to check on the boys. His call was connected to the neonatal resident.

'Dr Spencer, I've just finished reading the boys' notes for today. I did try to call Miss Monticello but had no luck getting through.'

'It was a big day for Claudia and she's taking a nap

now so that's why I've called. I will pass any updates on to her.'

'Thomas is still progressing well, as he did from day one, and Luca's PDA appears to be self-correcting. He'll be having another echocardiogram tomorrow but Dr Wilson is confident no further treatment will be required. So please let Miss Monticello continue to rest. She can come in the morning to see them. Both boys are asleep and will have their gavage feed in another two hours. There's no need for Miss Monticello to be here when the rest would do her more good.'

Patrick thanked the young doctor and hung up the telephone before he ran upstairs to change into shorts and a T-shirt. He would take a dip in the pool later but first he would cook some dinner for the two of them. He knew it was stupid to think there would be anything between them after the next few weeks but she was getting under his skin and he couldn't deny it.

For some inexplicable reason, he didn't want to let the dim future get in the way of a happy few weeks.

Life was short and so he intended to enjoy whatever time he could with her. She challenged him and just being around her made him feel alive. Her accent and her very British mannerisms surprisingly made him think almost fondly of London and even fleetingly of his family. And, in a deep dark corner of his mind, he thought perhaps there was a chance, however slight, that she could change her mind and stay in the US.

Claudia woke to the smell of cooking. Her eyes struggled to focus and for a moment she forgot where she was until suddenly it came back to her. She had lain down for a moment in Patrick's guest room. It was dark but she could feel the light weight of a throw rug over her. She didn't remember pulling it up so assumed Patrick must have returned home and covered her. The curtains were billowing with the cool evening breeze and there was light creeping under the now closed bedroom door.

Suddenly she sat bolt upright. She hadn't called a realtor. She reached for her phone and discovered it was after six, in fact closer to seven.

'Darn, bother, you silly cow,' she said as she rubbed her forehead and silently continued berating herself for falling asleep. Now she would have to find a hotel as soon as she had visited Thomas and Luca. She swung her legs down and felt around for her shoes before she headed in the direction of the light. She would thank Patrick for his hospitality and get a cab to a hotel, check in with her bags and then head straight to the Mercy.

There was no way she could accept his hospitality. Their relationship had already overstepped the boundaries of common sense.

Moments later, Claudia stood in the doorway to the kitchen, watching Patrick stirring something that smelt delicious on the stovetop. Suddenly her heart felt lighter. But her head felt terribly confused. He turned to see her watching him and she felt very self-conscious. A tingling sensation crept up her neck and onto her face and she felt certain the blush had spread across her cheeks.

'Well, hello sleepy-head. Did you have a nice nap?'

His eyes twinkled as he spoke and she tried to ignore her increased heartbeat.

'I did, thank you, but you should've woken me. I

slept for far too long. I need to get to a hotel and then see the boys.'

He lowered the heat underneath the pan and turned around to face her. He was wearing a tight white T-shirt and cargo shorts. His toned physique was cutting through both. His feet were tanned and bare on the large terracotta tiles.

'I've checked on Thomas and Luca and they are both doing very well. They were sleeping when I called but,' he said, glancing at the roman numerals of the large wall clock and then back to Claudia, 'they will have been fed again and should be tucked in again for another four hours or so.'

'I should have been there for that feed.' She was angry and disappointed in herself. She was convinced her boys needed her more than she needed sleep.

As if he sensed her self-reproach, he added firmly, 'You can't do everything, Claudia. The rest you had this afternoon was important. In fact, I told the neonatal unit that you wouldn't be back to visit the boys until tomorrow.'

Claudia was taken aback by his announcement and she felt her body tense. 'Why would you say that to them without asking me? Whether I see my sons or not is not your decision to make.'

'Well, in my capacity as a doctor it is. You need to get your own strength back, as I have said to you more than a few times. You'll be no good to your sons if you run yourself into the ground the first day out of hospital.'

'But I want to be with them.'

He shook his head and turned back to the stove.

While he admired her strength, he found her stubbornness in ignoring her own wellbeing frustrating.

'I'm all they have in the world.'

There it was again. Her reference to Thomas and Luca having no one but her.

Patrick nodded his understanding of her need to be with them but he wanted to at least get some food into her so she could keep up her strength. 'Then I'll take you there after dinner.'

'There's no need for you to take me. I can do it after I book into a hotel.' Her arms were crossed across her chest and her eyes were narrowed.

'Claudia, I know you have a need for independence above all else, but you have to look after yourself. And since you don't seem to understand the importance of taking care of yourself I'm more than happy to step up to do the job.'

'I'm perfectly capable of looking after myself and my boys on my own. I'll be doing that when I return to London in a few weeks.' She felt her neck tense with the thought of depending on any man again.

Her words cut through him like a knife. He wasn't sure if that was her intention but, if it was, she had succeeded.

'Point made,' he replied as he returned to the task at hand. Listening to his heart had been something he'd successfully avoided for many years and it appeared, from Claudia's reaction, it was something he needed to continue avoiding.

Disappointment suddenly coloured his mood. The heat was still under the large pan of boiling water so he dropped in the fresh pasta. 'If you want to share dinner before you grab a cab then you're welcome. If not, then I can help you out with your bag when the cab arrives.'

Claudia looked at him as he turned his attention back to preparing dinner and wished they had met under different circumstances. Before she had been so badly hurt and disillusioned. He appeared to be everything she'd once dreamed of finding in a man…but she was no longer looking and she doubted she ever would again.

He turned back to her for a moment. 'I don't want you to feel pressured, Claudia. That was never my intention.' His reply was truthful, his voice gentle and low—almost a whisper. 'I just wanted to help you… but I would never force you to do anything or stay anywhere you didn't want to be.' His voice trailed off.

Claudia wasn't sure how to respond. He had been a gentleman up to then and she doubted that would change…unless she invited him to alter his behaviour towards her. She started to wonder if perhaps she had overreacted. Once again since meeting him, she had been rude.

The first time had been due to her aversion to men and now, looking back, she knew he didn't deserve to be punished for another man's mistake. At the time she couldn't seem to help herself. But this time it was something else driving her to push him away. It wasn't his fault she was starting to have feelings for him. She wished she had Harriet on speed dial to give her logical, solid advice but it would be selfish to pull her sister away from something far more important in Argentina to ask her whether she should stay for dinner, stay the night or stay for a month.

No, she had to do this alone. She had to make a decision not based on another man's behaviour or her own doubts and insecurities. She had to make a decision based on Patrick's behaviour. And that had been nothing other than exceptional.

Just as exceptional as his broad-shouldered silhouette looked while stirring the delicious-smelling pasta sauce.

'If the invitation is still open, then perhaps I'll stay for dinner. But only for dinner.'

CHAPTER NINE

As CLAUDIA HUNG up her clothes in the walk-in wardrobe she prayed she had made the right decision. This was the second time she had rushed into moving in with a man she barely knew. Her life had changed so completely in the time since she'd arrived in Los Angeles and not much of it had been for the better, except for the arrival of her sons. She longed to return home. To where she felt life was a better fit and to where she felt a sense of family. Her internal compass was directing her back to London.

But she had unexpected mixed emotions about Patrick.

Where did he fit into her life? Would he be a part of it once she left Los Angeles or would he become a memory? A sweet memory, but nothing more.

Claudia had tried to think logically about moving in. They had only known each other a short time, but she and Patrick had a bond that she knew she would never share with another man. He had brought her sons into the world, saved their lives and saved hers as well. He was a brilliant obstetrician and while she wondered why he had not continued in that line of work, it was not her place to question him.

Was the fact he too was of English heritage a deciding factor in her feeling comfortable enough to move in? she wondered. Did he remind her of home? Did that make her feel safe? She prayed it wasn't a false sense of security.

There had been absolutely no pressure from Patrick over dinner; in fact he had even suggested a couple of hotels near the Mercy Hospital for her to stay in that night. His lack of insistence that she stay in his home but his genuine offer made her feel more comfortable to accept his invitation. And to apologise for being rude.

Everything happening in her head, and her fear of accepting Patrick's help, was her problem to deal with and in no way related to him.

'I will pay you exactly what I would be paying at a hotel,' she'd told him as they'd put the dishes into the dishwasher and sat down in the living room.

'The going rate for a hotel around here is just over a dollar a night.'

'Beverly Hills certainly isn't as expensive as it's alluded to be,' she joked. 'In all seriousness, I must insist...'

'Here's my business proposition,' he interrupted as he looked into her eyes, melting her heart a little further. 'Since I arrived in the US I haven't been able to find my favourite English toffee with almonds. It's amazing and nothing comes close. The almonds are toasted and the toffee's covered in dark chocolate. If you manage to find some, we'll call it even. Perhaps even arrange some to be shipped over after you return home. It used to be available at Harrods. There's no deadline, just a promise that one day I'll get my toffee.'

'English toffee in exchange for living in a home this beautiful?' She turned her head and, from her seat on the sofa, she surveyed the beautifully decorated room. It was elegant but simple. It wasn't stark but nor was it cluttered and the colours were warm earthy tones and the lighting softly added a glow to the room.

'You don't like the terms? Too steep?' he asked, staring into her eyes when they came back to meet his gaze. His lips curved to a smile and softly lined the stubble-covered skin on his jaw.

His voice sounded like the warm dark chocolate he was describing as the words flowed from his lips and Claudia involuntarily bit her own. Her heartbeat picked up unexpectedly and she closed her eyes and tried to blink away thoughts she was having about her landlord. He was far too gallant and handsome for his own good and most definitely for her own.

The French windows onto the balcony were open and the warm July breeze felt wonderful after the hospital air-conditioning so she carefully stood up and made her way to the door. Each day the physical scars were healing, but she just wished the emotional scars inflicted by the city would fade as quickly.

At that moment she needed to move away from Patrick, and the feelings she was having, being so close to him. She needed to step outside and clear her head in the balmy night air. She looked over the balustrade to the moonlight on the gently moving water of the pool. It was a perfect evening. The perfect house. The perfect man.

But, in Claudia's mind, she was so far from perfect. And life for her had never been perfect.

Patrick watched Claudia from his vantage point on the sofa. Her feet were bare and her short hair was gleaming in the moonlight. She seemed so at peace with the world at times, but at other times almost tortured. And so vulnerable. He had to control the urge to step behind her, pull her into his arms and tell her that everything would be all right. Protect her from whatever had hurt her or could in the future.

But he had no clue what the future held for her or for him. He barely knew anything about Claudia's past, apart from her losing her father and mother. Where had she gone to school? What had made her take the position in Los Angeles? And why didn't the father of her children want anything to do with them…? But, strangely, nothing about where she came from mattered to him any more. It wasn't her past, her family or her career that made him want to be with her. It was her attitude to life. Her strength. Her independence. Her beauty.

And her love of her children.

The next morning Claudia woke early and dressed in the shorter of the two nightdresses before making her way to the kitchen for breakfast. She thought she would make something to eat for them both and then head in to change before Patrick rose. Cooking breakfast would be her way of repaying his kindness.

But he was already up. And he took her breath away. Standing at the bench with a knife in his hand, he was cutting vegetables and fruit and placing them into a large glass bowl. Nearby was a small high-tech food processor. But her eyes were drawn to his bare chest and his low-slung shorts. Swallowing and trying not to stare at the perfection of his body, she looked out onto the patio, where she could see a gym bench and weights.

'Good morning, Claudia. I hope you slept well. If you need more covers or anything just let me know.'

She coughed to clear her throat. She needed to be polite and meet his gaze but that meant looking at his half-naked body again and worrying about her clothing being a little skimpier than she would normally choose. Ordinarily, that would not be a problem, but Patrick had to remain in the generous landlord category and she had to stay inside those parameters. She couldn't afford to entertain fantasies. She vigorously rubbed her arms as if she was cold. She wasn't. His presence was making her hot and self-conscious.

'Good morning,' she managed, trying to look around the room and avoid the obvious. Gorgeous, jaw-dropping Patrick, with both a body and smile to die for. And, first thing in the morning when most were struggling to open their eyes and look human, he was poster perfect. 'So you've been working out.'

He smiled back. 'Yes, I like to get up early and start the day using the outside gym. There are deck lounges out there so be my guest today and enjoy the stunning weather.'

'Stunning…weather.' She found it difficult to look at him and not have her eyes wander over his body in appreciation.

'I'm making a health blend with kale, carrots and a bunch of fruit. I didn't want to turn it on until you woke up since it sounds like a small lawnmower,' he said with a smile. 'Would you like one—I've prepared enough for both of us.'

'I'd planned on getting up early and cooking for you. You're already done so much for me.'

He shook his head as he crossed to the sink and washed the stickiness of the fruit from his hands then he slipped on a T-shirt that was hanging over the back of the high-backed kitchen chair. 'I'm always up at the crack of dawn in summer and I like a liquid breakfast after a workout. It gives me energy to face the day and I've got a full day of surgery scheduled so this will keep me going. Will you join me?'

Claudia was relieved that he was partly covered and her breathing had slowed accordingly. 'I'd love to, thank you.' She sat on a chair near to the bench where he was working and thought she would steer the conversation towards his work. 'So what surgical procedures are on today? Which starlet is going double D?'

He was dropping the chopped fruit in to be blended but paused to answer her question. Both of his lean hands rested over the top of the machine as he looked at her. 'I have two post-mastectomy reconstructions. A young mother in her early thirties and a slightly older patient who just celebrated her sixtieth birthday.'

Claudia felt so stupid. 'I'm sorry.'

'Don't worry; everyone does it…'

Shaking her head in frustration at herself, she continued. 'Just because everyone thinks the same way doesn't make it right. I was condescending and I made a sweeping generalisation. I'm so stupid for saying that. I should have known there would be more to your practice.'

'Thank you. Most people just shrug and don't apologise so please don't feel bad.' He paused for a moment. 'And, to be honest, I do my fair share of purely cosmetic augmentations. The holy grail of boob jobs, the double Ds and a few Es. Those surgeries allow me to perform the worthwhile ones at a much lower cost.'

'That's wonderful.'

'Well, I have a lovely home. Don't go putting me up on a pedestal.'

Despite what he said, in Claudia's mind he was a true gentleman and already up on a pedestal and she doubted he would fall off anytime soon.

One morning after Patrick had left for work, Claudia thought she would sort out the matter of the generous benefactor before she left for the hospital. She found the delivery docket in her purse and called the Rodeo Drive store. She was determined to repay the stranger's kindness and at the same time ensure she was not in their debt.

'I'm sorry, madam, but I can't divulge the sender's details. As with all of our account holders, they're a highly valued customer. This is an awkward situation and I would truly like to help but store policy won't allow me to do so. However, you are very welcome to exchange anything that you don't like or need in another size.'

'No, I don't need to change anything. It's all perfect.'

'We do pride ourselves on the styling and quality of all of our garments.'

The young woman's delivery was very eloquent and her tone leaning towards pretentious but Claudia knew that came with the location of the store. She bit the inside of her cheek. She wasn't going to accept the gift. She had to repay the sender but she needed to think of a way quickly before the young woman ended the conversation, no doubt politely, but, however it ended, her chance to repay her benefactor would be over.

'I have an idea,' she began in an equally polite tone, hoping to sway the sales assistant to agree to the thought that had popped into her head. 'Could I buy a gift certificate to the same value as the gift sent to me and you could mail that to them? If they have an account then you would have their mailing address. You are not breaking confidentiality because their details have not been given to me and you have just doubled your sales because they will have to visit your store to spend the certificate.'

There was no answer for a moment and Claudia assumed the sales assistant was considering her proposal. 'But they may want to know who sent it.'

Claudia wondered at the slight double standard when it came to account holders and mere mortals.

'That's fine. I don't have any problem if you let the sender know it was from me. In fact, I would be happy for them to know I had repaid the gift.'

The deal was done. Claudia gave her credit card details over the phone but the amount was even more than she had imagined. But, since she wasn't paying rent, she could afford it. There was nothing more she needed to buy for herself. She drew a deep breath at how extravagant the anonymous benefactor had been and would be hand-washing everything, hoping that it lasted for a few years, knowing what it had cost.

Claudia watched her little boys grow day by day, week by week. She was able to hold them and bottle-feed them and on the twentieth day they moved from the neonatal nursery into the general nursery. The warmth and serenity that she experienced every time Claudia held them made her happier than she thought possible and she didn't want them to be out of her arms. As she touched their soft warm skin and looked into their big trusting eyes she knew her life was complete. There was nothing she wouldn't do or give to Thomas and Luca for as long as she lived. Each milestone they reached in weight or developmental markers made her heart sing. She could imagine decorating Christmas trees with them and watching the joy on their faces as they unwrapped their birthday presents.

The boys' little faces filled out a little more every day and she could see subtle differences. Thomas was a little bigger and his mouth a little fuller and his mop of hair was thick and straight, while Luca's hair was curly and he was a leaner baby. Whether that had anything to do with his initial heart problem, she was unsure.

Claudia would arrive first thing in the morning at the Mercy Hospital and leave just after the sun set as the boys had settled into a routine and were ready for sleep. They had two feeds during the night, one at eleven and another at three in the morning, but the nursing staff insisted she get rest and come in the morning. The first time she was allowed to bathe them one at a time she had tears of joy in her eyes that fell from her cheeks into the tepid water. She was so nervous as she supported their tiny bodies in the water and then gently let the water splash over them before she wrapped them in a soft white towel and held them for the longest time.

When the weather cooled just a little so it wasn't too extreme, Patrick suggested a picnic outside for the four of them. At first Claudia was uncertain but when he walked her downstairs she caught sight of the checked blanket on the ground, complete with picnic basket, she nodded her approval. Together they collected the boys after their feed and took them down to the shady place beside the small pond. The sound of the water trickling over the rocks and running into the pond filled with oversized goldfish was relaxing.

'I think they'll enjoy fishing.'

'And what makes you think that?'

'It's just a feeling I have.'

Patrick didn't want to say that if they were his sons he would teach them about fishing, the way his father had, and they would learn to love it as he did.

Claudia watched him fussing over her sons and she had the feeling that, despite what he said, he would be a wonderful father.

The basket was brimming with wonderful picnic food; there were assorted sandwiches. It truly was a family outing. Whatever family meant, moving forward.

Claudia took photos of the boys with her phone camera every day as they grew. It would be a reminder of how far they had come and a keepsake for them when they were older. She decided to have a photo of each of them framed for Patrick. He had been so wonderful and she wanted him to have a memory of the little boys he had brought into the world. It saddened her that soon they would be worlds apart but it was a fact she had to accept.

She stopped at the drugstore on the way home one day and had two of the cutest photos printed and bought two silver-plated frames. And as she walked into his bedroom that afternoon to place them on the dresser as a surprise, she felt strangely at home. The room had a masculine feel to it but it was also warm… and inviting. It was decorated in muted warm tones of grey. Heavy deep grey drapes framed the window and the softest pale grey carpet covered the floor. The bed and bedside cabinets and the dresser were black and there were three large charcoal drawings on the wall behind the bed, also framed in black. The bed cover was the same tone as the drapes. It was a simply decorated room but stunning. The longer she stayed, the more she felt at home. She would have preferred that she felt like an intruder but she didn't.

Placing the frames on his bedside table, she left the room, her eyes surveying one final time where he slept every night. She wondered if his bed was as soft as hers and if he slept on his back or on his side. Did he toss the covers off or did he sleep peacefully…?

Every few days Patrick would stop at the hospital to check up on the three of them. And each time he did, Claudia felt her heart flutter as she watched him tenderly hold one of her sons. She couldn't help but notice that he was completely and utterly consumed by whichever baby he was given. He didn't take his eyes away for even a minute and he spoke to them in great detail as if they understood every word. Claudia had to remind herself that he was not their father. He gave such attention and love to them, it was often difficult for her to remember that simple fact.

Patrick gave her the use of his silver imported SUV to travel to Mercy Hospital. He knew it would help her to feel independent by not asking to be dropped off or catching cabs at all hours. He wanted her to feel the freedom she needed but still feel a sense of belonging. And it worked. She was extremely grateful to him but he did not exploit that gratitude in any way. She initially refused, as he expected she would, but when he pointed out the safety of late night trips back from the hospital she reluctantly agreed. But she insisted on putting in the gas and having it washed each week.

She cooked dinner for him two or three nights a week. And he continued to rise early and make smoothies in the morning. Occasionally Claudia would eat at the hospital so she could stay a little later with Thomas and Luca. And Patrick made Friday night their night together at the hospital. He brought fish and chips from a store owned by an expat from North Yorkshire who had relocated to LA and opened a café on Melrose. The shop was always busy and he would line up for thirty minutes just to place his order. Then Claudia would meet Patrick downstairs in the visitor gardens to eat their fish and chips together. It felt so good for both of them to step outside. They had enjoyed four Friday date nights and they were planning the fifth, the date they both knew would be the last. Claudia would be heading back to London in less than a week and, while she was looking forward to returning home, she realised leaving Patrick would be one of the hardest goodbyes she would ever have to say.

But she had no choice.

As they sat together on the patio at home one evening, Claudia sipped on her iced tea and looked up towards the stars, wondering if her parents approved of the man sitting beside her. She felt certain they would and it made her want to be honest with him about something they had never discussed. She curled her bare feet up under herself and turned to him.

'Is there anything you want to know about me? I mean, I've been living here and you've never pressed me about anything.'

'You have a sister, whom you adore. And she's over working in South America. And you worked in television.'

'What about the big elephant in the room? The one we've walked around since we met.'

'And that would be?'

'The fact you've never asked me anything about Thomas and Luca's father.'

He studied her for a moment. 'It's not my place, Claudia. I've just thought all along, if you want to tell me you will but if you don't then I respect you. You must have your reasons for wanting to keep it private,' Patrick told her honestly. He knew he had no right to ask. After all, he'd kept his past to himself.

Claudia smiled at his reply. It was so refreshing in a town where everyone wanted to know everyone else's business and it somehow made her want to tell him. Many times over the weeks they had spent together she had wanted to open up but hesitated, a little scared that his opinion of her might change if he knew the truth. Then she questioned why it mattered so much what he thought of her.

'I assume it's over between you.'

'Over as soon as he discovered I was having a child.'

'Don't you mean children?'

'No, he never stayed long enough to find out I was having twins. His lawyer informed me early on that he didn't want to have his name on the birth certificate and relinquished all parental rights. He's actually...' She paused as she stumbled over her words.

'There's no need to go there,' he cut in angrily. He was furious any man would behave so poorly and sensed she was feeling torn about discussing the boys' father. 'Unless you're in witness protection and hiding from a mobster, I have no interest in knowing about a man for whom I have no respect.'

Claudia smiled. 'I'm not in witness protection.'

'That's good news then...nothing else matters.'

Claudia nodded in silence. Up until now, she had given too much thought to telling anyone, let alone Patrick, that her sons' father was a married man. *Don't do it now*, said a voice inside her head. She felt confused by her desire for him to know everything about her. 'I thought he was a good man when I met him...'

'Claudia, any man who would leave you alone and pregnant with his children is a low-life bastard. I never want to lay eyes on him. If I did I wouldn't hold back so maybe it's best I don't.' His voice was loud and filled with anger.

Claudia was taken aback. She had not seen that side of Patrick. His emotions had always seemed so moderate but hearing that reminded her of her father. She knew he would have said the same if he was still alive. Suddenly she felt more protected than she had since her parents died.

'I didn't expect that response from you.'

'I don't sit on the fence, Claudia,' he responded. 'I don't tolerate cowards or fools and the man was both.'

Claudia was compelled to confess her part in the ugly situation. She was shaking inside because she was so aware that his opinion about her might change but all of a sudden she knew she wanted to tell him anyway.

'It's more complicated than that,' she began and then paused for a moment. 'The boys' father…he was married.' The words just came tumbling out. Her heart began racing as she saw his jaw tense and his eyes become more intense.

'Married! The guy is a bigger low-life than I thought. How dare he hide that from you and disrespect his wife at the same time?'

'You're assuming I didn't know he had a wife without me saying anything?'

'Claudia, I know that you would never have become involved with a married man if you'd known he had a wife. It's not who you are. It's obvious he kept it from you.'

'He did,' she said with her head bowed a little. Patrick was visibly distraught but Claudia realised with relief that he wasn't disappointed in her. His anger was towards the man who had betrayed her. But she wanted him to know the full story. She had to take the blame for her part.

'I should have asked more questions. I was naive…'

'He was probably a seasoned cheat and wouldn't have told you the truth anyway.'

'Perhaps,' she agreed.

'This town is full of predators. I've *freshened* up a few of them. Actors, producers, agents.'

'He's a producer, quite well known in the soap opera industry. I was working on his show and, as I said, I had absolutely no idea that he was married. He managed to hide it because his wife was away overseas, working on a remote set. She's an actress, much younger than him but not well known, not yet at least. She was apparently heading back to LA about the same time I discovered I was pregnant. He left the apartment we were sharing the day I announced we were to have a baby and I haven't heard from him since. Only his lawyer.'

Patrick ached inside to reach for her but he didn't. He didn't look at her; he stared straight ahead, scared that if he did look into her eyes he would sweep her into his arms and never let her go. It had only been nearly six weeks since they had met on the day the boys had been born but it seemed longer to Patrick. All along he'd suspected she had been hurt and now he knew by whom. The father of her children had been the one who'd inflicted the heartache.

He wanted her more than any woman he had ever met but he needed to wait until she was ready. If that never happened then so be it. But if she did open up and let him know she wanted him then he would make love to her with every fibre of his being and he would hold her in his arms all night long for as many nights as she would give him. He would try to heal every hurt she had every experienced. He would make her whole again, if she would let him.

'He'll pay the price for the rest of his life by not knowing his sons.'

Claudia opened her mouth to respond but couldn't think what to say. He had not questioned her or doubted her for a moment and she wondered how and why such a wonderful man had come into her life. Without thinking too much, she leant in to kiss his cheek but he turned his face at that moment and the softness of his lips met hers. It was an unexpected kiss but neither wanted it to end. She willingly pressed herself against his hard body. She wanted him as much as he wanted her. A welcome vulnerability washed over her as she realised how much she trusted the man she was kissing.

She trusted him more than she'd ever thought possible. And she was falling a little more in love with him by the day.

His hands trailed down the curve of her spine and she could feel his heart racing through the cool fabric of his shirt. Her heart synchronised with the beating of his and their kiss deepened as he explored her mouth. Without warning, he slowly and purposefully stood and reach for her hand to pull her up from the sofa. Once she was on her feet, he swept her up off the ground and into his arms, his mouth possessing hers again. Claudia's hands wrapped around his neck as he carried her into his bedroom, where he slowly removed every piece of her clothing. And then his own.

That night they both opened their lives, their hearts and their bodies to each other.

CHAPTER TEN

THE EARLY-MORNING SUN slipped through the gaps in the drapes and filtered onto the bed where they lay entwined in each other's arms. Claudia opened her eyes to see Patrick's handsome face only inches from hers. He was still asleep and she could feel his warm breath on her skin. Gently, she eased herself from his arms and moved to the edge of the bed in search of her clothing. It was his room, not hers, and there was no clothing in reach. Her eyes roamed the room, to find her things scattered all over the floor in a trail that led to the bed.

'Looking for something?'

She turned to see him propped up on his elbow watching her.

'My underwear.'

'I don't think you'll need that today,' he said, a spark in his eye as he pulled her back into his arms.

An hour later, Claudia woke to the smell of freshly percolated coffee. They had made love again and she had drifted into a deep and wonderful sleep. Patrick appeared in the doorway in denim jeans but no shirt. His face was freshly shaven. His hair was wet and slicked back.

'Why didn't you wake me?'

'Because, my darling, you needed your sleep.' He crossed to the bed and kissed her tenderly. 'You can have a shower and, when you're ready, there's breakfast on the patio.'

'You are spoiling me terribly.'

'I hope so,' he said as he kissed her again and she melted into his arms.

'I should get ready now,' she finally said as she pulled herself away. 'I want to be at the hospital for the boys' feed and bath.'

'Not a problem. We can eat and head over there together—it's still early.'

With that he disappeared and left her alone in the still warm bed with even warmer thoughts of him.

'There's one thing I really want to know,' she said as she traced circles with the tip of her finger on his warm bare chest and looked up lovingly at the man who had captured her heart as they sat together on the patio sofa enjoying the morning sun as they shared breakfast. She had showered quickly and they planned on being at the hospital by ten. 'Why did you really change career?'

'I found something else I enjoy—something that's rewarding and important.'

'I know, and I appreciate that you're not just fixing starlets' noses and breasts. I understand the other wonderful work you do, but you're very good at delivering babies too.'

'You only have your delivery to go on so I think your opinion may be somewhat biased.'

'There's no bias; I'm serious. You stepped in and saved us all. We owe our lives to you, Patrick.'

'You were the perfect patient...'

'Perfect patient?' She laughed and she lay back on the soft oversized outside pillow, staring at the cloudless sky as her thoughts rushed back to the day she'd given birth. It was overwhelmingly frightening sometimes when she thought about that fateful day and other times she felt so blessed and fortunate, as if the stars had aligned to place them both in the elevator. That morning, as she snuggled next to Patrick, she felt as if it must have been serendipity and she was so very lucky. 'I was perfectly horrible to you.'

'Initially, perhaps, but when labour started I think you handled yourself incredibly well. You were braver than any woman I know.'

'I don't know about the brave bit, but I do know that I was flat-out rude and chose the most inconvenient place for you to deliver the boys.'

'You didn't have much say in choosing the venue.'

'That's true...' she began but her words were cut short when his warm, soft lips pressed hard against hers and he didn't let another word escape until he had tasted her sweet mouth for the longest time.

Finally he released her. Her head was spinning, her heart was racing and it took her a moment to catch the breath he had stolen. Her thoughts about everything except the man beside her were muddled. Those thoughts were crystal-clear. She was unashamedly falling in love with him. She knew they had no certain future and they had no past, having known each other for not long over a month, but they had the present. She was falling for Patrick the way she had never fallen for a man in her life and knew she never would again.

'Let's get to the hospital and see your strapping

young sons—they may have gained weight overnight and be ready to come home.'

It wouldn't be *come home*—it would be *go home*—to somewhere far away, she thought with a pang of sadness in her heart.

Claudia smiled as Patrick helped her to her feet but his words had cut like a hot blade, piercing her heart and reminding her that home for the boys and her would be London. And Patrick's home was in Los Angeles. Their brief romantic affair would be that.

Just a short, sweet affair.

As they drove to the hospital, Claudia glanced over at Patrick. His slender masculine hands that now held the steering wheel had only a few hours before been stroking her naked skin and bringing her such pleasure that she'd never wanted it to end. His profile in the morning sun was the same handsome face that had woken next to her that morning. And she hoped they would wake together every morning until she left.

But, no matter what the future held for either of them, she wanted to know more about her devilishly good-looking obstetrician. And that meant understanding the decision he had made over a decade before. She wanted to be able to answer any questions her sons might have over the years. And even if they never asked a single question, she still wanted to know all there was to know about Patrick. He was such a wonderful man, but she sensed there was something he was hiding behind the sunglasses resting on his high cheekbones, gently shaded by morning stubble. It still seemed unusual to move to the other side of the world and begin all over again. To study another medical specialty and leave behind his family and friends. To never return home when there were clearly no financial barriers was all very puzzling. And, for an inexplicable reason, she had to know what had driven him away from the country she loved.

'Patrick,' she began softly as they pulled up at traffic lights only two blocks from the Mercy Hospital. 'Can I ask you a question?'

He turned to her with a smile that melted her heart. 'It depends.'

'Depends on what?'

'Will you let me plead the Fifth Amendment if I don't like the question?'

'The Fifth Amendment? But you're not an American citizen!'

'No, I'm British—we both know that,' he replied as he changed gear and took off as the traffic lights turned green. 'But I've been here long enough to feel comfortable using their constitutional loopholes.'

Claudia watched him smile. He was obviously trying to find a way to make light of something about his past he didn't want to discuss and his expression showed her he thought he had won.

'You know what, let's talk tonight.'

'Sounds fine to me,' he said as they drove along in the traffic heading towards the hospital.

Later, as they sat together on the patio in their swimsuits after a late-night swim, Claudia broached the subject again.

'I think you know everything there is to know about me,' she began as she ran her fingers through her wet curls to push them away from her still damp face.

'Where exactly is this going?' he asked as he began to kiss her neck where the water was trickling down from her hair. 'Because I would like to take it back to the bedroom.'

'Me too…in a minute, but first I want to take it back to the question I wanted to ask this morning.'

He stopped kissing her. 'Do we have to go there?'

'But you don't even know the question.'

'Do I really want to know? Let's leave the past where it belongs… I'm doing very nicely without it.'

Claudia sat up and turned to face Patrick. She doubted what he said was accurate. He had left everything behind. The reason had to be enormous. 'What is the deal with your family? Did you fall out?'

'I'm definitely pleading the Fifth Amendment. I told you I would this morning. Nothing's changed.'

His smile seemed forced. There was more behind it. She intended to find out exactly what. A man had once hidden a secret from her that not only changed the course of her life but that of her children. She would not and could not accept a man at face value, no matter how handsome that face.

'Patrick, I need to know a little more about you. It's important to me.' She drew a deep and slightly nervous breath. 'My cards are on the table. You know everything, good and bad, and you still want me in your bed, so please give me the same credit.'

Looking into Claudia's deep brown eyes, Patrick felt her searching his face for answers and realised that she wasn't going to let it go. Perhaps she had a right to know. She had opened up to him about her life. Perhaps it was his turn. Maybe if she understood his reasons then she would consider staying in Los Angeles and they could be together. He suddenly had to face the truth that he had more to lose by not opening up.

He could lose Claudia.

'Fine. We are…estranged. There's been no contact with anyone from my past for close to twelve years.'

'That's sad; I couldn't imagine life with Harriet.'

'Well, I suppose that's where you and I differ then,' he said flatly. 'I can live quite nicely without my family.'

Claudia suddenly felt as if the man beside her was not the same person. How could he not want to be with his family? Family meant everything to her. Losing her parents had been a crushing blow and to think he'd just walked away from his confused her.

'Have you tried to sort out your differences?'

'This is a little deeper than simple differences. I've rebuilt my life and don't want to look back or go back. My past and my family are not relevant to me.'

As he said it he knew it wasn't the truth. Every day he thought about his family. Where his mother was, what she might be doing. His nephew would be twelve now and he had not seen him grow up and it saddened him. But there had been no other option but to walk away and let them live their lives without him.

'It's relevant to me…I mean it was significant enough to make you pack up and leave,' she replied softly. 'I don't want to open old wounds but I do want to understand you better, understand why you won't return to the place you were born.'

He stood and reached for Claudia's hand and helped her to her feet 'Then let's go inside and forget about this conversation. Just accept my past is something I don't want to relive. It will do no good. My family and I have all moved on from each other. End of story.'

Claudia lay in Patrick's arms that night but they didn't make love. Nor did she sleep well. She couldn't. It worried her that there were things in his past he wouldn't share but they were significant enough to make him leave the country he had called home, leave behind his family and never make contact again and even change his profession.

It was all so confusing.

Who was the man lying beside her? Had she made a mammoth mistake in letting him have a piece of her heart?

She climbed from bed early the next morning and had a shower before he woke. She didn't want to pry any further. Clearly he had shut down her attempts and she was not going to push him for answers. But she knew she couldn't continue to see anything between them. Honesty and openness could not be a one-way street. And while he had not promised he would open up to her, in fact he had made no promises at all, she couldn't plan a future with a man who didn't have the same values as her.

What if she and the boys did stay in LA to be a family with him and he walked away from them all and never looked back if it became too difficult? Family was everything to her and she and Harriet had already lost those they loved most. How could he not value family the way she did? To not reach out in so many years, to patch up differences and make amends— it was all incomprehensible to her. Even if she had planned on staying in LA, it wouldn't work between them if he could place such little value on the importance of family and not explain why.

She gathered up her belongings, set them by the front door and sat on the patio and waited for him to wake.

'I'm guessing you can't leave this alone?' he said as he appeared in the doorway, dressed in shorts and a T-shirt. His expression was serious.

'No, I *can* leave it alone; in fact it's what I'm planning to do, but if I do then I have to leave us alone too. I rushed into this,' she said, shaking her head as she looked around the lovely home they had shared for over a month. 'I didn't really know you when I moved in. And I shouldn't have shared your bed for the past two nights. We're too different.'

'We're not different...'

'We're so different,' she argued. 'I would give anything to have my mother in my life. And you haven't spoken to yours in years for a reason you won't explain so I can't begin to understand. I think in time we will find more differences and I can't bring the boys into something that maybe won't last. What if you up and walk away one day and don't look back at the boys and me? My life back in London will last. My family is there. My sister. It's where I belong.'

'You don't think we have any future?'

'Not when you won't share a past that has fundamentally changed everything about who you were.'

Patrick sat down on the chair opposite her and took in a breath that filled his lungs. His long fingers ran through his hair as he looked at the ground. He realised he had no choice but to share his past or risk losing Claudia completely.

'It was almost twelve years ago,' he began without prompting. 'August seventh, to be precise.'

She remained silent but the fact that the date of his story came so easily to mind showed her just how traumatic the memory was for Patrick.

'It was a Thursday night and I took a call to assist with a high risk delivery in the county hospital where I worked in Durham,' he volunteered but the strain in his voice was obvious. 'I was an OBGYN resident and I loved what I did.'

She waited in silence for him to continue, which he did without any prompting.

'It was late, about ten o'clock, when a young woman was rushed into Emergency, presenting at the hospital in the early stages of premature labour.'

'You said you were called in; you weren't on duty then?'

'No, I had the night off. I was at the local pub with some friends from med school. It was a warm summer night; one of them had secured a placement at a hospital in New Zealand and we were giving him a send-off. Anyway, I got the call to head back. The senior obstetric consultant had left for London to speak at an OBGYN conference and couldn't get back until the next morning.'

'But if you were at the local pub you would've been drinking,' she cut in, her frown not masking her concern at the direction of his story.

He shook his head. 'Normally the answer would be yes, and by ten o'clock I would ordinarily have had a pint or two. But that night I'd finished my shift at the hospital with a bit of a headache coming on and, since I had an early start the next morning with a surgical schedule, I thought if I had even one glass of alcohol that I wouldn't pull up well. I stayed on ginger beer all night. I was perfectly fine to take the call—to be honest, I wish I had been drinking and had to refuse but I accepted and headed in to what would essentially be the end of my career in obstetrics.'

Claudia began nibbling on her lower lip. 'I still don't understand. You did nothing wrong; you hadn't been drinking...'

'I hadn't...but, with the tragedy that unfolded, some thought otherwise. That was the only conclusion they could find for what happened in the operating theatre. They couldn't accept that a high risk pregnancy extends to a high risk delivery. Anyway, I scrubbed in and began the Caesarean, but very cautiously as there was a complication, as I mentioned. The placenta was growing outside of the uterus wall and, despite me doing everything textbook and taking precautions along the way, the patient began to haemorrhage. I lifted the baby boy clear of the womb but as there was so much blood I couldn't see where to begin the repair. The blood loss was too great and, despite the whole team doing everything we could, we lost her on the table. There was nothing I, or anyone, could do. The theatre staff knew I had done everything right and told me as much but the jury were sitting outside in the waiting room and, to be honest, the worst juror was myself. I took the blame before I saw them—they just reinforced my feelings.'

'Why would you do that? You knew it wasn't your fault and the medical team knew it wasn't...'

'For me, overwhelming guilt that I had not been able to save her and, for them, their own grief turned to anger when they were told I had been seen having *drinks* at the local only an hour before. It cemented it in the minds of the family that I had to have been drinking and that was why their little girl died giving birth.'

'Why didn't you fight? Surely there must have been something you could have done? It's so unfair that you did the right thing in returning to the hospital and you tried to save the woman and you had the family blame you on circumstantial evidence.'

'It shattered my world. I was grieving too, and they needed someone to blame for the loss of her life. I decided it was my duty to take that blame.' Patrick paused and stared at Claudia thoughtfully and in silence for a moment. He didn't want to tell her any more. He had omitted the most important fact in the entire tragedy. The one that had changed his life completely. But he had to be honest. She deserved to know the truth.

With a heavy heart, he closed his eyes. 'The young woman who died…was my sister.'

CHAPTER ELEVEN

'Your sister died having her baby?'

He nodded, unable to bring himself to say the words again.

'So it was your own family that blamed you? It's so sad that she died, but why would they do that? I don't understand—families don't do that to each other.'

'It's not their fault. It was complicated,' he said, trying to validate their behaviour. 'No one knew Francine, or Franny, as we always called her growing up, was a high risk so to them her death had to be due to negligence.'

'Surely your brother-in-law knew there were complications?'

'No, he had no idea.' Patrick shook his head. 'I assume she kept her medical condition from us because she didn't want anyone to worry. We had just endured another tragedy a few months before, so she was trying to protect everyone.'

'What sort of tragedy?

'My younger brother, Matthew, died six months before.'

Claudia covered her mouth with her hands as she gasped, 'Oh, no.'

'My father and mother had divorced a long time before; I was young when it happened. My mother raised us. One Saturday my mother went up to Matthew's room to wake him as he had friends waiting downstairs to head to Brighton for the day. She found him in bed, which was unusual since he was an early riser. She patted his legs to wake him, but my brother was unresponsive so she pulled the covers down and found he was bleeding from the nose and mouth. My mother called out for help from his friends and dialled for an ambulance, hoping the paramedics would somehow revive him. They couldn't and he was pronounced dead on arrival at the hospital.' Patrick's jaw was clenched and Claudia could see he was struggling to make eye contact.

Claudia's brow was knitted in confusion. She wondered if it might have been a drug overdose but she said nothing. Asking such a question seemed cruel and unnecessary. The details made no difference. Patrick had tragically lost his younger brother.

'The autopsy report from the coroner's office came back with suspected lung aneurism,' Patrick offered without prompting. 'In simple terms, it's a ruptured artery in the lungs, which meant he drowned in his own blood. It's extremely rare and nothing that could have been predicted. Matthew had been a medical time bomb for a very long time.'

'I'm so sorry.' Claudia couldn't find any other words. Nothing she thought to say seemed to be adequate for the tragedy she had heard. His family had been dealt an overwhelmingly sad time.

'It was the worst time in my mother's life, in all of our lives. My father attended the funeral but after that he kept his distance again. My maternal grandmother was alive, but only barely, as she was living in assisted care; the shock of the broken marriage was difficult but hearing that her grandson had died was what I believe sent her into a depression that she never really recovered from.

'Then Franny discovered she was pregnant. It brought some joy back to our mother and to our family. She was focusing on the new baby on the way and I don't think that Franny wanted to bring her down with worry. She wanted her to hold on to something. The thought of a baby arriving gave us all a light at the end of the tunnel. We knew she was having a boy, that part she shared, and in some way I think the fact another boy would join the family made losing Matthew *almost* bearable for our mother. I'm assuming Franny didn't want our mother to be anxious and, while I understand her wanting to protect her, she should have confided in me. I could have ensured the best antenatal care and would have been prepared, going into surgery.'

'So she never took her husband to any of her obstetric visits?'

'No, Will never attended any of them.'

'Still, whether they knew or not, I can't believe they would blame you.'

'They didn't understand, even when I explained that her medical condition translated into a high risk delivery.'

'But, without any medical knowledge, it still doesn't make sense to throw the blame your way; it all seems unfair and so wrong.'

'Don't forget I'd been seen in the pub; they forgot

everything about her condition and focused purely on my supposed drinking.'

'But you hadn't been drinking. Couldn't you have a blood test and prove it?'

'I didn't think to have the test the night she died as, since I hadn't been drinking, it didn't cross my mind to cover myself and the allegations came out the next day from my brother-in-law's family. One of his cousins had seen me at the pub and, despite me telling them otherwise, they didn't believe that I had been completely sober.'

'But couldn't your friends corroborate your story?'

Patrick nodded. 'They tried, but his family was convinced it was just my medico mates covering for me. The whole medical fraternity banding together to protect each other conspiracy theory.'

'And your brother-in-law believed them?'

'He was upset, he was half out of his mind and he got swept up in the witch hunt. There was even footage taken on a mobile phone of another celebration in which I featured in the background. It was all over. You have to remember I lost my sister that day. I couldn't argue in my frame of mind. I was grieving too.'

'What about the rest of your family? Your mother and father?' Claudia frowned in perplexity. It all seemed so wrong.

'My mother was barely functioning and she believed what she was told. My negligence had taken away her beloved daughter.'

'But you had tried to save your sister, with no knowledge of her medical condition…and I know it couldn't bring her daughter back, but she had a grandchild. The grandchild that you had brought into the world.'

Patrick ran his hands through his hair in frustration. 'I was hung, drawn and quartered by the town. There was no coming back from that so I left. It was best for everyone.'

'Are you sure about that?'

'The grief blanketed both families and I guess I just couldn't face the arguing. I made the decision to leave. If either family wanted to look into it further I left the name of her obstetrician, but they never called. They didn't want to look further than me for the cause. It was their choice to direct the blame at me and it was my choice to walk away.'

'It's all so terribly unfair.'

'Yes, but it's done.'

'And your brother-in-law and his son…?'

'Will named the little boy Todd after his father. Todd turned twelve this August. He's a tall boy like his father and doing well at school.'

'So you speak with your brother-in-law then?'

'No, I haven't heard a word from him since I left. A friend from university lives not far from him; their boys go to the same school. He keeps an eye out for them and keeps me up to date. I set up a trust fund to cover his college education. Will gave up work for a period to raise Todd and then found it hard to get back into the workforce so had to start again at entry level. I feel I owed him to take care of Todd.

'So now you can understand why I choose to live over here. It's simpler for everyone.'

Claudia saw everything so differently. 'While I understand your need to leave, and I think what happened to you is almost unforgivable, it's still your family. You can't turn your back on family. Your mother lost her daughter and both sons within months of each other.'

'I'm still here. I didn't die.'

'No, but you left her life. For a mother it would be the same level of grief.'

Patrick leaned back against the chair. 'No, it's not the same. I'm here but she chose not to contact me. Nor did Will.'

'Perhaps your absence cemented their doubts about what happened. You could have gone back anytime over the last twelve years and cleared it up.'

'I'm not about to stir up all that again. I have built a new life here and reconstructive surgery has been good to me.'

'So you gave up obstetrics because you couldn't save your sister.'

'Yes,' he said solemnly and without hesitation. 'I had nightmares about her lying lifeless on the table at my hands…I lost the will and drive to practice.'

'But it wasn't because of anything you did.'

Patrick felt his body tense. 'I couldn't face that sense of helplessness again. Being unable to save Franny was something I could not relive.'

'But you did…with me. And you saved me. You didn't know I had a serious condition and you saved me from dying.'

'No, the paramedics came in time to save you.'

Her face became even more serious. 'They took over but you had kept me alive.'

Patrick knew the best thing he had done was to walk away from obstetrics and his family. And he knew that Claudia was testing that resolve. 'Fine, I kept you alive but I can't go back to that. I'm content with my work. I live here now and I'll never set foot back in the UK.'

'But your work here, now, it's not your first love.'

'No, but you can't always have everything you want, Claudia, including your first love.'

She couldn't ignore the resolve in Patrick's voice. 'Have you never thought about returning to Durham and facing your accusers and telling the truth?'

Patrick rolled his eyes and did not hide his exasperation. 'There was no evidence. Nothing to support me and everything to support their accusations.'

She shrugged. 'But you walked away from your career…and your life…because of lies.'

Patrick's body went rigid and his voice became harsh. 'I didn't walk away from anything. I left to make it easier for everyone.'

'Why can't you face the past now then? Rebuild your life in London? It was twelve years ago and I'm sure your mother would give anything to hold you in her arms again. You're her only living child.'

'No. I can't and I won't go back. My life there is over. It ended the day I left.'

Gaping at him, Claudia exclaimed, 'That's so dramatic!'

'My sister died, Claudia. They all think I caused her death. *That* is dramatic.'

Claudia frowned at him while she scrutinised his face. His expression was severe. His jaw appeared more pronounced. 'I'm just saying perhaps you could explain it properly. Have your peers explain it again. Franny's obstetrician could sit down with your mother and tell her the truth. It would have been near on impossible for your mother to pick up the telephone and speak with him. But you could facilitate that conversation. Make her see reason. Would that be so hard for you to do?'

'It's too late. They've moved on with their lives.'

'It's never too late. No mother moves on from a child.'

'I'm not so sure.'

'I am. I couldn't imagine a day without Thomas and Luca in my life. I would travel to the end of the earth to be with them and you should do the same for your nephew. You've chosen to give up without a fight.'

'Fighting is overrated.'

'Not in my books. I need a man who will fight for family.'

Patrick stood up and crossed back to the doorway. His face was taut as he knew at that moment exactly how Claudia felt.

Claudia sat staring ahead. Her heart was aching with the reality that had just been spelt out to her. 'It's been a long time and your mother would probably be stronger now. Don't you think you owe it to her to let her know what really happened? I would want to know.'

'Claudia, let it go.'

'You mean let us go?'

He rubbed his clenched jaw. Claudia noticed his eyes suddenly looked tired, almost battle-worn as he spoke. 'The choice is yours.'

CHAPTER TWELVE

PATRICK STIRRED FROM a tortured sleep the next morning, knowing that his every reason for waking up was gone. Claudia had left. She had grabbed her belongings and caught a cab. She'd told him where she would be staying if he changed his mind and wanted to talk but he left the slip of paper by the bed. He had no intention of calling. She was right—she deserved to be with Harriet. Family was important to her. He had learned to get along on his own for a long time. He missed his mother and his brother-in-law and wished with all of his heart some days that he could be there to watch his nephew grow up. But he couldn't. The wounds had healed on the outside and he didn't want to rip them open by travelling home.

It was better to let her rebuild her life back in the UK. She would settle in quickly and no doubt move on.

She would forget about what they'd shared in time and someone else would take his place.

But he wasn't sure he would ever move on.

Claudia had brought more joy and happiness into his life than he had dreamt possible. She was everything he could wish for in a woman and more. And he had let her walk away.

He had never felt so empty and it filled him with regret to walk away from Claudia but there was no other choice. What she expected from him was impossible. How could he face his family again? Where would he start? Would the blame still be there? The desolation in his mother's eyes—so empty, so blank, so lost and hurt by him that he could never go back. He just couldn't. It was better to leave the past behind.

When he'd discovered she had left that morning he had tried to push what they had shared from his mind but, waking on the second day, it became a reality. And he could no longer ignore the way he felt. A cloud had moved over his world and it was suddenly a much darker place, devoid of everything he had come to love.

Glancing around the room, his eyes came to rest on the bedside table, where the framed photos of Thomas and Luca were resting. It was the first time she had reached out to him and let him into her world. He now knew how difficult that had been for her but she had fought her doubts and insecurities, and waded through the hurt, to let him know that he meant something to her and the boys.

Next to the photographs was the note she had left— and her pearl earrings.

A rush of memories assailed his mind.

The day they'd met in the elevator. How beautiful he'd thought Claudia was and how he'd quickly discovered her looks were matched with her feisty spirit. She was a strong woman on the outside but inside she was filled with love. That day he had witnessed the level of that love for her sons and, weeks later, experienced first-hand her capacity for love when she'd shared his bed.

And he had let her leave.

Perhaps she was right. He had taken the easier option. But that suited him. He had adjusted to the values in the city. At least that was what he would have to tell himself. He climbed from bed and headed for the shower. He had the day off and no idea how to spend it. Claudia was gone and he couldn't visit Thomas and Luca. He had to become accustomed to life without them and that wouldn't happen if he tried to reach out to them even one last time.

After a quick shower, he dressed in a polo shirt and jeans and, looking for something to occupy his mind, he decided to head to his practice. His hair was still wet and he was unshaven but he knew he wouldn't be seeing anyone at that hour. There had to be some paperwork to finish, reports to finalise and mail to check. Anything to stop him rethinking the decision he had made.

As he entered the garage he looked at the SUV that Claudia had been driving and made a mental note to call a dealership and trade it in. He didn't want to be reminded of what he had lost every time he saw the car that he now considered to be hers.

There was little traffic that early in the morning and he was at work in less than ten minutes. The cleaner was leaving as he pulled into the undercover car park; they acknowledged each other with a wave before the young man climbed into his van and left. Patrick took the stairwell to his first floor office. It was empty and quiet. So quiet that his own thoughts were almost deafening. He wished the cleaner had stayed so the sound of the vacuum could drown out the doubts that were pounding inside his head.

He rifled through the papers on his desk and then noticed the pile of mail that his receptionist had sorted and put aside as not urgent. He hadn't looked at it for a few weeks but he trusted Anita would have brought anything important to his attention.

He read them one by one but nothing brought even a hint of enthusiasm to him. There was an invitation to attend a benefit for the Screen Actors Guild at the Beverly Wilshire; an invitation to drive a new luxury sedan that had arrived at a dealership in Santa Monica; a bi-monthly magazine from the Cosmetic Surgeons of America and numerous professional association offers and advertisements. It was all as he'd expected.

Then he spied a gift certificate from an expensive women's store on Rodeo Drive; it was only three doors down from his practice. He picked up the beautifully presented certificate and noticed it was for a sizeable amount. He wondered if they had made a mistake sending it to him, then he froze. This was the same store where his receptionist had ordered some pyjamas and toiletries for Claudia all those weeks ago. But why would they be sending him a gift certificate? It was far too generous to be a thank you in return for his business. He turned it over and found a note on the back.

Dear Dr Spencer
Miss Monticello insisted that she repay the kind-
ness of the 'anonymous' customer. We did not re-
veal your details; however, she insisted that she
provide a certificate of equal value to you. We

hope a lovely lady in your life can enjoy shopping in our store in the near future.
Warmest regards
Camille and staff

He closed his eyes and dropped his head back to look up at the ceiling. He knew he had to be the most stupid man in the world. She still had no idea that he had sent the parcel. She'd just wanted to repay a stranger. She could have just walked away but she had so much pride and honesty she had found a way to return what she didn't feel in her heart was hers. In a city of people who were only too willing to take, Claudia wanted only to give. And he knew she would have struggled to have covered the cost. She had so little money but she still did the right thing. She never let her values slip or chose the easy way out.

She'd fought so hard to bring her boys into the world. She never gave up on who or what she loved, no matter what obstacles she faced.

Claudia was an amazing, wonderful woman and he had just let her go.

She had dropped her walls, despite all the disappointment she had endured; she had let him into her life and her heart, and how had he repaid her? He had been as cruel as the father of her children. Perhaps even worse, he berated himself, because he knew what Claudia had been through. And she had allowed him to become a part of her babies' lives.

His head was upright as he stared at the door. His jaw flicked with mounting fury. At himself and the lies that had changed his life. He drew breath and filled his lungs, and suddenly felt adrenaline rush through his body.

He wouldn't let it happen again. Walking away from a life with Claudia, Thomas and Luca was not what he wanted to do. Not now, not ever. He wasn't sure he deserved them but he knew he wanted to fight to have them in his life. The thought of the boys' birth certificates having no father listed made him want even more to be the father figure in their lives. To guide them and to love them. If Claudia would let him, he would willingly take on that role. Forever.

He knew that meant reconciling with his family, no matter how difficult that might be. Perhaps time had healed some wounds, perhaps not. But Patrick wasn't about to base his future on assumptions. He would visit and see first-hand. And if they didn't want him back, then he would accept it but he wouldn't run away. He wanted a life back in London with Claudia...if she would have him.

He threw down the certificate and raced from the office. He had to prove to Claudia that he would fight for her and her boys and their future. He would do whatever it took. It was time to take a stand.

There was just one thing he had to do before he left to find her—he had a flight to book to London.

Claudia had packed her suitcase and left it by the door for the concierge to collect as she made her way to the hotel lobby to check out. Her tears had finally dried. She told herself firmly that Patrick Spencer would be the last man she would waste precious tears on. She would concentrate on raising her sons and forget about any other love. Her boys would be enough to fill her life and she knew they would never let her down. And, more importantly, she would never let them down. She would be there for them and give them everything they needed, growing up. And she hoped one day as grown men each would find their true love and she would be happy for them.

With a sigh for what might have been, she approached the reception desk.

'Good morning, Miss Monticello, are you checking out today?'

The young woman was dressed in a corporate charcoal suit, tortoiseshell glasses and a pleasant but predictable smile. Her hair was pulled back in a sleek chignon.

'Yes, I am. Can you please add a bottle of lemonade I took from the minibar to my credit card along with the room charges? I was staying in Room 303.'

The receptionist checked the computer screen and handed over the account.

Claudia passed over her credit card then tucked her hair behind her ear as she stood waiting for the card to be processed. She felt for her pearl earring, the way she always did when she was nervous. But it wasn't there. Her hand switched to the other ear. That one was missing too. She hadn't even thought about them for two days. Her head had been filled with thoughts so much more demanding of her time than her jewellery. She suddenly remembered she had left them on the bedside table. Patrick's bedside table.

'Are you looking for these?'

Claudia spun around to find a dishevelled Patrick standing behind her, her earrings in his outstretched hand.

'I would like to speak with Miss Monticello in private,' Patrick told the young woman at the desk, now looking at both of them. 'Do you have a room available?'

'The business centre has some private meeting rooms,' the receptionist told them, adjusting her glasses. 'You're more than welcome to use one of those.'

'Thank you,' Patrick replied, glancing around the lobby and spying the business centre.

'There's no need to thank her; we won't be using the room,' Claudia retorted, shaking her head in defiance. 'There's nothing I need or want to say to you, Patrick. I'm leaving today. We're over.'

'There's so much I want to say to you and I'd like to say it in private.'

With a look of discomfort Claudia felt certain was due to the potential for a situation to play out in her lobby, the receptionist interrupted. 'As I said, you're both more than welcome to use any of the meeting rooms and at this hour they're all free.'

Patrick led the way and crossed the lobby foyer with long purposeful strides and waited by the door of the business centre for Claudia's response. In silence she begrudgingly walked up to him. With each step across the large Mexican-inspired tiled floor of the lobby, the ache in her heart made her more resolute in her decision to end this meeting as soon as possible and never see Patrick again. She was angry and hurt in equal proportions that he had made her so vulnerable. She would hear him out then leave before she weakened and let her heart tell her what to do. She couldn't live her life with a man who had such different values to her own.

He softly closed the door behind them. 'I've got

so much to say to you, Claudia, and it begins with an apology.'

'There's no point. I don't want an apology.'

'But you deserve one. I should never have let you walk out of my life and I apologise for that. I've been the biggest fool and you were right. I need to fight for what's important. That's you *and* my family. Claudia, I don't want to lose you and I'll do whatever it takes for us to be together, if you'll let me.'

'What do you mean *if I'll let you*?' she demanded. 'What are you telling me?'

'I want a life with you and your sons.'

'I can't stay here in LA; I told you that.'

'I know that and I wouldn't want you to stay here,' he said, taking her hands in his. 'I want to come home with you. I want to go back to London and do what you made me realise I should have done years ago. I want to set things right with my family. At least try to anyway.'

Claudia didn't pull her hands free as her expression turned from confusion to something closer to joy. 'Are you really serious about that?'

'I've never been more serious.'

'But why now? What's changed in two days?'

'I had time to think. Time to miss you and realise it's something I should have done a long time ago. Because I don't want to lose you or the boys.'

'And when are you planning on doing this?' Her voice did not betray the happiness she felt building inside. She did not dare to allow herself to believe he wanted a life with her, only to be disappointed again.

'As soon as I can sell the practice, I will move home to the UK permanently. You're right, my first love has always been obstetrics. And I can do it. I can honour my sister's life and her bravery by bringing more children into the world, not trying to forget what happened.'

'You really want to go back to what you had before?'

'It won't be exactly what I had before. So much has changed, but I will deal with everything if I have you in my life.'

'This is a huge commitment to change everything about the life you lead. It's a big adjustment.'

'And it's one I need to make.'

'Then I will see you when you arrive,' she said, hoping with all of her heart that it wasn't an empty promise. She had become a realist and knew it might take time to sell the practice. In that time he might change his mind.

'You will see me sooner than that. I'll be travelling with you in about four hours' time,' he told her as he looked at his watch. 'You'll need help with the boys on the long haul flight…and to settle into your home.'

'You're travelling from LAX to Heathrow with me tonight?'

He pulled the airline ticket from his back trouser pocket. 'If you'll let me.'

Claudia smiled in return and immediately felt herself being pulled into Patrick's strong embrace and his lips pressed tenderly against hers. He pulled back for a moment to look lovingly into her eyes.

'I love you, Claudia Monticello, more than I ever have or ever will love anyone and more than I thought possible. You've given me the reason and strength to fight for what I want. Don't doubt, even for a moment, that you're my reason for waking up every day because that is what you've become. I don't want to live without you and if you'll marry me you will make me the happiest man in the world.'

Tears of happiness welled in her eyes as she nodded. 'Of course I'll marry you, Dr Spencer.'

EPILOGUE

'DADDY!' CRIED THOMAS and Luca in unison as they ran to greet Patrick.

Thomas was a little taller than Luca but they both had mops of thick black hair and smiles as wide as their chubby, and slightly ruddy, little faces.

'How was your first day at school?' he asked as he scooped both of the boys into his strong grip, resting one child on each hip as they wrapped their little arms around him. 'Did you enjoy it?'

'I like it home with Mummy and you better,' said Luca and he nestled his head onto Patrick's broad shoulder.

'Me too, Daddy,' Thomas agreed. 'But there's a turtle in the classroom so it'th not too bad.'

'Yeth, I like the turtle very much.' Luca lifted his head from Patrick's shoulder and chimed in. 'I think I might ask Father Christmas for one.'

'And Mummy got some of your favourite toffee from the lolly shop today too,' Thomas exclaimed. 'The special one with the yummy chocolate all over it.'

Just then, Claudia walked down the hallway of the beautiful Knightsbridge townhouse they had called home for almost five years and a smile spread over

Patrick's face. She looked as stunning as she had the day they married and he loved the thoughtful things she did, like buying his favourite chocolate-covered almond toffee and kissing him every day, the same way she had done the very first time. He placed the boys both down on their feet again and ruffled their hair with his hands before they ran off to play outside.

'And how was your day, darling?' she asked as she threw her arms around Patrick's neck and kissed him.

'Not too bad, but it just became much, much better,' he told her as he kissed her tenderly and pulled her closer to him.

Claudia held her body against his, relishing the warmth of his embrace. Every morning she woke in his arms and fell a little more in love with the man who had made her believe in love again.

'Did you deliver any gorgeous babies today?'

'Two, actually,' he replied with a proud grin. 'And I'm inducing one of my IVF patients tomorrow morning. She's overdue, so she's been admitted to hospital this afternoon. The whole family is on standby and very excited.'

'Well, my day was wonderful too. Harriet and Matteo have finished renovations on their kitchen and want us over for an early dinner on Saturday. Matteo built a sandpit for the twins so the four of them can get messy together.'

'Sounds great. Matteo's quite the handyman. Perhaps he can help me to build one for the boys.'

'Oh, and Will called and he's coming over on Sunday with Todd and your mother for a roast. Todd's looking at universities for the year after next and wants your advice. His heart's set on studying medicine like his uncle. Thinks he wants to specialise in OBGYN.'

'Well, I'll do my best to talk him out of that.'

'You'll do no such thing. Where would I be today if you hadn't studied obstetrics?' she argued playfully. 'Just tell him to always have his medical bag handy when travelling in elevators and be prepared for anything if there's a pregnant woman in there with him.'

'Even falling in love.'

'Yes, even falling in love,' Claudia replied as she looked lovingly at her husband.

He pulled her close to him and kissed her again. 'Did I ever tell you that I am the luckiest man in the world and that I couldn't possibly love you any more than I do now?'

'You haven't told me today, Dr Spencer,' she said, running her fingers lightly down his chest. 'But you have mentioned it once or twice over the years.'

'Once or twice?' He laughed as his hands slipped down her spine and rested on the curve of her bottom. 'Well, just so you know how much, I will show you, Mrs Spencer. Once the sun has set and our boys are in bed, of course.'

She kissed him again and, hand in hand, they walked down the hall, both hoping the sun would set early that night.

And every night for the rest of their lives.

* * * * *

MIRACLE TIMES TWO

JOSIE METCALFE

PROLOGUE

'PLEASE, Colin, I said no,' Jenny repeated, wondering why it seemed so hard to get the words out. It almost felt as if her tongue was tied. 'Th-thank you for bringing me home, but now it's time for you to go.'

'You don't really mean that, sweetie…not after all these weeks. Your family is just waiting to see my ring on your finger.' Colin nuzzled the side of her neck and when she could barely breathe for the pungent aftershave he was wearing, she remembered all too clearly why she'd always hated the smell of scent on a man.

She hitched her shoulder and tried to twist her head out of reach when his lips started to slide their way towards her mouth.

'Well, my family will just have to w-wait,' she said, but the words just didn't seem to emerge with the same degree of vehemence that they left her brain…and her tongue now felt as if it was too big for her mouth…and as for her eyes…it was almost impossible to focus and the lids were so heavy…

'I only w-went out with you tonight because…because it had been arranged before we…we broke up.'

'We didn't break up, sweetie,' he argued in that patronising way that managed to set her teeth on edge even when it seemed as if it came from several miles away.

'You must have had a bit too much to drink if you think that was anything more than a minor tiff. Anyway, you'll have forgotten all about it by the time you wake up in the morning with my ring on your finger...'

'*N-no!* No ring!' she said as vehemently as she could, but when she shook her head she lost her balance and nearly fell over.

'Excuse me?' said another male voice from an impossibly long way away. 'Is there a problem, here?' There was something very familiar about that new voice and she just about managed to focus on the face of the man who was able to grab her before she landed on her bottom in the hallway.

She felt curiously disconnected from everything around her, almost as if she was watching it all happening to someone else; watching as her rescuer retrieved her key and sent a clearly furious Colin away.

When her knight in shining armour swept her up into his arms she couldn't even summon up the coordination to wrap her arms around his neck, but with her head lolling on his shoulder she drew in a deep breath of soap and male skin that was oh, so familiar...trustworthy...safe.

The last fleeting memory she had was of this new but familiar man carrying her into her flat and depositing her on her bed, shoes and all, and pulling the covers over her.

CHAPTER ONE

'UM...THANK you for the other night,' Jenny said, the heat of embarrassment crawling visibly up her throat and into her face.

'No thanks necessary,' Daniel Carterton said lightly, guessing that the newest member of his team must have spent the whole of her day off working up to this apology. 'I just happened to be in the right place at the right time.' And if she believed *that*, there was a rather ornate bridge in central London on special offer.

He'd chosen his seat at the banquet honouring her father so that he could lighten the boredom of the affair by catching glimpses of Jenny across the room. That self-indulgence had been the only reason why he'd noticed the surreptitious way her companion had been topping up her glass throughout the evening. His suspicions were raised by the smug look of satisfaction on the man's face when Jenny had been less than steady on her feet when she'd finally got up from the table, but that didn't stop him from feeling almost like a stalker when he'd decided to follow them to make sure she arrived home safely.

'Do you want to answer that thing?' Daniel asked as Jenny's phone rang.

'Not in this lifetime,' she said grimly after a glance at the screen, silencing the noise with a press of a button to send the call direct to voicemail. 'And if I knew how to bar him from connecting with my mobile at all, I'd be happier still.'

'Trouble in paradise, Jennywren?' he teased, knowing he should go straight to hell for crossing his fingers that he was right. Jenny Sinclair was a genuinely lovely person who deserved a happy life with someone her equal…something he could never be. He'd been born so far on the other side of the tracks that he couldn't even hear the train from there.

And it certainly wouldn't make any difference that he'd worked his cotton socks off to become one of the youngest consultants in his field. As someone who'd only scraped into one of the lesser medical schools at his second attempt, he wouldn't stand a chance of gaining her parents' approval. Their blatant professional elitism meant that the fact that he'd been self-supporting and working crazy hours to earn every penny necessary to put himself through his training would count for nothing…even if he were ever to tell them about it. It certainly wouldn't make them look any more favourably on him for daring to look at their daughter.

So, he'd resigned himself to the fact that the only woman who could make his heart give that extra beat just by thinking about her was the one he could never have.

Well, if he was forever condemned to the role of colleague, occasional guardian angel and potential friend, he might just as well enjoy it while he could. Since Jenny had joined his unit he'd already seen a number of men make a blatant play for her, but without apparent success. Whoever was trying to ring her wasn't going to fare any better, if the expression on her face was anything to go by, but it wouldn't be long before another took his place, not with someone as special as his little Jennywren.

Except…there was something different, this time. A shadow that hadn't been there before?

'Come on. Spill the beans,' he coaxed lightly, knowing he was venturing into new ground. 'Which one's causing a problem? Tell big brother all about it.'

'Big brother?' She threw him an old-fashioned look from those fascinating hazel eyes before she pondered darkly for a moment.

He was almost holding his breath hoping she would confide in him when she suddenly burst into speech.

'It's Colin Fletcher,' she revealed grimly. 'He's obviously so thick-skinned that he can't take a hint…even after you sent him off with a flea in his ear the other night.'

'That man was Colin Fletcher? As in, your father's blue-eyed boy, Fletcher?' That *did* surprise him. He knew the name from hospital gossip but hadn't realised the man had been Jenny's escort that night. He was reputed to be a born social climber from an apparently well-to-do family, and it had been hinted that the man had his eye set firmly on taking over Jenny's father's prestigious position at the hospital, to say nothing of inheriting his lucrative private practice when the great man could be persuaded to retire. It was now blindingly obvious to Daniel that, as his son-in-law, Fletcher would be the obvious choice, and if he were to have a glowing recommendation from the great man himself, it would practically make any interviews for a replacement unnecessary.

He saw her shudder with something more than distaste in her expression, and knowing that she was remembering what had happened that night, every protective instinct leapt to attention.

'He must be the slimiest, most insincere, self-serving… *weasel* in the whole hospital,' she continued heatedly, sparks almost radiating from her. 'He insisted on holding me to the arrangement to sit at my parents' table at that big "do" the other night—in spite of the fact we weren't going out any more. He then plastered himself to my side as if we were Siamese twins, and even though I *never* have more than two glasses of wine when I go out, he must have been topping up my glass on the sly all evening, so he'd have the perfect excuse to see me home.'

'You'd already told him you wouldn't be going out with him any more?' Daniel gave her points for working out exactly what had happened at the same time as he added another item to the list of why he didn't like this Fletcher character. Top of the list was the fact that the man was the immaculately groomed poster boy for the perfect man for Jenny, unlike himself.

'I'd told him in words of one syllable that I had no intention of *ever* going out with him again—and that was more than two weeks earlier—so where he got the idea that he had the right to insist on partnering me for the evening… to virtually take over control of my life…' It did Daniel's heart good to hear the anger in her voice, knowing she was coping with her near miss. The fact that she was talking about it at all was far better than bottling it up inside, and that she was comfortable using him as a confidant…

'Well, he could hardly leave you to make your own way home if you were three sheets to the wind,' he pointed out, trying to be fair even while he was rejoicing, inside, that she'd obviously seen through the little toady.

'I suppose not, even if it *was* his fault for topping up my glass without asking.'

Just the thought that the man might have set the whole thing up deliberately, that he had been within seconds of locking the two of them in Jenny's flat, was enough to have a red haze of protective fury descend over him, again, and he had to force himself to swallow the bile that rose in his throat at the very idea of this precious unattainable woman being at the mercy of that.

'I just feel so stupid that I didn't realise what he was doing until it was nearly too late. I'm just so grateful that you were there to...'

'No thanks necessary,' he said, again, hoping she wouldn't think to ask why he'd 'just happened' to be there at that time of night. He could hardly tell her he'd been watching her during the dinner and had a bad feeling about her escort's intentions, could he?

'Well, I certainly won't be getting into that sort of situation, again, even if it means suffering from dehydration,' she announced grimly. 'At least, then, I'd be sober enough to kick him out of my flat.'

'You? Kick someone out?' He raised an eyebrow and ran a teasing glance over her slender frame, mentally estimating that, while Colin wasn't particularly overweight—yet—he must be more than a head taller than she was and weigh at least half as much again. Any future escort was unlikely to be very much smaller, so her chances of overpowering an adult male were virtually nil.

'Remember, I went to those self-defence classes?' she prompted, and he almost groaned aloud at the swiftly repressed memory of the one and only time when he'd been cajoled into being her practice partner. He'd barely survived with his sanity intact after an hour of Jenny's sweetly curvaceous body climbing all over him in her attempts to pin him to the floor.

'Actually, I probably wouldn't need to do much more than twist his arm behind his back to frogmarch him to the door. He'd probably be squealing that I was damaging his hand and destroying his career,' she muttered and he couldn't help snorting with laughter.

'The mouse that roared,' he teased and tapped her on

the nose, wishing he dared linger long enough to enjoy the silky texture of her skin, but they could never have that sort of relationship.

'Hey! Who are you calling a mouse?' she demanded, smacking his hand away. 'Not that I'm not grateful for your help, but I'm sure I'd have been able to deal with him if he hadn't been topping up my glass all evening.' Then her shoulders slumped and she sighed into her coffee. 'Unfortunately, he's been bombarding me with calls, messages and texts ever since. If there was a way I could strong-arm him into leaving me alone...'

'Do you want me to have a word with him?' he offered, relishing the thought of even the slightest chance of messing with pretty boy's perfect dentistry.

'I couldn't ask you to do that,' she said, the light striking coppery sparks off her hair as she shook her head, adding firmly, 'I'm a grown woman. I should be able to deal with situations like this for myself. Anyway, he's bound to get tired of it, eventually.'

'Well, at least I can sort your phone out for you.' He held out his hand. 'Tell me the weasel's number and I'll set it up so his calls are barred.'

'How come you know how to do that?' She pushed the slender gadget across the table with a surprised expression on her face.

'Perhaps it's a boy thing,' he joked and had to duck her retribution as he accessed her contact details and pressed the relevant buttons to refuse all future calls from Colin Fletcher's mobile even as he added his own number to her phone book. 'There you are; all done. He's history.' He paused a second, but his ingrained sense of honesty forced him to admit what else he'd done. 'I've also put myself as number one on your speed dial—in place of the Chinese takeaway. So if you have any further problems...'

His offer was cut off by the insistent sound of the pager clipped to his belt and he reached for his own phone to return the call.

'This is Daniel Carterton. You paged me?' he said tersely, knowing the call was unlikely to be trivial. It very rarely was in his chosen specialty.

'One of your at-risk mums is on her way in,' the voice on the other end responded equally crisply. 'It's Aliyah Farouk. She says she's started having contractions.'

'Send someone down to A and E to bring her straight up to the unit. Whatever you do, don't let her get trapped down there by the paperwork police. I'll be there in four minutes.' He cut the connection before he swore ripely under his breath.

'Problems?' Jenny demanded, already on her feet and straightening the hem of her top and smoothing both hands over her hair to ensure it was tidy, all trace of laughter gone from her lively face.

'Apparently, Aliyah Farouk's having contractions,' he said, knowing he didn't need to say any more to Jenny for her to know the seriousness of the situation.

'Damn,' she muttered forcefully. 'We thought we'd got away with it; that she was finally on the home stretch,' she added as she followed him out of the door at a rapid clip, and sudden warmth wrapped around his heart that she'd automatically referred to the two of them as *we*. That was *something*, he consoled himself as he strode along the corridor. At least he could savour the two of them linked together as *we* in a work situation.

'If she *is* in labour, let's see if we can do something about slowing things down…at least long enough so we can do something to give the babies' lungs a chance,' he said, putting such thoughts to the back of his head with all the other things about Jenny that he had to ignore, like her

surprisingly long legs that almost enabled her to keep pace
with him. Instead, it was time to concentrate, setting his
brain working to produce a list of possible complications
that could have sparked this situation with Aliyah.

'Hi, Aliyah,' Jenny called as soon as she caught sight of
their white-faced patient being wheeled swiftly into the
unit by a uniformed paramedic. 'You love us so much that
you couldn't stay away?'

'S-something like that,' the young woman muttered through trembling lips, then burst into noisy sobs.
'P-please help me,' she begged, clutching at Jenny's hand
as tears coursed down her elegant cheeks. 'I can't lose my
babies. I can't…not after everything we've gone through.
You must save my little boys, even if you can't save…'

'Aliyah, no!' her darkly handsome husband interrupted
fiercely before dropping to his knees in front of the wheelchair. 'I couldn't bear to lose you,' he said before breaking
into an impassioned speech in his own language.

'Jenny…' said Daniel's familiar deep voice behind her,
and instantly she snapped out of her unexpected fascina-
tion with the scene in front of her.

She quickly slipped into her proper role, escorting
Aliyah through to Daniel's examination room and taking
her vital signs in preparation for his evaluation of the situation, but that didn't mean that she couldn't feel a residual
ache of envy for the depth of love between Aliyah and her
husband.

'So, let's see what's going on, then, shall we?' Daniel
said as she finished adding the latest findings to Aliyah's
file. 'Your blood pressure's up and so is your pulse—
which is perfectly logical in a stressful situation—but they
shouldn't be raising your temperature.'

Jenny had thought the same thing and had the necessary

vials ready when the decision was made to do a range of blood tests.

'In the meantime, you say you haven't been spotting but you have been experiencing pains.' His dark brows drew together thoughtfully. 'Shall we do an ultrasound to check up on your little passengers before we do anything else?'

'Please!'

'Yes, please!' The Farouks answered almost simultaneously, making everyone smile in spite of the tension in the room.

'Well, let me get you a nice big glass of water before we set everything up,' Jenny said. 'For some reason, that's the preferred method of torture used by ultrasound technicians…to make pregnant women waddle around with a baby pressing on a full bladder.' It was a joke that she often told to pregnant women in an attempt at sidetracking their thoughts, but it rarely worked very well with women as stressed-out as Aliyah Farouk, finally pregnant after a string of unexplained spontaneous abortions.

This whole side of the unit was relatively new to Jenny, who'd spent several years working with the most fragile of their premature babies under the unit's director, Josh Weatherby. Then Daniel had joined the team, the focus of his attention being the at-risk mothers and babies—those who needed his special skills if they were to have a hope of a successful pregnancy—and she'd found herself fascinated by the new field.

Of course, as soon as word had gone round that he was good-looking, heterosexual and single, there had been much laughter among the existing staff about the sudden influx of nurses wanting to join his specialist side of the unit even if it meant undergoing further training, but for Jenny, that had just been a particularly delicious bonus.

She had decided to take advantage of the opportunity

when it was offered, as a way to step back from the constant minute-by-minute stress of caring for babies who
could stop breathing at any moment, or suffer from a
catastrophic intracranial bleed with very little warning,
or develop necrotising enterocolitis, or any one of dozens
of other complications.

She hadn't realised until it was too late that it could
be every bit as stressful caring for the pregnant women
referred to the unit and the children they were fighting to
carry, especially as she grew to know them over the weeks
of their pregnancy. Anyway, by the time she'd realised it,
she was hooked on the job and the delight of working with
someone as focused and professional as Daniel. The fact
that he also had a wicked sense of humour and was one of
the best-looking and sexiest members of staff, causing a
spike in her pulse rate whenever he entered a room, had
absolutely nothing to do with it.

Aliyah Farouk had been one of the first patients she had
met in the at-risk category, and she'd immediately warmed
to the woman, feeling an empathy for her desire to continue
with her legal work as long as possible. It had been during
a wait for an earlier ultrasound that Aliyah had confided
the details of her battle with her ultra-traditional parents
to be allowed to study the law that had struck a chord with
Jenny's own battles after her decision to become a nurse
rather than follow her parents' preferred route as a third-
generation doctor.

'Let's see if we can get a clear picture, yet,' the ultrasound technician said a while later as she squirted a small
mound of clear pale blue gel on the neat swell of Aliyah's
belly. 'And there's absolutely no truth to the rumour that
we keep that gel in the fridge so we can shock the baby
into running around.'

A shoulder pressed firmly against hers as Jenny craned

her neck to see the shadowy image appearing on the screen and she didn't need to glance at the lean muscled body or draw in the mixture of soap, hospital laundry starch and warm man to know that it was Daniel standing beside her. Her galloping pulse had already told her that.

'Well, baby one is still definitely there,' the technician said as she gestured towards the patterns of dark and light that differentiated between foetus and the surrounding water and maternal tissues. 'And there's a second very healthy heart there, too. Listen.'

The rapid patter of two foetal heartbeats, one after the other, filled the room and one of the little creatures suddenly seemed to react to the fact that they were all intruding on what should have been a private place, almost seeming to wave a fist at them.

'All right, little ones,' the technician chuckled as she tapped the necessary buttons to record the scan and silence the Doppler. 'We've seen that you're both safe and sound in there, so we'll go away and leave you in peace, now.'

Aliyah burst into noisy sobs of relief and Jenny was certain that there was a suspicious gleam in her stoic husband's eye, too, as he cradled her dark head against his shoulder.

'So, if there is nothing wrong with the babies, why is Aliyah having pains?' he demanded, apparently only allowing his fear to show now that his wife couldn't see his face. 'Is there something wrong with *her*?'

'That's what we're trying to find out with the tests we've taken,' Daniel explained calmly. 'It shouldn't be long before we have the first of the results back.'

'Now that the ultrasound's been done, it would be a good time to do some urine tests, too,' Jenny suggested. 'Aliyah's probably desperate for the bathroom by now.'

'Good idea,' Daniel agreed. 'And then, could we find

her a comfortable place to rest until we know what's
going on?'

'You think I need to stay in hospital?' The idea clearly
horrified her. 'You think it's something so serious that I
can't go home?'

'I've no idea at the moment,' he said and Jenny registered that, although she hadn't known Daniel for very long,
in that time he'd never been anything less than absolutely
honest with a patient. 'But it would be a good idea if you
tried to stay as calm as possible until we get all the results,
if only for the sake of your blood pressure. It would be
better for the babies, too.'

'And for me,' her harried husband added.

Jenny stayed until Aliyah was as settled as she was
going to be in one of the side rooms closest to Daniel's
office, adding her voice to the young woman's when she
urged her husband to go back to the important business
meeting he'd been called out of.

'Your wife and baby are safe here,' she pointed out logically. 'They're surrounded by doctors and nurses, and if it's
a problem caused by some sort of infection, the antibiotics
we've given her will already be starting to do their job.'

'I have this mask to hand if the pains return,' Aliyah
added as she held up the clear plastic face mask attached
to the Entonox. 'And anyway, this is a room where I can
have my mobile switched on, so I can call you or receive
your calls whenever you wish.'

It took several minutes of reassurance and then several
more supplying the suddenly tearful woman with tissues
after her husband left before Jenny was free to set off in
search of Daniel.

She found him just as he was reaching for a piece of
paper being spat out by the printer.

'Please, tell me that's the preliminary report from the

lab and it's just a simple waterworks infection; bladder or kidney, I don't mind which, just as long as there's nothing wrong with the pregnancy,' she demanded and was rewarded with a broad grin.

'Your every wish is my command,' he said with a flourishing bow, then handed her the paper to add to Aliyah's file. 'Obviously, there hasn't been time to isolate the particular bug causing the problem, but as we put her on trimethoprim in the interim…'

'She could have relief from her symptoms within an hour,' Jenny finished for him.

'Within one to four hours,' he temporised. 'It would probably be quicker relief with ciprofloxacin, but that's not so good for the pregnancy.'

He went on to run through the progress on several other cases, but Jenny suddenly knew that he was feeling every bit as relieved and delighted with the prospects for Aliyah's pregnancy as she was.

The realisation was so unexpected that, for a moment, she completely lost track of what Daniel was saying.

Was she just imagining that she could read his feelings, or was she actually beginning to be able to see beyond the cheerfully professional persona he showed the world?

It was always unlikely that one person could be that unfailingly even-tempered and still be human, and that opened up a whole new world of possibilities in the mystery of the gorgeous specimen of masculinity that was Daniel Carterton. Possibilities such as, if his smiles *were* a camouflage for other, deeper thoughts, was he hiding secrets…and if so, what sort of secrets?

Not that it would ever be something dark—such as Colin's underhanded ploy to get her alone when he obviously cared very little for her other than the fact of who her father was.

No. If Daniel had secrets they would be...what?

'What?' the man in question echoed, snapping her out of her crazy thoughts and into the real world and the recognition that she had absolutely no idea what he was talking about.

'What?' she repeated, feeling stupid and horribly afraid that she was going to blush.

'That's what I asked you,' he said with a puzzled frown. 'You were just standing there, staring at me as if you were trying to unravel the secrets of the universe on the end of my nose.'

She closed her eyes for a second, grateful that at least he hadn't realised it was those gorgeous deep blue eyes and their unfairly long lashes she'd been gazing at, or the rogue curl of dark hair curving forward onto his forehead as he worked his way through the basket of correspondence waiting for his attention.

One envelope contained a photograph of a perfect set of twins, obviously identical, even down to the slightly cross expression on their faces, and she couldn't help chuckling.

'Anybody you know?' she asked.

'Their mother was one of the earliest patients I saw when I came to work here—before you joined the unit,' he said and reached for a manila folder standing beside his computer to slip the photo inside with what looked like quite a few others.

'Are they all your babies in there?' she demanded, holding out a hand for the folder before she thought how intrusive he might find it.

'Sometimes parents send me a picture to let me know their babies have arrived safely,' he said, upending the folder in the middle of his desk to reveal dozens of babies, from the smallest, wrinkliest preemie to some that looked to be at least three months old when they were born.

'Why have you got all these hidden away?' she demanded as she spread them out across his paperwork. 'These should all be on display somewhere.'

'On display?' He looked as if the idea had never crossed his mind. 'Why?'

'For reassurance,' she said impatiently. 'You deal with at-risk mums and babies, so you have a far higher mortality rate than an ordinary Obs and Gynae department. Most parents-to-be come here expecting the worst and it would be so good if the first thing they saw when they came into your room is a whole array of photos of the healthy happy babies you've helped on their way...far more babies than the number that *don't* survive,' she pointed out.

His attempt at a response was cut short by the strident ring of the telephone and she'd only taken a couple of steps towards the door to afford him some privacy for the call when the sudden tension in his voice stopped her in her tracks.

'When? Where? How long ago?' he snapped out in short order. 'Well, find out and ring me back as soon as you do. Have you notified Josh Weatherby?'

With the mention of the senior consultant a shiver of dread ran up Jenny's spine, every hair standing up on end in its wake.

Whatever it was, this did not sound good; not if it involved the man who took charge of all the seriously premature babies or those with peri-natal problems.

'What's happened?' she asked as soon as he took the phone away from his ear.

Her words collided with his as he rapped out, 'There's been an accident, right outside the hospital.'

'Not one of *our* mums,' she pleaded, but the grim expression on his face was enough to confirm the bad news.

'Sheelagh Griffin,' he said, already tapping to access the young woman's file on the computer. 'Apparently, she started spotting heavily and cramping this morning, so her husband insisted on driving her in. He hit a pedestrian as he was turning in through the gates and smashed their car into one of the granite pillars.'

'Do you need me to come down with you?' It was a given that he would be going down to A and E to speed the young woman's admission to the unit, otherwise she could be caught up in the nightmare of paperwork until it was too late to do anything for the precious babies.

'Stay up here, for now,' he said after only a moment's hesitation. 'I can call you down if I need to, but you'll be my eyes and ears up here while I'm away.'

Jenny was immensely flattered that he would already think her competent for such a responsibility. She had done extra training for this new position but she was a nurse rather than a doctor—much to her parents' enduring disappointment.

'Let me know if you want me to get anything organised,' she said, startled to realise that what she'd really wanted to say was *Hurry back.*

And how stupid is that? she berated herself before he was even out of sight. She and Daniel didn't have that sort of relationship, and there was very little chance that they ever would. After all, no matter what her parents' narrow-minded view was of people who had risen to the top in spite of starting off at one of the less elite medical schools, Daniel was something of a high-flier, and as such, was stratospherically beyond the reach of a humble nurse, no matter how well trained and good at her job.

Anyway, hadn't Daniel categorised their relationship just a short while ago when he'd invited her to *'tell big brother'* about her troubles?

Colleague…little sister…*friend*, perhaps? She might slot into several niches in Daniel's life, but there was very little chance that he would be interested in seeing her in a role that she was only now beginning to realise might be the one she really wanted.

The phone rang stridently at her elbow, snapping her out of her pointless reflections and doubling her pulse rate with the expectation that she would hear Daniel's voice when she answered it. It was a complete letdown to realise that the caller had simply been connected to the wrong department.

'Jenny?' Daniel's voice behind her had her whirling to face him, the first of at least a dozen questions on the tip of her tongue until she saw his face.

'Daniel? What's happened?' she demanded, automatically reaching out to take his arm. 'Are you ill?' He looked positively grim, and in the short time he'd been away from the department, his face had somehow become hollow-looking, his eyes filled with shadows.

'I was too late to do anything to slow down Sheelagh's labour,' he said bluntly, and she could hear the same defeated tone that always emerged in his voice whenever something happened to one of their special babies, but this time there was something more, something infinitely darker.

CHAPTER TWO

'ARE the babies still alive? Have they gone to Josh's unit?'

Even babies that premature were often born alive and a few of them actually pulled through, albeit with a legacy of permanent disabilities, but it was an outside chance that they would have survived anything other than a Caesarean birth.

'One is.' Daniel grimaced, silently, the brilliant colour of his dancing blue eyes strangely flat. 'I've admitted Sheelagh into the isolation room overnight. I told her it was in case of complications, but they both know it's just a matter of time before…'

She nodded her understanding even as she thought that they really should think of a better name for the little suite at the furthest end of the unit. Apparently, that little area had been one of the arrangements Daniel had instigated within the first few days of his appointment—a place where mothers who had lost their babies could stay for monitoring and treatment without fear that their devastation would be made worse by the sights and sounds of pregnant women or healthy newborn babies all around them.

'Did it happen because of the accident?' Jenny demanded, something about the tension surrounding him like an electrical field warning her that there was worse news to come.

'My guess is that one of the babies died *in utero* and that triggered a spontaneous abortion of both foetuses.' He sank heavily into the chair and came to rest with his hands tightly linked together on the array of happy photos still spread over the inevitable pile of papers in front of him. He gazed blankly at them for several endless seconds while she fought the urge to go to him and throw her arms around him, to cradle his head against her and ask if there was anything she could do.

'The person they ran down was Aliyah's husband,' he announced rawly, and his devastated expression rocked her back on her heels.

'Dear Lord,' she gasped, sinking heavily onto the edge of the nearest chair when her legs refused to support her. 'Is he...?' She couldn't bring herself to say the word, but she didn't need to for him to know what she was asking.

'He's in theatre. Depressed skull fracture, punctured lung, broken leg...you name it, he's got it,' he listed grimly and she felt her eyes widen with each additional injury on the list.

'But he's still alive?' she pleaded anxiously.

'For the moment,' he agreed and it only took the tone of his voice to know that the prognosis wasn't good.

Her heart sank like a stone. 'What are you going to tell Aliyah?' The image in her head of how tenderly the injured man had been supporting his wife less than an hour ago was so clear that it was almost painful.

'How on earth was he injured so badly?' she demanded on a sudden surge of anger for the destruction of such a perfect couple made even more tragic by the fact they were finally expecting the babies they both wanted so badly.

'Did he forget where he was and step out into the traffic, or…?'

'Apparently, the Griffiths' car went out of control and mounted the pavement at the entrance to the hospital. He was slammed against one of the pillars and trapped.'

Jenny winced as she imagined a human head coming into contact with that impressive construction of unforgiving Cornish granite.

'And I have absolutely *no* idea what I'm going to say to Aliyah,' he said finally, his voice as rough as gravel. 'She's still shaky after that scare with the baby and we're waiting for the antibiotics to do their thing. I don't know whether I should hold off telling her in the hopes that he comes out of surgery with some sort of positive prognosis, or whether I should go to her straight away in case she needs to prepare herself to say her final farewell while he's still alive.'

'Or at least given a semblance of life by various machinery,' she muttered, feeling sickened by the awful possibility.

How would *she* feel if she were in the same position?

Would she rather know, immediately, that the man she loved had been terribly injured and was not expected to live, and have to agonise for hours imagining what was going on in theatre? Or would she prefer to receive the news after every effort had been made to repair the damage?

'If she weren't pregnant…' Daniel muttered and she knew he was weighing up exactly the same options and trying to balance their patient's right to know against the increased risk to her pregnancy such a shock might cause.

A sudden unearthly scream from further along the corridor sent all the hairs up on the back of Jenny's neck.

'What on *earth*…?' She whirled and took off out of

Daniel's office at a fast clip, almost colliding with a young nurse catapulting out of Aliyah Farouk's room.

'*Nooo!*' The unearthly scream sounded again, then was replaced by a wail that degenerated into inconsolable weeping.

'What's going on here?' Daniel demanded, glaring fiercely at the shocked-looking nurse.

'I don't know, s-sir!' The poor girl's teeth were almost chattering. 'Sh-she was trying to phone her husband's work to leave a message and they said he hadn't arrived. S-so she said she was going to try his mobile phone and…and…'

Jenny winced as she put two and two together. It didn't take much to imagine the scene in a busy A and E, especially as her husband's clothing would have been summarily cut off his body to enable swift access to his injuries. Keeping track of his mobile phone would have been a low priority, everything being stuffed into the same bag for later retrieval.

It was all too easy to imagine the junior member of staff detailed to take charge of yet another patient's belongings to think it was a good idea to tell a seriously injured patient's wife that she needed to come to the hospital as soon as possible.

'Okay, Joanne. Go and get yourself a cup of tea and don't come back until you've stopped shaking. Let someone know where you're going,' Jenny said.

'Th-thank you,' she stammered, but Jenny was already following Daniel into the room, shutting the door firmly against any intrusion.

She was just in time to see him reach out to the keening woman and gasped in disbelief when Aliyah turned on him like a rabid dog, her eyes wild and her fingers stiffly curved as though ready to rip him to shreds.

'No, Aliyah, no,' Daniel said, his deep voice almost

crooning as, far from backing away, he stepped straight into the danger zone and wrapped a consoling arm around her shoulders. 'Gently. Gently,' he said. 'This is not good for the babies. Think about those precious babies.' His words were almost hypnotic in their gentle rise and fall, but it took several racking moments before Aliyah's devastation would allow her to hear what he was saying.

Suddenly, she flung herself into Daniel's arms and he had to ease himself onto the side of the bed to support her weight as she sobbed, clearly broken-hearted.

'Why?' she wailed at intervals, but there was obviously no answer for the randomness of chance. If her husband had decided not to go back to his office, or if he had decided to leave even a couple of minutes earlier, this would not have happened.

It was only when she finally drew back from Daniel's comforting hold and looked up at him from tear-swollen eyes she demanded, 'Why did he have to die before he could even see our sons?' that Jenny understood the enormity of her devastation.

For a moment, she wondered whether the information was true. Then she put her rational head on and recognised that the person who had answered the phone in A and E was unlikely to have more up-to-date news than Daniel.

Still, she reached for the phone and pressed the relevant numbers.

'Theatres,' said a crisply efficient voice when the call was answered.

'This is Jenny Sinclair calling on behalf of Daniel Carterton,' she announced. 'Can you give me an update on Mr Farouk's surgery? His wife's a patient in our unit.'

'Oh, no!' the voice exclaimed, instantly sympathetic, then, 'Just give me a minute to check,' but Jenny wasn't worried about a moment or two's delay. It might give

Aliyah time to comprehend the fact that her husband hadn't died at the scene of the accident, as she seemed to believe.

'Surgery's still ongoing,' the voice reported in her ear while she watched Daniel try to calm his patient enough to listen to what he needed to explain. 'There are three of them working on him at the moment—a thoracic surgeon, an orthopod and a neurosurgeon. They said they've managed to stop the bleeding but there's still a long way to go before they'll know anything definite. Do you want someone to phone with updates?'

'Please,' Jenny confirmed. 'Updates would be good,' and she put the phone down.

'He's still alive?' Aliyah breathed with tremulous disbelief, her thick dark lashes clumped by tears. 'Please, tell me he's still alive.'

'So far,' Jenny cautioned, stepping close enough to take the hand the young woman held out to her. She squeezed it reassuringly between both of hers as she paraphrased the information she'd just been given. 'So far, they've managed to stop him bleeding, but that's only the first step.'

'What else do they have to do? When will I be able to see him?' She flipped back the covers and started to slide her feet over the side of the bed. 'Please, can I go to him? I need to be with him.'

Daniel had to step in with a doctor's authority before they could persuade their patient that there was absolutely no point in trailing through the hospital only to have to sit in a surgical waiting room.

'We'll probably receive news, here, before you would, there,' Daniel pointed out. 'Jenny has arranged for someone in the surgical department to phone through updates as soon as there is anything to tell us.'

'You promise?' Her dark eyes flicked frantically from

one to the other. 'You will tell me as soon as you hear anything?'

'I'll promise if you'll promise, too,' Daniel said firmly, then pointed to the figures on the monitor panel. 'You must lie back and relax and concentrate on bringing your pulse and blood pressure down, for your babies' sakes. Do you think your husband would forgive himself if worrying about him damaged your sons?'

The rest of her shift seemed interminable and it almost felt to Jenny as if they were all holding their breath while they waited for news of the surgery.

The report that Aliyah's husband had survived the removal of several large shards of bone from his brain and that the plate of skull they'd removed to access them would not be replaced until some of the swelling had gone down was the final part in the lengthy process.

Not that surviving the complex operations would guarantee the patient's survival, and there was still an extremely long way to go before they would even begin to know how much permanent damage his brain had suffered in the impact and its aftermath.

'Are you as exhausted as I am?' Jenny demanded as she emerged from the locker room still sliding her arms into the sleeves of her jacket to find Daniel performing almost exactly the same task as he walked towards her.

'Probably,' he grumbled. 'And it's not as if the day was unusually busy.'

In fact, the unit had been relatively quiet, beyond the usual round of clinics and assessments. Of course, there was an almost electric buzz in the air every time the phone rang, with everyone seeming to hold their breath in case it was news about Sheelagh Griffin's desperately struggling baby or the outcome of Faz Farouk's lengthy surgery. It was always that way when one of 'their' patients had bad news, and in a unit that saw the highest-risk patients, they saw more sadness than most.

This seemed somehow different, almost as if the whole world was waiting to hear the outcome. And still the tiny baby clung to life as though oblivious to the fact that his fight was doomed to failure, while Aliyah Farouk waited impatiently to be given permission to go to her husband's side.

'I never realised that tension could be so draining,' she said as she automatically fell into step beside him, both of them heading towards the exit after their brief detour to glimpse the tiny scrap that was barely as long as her hand. 'But I suppose that when everything revs into high gear every time the phone rings...'

'And your body gets flooded with adrenaline in anticipation of news,' he added.

'So your pulse and respiration speed up, causing you to burn up so many calories that you feel completely limp and empty even before the situation resolves itself.'

'So, you're saying that you're about to collapse with lack of nourishment and are in imminent need of sustenance?' he asked and she was grateful that he'd changed the topic to something so mundane and normal.

'How did you guess?' Jenny pulled a face as she rubbed a hand over the noises coming from her stomach. 'I know it's not the best thing nutritionally, but I think I'm going to get a takeaway, for speed.'

'I could do *tagliatelli carbonara*, if you're interested?' he offered tentatively and she blinked in surprise, then wondered if, like her, he didn't want to be alone with his thoughts just yet.

She had to squash the bubble of excitement that started to swell inside her at the idea that she'd be spending some off-duty time with him. After all, it hadn't been so long ago that he'd let her know he saw her as more of a little sister than an attractive woman.

'How long would I have to wait to eat?' she demanded, concentrating on looking suspicious. 'Is that a crafty way of getting me to do the shopping so you'll have the ingredients to cook?'

'I'm mortally wounded that you could think me so devious!' he complained as he stepped aside to allow her to exit the automatic doors first. 'When have I ever given you cause to think that I'm anything other than honest and straightforward?'

His teasing words died away as she came to a halt, her way blocked by a darkly scowling Colin Fletcher.

'There's something wrong with your phone,' he announced bluntly. 'I've been trying to ring you all day to tell you I'd be picking you up at the end of your shift.'

Jenny swallowed hard, tempted to close her eyes tightly to pretend that the obnoxious man wasn't standing there, clearly unconcerned that he was about to cause a scene in front of goodness knew how many colleagues, patients and visitors.

'There's nothing wrong with my phone,' she said quietly, not certain whether she was glad to have Daniel's silent presence at her back or embarrassed that he was a witness to the result of her stupidity in ever agreeing to go out with Colin in the first place.

'There *must* be something wrong because I haven't been able to get through,' Colin argued with a pointed glance at his watch then a disparaging look at her favourite pair of well-worn jeans. 'You'll need to get yourself tidied up enough to go somewhere decent like the Pastorale. I'd better give you a lift to your flat or you're not going to have enough time to make a good job of it.'

The classy French restaurant that had opened recently at the top end of the high street had quickly made a name for its elegant ambiance and superb cuisine, but it certainly wasn't the place she wanted to go after a stressful day like today…nor was Colin the company she'd ever choose.

'Thank you for the invitation, Colin,' she said, so perfectly politely that even the pickiest manners maven couldn't have found fault, 'but I'm really not in the mood for—'

'Not in the *mood*!' he interrupted angrily. 'Do you realise how exclusive Pastorale is; how hard it was to organise a reservation at such short notice so I could stage the romantic—?' He stopped himself suddenly, almost as if he'd said more than he'd intended, then continued, sounding angrier than ever. 'And you're standing there saying you're not in the *mood*?'

'Excuse me.' It was Daniel's turn to interrupt and Jenny almost giggled when the unexpectedness of it left Colin with his mouth agape.

It was tempting to allow the strong silent man at her back to take over for her, but she'd never been one to back down from a battle that was important to her, and this one definitely qualified.

'Colin, there's no point in trying to browbeat me into going for a meal with you, because it isn't going to happen,' she said firmly.

'Well, I'd have been able to get hold of you to arrange it properly earlier on today if your phone had been working,' he began again, but this time she interrupted him herself.

'There is absolutely nothing wrong with my phone,' she declared. 'I've already told you that I won't go out with you, several times, in fact. So I've had my phone programmed to refuse any of your calls. Now, if you'll excuse me, there's an enormous plate of *tagliatelli carbonara* with my name on it and I'm starving. Goodnight, Colin.'

Her knees felt rather wobbly as she forced herself to stride briskly past the man, but the matching echo of Daniel's feet following close behind fanned the spark of defiance that kept her chin in the air and bolstered the confidence that her nemesis would never know how uncertain she'd been that she could cope with such an uncomfortable confrontation.

'So there's an *enormous* plate of *carbonara* with your name on it, is there?' Daniel mused as he lengthened his stride to catch up with her as they set off across the vast car park to the other side of the hospital grounds. 'I'm not certain that I've got enough ingredients for that. Perhaps we *should* detour to do a bit of shopping, just to be sure.'

Jenny had no idea why his teasing should suddenly make her feel like crying and laughing aloud at the same time, but it took a real effort not to do either...or both.

'*No* shopping,' she decreed imperiously, warmed beyond words that she had such a friend and overwhelmingly grateful for his ready sense of humour. 'I need food *now*!'

A leisurely hour later they were both coming to the end of plates full of perfectly cooked *tagliatelli* smothered in the most delicious creamy sauce, and Daniel's light-hearted banter had temporarily managed to push their concerns about their patients to the back of their minds. It had also all but banished the memory of that unfortunate scene at the entrance to the hospital's main Reception. In fact, she was feeling so relaxed that that she wasn't sure she was going to be able to summon up the energy to walk to her own flat, and there was a real danger that she would fall asleep where she sat if she stayed much longer.

Regretfully, she began to fish under the table for the shoes she'd kicked off soon after she'd arrived, trying to find the words to thank him, not only for the delicious meal but also for standing by her while she faced Colin down, yet still allowing her to deal with the situation herself.

She was just drawing a breath to bring the evening to a close when his mobile phone began to vibrate its way across the centre of the table.

'Carterton.' His brisk response told her she wasn't going to have to eavesdrop on a one-sided private call and the resigned expression that came over his face was enough to tell her that Sheelagh Griffin's baby had lost his fight.

'Poor woman,' she whispered, her heart heavy for the couple who would have to start the whole IVF process all over again if they were ever to have the family they wanted.

Before Daniel could comment his phone was ringing again, but this time the shocked way his eyes widened told her the news he was getting was totally unexpected and it wasn't good.

Listening in on a call that largely consisted of one-word questions was both frustrating and frightening, especially when she saw the regret fill his face.

'What?' she demanded as soon as the call ended. 'What's happened? Oh, no! Is it Aliyah? How bad is it?'

He raked his fingers through his thick dark hair and swore ripely, something she very rarely heard him do.

'It's not Aliyah,' he said but before she could let the relief flood through her he added, 'it's her husband. He coded in ICU and it took five tries to get him back.'

Jenny felt close to tears when she remembered what a lovely caring man Faz was and how concerned about Aliyah and their baby. 'How long was his heart stopped? Do they know why?'

'They've taken him back to theatre. There's blood building up in the pericardium that's stopping the heart from working properly. It nearly stopped it permanently.'

'Surely they would have checked for other sources of bleeding when they were retrieving the bone fragments from the broken ribs and sorting out the collapsed lung?'

Daniel's expression was wry because they both knew that such things could be missed when a patient presented with so many life-threatening injuries at once, especially if the damage was small enough to make any bleed insignificant amongst all the other gore.

Sadly, she realised that their almost idyllic evening was over—the outside world back with a vengeance—and suddenly her exhaustion made everything more than she could bear—the situation with Colin and their embarrassing confrontation, the worry that Aliyah might be losing her longed-for babies, Sheelagh Griffin's accident right at the hospital's gates and the loss of both of her precious babies. Now this! The horrible events still seemed to be piling up.

With barely a second's warning her breath caught in her throat and her eyes burned as they filled with tears.

'Oh, Daniel,' she wailed, then whirled towards his door, wanting nothing more than to escape before he saw them start to stream down her face.

'Hey!' He caught her arm as she fumbled with the lock on the front door and swung her gently around. 'Are you going without your shoes?'

The concerned frown pleating his forehead was the final straw, releasing the first sob from the dammed-up agony in her throat, and when he pulled her into the sanctuary of his arms the floodgates burst.

'Shh!' Daniel soothed helplessly as he awkwardly patted her back, realising wryly that, for all his extensive education, he had no more idea of how to deal with a crying woman than any other man.

And the fact that a large part of his brain was taken up with registering just how perfect Jenny felt in his arms wasn't something he had any control over, either.

She was such an energetic person with such a lively personality that it was all too easy to forget just how slender she was, especially when she was swathed in a shapeless uniform or several bulky layers of off-duty clothing—one of the down sides of spending her working days in a heated building.

Now that he had her wrapped in his arms he realised that she was more than a head shorter than he was, easily able to burrow herself into the angle under his chin as she clung to him.

The hand that started stroking her back traced the perfect curve of her spine from the silky hair at the base of her skull all the way down to the top of her jeans, and he was almost certain that, had he tried, he could have wrapped both hands completely around her waist, fingertip to fingertip.

And as for her legs, those deceptively long legs, one of which he was bracketing with his own as she leaned against him, sparking his imagination to fill with images of how they would feel without the layers of fabric separating them, how it would feel if they were both naked with those endless legs wrapped around his waist as he...

'Oh, Daniel, I'm sorry,' she whimpered against his throat and he had to swallow a groan as the puffs of moist warmth on his bare skin ratcheted his pulse still higher even as he tried to remind himself that he was supposed to be supporting and comforting her, not wasting his time imagining impossible scenarios in which...

'There's nothing to be sorry for,' he growled, hoping

she couldn't hear the way his voice betrayed the effect she was having on him.

'I sh-shouldn't be falling apart all over you,' she hiccupped. 'It's not fair to you to have to m-mop me up.'

'You let me worry about that,' he reassured her, even as he tried to push to the back of his brain all the other things he'd be willing to do for her. To her. With her. 'Everyone needs a friend they can let the barriers down with, otherwise we'd all go crazy in a high-stress job like ours.'

He rested his cheek briefly on the crown of her head just long enough to draw in the fresh scent of the shampoo she'd used earlier mixed with the indefinable something that belonged to no one but his little Jennywren.

'It never seems to get to you,' she complained. 'Even when you came back up to tell us about Sheelagh Griffin's babies.' The thought sent her off into renewed sobs and he realised that, as it didn't look as if she was going to be fit to leave any time soon, it was time to make them both more comfortable.

She was weeping so hard that she was probably almost unaware that he'd half-led, half-carried her back into his living room. In fact, she only reacted when he lowered himself into the corner of his oversized settee and tried to settle her on his lap.

'Daniel, no,' she objected, floundering in her attempts at getting her feet on the floor. 'You don't have to do this. It's not… You can't want… I shouldn't…'

'Calm down, sweetheart,' he said, thwarting her half-hearted efforts by drawing her closer to his chest. 'It's not a problem.' Well, that was a blatant lie for a start, because having her squirming on his lap was quickly becoming a big problem, and if she squirmed much more, she would discover just how big.

'It's difficult to calm d-down,' she sobbed against his

throat. 'All I can think of is those poor people and everything they've l-lost and…and…'

She turned her head to look up at him just as he angled his to press his face against hers and somehow, accidentally, fleetingly, their lips brushed.

He froze, unable to breathe, convinced that even his heart had stopped beating for several timeless seconds as he savoured the softness of her mouth against his for the first time.

'Daniel?' she whispered huskily, and while he was utterly amazed that she hadn't immediately broken the contact between them, he was intimately aware that he could taste the salt of her tears.

The last thing he wanted was to draw back, afraid of what he would see in her eyes. Shock? Rejection? Or worse, disgust if she thought he was taking advantage of her emotional state?

In the end it was Jenny who moved just the few inches that would allow them to see each other's expressions, and the wide-eyed wonder on her face as her gaze flicked from his eyes to his mouth and back again jolted his heart into double time.

'Jenny?' It sounded more like a growl than a question and he wasn't really sure what he was trying to ask her, but to his everlasting relief she seemed to take it as an invitation.

'Please,' she whispered as she angled her head and leant forwards just far enough to stroke her lips over his…once… twice… 'Please, Daniel,' she said again as she wreathed her arms around his neck, this time pressing not only her lips against his but the whole of her body, too. 'Please, Daniel. I need you,' she begged breathlessly before she plunged them both headlong into the kind of kiss he'd been dreaming of ever since he'd met the tantalising woman... only better.

CHAPTER THREE

DANIEL woke to find Jenny still in his arms and an unexpected image suddenly sprang into his mind.

He'd been sent to stay with his grandfather one summer, and every morning he'd been woken by the elderly man's favourite cockerel that used to fly to the top of a big wooden gatepost and crow.

Now, for the first time in his life, Daniel knew exactly how Ruben the Rhode Island Red rooster had felt. After the night he and Jenny had just spent together, he almost believed he could leap to the top of the roof to shout to the world how good he was feeling.

Except…

Except there was a very honest part of him that was kicking himself for his loss of control. Guilt was telling him that he should have been stronger when Jenny had been falling apart; that he should have been able to comfort her without succumbing to the desire that had been building in him ever since he'd met her.

And while he was relishing the fact that he had this precious time with her in his arms, he was dreading the moment when she woke, afraid he would see the same expression in her eyes that she'd had when she'd spoken about Colin's attempt to take advantage of her.

It was easy to push that thought to the back of his mind

when he was looking down at her curled up trustingly at his side, her head nestled into his shoulder and her forehead against the curve of his neck. He couldn't think of a more arousing way to wake up than with the warmth of her breath soughing over his chest, ruffling and teasing the hairs and tightening his nipples into hard points that were begging for more of her attention.

Even then, with the evidence all around him, the tumbled bedding, the scattered clothing, the musky, totally arousing scent that was partly his and partly hers…he still could hardly believe that it had really happened.

It wasn't simply the fact that it had happened at all that had him reeling, either; it was the sheer scale of it that had been enough to blow his mind for the next millennium or so.

That hadn't been the Jenny he had thought he was coming to know at the hospital. *She* was the calm, caring, concerned professional who could be counted on to go the extra mile for every one of their patients with sympathy and tact. It hadn't been the off-duty Jenny, either; the cheerful, friendly young woman with a welcoming smile for everyone even while surrounded by an indefinable air that sometimes came across almost as naïveté.

No, the Jenny he'd discovered last night had been a complete revelation; an unbelievably arousing combination of uncertainty and boldness; of alternating shyness and daring that had rendered him speechless and breathless and utterly captivated.

Making love with her had been more—*much* more—than he'd ever imagined, and it was something he'd be delighted to repeat on a daily basis far beyond the foreseeable future but…

He drew in a controlled breath as he fought down a feeling of dread.

Yes, it had been, without exception, the most spectacular night of his life, and hers, too, if her eager reaction was anything to go by, but would he still be basking in this contented glow thinking the night's pleasure had been worth it if it meant he'd lost her friendship?

He'd already admitted to himself the fact that there was little chance of anything permanent between them, but he'd hoped that at least in the time they spent together they could be friends as well as colleagues. Had he ruined that, now?

A glance at the alarm clock told him that it was still early. Too early to get ready for work. In fact, it was early enough for a leisurely repeat session that he was craving more with every second, even though he knew he couldn't have it.

He should leave the bed, *now*. Leave her in the hopes that she wouldn't be too angry that he'd taken advantage of her distress.

His mobile phone suddenly buzzed into life, the vibrate function making it rattle noisily on the chest of drawers beside the bed.

Daniel was glad that at least he'd had the presence of mind to switch off the noisy ring tone. Now all he had to do was silence the wretched thing quickly enough that it didn't wake the sleeping woman in his arms. It was going to take a while longer before he'd be ready to face her.

But before he could untangle an arm to reach for the infernal gadget, her eyes flicked open, their hazel irises glowing with golden fire as they gazed straight up into his.

The phone buzzed again and she glanced fleetingly at it before her eyes returned to his, the slumberous expression in them almost making him groan aloud as his body started to respond.

'Are you going to answer that?' she prompted with a hint of a grin. 'It doesn't sound as if they're going to give up.'

The impish curve of lips that had met his own time and time again during the night was almost enough to make him forget his name, but there was no way he could ignore his phone when there were vulnerable patients relying on him.

'Car—' he began then had to clear his throat before he could continue, the husky tone far more suited to the bedroom than his professional persona. 'Carterton,' he announced crisply on his second attempt, mentally switching gears. The last thing he needed to be thinking about was bedrooms when he was taking a call from the hospital.

'Hello. I'm sorry to disturb you so early, Dr Carterton, but you wouldn't happen to know where Jenny Barber might be?'

'What?' He could feel the unexpected heat of a blush searing up his throat and into his face, hardly able to believe that the woman in question was still curled sleepily against him as if she was totally unaware that the two of them were wrapped around each other, completely naked.

'Oh, I'm *so* sorry!' the voice on the other end of the line exclaimed. 'That must have come out of left field, especially this early in the morning. And I didn't even tell you who I am…and I probably woke you up, too. I'm *so* sorry!'

'You didn't wake me,' Daniel reassured the flustered woman. 'How can I help?'

'This is Fiona Tarbuck. I'm a Staff Nurse in Cardiac ICU and I'm trying to track down one of the nurses from your unit—Jenny Barber. You wouldn't happen to know where she is, would you? We've tried her landline in her flat and her mobile but there's no answer on either phone. Either she's switched them off, or else her battery's…'

Daniel's attention had been caught by the woman's introduction.

'CICU?' he questioned, interrupting her rambling speculations.

'Yes, that's right. Unfortunately, her father was brought in during the night and her mother's been trying to contact her to let her know. Apparently, their daughter's not on duty, today, but one of your staff suggested she might have told you what she was going to be doing on her day off?'

'No, she didn't say, but—'

'In that case, I'm very sorry to have disturbed you,' she interrupted before he could find the words he needed. How could he say he'd pass the message on without ruining Jenny's reputation for ever by revealing that she was here in his arms?

When the voice was swiftly replaced in his ear by the buzz of a finished call he was left with the task of finding a new set of words—the ones that would break the news that her father was in CICU.

'Daniel?' A concerned frown had appeared, deep enough to pleat the smooth skin of her forehead as she'd tried to follow his cryptic questions and answers. 'You said CICU. That wasn't about Aliyah's husband, was it? Please tell me he hasn't taken a turn for the worse,' she begged, her empathy for their patient completely transparent.

He hated the fact that the news he had to break would cause this caring woman even greater stress, but he had no option. If her father's condition was serious—and the very fact that he was in CICU was proof that it very well could be—then every moment's delay could jeopardise her chance of reaching his bedside in time.

'I'm sorry, Jenny,' he began, desperately fighting the urge to wrap her tightly in his arms in an attempt to soften the blow. 'That was CICU—as you probably gathered. They've been trying to reach you to—'

'*Me?*' she echoed, clearly startled, then panic flared in her eyes. 'Who…? What…? Not *Dad*?' she gasped in sudden comprehension, her body totally rigid against him.

'Unfortunately, yes,' he confirmed. 'He was taken ill during the night.'

'What happened?' she demanded, suddenly frantically fighting her way out from under the cosy nest of bed-clothes, still apparently uncaring of the fact that she was utterly, tantalisingly naked.

'I've no idea of the specifics,' he admitted, battling the urge to gaze his fill of her beautiful body in case it was the last time he ever got to see it—all those lean, slender curves that set his pulse throbbing anew with the urgent need to trace them and savour them and… 'The Staff Nurse didn't go into it,' he admitted as he forced himself to drag his eyes away, turning to reach for clean underwear in the top drawer beside the bed. 'All I know is that they haven't been able to reach you on your landline or your mobile and wondered if I had any idea what you were planning to do today.'

He was already slipping his feet into his shoes while he thrust his arms into a clean shirt, having long ago perfected the knack of speedy dressing. When he turned back to her, Jenny was still trying to find the last of the clothing he'd tossed aside so cavalierly in his urgent need to have her in his arms and in his bed.

'And I was here, with a flat battery in my mobile,' she wailed, self-recrimination obvious in her voice. 'Oh, Daniel…!'

'Hey, Jennywren!' he soothed, discovering her second shoe buried under the pillow that had been tossed to the floor some time after midnight and handed it to her. 'She didn't say the situation's urgent, so don't automatically assume the worst.'

'But she was ringing round trying to find me…she rang my *boss*, for heaven's sake!' she exclaimed. 'That hardly sounds like *"Oh, it's all right, Mr Barber, patients confuse indigestion for heart attacks all the time"*, does it?'

'It doesn't sound like *"It's time to organise the funeral"*, either,' he pointed out sharply, walking the tightrope between sympathy and helping her to keep herself together. 'If you're ready, let's go.'

'Go?' There was a wildly unfocused look in her eyes as she gazed around his little hallway as though she couldn't really work out what she needed to do next.

'I'll drive you to the hospital,' he said, holding up his keys.

'Oh, you don't need to do that. I can take a taxi,' she said immediately, but he was already shaking his head.

'You could, but do you really want to make a phone call to order one, then stand here waiting for it to arrive? It'll be quicker if I take you and drop you off at the closest entrance to CICU.'

He was relieved when she acquiesced, hating the thought that she might have preferred to get herself to the hospital; hating even more the thought that she might not have wanted to have him with her, especially after what had happened between them last night.

Somehow, the attraction he'd felt towards her right from the first day he'd met her—the impossible attraction he'd tried so hard to subdue under the twin guises of professionalism and friendship—had not only exploded into passion, but that passion had given birth to a deeper emotion… a feeling of *connection* that he'd never felt before, with anyone.

* * *

'Thank you so much, Daniel,' Jenny managed in spite of the fact that her thoughts were so impossibly scattered that manners were absolutely the last thing on her mind.

'You're welcome, Jenny,' he said, and his hand came out to trap the one she'd left hanging in mid-air, uncertain whether what had happened between them the night before gave her the right to curl her fingers around the back of his head and pull him close enough for a kiss, the way she wanted to. Blandly shaking his hand certainly didn't feel right...but then, she doubted whether any sort of contact between them would ever feel bland again.

'Let me know how your father's getting on,' he continued, his expression apparently every bit as calmly caring as it always was when he added, 'or if there's anything I can do for you.'

You could come up to be with me while I find out whether Dad's going to be all right, she thought, knowing she definitely didn't have the right to ask that of him. But the thought of having Daniel at her side, of having his hand to hold on to while she learned the worst...

'Thank you,' she said again, knowing that this was something she was going to have to face by herself. Then, when she would have climbed out of the car he suddenly reached out again to put a hand on her arm.

'I mean it, Jenny,' he said, the unexpectedly intent expression in his eyes stopping her breath in her throat for several seconds. 'If you don't call me, I'll come up to look for you...to find out what's going on.'

'Okay,' Jenny agreed breathlessly, suddenly warmed by his evident sincerity even as her heart kicked out an extra couple of beats when she remembered just how potent those eyes could be when they were focused on her. 'I promise I'll let you know as soon as there's anything to tell you.'

'And just for the record,' he added even as she had the door open and one foot on the ground, 'I might seem cool, calm and unaffected by the tragedies we sometimes see, but *seem* is the operative word.'

It was several hours before she had the chance to tell Daniel that her father had undergone balloon angioplasty… at his own insistence. In spite of the advice of the cardiac consultant and the urging of his wife and daughter, he had completely refused to agree to bypass surgery on the grounds that he couldn't afford to take that much time away from work.

Jenny had serious doubts that the procedure would be a long-term success at restoring adequate circulation through her father's heart. The wretched man was so firmly set in his ways that his terrible diet and dire lack of exercise would only cause the whole situation to recur. As heartless as it might seem to anyone else, she had the feeling that only the enforced absence from work that major surgery would entail would give the man the incentive to take a long hard look at what his lifestyle was doing to him.

At least, that was the conclusion she'd reached as she'd sat in the relatives' waiting room, ostensibly to keep her mother company—although what company the workaholic woman needed when she'd spent a good part of her time on the telephone while her husband was undergoing the procedure, Jenny wasn't sure.

Forty-eight hours later, the situation hadn't changed much and Jenny was almost at her wit's end, especially as her father was insisting on discharging himself and her mother was calmly proposing that, if he needed anyone to watch over him, it would have to be Jenny as her own patients certainly couldn't do without her.

For a moment Jenny was completely speechless at the

arrogance of the assumption that a nurse's worth was so much less to her patients than a doctor's. That was apart from the fact that the man in question might be Jenny's father, but he was Helen Sinclair's husband, and as such, should be *her* primary concern.

Of course, the fact that Jenny had already had to take a leave of absence from her own job for the past couple of days on compassionate grounds, and hadn't had a chance to speak to Daniel beyond leaving updates on his voicemail, had absolutely nothing to do with it.

'No, Mother,' she said firmly, stopping the woman in her tracks when she was already halfway out of the door.

'What?' Helen's brain was obviously already focusing on the place she would rather be…with her patients. 'No… *what*, Jennifer?' She glanced at her watch and made the swift double-click of exasperation with her tongue that had been a constant soundtrack to Jenny's entire childhood. 'I really don't have time for pointless riddles.'

'In that case, let me make myself very clear, Mother,' she said, keeping a pleasant smile on her face in spite of her sad resignation to the fact that the woman was unlikely ever to change. She certainly wouldn't have been expecting outright rebellion from the daughter who sometimes felt as if she had spent her whole life trying to please…and failing. 'I will be returning to work tomorrow morning because my colleagues have been left short-handed by my absence and we have patients who could die if there aren't enough of us there to look after them.'

'But… You…' her mother spluttered, clearly as stunned as if the rather etiolated potted plant in the corner of the room had started speaking to her, but Jenny had no intention of letting her speak before *she'd* finished what she needed to say.

'Apart from that, he's *your* husband, not mine, so it's

only right that he should have *you* at his side while he recovers. I'll visit, of course,' she added swiftly when it looked as if her mother was starting to rally her thoughts to mount a counter-offensive. 'I'll come every day, either as soon as I finish my shift, or in the morning if I'm on a late. You can always send me a text if there's anything you need me to bring.'

She hoped that her mother couldn't tell how badly she was shaking as she bestowed their usual cursory cheek-to-cheek excuse for a kiss before she strode briskly out of the waiting room, taking with her the familiar scent of her elegant parent's signature perfume.

She was still shaking when she reached the familiar surroundings of the unit and tapped in the code to open the security lock.

'Jenny! You look dreadful!' Daniel exclaimed…the very last person she'd wanted to meet until she'd got herself a little better under control but absolutely the first person she would have chosen to pour out her latest troubles. 'Is your father worse?' he demanded as he took her elbow and led her into his office. 'I thought he was on the mend.'

'He is…sort of,' she agreed, her concentration scrambled by the solicitous arm he'd wrapped around her shoulders. 'Everyone knows that the angioplasty is only ever going to be a short-term fix for the problem and now he's insisting on signing himself out first thing tomorrow morning… AMA, of course.'

'And you're worried that he's not going to be able to help throwing himself back into the thick of things before he's properly recovered?'

'That goes without saying,' she said wryly. 'There are always more patients waiting to see him, but at least he can't start operating before he's been signed off as fit. That doesn't mean that he won't push himself to do everything else, though.'

'But that's not why you're upset, now,' he said after the briefest of pauses, and the fact that he'd made it a statement of fact rather than a question left her uncomfortably aware that he was the first person who'd ever been able to read her so accurately. 'Did you have an argument with him about going home too soon?'

She shook her head. 'Not with him. There'd be no point,' she said with a resigned shrug. 'He's always been a law unto himself. Even his surgeon admitted it when he couldn't persuade him to have the bypass surgery he should have had…or at least to have stents put in to hold the arteries open far enough to allow some sort of normal circulation.'

'So, what did happen?' He'd perched on the front corner of his desk with one foot propped on the edge of the chair beside hers so that he was distractingly within touching distance. At least his proximity had provided enough of a diversion to stop her shaking.

'I told my mother, categorically, that I would *not* be extending my leave of absence to take care of Dad when he goes home…that he was *her* husband and *she* should be the one to spend that time with him.'

'And she thought you should be the one to stay with him because…?' He did that raised-eyebrow trick that always fascinated her when he used it to signify that he was waiting for her to fill in the blanks.

'Because *I'm* only a nurse while *she's* a doctor and therefore her work is *so* much more important than mine,' she finished for him, clenching her hands into fists when the angry tremble came back into them.

'If you're talking about balancing life-saving surgery against emptying a bedpan, then she would have a point,' he said, then put up a staying hand so that she wouldn't interrupt before he'd finished. 'But if you're balancing an hour or two's attention in an operating theatre with an unconscious patient against days—possibly weeks—of the sort of minute-by-minute, face-to-face, meticulous nursing that can be required to return that patient to good health, then the scales would come down heavily on *that* side of the fence, every time.'

'But just because *you* understand that, it doesn't stop me feeling sick that my parents will never be able to accept my choice of profession; that I'll never be the daughter they hoped for.'

'I take it you're an only child,' he commented, 'or she'd have a second choice of babysitter for your father.'

Diverted by the personal remark she gave him a thoughtful look. 'Whereas you are either the youngest of two or an only, like me,' she decided.

'What makes you say that?' There was a quizzical smile hovering while he waited for her explanation.

'Well, most "onlys" I've known…provided they haven't been spoiled rotten by their parents…have been driven to succeed, and the fact that you reached consultant as early as you did would bear that out.'

'And second children?' he prompted.

'All the ones I've met have been either fiercely resentful of their older siblings or fiercely competitive.' She paused, waiting for a reply, then prompted impatiently, 'Well, which is it? If I were a betting person I'd say you were an only child.'

'Spot on, but in my case it was also single parent as my sperm donor decamped as soon as he learned I was on the way.'

She blinked, surprised that he'd volunteered quite so much and even more surprised by the feeling of connection that knowledge brought with it when she'd only seized on the topic to keep his attention away from her previous lack of control.

She'd had absolutely no idea that she was going to give vent to all those feelings that had been boiling inside her for almost as long as she could remember. It wasn't like her. Usually, she was far too aware of her parents' standing in the hospital to be so indiscreet, but there was just something about Daniel Carterton—about the way he seemed to value her as a colleague—that had made her drop her defences, but had she dropped them a little too far?

In spite of the new feeling of connection that the revelation of their matching only-child status seemed to have formed, she would have to watch out for that and guard against doing it again.

That was especially important in view of his response to the night they'd spent together. Much to her disappointment, instead of taking their tentative friendship to a new level of intimacy, he seemed to have completely backed off from any sort of personal contact with her. In fact this was the first time she'd seen him since he'd dropped her off at the hospital the morning her father had been admitted.

'So much for being guided by your instincts,' she muttered under her breath, later, as she double-checked the equipment trolley, case notes and test results ready for the clinic that afternoon, wondering how she could have got it so wrong. She certainly hadn't taken Daniel for being in the same league as Colin, only interested in her company for what he could get out of it.

In Colin's case, it was blatantly obvious that he saw her as the fast track to a giant leap in his career. In Daniel's…what? Had she been nothing more than a one-night stand when they both needed consolation after a horrendous day?

'Live and learn, Jenny,' she murmured softly, determinedly ignoring the ache around her heart. 'Live and learn.'

Except she had a horrible feeling that it was going to be harder than that to do it. Idiot that she was, she'd probably fallen for Daniel the first time she'd met him; the first time she'd seen the way his smile had lit up those beautiful sapphire eyes.

Then, of course, there was the small fact that, in spite of the overwhelming emotional tension of that day, she would never have made love with him *without* loving him. But that was *her* problem, not his, as was the fact that she couldn't see that situation changing. With her luck, she would probably still be hopelessly in love with him when she was a creaky-limbed eighty-year-old.

So, it all came down to looking at the situation logically, not emotionally, she told herself firmly. For now, they had to work together and she would have to make certain he never guessed how she felt, because that would just be too awkward to bear on a daily basis and she really didn't want to have to leave, not when it was obvious that working with him was all she could ever have of him.

Anyway, there wasn't much she could do about the situation if he was happy with things the way they were between them.

CHAPTER FOUR

DANIEL wasn't happy.

It had been nearly a month since the night he and Jenny had...since her father's collapse, he continued inside his head, not even allowing himself to *think* about what else had happened that night.

And that was part of his problem. The fact that he refused to think about it didn't mean that the events of that night weren't stored in exquisite detail in his brain, just waiting to be resurrected on a nightly basis as soon as his head hit the pillow.

It was slowly driving him crazy.

Or, maybe not so slowly, he thought when he saw her coming out of the staffroom with a worried expression on her face and immediately felt the need to find out what was wrong. Perhaps he'd already gone right around the bend when his concern for one particular member of staff could push everything else completely out of his head.

There were so many unassailable reasons why there should be nothing more than a professional relationship between the two of them, the fact that she was a junior member of staff in the same department being just the least of them, but he was definitely going to go demented if he couldn't talk to her—to have at least one conversation to try to clear the air between them. After all, trying to ignore the fact that the two of them had spent the night together wasn't going to help the memory fade from his mind any time soon, and he needed his brain back in working order *before* he made a serious clinical error.

'Jenny, do you think you could—?' he began.

'Daniel, I need to talk to you—' she started simultaneously.

'After you—' he said, utterly relieved that he wasn't going to have to find the words to ask her if she would go out for a drink with him. He was uncomfortably aware that it felt horribly like the first time he'd ever tried to ask a girl out…and got shot down in flames for his trouble.

'No, after you,' she demurred after a silence that seemed to stretch out into infinity, then leapt into the void, anyway. 'I was just hoping you would have a few minutes free after work this evening, that we could have a coffee, or something, and talk.'

Finally, she ran out of words, like a child's toy that needed winding up before it could chatter its way around the floor again.

'Of course.' Was it really going to be this easy? 'What time were you thinking? Sevenish?'

She pulled a wry face, wordlessly acknowledging the fact that shifts in a hospital rarely ended on time. 'Sevenish,' she agreed, her expression gratifyingly lighter than it had been just a few minutes ago, although there was still an unfamiliar shadow lurking behind those beautiful eyes.

Well, now was not the time to worry about it. There was obviously enough left of their fledgling friendship for her to have felt she could come to him when she needed a sounding board for whatever was on her mind. And if she had secrets and had chosen him to confide in, well, he couldn't help but be aware of the little bubble of hope that started to swell inside him, or stop himself from glancing at the clock to see just how many minutes there were until he'd be seeing her again.

'Can I get you something to drink, Jenny?' he offered, his wallet already in his hand as they reached the softly lit bar. 'White wine, or something stronger?'

She shook her head and hoped her smile didn't look as shaky as it felt.

'An orange juice, please, topped up with lemonade… I'm always desperate for fluids when I come off a shift. I suppose it's a combination of spending so many hours in such a warm environment and not taking in enough liquids during the day—not having enough time to drink at all, most of the time—a common complaint among doctors and nurses. And if the liquids you *do* drink are coffee, which acts as a diuretic…'

She closed her eyes as soon as he turned away to place their orders, mortified that she was doing that nervous-chattering thing again but totally unable to bear any silence between them, afraid that she might say too much, too soon.

Thank goodness, for the sake of her sanity, Daniel took over the conversation at that point, telling her how he'd come across this little out-of-the-way pub almost a year ago on a similarly bitterly cold night.

'This little valley seems to catch the worst of the weather every winter and the frost was so hard that it almost looked as if there'd been a light fall of snow. The roads were getting treacherously slick and I'd just decided to look for somewhere safe to turn around when I saw the lights of this place up ahead and couldn't resist,' he related as they navigated a route through the scattering of wooden tables with drinks in hand and found a quiet table in the bay of one of the front windows.

The cosy room wasn't big enough for any true seclusion, but there was just enough chatter from the other patrons and the group bantering with the landlord at one end of the bar that it was doubtful that anyone would overhear their conversation.

Still, the subject she wanted to bring up meant that relaxing was impossible, and Daniel didn't look as if he was sure how to begin now that he'd exhausted the topic of how he'd initially found the place.

Her heart sank as she realised just how little likelihood there was that this evening would end well. She'd known before she'd even approached him earlier today that it was highly unlikely that they would ever be on their old friendly footing again, but...

'I hope you don't mind, but I ordered two plates of lasagne, as well. It's home-made and rather good,' he added hurriedly, a look of apology on his face when she just sat staring at him, wondering when he'd managed to organise that without her hearing a word of it.

'Jenny?' he prompted gently and reached out to touch the clenched fists resting in her lap. 'One thing at a time, one decision at a time. First decision, would you like lasagne or no lasagne?'

She had to blink hard against the sudden hot press of tears brought on by his typically Daniel consideration, but she managed to find a glimpse of the smile he deserved. 'Lasagne, please,' she confirmed. 'I'm starving.'

'So, how's your father doing?' he asked and she almost leapt on the new topic with relief, glad that she was able to make him laugh as she told of her mother's exasperation with a husband she swore was as recalcitrant as a two-year-old.

The meal was every bit as good as he'd said it would be. Unfortunately, the last few mouthfuls were spoiled by the knowledge that the time for one of the most important conversations of her life was approaching with the speed of an express train; the knowledge that her relationship with the man who had been slowly winding himself around her heart from the first time she'd met him would never be the same after she told him—

'Oh!' She felt herself shriek as something crashed into her side, sending her flying, and the peaceful atmosphere around them was shattered by the most unbelievably loud mixture of noises. Sounds that convinced Jenny that a bomb had been detonated in the room as glass and furniture thudded and crashed around her.

Just seconds later all was relatively silent for the space of a single breath, then the screams and moans of the wounded rose up all around them, almost hiding the sound of running feet somewhere outside the enormous hole now letting the icy air blow across her.

'Jenny? Are you all right?' Daniel demanded urgently from the other side of their upturned table. 'I'm ringing for the emergency services but we'll need to start some sort of triage.'

'I'm okay,' she told him, wincing as she tried to wriggle out from under the surprisingly heavy table without Daniel knowing. There could be far worse injuries to deal with around them than the few bruises she would have to show. 'Can you find out what happened so we have some idea what we'll be dealing with? Was it a gas explosion in the kitchen, or what?'

She heard his feet crunching over broken glass somewhere nearby, but with the sudden darkness pressing down on her she was barely able to stop herself from begging him not to leave her. And how stupid was that when she was perfectly able to extricate herself and do something to help others unable to help themselves?

'It was a car,' he announced, appearing just as she'd managed to struggle to her feet, looming through the thick pall of dust hanging in the air. 'It must have been travelling too fast when it hit a patch of black ice on the hill outside this place and couldn't stop. We're lucky it only hit the wall before it stopped or we could have had a car parked inside the pub.'

'Is anyone trapped in it?' she demanded as she shook her head gingerly, grimacing at the sound of the falling shards of glass.

'No. I heard whoever was in it legging it, so either they'd stolen the car or they were driving under the influence and didn't want to be breathalysed.'

'I hope they weren't hurt,' she murmured as they moved in tandem through the dimly lit room, grateful for the candles the publican was lighting as they righted chairs and tables in their path, checking each place where, such a short time ago, people had been enjoying a peaceful evening. 'What happened to the lights?'

'Obviously the circuit's been damaged somewhere and tripped the fuses. The publican said it's probably safer to leave it off till it's been checked,' he explained. 'Give me a shout if you need any help.'

Jenny was grateful for the pub's plentiful supply of water and paper serviettes as she came across several patrons who had been wounded by flying glass over the next few minutes. It took longer to reassure them that help was on its way than it did to provide makeshift dressings for those that needed covering.

She suspected that the older lady who'd put out a hand to save herself when she'd tripped in the dark had probably broken her wrist, but that was the most severe injury she encountered, and the landlord's first-aid supplies provided the sling she needed to make the stalwart lady comfortable enough to await transport to hospital.

She'd been so busy going from person to person, certain that there must have been some more serious injuries from such a catastrophic accident, that she'd all but forgotten her own injuries. It wasn't until Daniel called and she twisted to check on his whereabouts that the pain in her ribs grabbed her with vicious claws and she nearly passed out.

Lightning flashes filled her vision and she was totally unable to draw breath for several endless seconds before she was able to loosen her desperate grip on the back of a nearby chair, suddenly realising with a sinking feeling that she might have been a little more severely injured than she'd initially thought.

'Fire and Rescue,' said a voice from somewhere out in the cold darkness.

'Thank God,' Jenny said, glad that their ordeal was nearly over, even as she wondered when she would have a chance to go back to the conversation they should have been having by now. Part of her was relieved that the fateful moment had been delayed, but the greater part wished that it was already over; that she knew what his reaction had been when she'd told him—

'Are you injured, Miss?' called a voice somewhere behind her and she gingerly turned just far enough to see the paramedic's uniform.

'I'm fine,' she tried to reassure him, squinting against the bright torch he was aiming in her direction.

'Are you sure?' he challenged and she had to give him points for his powers of observation. 'You look as if you've got a very sparkly case of dandruff, there. Rather a lot of glass obviously landed on you.'

'I can shake it off when I get outside,' she said dismissively then gestured in the direction of the elderly lady she'd just been tending. 'Gladys, here, is your next patient. Query Colles' fracture, left arm.'

When the time came for her patient to be loaded into the ambulance, she suddenly became very tearful and begged Jenny to come with her.

She was torn, one part of her only too willing to give the shaken woman the reassurance of a familiar face while the other wished that there was enough time to speak to Daniel, to say something before she went, to tell him… what?

Tell him that she was sorry that she'd made a mess of things by falling apart on him that night. Tell him that she missed his smiles, his jokes, the way his eyes used to sparkle at her when they were sharing a moment of triumph when a woman who had tried to start a family for years without success was finally able to hold her precious baby. Tell him that she missed spending time with him, even if it was only for a cup of coffee at the end of a long shift. Tell him that she loved—

'Go with your patient,' Daniel said easily, giving her hand a little squeeze that shouldn't have had any effect on her pulse. 'Get yourself checked over at the same time. I'll catch up with you in A and E,' and the decision was made.

Mounting the steps into the back of the ambulance without revealing her discomfort hadn't been easy, but the sharp shards of agony that any movement sent through her ribs was marginally relieved by wrapping her arms around herself.

Still, at least Daniel wasn't there to see that she was in pain. The last thing she wanted was for him to treat her as an injured patient. For her own peace of mind, it was important for the sake of any future relationship between the two of them that he should see her as a competent professional colleague.

'Here,' said the paramedic as he grabbed a thick cellular blanket from a nearby locker and wrapped its soft warmth around her.

'How is she doing?' she asked with a nod towards the older woman, noting that she looked rather wan.

'Not very comfortable, but definitely happier now you're with her,' he reported cheerfully.

Well, at least that was something, Jenny consoled herself while she tried to brace herself against the movement of the ambulance without giving any hint of her growing discomfort.

She'd heard that broken ribs were inordinately painful, but she was desperately hoping that wasn't what was causing the agony every time she moved. She really didn't want to be forced to take time off work so she was hoping that she'd be able to convince anyone who asked that she'd suffered nothing more serious than bruising.

As for her hip, at her age it was highly unlikely that she would have broken it in a mere fall, so it was just a case of putting up with the ache until the discomfort of the bruising resolved itself.

'You'll have to get out first, so we've got room to manoeuvre,' the paramedic announced as the ambulance braked before reversing into position in front of the emergency entrance. 'As you're staff, you'll be allowed to follow us through.'

The double doors swung wide and Jenny gingerly stepped out first as the paramedic helped Gladys out of the ambulance and into the waiting wheelchair. Then she was hobbling in its wake, glad that Daniel wasn't there to catch sight of her struggles.

With Gladys whisked out of sight, no doubt destined for

X-rays and the plaster room, Jenny made her way towards the A and E waiting area feeling decidedly at a loose end until Daniel arrived.

Tentatively, she lowered herself into one of the ubiquitous plastic chairs, barely suppressing a grimace as her painful hip came into contact with the unforgiving surface.

'So, you didn't escape without a bump or two, did you?' said a man's voice and she looked up in surprise to see several of the people to whom she'd given assistance back in the dusty nightmare of the damaged pub.

'Just a couple of bruises,' she said dismissively. 'How are you doing?'

'Not so bad,' said his wife with a smile. 'The nurse said they'd get to us as soon as possible—that we're both going to need a couple of stitches when they've checked that there isn't any glass left in the cuts—but we know we're not emergencies and there are people who need help before we do.' Suddenly, a thought struck her. 'My dear, you wouldn't know what happened to the people in the car, would you? Were they very badly hurt?'

'We don't know whether they were hurt because they ran away from the scene,' she said.

'Ran away?' the woman said in amazement. 'Why on earth would anyone…?'

'Joyriders!' her husband interrupted in disgusted tones. 'Although why it should be called that, I'll never know because it certainly doesn't seem to bring much joy…to the car's owner, the police, even to the stupid kids if they injure themselves driving too fast, to say nothing of the other people they injure. The government should bring back conscription. That would teach them some discipline and a sense of responsibility.'

'Don't you start, John,' his wife scolded in what was obviously a well-worn argument, and Jenny was able to tune them out, wondering if she shouldn't just take herself home rather than wait for Daniel. All she really needed was to hang her head over a large sheet of newspaper with a brush to get rid of the glass, and as for her ribs and her hip, nothing but time was needed to cure her bruises.

If that was all true, why was she still sitting there with her eyes flicking constantly towards the door, waiting for Daniel to appear?

Admit it, she berated herself silently. *You're just looking for an excuse to spend more time with the man.*

She could hardly argue with that thought, because it was true. In the last month, she'd missed those precious off-duty moments they'd spent together and had been storing up the unexpected bonus of eating a meal together this evening before she had to broach the conversation that could put a permanent barrier between them.

She shifted uncomfortably in her seat, again, and this time it was her ribs that caused her to draw in a sharp hiss of breath.

'Jenny?' said a voice beside her as her elderly companions chimed in.

'There you are, young man! How is everyone? Did that poor woman break her arm?'

'She's in good hands, now,' Daniel reassured them without breaching patient confidentiality, just as she had.

'That's good to hear. Very good to hear. Now, have you come to look after this young lady?'

'This one?' Daniel asked with a frown as he finally met her gaze.

'Yes. That one,' the elderly man said firmly. 'She spent all that time taking care of everyone else, and all the while she was injured, herself.'

'Injured?' She saw Daniel's eyes darken with concern

as he reached out a hand to lift dusty wisps of hair off her forehead. 'Where are you injured, Jenny?'

'It's nothing,' she tried to reassure him, but she might as well have saved herself the effort; he obviously wasn't buying it.

'Come with me,' he said, holding out a rather scratched hand to her. 'I'll get someone in Triage to check you over.'

'It's really not necessary,' she began but it didn't look as if he was taking no for an answer when he wrapped those long fingers around her wrist and tugged, making both her hip and her ribs stab her simultaneously.

'No arguments,' he decreed as he led her across the room towards the central desk. 'Is there anyone free to check this stubborn woman over?' he demanded. 'She's one of the victims from the pub crash and hasn't been seen by anyone, yet.'

She was going to point out that she was perfectly capable of asking for help if she wanted it, but when Daniel turned towards her she caught a brief glimpse of something that looked like abject guilt and, much though she didn't want to have her personal diagnosis of cracked ribs confirmed, couldn't deprive him of the peace of mind that allowing herself to be examined would give him.

In a very few minutes she was in a cubicle behind a drawn curtain and had finally had to admit that she might need some help when she couldn't pull her jumper over her head to get the voluminous cotton gown on.

'Dammit, Jennywren, why didn't you tell me you'd been hurt, too?' Daniel growled when he stepped behind her to tie the inevitable gown and caught sight of her bruises for the first time.

He felt sick when he saw the livid purple welt across

her ribs, and so guilty that he hadn't even suspected that she might be in pain.

'How did this happen? Why didn't you say something?'

'For the simple reason that it wasn't important when there were patients to triage,' she declared. 'It's only a couple of bruises caused by the edge of the table and when I fell on the floor, neither of which were your fault, so take that guilty expression off your face.'

'Fine!' he exclaimed, and found himself flinging both hands up in the air in a most unlikely gesture of surrender. 'We'll agree not to argue, then. I'll agree not to argue about who's responsible for your injuries if you'll agree not to argue about having X-rays to check that nothing's broken. Deal?'

If anything, her face went even paler, especially when she shook her head and had to grab for her painful ribs.

'*No* deal,' she said, her strained voice only serving to make him more determined to get those pictures. 'The National Radiological Protection Board frowns on the taking of unnecessary X-rays.'

Daniel gritted his teeth at her obstinacy and wished heartily that they were having this discussion somewhere rather more private than a curtained cubicle surrounded by dozens of other people, both patients and staff.

He doubted she'd punctured a lung—her symptoms were obviously uncomfortable but weren't severe enough for that—but there was definitely something more than a couple of bruises going on, colourful though they may be, and he was determined to find out what. He was sure there must be something that needed attention, or Jenny wouldn't be standing there with a chalk-white face clutching her ribs and avoiding putting her weight on one hip. He didn't need to be an A and E consultant to make that diagnosis.

'On the other hand,' he argued, 'the GMC would frown heavily if a doctor were negligent in the care of a patient, for example, in not taking X-rays when their use was clinically indicated.'

'Except if the patient were to exercise his or her right to refuse treatment,' she countered stubbornly. 'And anyway, I'm not your patient.'

'Dammit, Jenny, what is wrong with you?' he growled, hanging on to his temper by a fraying thread as he positioned the purloined wheelchair beside her, ready to push her wherever she needed to go. And all the while the thought that he'd blithely directed her to help everybody else when she was injured herself—injured and had never so much as hinted that she was in pain as she'd spent time examining people and reassuring them—had his guilt ballooning.

'It's only an X-ray, for heaven's sake!' he exclaimed as she folded her arms around her ribs, evidently refusing to budge in spite of the fact she could be risking a punctured lung. 'You know as well as I do that it will only take a couple of seconds to be certain you don't have any serious injuries, and it won't hurt a bit.'

'Won't hurt *me*, you mean,' she whispered through trembling lips, her hazel eyes wide and fearful as she focused them on him.

For several heartbeats he stood there as the overwhelming significance of that tiny sentence detonated inside his brain, his gaze trapped by the mixture of emotions in her expression.

Helplessly, he found himself staring at the slender body lost in voluminous patterned cotton, even though he knew it was far too soon for there to be any evidence of the miracle going on inside her.

'Jennifer?' called a commanding voice as the curtain

behind him was drawn swiftly aside. 'Have you been for an X-ray, yet? Have you broken anything?' demanded her father, flanked by not only his wife but the smugly loathsome Fletcher, too, and when he saw the gaggle of interested bystanders clogging up the corridor, Daniel knew that this definitely wasn't the place where this conversation should be taking place.

CHAPTER FIVE

'WHAT'S going on? *Has* she had any X-rays yet?' her father demanded again almost before the door of the interview room had closed behind them, as usual hating not to be in charge of whatever was going on.

It hadn't taken Daniel long to whisk them along the corridor to the relatives' interview room and Jenny could almost have thrown her arms around him in gratitude for his consideration. There must have been almost a dozen people within sight of that curtained cubicle, and heaven only knew how many more within earshot.

'Jenny won't be having any X-rays,' Daniel said as he stood beside her, one reassuring hand warm on her shoulder, and for the first time Jenny knew the delightful feeling of knowing that she wasn't going to be facing her parents alone. 'It's not considered advisable in the early stages of a pregnancy.'

'You're *pregnant*?'

The words were spoken almost in unison in equal tones of incredulity by the three people facing them and Jenny didn't think she'd ever been so embarrassed before, but it wasn't the embarrassment that would remain in her memory for ever so much as the different expressions on her audience's faces.

Her parents wore almost identical masks of disapproval

and disappointment…but when had they ever looked at her in any other way?

After his initial blank-faced shock, Colin's expression had become a strange mixture of calculation and determination as he worked out how to turn this unexpected situation to his advantage. She could easily imagine him rubbing his hands with the gleeful thought that her father's shoes were about to be handed to him on the same platter that would hold her head.

She couldn't even bring herself to meet Daniel's eyes, knowing just how much he must hate being mixed up in such an unsavoury situation, and her heart felt like a lump of lead in her chest at the opportunity she'd missed to tell him her news in a less public way; to explain that, despite the fact her stupidity had forced him into the position of becoming a father, she had absolutely no intention of trying to use the pregnancy to tie him to her…much as she might want to.

'Oh, but this is *wonderful* news, darling,' Colin burbled with a smile as wide as a letterbox showing every one of his thirty-two chemically whitened teeth. 'Now you'll have to get busy organising the wedding, won't you?' he added gleefully as he walked towards her with his arms spread wide, only to have Daniel step in his path with a determined expression on his face.

'Just a moment, Fletcher,' he said in growling tones reminiscent of a very big, very powerful guard dog with a trespasser in his sights. 'I wouldn't go counting your chickens *just* yet.'

'This is hardly any of *your* business,' the shorter man sneered smugly. 'You might be Jennifer's boss, but her parents already know that I've proposed to her. All this does is brings the date forward a bit.'

'Hardly!' Daniel snorted dismissively. 'I know for a

fact that Jenny has refused your proposal, in no uncertain terms, so I think it's highly unlikely that she'll be hurrying to organise a wedding with you under *any* circumstances, and certainly not these.'

The whole situation was already making her feel distinctly uncomfortable, and the only redeeming factor she could think of was that neither Clive nor her parents knew about the night she'd spent with Daniel. In her parents' eyes, the very fact that she was pregnant without being married was tantamount to a declaration that she was totally without morals.

She was overwhelmingly grateful that Daniel had transferred the whole conversation behind closed doors. The last thing she needed was for this information to be broadcast right around the hospital. Her parents would never forgive her for bringing such shame on the family.

The fact that she was now shut in a room with both of her parents and with Colin doing his best to ingratiate himself with her father made her feel even more queasy, but there was no way out of it. The least she could do was face them on her feet rather than having them all talking down at her, but that was easier said than done when everything was hurting so much.

Then Daniel's arm wrapped gently around her shoulders to support her as she pushed her way out of the chair, and when he automatically made certain that the fabric of the flimsy hospital gown was wrapped firmly across her back to preserve her modesty, she suddenly felt the warmth of certainty that there was at least one person in the room who would stand up for her in the coming argument.

Not that her father was happy about his presence.

'Does *he* have to be here while the family's dirty linen is aired?' her father challenged her with a glare at Daniel.

Jenny had to turn her whole body so that she could

see Daniel's face, causing his arm to slip away from her shoulders. Immediately she felt its loss, but when his lean-fingered hand sought hers among the limp folds of her hospital-issue gown in a wordless gesture of support, she gratefully allowed him to wrap her own in it. The tingling warmth that permeated her whole body made it easy to ignore the glares aimed at them by both her father and Colin.

'*I* want Daniel to be here with me. He's become a good friend,' she said, and as the unexpected words emerged, she suddenly realised that she couldn't have meant them more, in spite of the fact that the two of them had hardly spoken since that fateful night.

'Is it true, Jennifer?' Now it was her mother's turn to take the floor. Her parents had always made concerted attacks when they felt that their daughter wasn't living up to their expectations. '*Are* you pregnant?'

There wasn't a hint of anything other than censure in her sharp tone or her expression; certainly no dawning joy at the realisation that her first grandchild might be on the way.

Still, why should she have expected anything different? It was hard to recall anything she'd done that her mother had approved of, right from her earliest memories of the scoldings she'd received for spoiling the pretty dresses she'd been forced to wear when she'd rather have worn something more suitable for climbing trees and riding bi-cycles.

Then Daniel's hand tightened just a little bit around hers, his thumb stroking across her knuckles reminding her that she wasn't standing alone, this time…but it also reminded her that she wasn't that little girl any more. She was an adult and it was up to her to deal with her own life's choices.

'Yes, Mother, I'm pregnant,' she agreed with a show of calmness that she definitely wasn't feeling. 'I did a test this morning.'

'Stupid girl!' the elegant older woman hissed, her perfectly unlined complexion a testament to her husband's skill with a knife. 'When have you *ever* managed to do anything right? I suppose it's up to your father and I to sort out yet another mess for you. There isn't time to organise a proper wedding so it'll have to be in the nearest Registry Office.'

'*No*, Mother!' Jenny exclaimed, but she might as well have tried to stop a Centurion tank with a feather duster.

'Colin, can I leave it up to you to find out the earliest possible appointment?' her mother continued, completely ignoring her. 'Jennifer will have to go with you to fill out the forms and I think you'll both need to take your birth certificates with you, but that shouldn't be any...'

'Mrs Sinclair, if I might interrupt for a moment?' Daniel said in a strangely soft tone that sent prickles over Jenny's skin. She didn't think she'd ever heard him speak like that before and certainly wouldn't want to be on the receiving end of it. She could well understand why even her mother went instantly silent. 'Don't you think that telling Fletcher to organise his marriage to your daughter to legitimise her baby might be a bit premature when you haven't even asked her if the baby is his?'

'Of course it's mine!' Colin blustered, suddenly redfaced at the turn the conversation had taken, but she noticed that he didn't make any attempt to meet her eyes. In fact, now that she looked closer, he was definitely avoiding everyone's gaze in a decidedly shifty way. 'And I had every intention of giving Jenny an engagement ring after the dinner dance,' he added suddenly, with the air of a magician pulling a rabbit out of a hat.

'Ah, yes! The dinner dance!' Daniel exclaimed with that steely edge of menace growing with every quietly spoken word. 'That would be the dinner dance that you forced Jenny to attend with you in spite of the fact that she'd already told you she didn't want to go out with you again, would it? The dinner dance where you deliberately got her drunk to make certain that you would have an excuse to escort her home?'

The stupefied expression on her parents' faces was something she'd never thought to see, but it wasn't nearly as riveting as the sickly pallor that was rapidly appearing on her erstwhile suitor's.

'And if you're now claiming that Jenny's pregnant with your child,' he continued inexorably, 'then I doubt that there would be any court in the country that wouldn't convict you of premeditated rape.'

Such an ugly little word and so full of evil that it made her shudder. And she had Daniel to thank that it hadn't happened. Colin's greed and ambition obviously so far outweighed any concepts of decency and honesty that he would even try to claim responsibility for the pregnancy as a way to force her hand.

As for the baby, her only regret was that it was going to be coming into the world without the benefit of a mother and father in a committed, loving relationship, and she had no one to blame for that other than herself.

'I didn't *rape* her!' Colin exclaimed in a panicky voice, suddenly seeming to notice the gaping black hole that had opened at his feet. 'I only topped her glass up a couple of times.'

'You *deliberately* got her drunk? *Why*, for God's sake?' her father demanded, looking utterly dumbfounded. 'Why on earth would you do such a thing to her? You told me you were in love with Jennifer…that you wanted to marry her.'

Colin had the frantic look of a trapped rat and didn't look as if he dared to open his mouth for fear of making the whole situation worse. In the end it was Daniel who put the whole shameful plan into words

'He's probably not honest enough to admit it, but he's *never* been in love with Jenny. He probably only told you that because he thought you would help him to persuade her to marry him. The only thing he really wants is to be your son-in-law,' he said succinctly and Jenny saw Colin flinch at the brutal way he'd worded it. 'At a guess it was part of his master plan…to become part of your family so that he would be at the head of the queue to step straight into your shoes as soon as you retire. Of course, if that part of his plan didn't work…if he didn't get the job in spite of the fact that he was your son-in-law, I don't doubt that the despicable worm was counting on the long-term benefits of marrying her…that all your family wealth and property would drop straight into his greedy hands when you die.'

'Dear God, Fletcher, are you really that venal? Did you really think you could get my daughter drunk and rape her to get an easy life?' Douglas Sinclair was roaring out the words by the time he got to the end, the veins standing out alarmingly at his temples. 'Get out of here and clear your desk. As of this minute you are no longer employed at this hospital. And don't even *think* about asking me for a reference. Oh, and just in case you think you can claim unfair dismissal and use employment law to screw some money out of the hospital, let me remind you that it would only take one word to the appropriate authorities for you to be struck off for what you've done, and for you to be spending time in prison… In fact that's still a distinct possibility, if my daughter decides to make a formal complaint against you…which I really hope she does!'

The look Colin threw in her direction was a disturbing mixture of terror and hate but she couldn't help herself taking personal satisfaction as she hammered the final nail in the coffin of his dreams.

'By the way, Colin, you should have done your research a bit better before you set your sights on me as the fast track to Easy Street and my parents' estate in the country. Didn't anyone ever mention that I'm only their *adopted* daughter; that I don't carry a single drop of Sinclair blood?'

Colin slunk out of the room like a dog with his tail between his legs and Jenny couldn't find a single scrap of regret for his misery because he'd brought it all on himself.

'So,' her father said, his colour slightly less alarming now that the object of his ire had left the room, 'how do you know so much about what's been going on in our daughter's life, Dr…?'

'Carterton. Daniel Carterton,' he supplied but Jenny wasn't willing to relinquish her hold on the security of his hand just yet, even if he'd wanted to offer to shake her father's hand. 'Jenny and I work together. We've been friends for several months…ever since she moved across from NICU.'

'But that doesn't explain how you could possibly know what Fletcher had planned; that he'd got Jennifer drunk to…to try to force her into marriage,' her mother broke in, her voice clipped and precise and obviously intent on getting answers.

Jenny knew of old just how relentless Helen Sinclair could be in one of her inquisitions and her heart sank that Daniel was about to be grilled just because he was here to give her moral support.

'I knew because…' He paused for a fraction of a second

before continuing. 'Because on the night of the party I happened to be in the right place at the right time to see what was happening,' he explained as simply and easily as if he was discussing the weather, apparently completely unaffected by the two pairs of eyes dissecting him. 'And because Jenny and I are close friends, I know that your daughter is far too choosy to want to go to bed with Fletcher voluntarily,' he added pointedly, but only Jenny knew that there was a hidden implication in his words... that she'd had no such reservations about going to bed with Daniel...had virtually propositioned him, in fact.

'So, has she told you who else could be the father of her baby?' It was her father's turn to take over the questioning. 'Do *you* know if she's been seeing anyone else?'

Jenny was just about to leap into the conversation to tell her parents that it was not appropriate to grill her boss about her social life, shuddering at the very thought of her parents' ire being turned on Daniel when it had been at *her* instigation that the two of them had spent the night together, when he answered.

'I'm afraid that is privileged information, sir,' he said formally but impeccably politely. 'Your daughter will have to be the one to tell you when she's ready. That's her right and I wouldn't presume to take it away from her.'

'But that's completely ridiculous and totally unacceptable!' her mother exploded, almost incandescent with rage. 'She's pregnant! In just a few weeks everyone will be able to *see* that she's pregnant! For the sake of the Sinclair name she should be respectably married before that happens.'

'No matter what anybody else deems *acceptable*, I doubt that Jenny would ever get married before she's good and ready, Mrs Sinclair.' Daniel turned just far enough that he could meet her eyes then deliberately held her gaze as he continued. 'She's an adult, and that means *she* gets to make the choices about her own life, regardless of your name.'

His words were an almost uncanny echo of her own thoughts at the beginning of this whole messy confrontation and she was so very grateful for them that she was close to tears.

'In the meantime, she's had a pretty harrowing evening,' he continued, pressing the hand he'd been holding throughout the whole encounter between both of his and smiling reassuringly. 'She was looking after other people in spite of her own injuries—a real credit to both of you—but she should be going to bed to allow her injuries to heal, as well as for the sake of her baby, so if you don't mind…?' He curved his arm around her shoulders again as he settled her back into the wheelchair then pushed her to the door, and to Jenny's absolute amazement, her parents didn't utter a single word of objection.

She held her breath all along the corridor until they turned the first corner before she spoke, her words trembling with a mixture of tension and relief.

'Oh, Daniel, I wish I'd met you at least twenty years ago. My life would have been so much more pleasant if you'd been there to run interference between me and my parents.'

'Oh, I doubt it, Jenny,' he disagreed with an unexpected edge to his voice. 'I was far more obviously from the wrong side of the tracks, back then.' And he doubted that her parents would have even let him in at the tradesmen's entrance to spend time with her, let alone the front door.

'Crazy man,' she chuckled, suddenly unutterably weary. 'Do you know, I don't think I've even got enough energy to get back into my clothes, let alone to get myself home?'

'Well, my car's not far away, so that's one less thing to worry about,' he pointed out so reassuringly that she was quite happy to leave him to make decisions for her while her brain no longer seemed capable of doing so.

In short order, he grabbed a clean set of scrubs and a passing nurse to help her into them, then brought his car right into the hospital forecourt and guided her gently into the front seat.

Instead of her minuscule home with the innumerable stairs, he took her to his own flat, where he insisted on dosing her with analgesia that was safe in pregnancy and tucking her into his own hastily remade bed.

She lay for several delightful moments luxuriating in the pleasure of being surrounded by the scent of freshly laundered bed linen underlain by hints of Daniel's soap and shampoo retained by the pillows and duvet, drawing in the darker notes that could only come from his own body. It was almost like being surrounded by the man himself... almost, but not quite. The bed definitely seemed far too big for one when the last time she'd been in it she'd been sharing it with its owner.

With her brain growing fuzzy with the combination of tiredness, adrenaline let-down and analgesia, it wasn't long before she drifted away into sleep, surfacing briefly when Daniel roused her to swallow the next set of tablets then settling gratefully back onto the pillow and wondering groggily why it felt so much as if it was Daniel's shoulder under her cheek and why his bedclothes cradling her felt so much like being surrounded by his arms.

It was a disappointment when her internal alarm clock woke her a few minutes before six to open her eyes and find herself alone in the bed. More than a disappointment when she'd been so convinced that Daniel had been sharing the bed with her.

'But life is full of disappointments,' she murmured philosophically, then yelped when she tried to roll over to get out of bed and was suddenly reminded in the most painful way that there had been a serious reason why she'd ended up at his flat rather than her own.

She raised her head experimentally, wanting to know just how far she could move before the pain in her ribs grew unbearable, and stopped, transfixed by the hollowed evidence that a head had recently been resting on the pillow beside hers.

'So, I *didn't* imagine it!' she whispered in delight, feeling a grin lifting both corners of her mouth at the realisation that she hadn't been dreaming. Daniel *had* been holding her gently, protectively, in his arms; she *had* been sleeping with her head on his shoulder and his arms around her.

She was tempted to bury her nose in that tantalising hollow to draw his unmistakable scent deep inside her when there was a sound at the bedroom door.

'Awake at last, Sleeping Beauty?' Daniel's voice sounded husky, almost as if he was still half asleep, and his eyes were heavy lidded as they travelled over her among the tumbled bedclothes.

'D-Daniel?' Her pulse accelerated to the speed of sound in the fraction of a second it took to realise that there was now a very intent expression in those wide-awake eyes; an expression that made her very aware of the fact that he was standing just feet away from the bed that they might have shared quite innocently last night, but it was the same bed that they'd shared far from innocently a month ago.

'I made you some tea and toast,' he announced, and finally allowed her to drag her gaze away from his to take in the mug and plate he was holding. 'I nearly made you coffee, but then I remembered...' And just like that, reality brought her crashing to the ground with even greater effect than that out-of-control car last night.

'I was going to tell you last night,' she said. 'That was why I wanted to see you, to talk to you. Well, not just to talk...' Oh, she was making such a mess of this.

'Stop stressing about it, Jenny. I had managed to work that much out for myself,' he said calmly as he deposited the gently steaming mug and the plate piled high with perfectly browned toast. And on the edge of the plate were two white tablets just like the ones he'd given her at intervals during the night.

The memory was clearer now, of him supporting her with a naked arm around her shoulders while she'd downed the glass of water he'd supplied to wash the tablets down. In fact, the memory was far too clear if she was going to be able to avoid blushing while she sat up enough to reach the breakfast he'd brought for her while still keeping the covers high enough for modesty.

'I *have* seen it all before,' he reminded her wickedly, making her fumble, and she lost control of both the bedclothes and her blush.

'Not while you were standing there fully clothed, you haven't,' she snapped crossly, dragging an armful of duvet up to her chin.

'Well, if that's what's upsetting you, it can be easily remedied,' he said as he reached for the hem of his sweatshirt.

'Don't you dare!' she squeaked, closing her eyes tightly then groaning when she realised what a fool she must look.

'Ah, Jennywren, I'm sorry. I'll stop teasing you... for now. Here...' He picked up the mug and plate that she'd almost forgotten about while she fought back her blushes, and passed them to her. Then, when she would have thought he'd turn and leave the room, she watched wide-eyed as he moved just one pace away to settle himself at the foot of the bed.

'Listen, we need to talk about a few things,' he said, all traces of humour gone.

'Things,' she repeated blankly, suddenly no more ready for this conversation this morning than she'd been last night, in spite of the fact he already knew the worst.

'Unfortunately, after last night, the hospital grapevine is probably already alive with rumours—'

'Thanks to my parents and Colin,' she interrupted grimly, despairing at the thought that her reputation could have been damaged beyond repair by that weasel, and through no fault of her own. Well, that wasn't strictly true if she were being honest because she had willingly made love with Daniel and *that* had resulted in her pregnancy. But after that less than peaceful meeting in A and E, how long would it be before the whole hospital knew that she was pregnant and the speculation grew about the identity of the baby's father?

Colin had been denied the chance to claim her baby as his, but that wouldn't matter to the grapevine.

'Fletcher's involvement certainly won't have helped matters, especially when word gets round that he's been summarily kicked out of his job,' Daniel agreed coolly, echoing her thoughts, but there was a glimpse of something dark and angry behind his apparent lack of emotion that she knew wasn't aimed at her.

'Nor were things helped by my mother's insistence on trying to arrange the details of a shotgun wedding in a less than soundproof room in the middle of a busy A and E department,' she added, her shoulders slumping under the weight of yet another instance where she'd disappointed her parents. 'I can't thank you enough for getting them all to go into the interview room, but neither of my parents seemed to care enough to keep their voices down.'

'By that stage there were already enough people around to have guessed what was going on so it was probably too little, too late; the damage had already been done.' He watched her silently for a moment while she took a bite and tried to enjoy the perfect toast he'd made for her even though she knew the conversation was far from over. She could tell from the contemplative expression on his face that his formidable brain was systematically working through the situation in the same way that he analysed the far more life-threatening problems they dealt with at work.

'Well,' he began again when she was starting to wish for a way to disappear, suddenly realising that she had no right to expect anything further from him; certainly not that he would be responsible for finding a solution to the situation. As he'd reminded her parents, she was an adult, now, so what she did with her life was up to her. Not that she wouldn't welcome his input, but...

'As the saying goes, *What can't be cured must be endured*,' she commented weakly. 'The gossip will die down as soon as the grapevine latches onto something or someone else.'

'In the meantime, we're left with deciding where we go from here,' he said steadily.

'We?' she echoed, desperately trying to subdue the sudden leap that her heart gave in her chest. Was that just a slip of the tongue or did he actually envisage some sort of...what? Collaboration over the pregnancy? An ongoing relationship?

Hah! As if that was likely.

Even if she wasn't guilty of virtually propositioning him that night, he was still the man he was—Daniel Carterton, her highly successful boss and a rising star in a very specialised field of medicine who had sex appeal to spare and a choice of any woman he wanted. Why would he be interested in someone that not even her parents valued very highly when his involvement in the whole messy situation had been the result of nothing more than a one-off emotional overload?

'Well,' he began again, his measured tone sounding as if he was having to search for words, something that was rare in his professional life, 'considering the fact that Colin's involvement is at an end, and add to that your determination not to allow your parents to dictate to you…'

She groaned at the reminder. 'You do realise that my mother hasn't given up, don't you?' she warned him. 'I wouldn't be surprised if she employed a private detective to hunt down a prospective groom. She'll be absolutely mortified if she doesn't get to stage the wedding to end all weddings for all their toffee-nosed friends, so you can bet that she's already drawing up lists and making phone calls to see just how quickly she can get something organised, preferably while the pregnancy can still be disguised under a voluminous meringue of a dress.'

'You? In a meringue dress? You'd look like the Christmas fairy!' He gave a snort of laughter that would have had her chuckling, too, if the topic hadn't been so serious.

'Don't laugh too hard,' she warned. 'You might end up having to leave the country because both my parents have gone away convinced that they're going to be able to get you to tell them who the baby's father is. You mark my words! You're going to have both of them cornering you time and time again until you finally tell them what they want to know.'

'You don't *honestly* think they'd do that,' he scoffed but there was a slightly thoughtful edge to his expression.

'You'd better believe it,' she cautioned. 'Once they've

made a decision, nothing will stop them, unless you can do something to make their goal impossible.'

'You sound as if you speak from experience,' he said. 'You've come up against their determination before, I take it?'

'At school,' Jenny said, feeling slightly shamefaced when she looked back at what an idiot she'd been as a rebellious teenager. 'According to them, I had two choices of career open to me—I was either going to be a lawyer or a doctor. But preferably a doctor, to follow in the family's illustrious footsteps.'

'And?' he prompted when she paused, heartily wishing she'd never begun this topic because it certainly didn't show *her* up in a particularly good light, either.

'And the only way I could think of to make them tear up all the application forms was to deliberately fail my exams.' She shook her head. 'I'll never forget the expressions on their faces when I handed them my exam results— my utterly *appalling* exam results—and announced, "Try to force me to go to law school or medical school with *those* grades," and flounced out of the room.'

'Ah, Jenny. Talk about cutting off your nose to spite your face!' he exclaimed. 'So when *did* you get those marks I saw on your CV when you applied to work on my team?'

She blinked at the realisation that he must have read all the way through her CV to know that she must have retaken the exams at some stage.

'I approached the local comprehensive school who contacted my previous school—my very expensive all-girls boarding school—for a résumé of my marks during my last year there. Then, with my promise that I'd produce any extra course work required and would put in the necessary hours of revision, they allowed me to resit the exams with their pupils the following year, even though I wasn't attending the school.'

'What were you doing if you weren't going to school?' Trust his quick brain to pick up on that.

'I got myself a job—as a hospital cleaner—and shared the rent in a flat with three other girls. I did most of my studying at the library, where there wasn't the noise of my flatmates getting ready to go out on the town to distract me.'

'Well, knowing you managed straight As, I know it wasn't a case of not having the brains to pass the exams first time round,' he commented. 'But if it was just the fact that you didn't want to be forced into doing something you didn't want to do—'

'That is *exactly* the same situation I'll be facing again, if my parents have their way,' she interrupted, amazed to discover that the man had actually registered the grades she'd entered on her CV when she'd applied for her current post. Did he have a photographic memory that he'd retained so much?

How much more did he know about her when she knew almost nothing about him?

CHAPTER SIX

JENNY couldn't believe how lonely her little flat felt when she closed the door behind her.

Just yesterday it had felt like a sanctuary, her first home that she actually owned—well, in partnership with her bank, that was; the first place where she had complete control of what went on inside it from the simple things like choosing the colour to paint her bedroom to the more costly things like the eventual remodelling of the outdated kitchen when she could afford it.

She dropped her sadly battered handbag in her favourite armchair and walked gingerly across to the kitchen and the kettle, desperately needing a cup of tea…well, actually she'd rather have a large mug of coffee, but that was off the menu for at least the next seven or eight months, so tea it would have to be while she mulled over the changes that a single day had brought.

Just a month ago she'd been perfectly content with her life as a whole, happy with her decision to take a sideways step within the department to concentrate on mothers and their at-risk babies in the months before they were born rather than the intensive pressure of nursing those whose arrival had happened before it was safe.

It was hard to believe that everything had changed in

the space of twenty-four hours, and not just because of the results of that pregnancy test, either.

She wasn't certain, yet, whether to be grateful that Daniel's analytical mind had enabled him to put the details together to face Colin with his foul machinations. Part of her would have been perfectly happy never to have known what the man was capable of. It certainly didn't do much for her self-confidence to know that his pursuit hadn't had anything to do with love—at least, not love of *her*.

On the other hand, it had been fantastic to know what it felt like to have someone's unconditional support for the first time in her life; to have Daniel stand up for her and demand that she be accorded the right to make her own decisions. The fact that she should have done the same thing for herself…well, perhaps she could excuse herself on the grounds that she hadn't been firing on all cylinders, last night, otherwise she'd like to believe that she'd have managed to knock the idea of a rushed marriage on the head without Daniel's assistance.

Well, she hoped that was true, even though the memory of her mother's anger at her pregnancy was still enough to make her cringe like a child.

What she could be utterly certain of was that there was absolutely no way she would have ever gone through any sort of marriage with Colin, no matter how much shame and blame her parents heaped on her head. Even if she'd never found out what he'd planned to do to her, she knew she could never have married him without loving him, and she could never love him because she had already given her heart to Daniel.

'And that, in a nutshell, is why I'm standing here, in my own flat with a solitary cup of tea, talking to myself,' she said, deliberately voicing the words aloud. 'I know I could be curled up on that perfect butter-soft leather couch in

Daniel's sitting room wrapped in his dressing gown waiting for him to come back from the hospital to cook a meal for us, but that would just be taking advantage of him.'

She allowed the words to die away because she knew that they were less than the truth.

Yes, she *did* feel a measure of that, now that her aches and pains were under control with the analgesics she was taking. It *had* seemed as if she was taking advantage of Daniel, delicious though it had felt to have him waiting on her, hand and foot. But by far the most pressing reason for calling a taxi to take her home was the fact that she was afraid that she was going to be so seduced by the bone-deep delight of knowing that he was going to be coming back to her that she wasn't going to be able to tear herself away from him if she stayed much longer.

So here she was, back in her own, oh, so lonely, little domain, and already bitterly regretting her impetuous departure; already kicking herself for being an idiot when she could be enjoying Daniel's company for another night and wondering if, when the time came to go to sleep, he would suggest that they should share that big comfortable bed again.

'And *that's* why you came home,' she reminded herself with a scowl, knowing that he would have only had to look vaguely interested in a repeat of that night a month ago for her to eagerly agree. 'What does it say about you that you'd be so willing to go to bed with someone who's not in love with you?' she scolded grimly, recognising that the fact that she was in love with him could never be enough, not for any sort of long-term relationship and especially not when a baby's happiness was at stake. And that was without taking into account the fact that Daniel could have any woman he wanted just by crooking his finger, so the likelihood that he would want to be burdened with her when he could have someone equally as high-flying as himself was infinitesimal.

It wasn't as if she was going to be desperate for his help in supporting the child. For all their faults, her parents would be unlikely to let the world see them abandon their only child and grandchild. Anyway, if all else failed, she could always fall back on the allowance that had been steadily mounting up, untouched, in a savings account. Pride and stubbornness had made her determined to forge her career under her own efforts, and so far she'd managed, albeit with a few spells subsisting on little more than baked beans on toast.

No, she certainly had no intention of trying to use her pregnancy to tie Daniel to her. The fact that she loved him was totally unimportant, unless he loved her, too. And as he'd obviously been keeping his distance from her ever since the night they'd spent together that clearly wasn't the case.

'So, you've got a couple more days to get your head together and then you'll be back to work and it'll be business as usual,' she lectured herself with a determined nod.

Except she had a feeling that she was only fooling herself if she thought it was ever going to be business as usual. Apart from the fact that day by day she was going to have the burgeoning reminder of her pregnancy, there was also the fact that she was never going to be able to look at Daniel without remembering the night when he'd made the rest of the world disappear.

Then, of course, she had no idea how he was going to react to her precipitate disappearance, today.

She'd written him a brief letter to thank him for his hospitality…well, her mother's years of training in the social niceties couldn't be completely ignored, especially when they were so appropriate. She really hadn't been in a fit state to look after herself last night, and it had been so nice, just for a little while, to bask in the illusion that the man she loved really cared about her, too.

The next morning, when she woke up at her usual time with the thought of two more days stretching ahead of her without seeing Daniel, suddenly her aches and pains didn't seem so bad any more.

With her decision made, she swiftly headed to the bathroom to get ready to go to work and actually arrived at the hospital nearly an hour before her shift was due to start.

'What on earth are you doing here, today?' Daniel growled under his breath when he slipped into the room and found himself next to Jenny in her usual spot during handover. 'You're supposed to be off for another two days.'

Ever since he'd arrived back at his flat to discover that his Jennywren had flown he'd been in a ghastly mood, and the sudden unexpected leap of delight that his heart had given as he'd opened the door to see her familiar face had just made his temper worse.

It was bad enough to realise that the prospect of missing seeing her for the next two days could affect him so strongly, but the significance of her leaving his flat as soon as she could had driven home the fact that she hadn't wanted to stay there nearly as much as he'd wanted her to stay; the realisation that he would have been perfectly happy if she'd *never* left.

But that was totally irrelevant to her turning up for her shift today when he knew exactly how much pain she'd been in during the night before last. He'd lain there with her in his arms and winced at every whimper as she'd moved in her sleep, guilt assailing him that she'd been the one who'd been injured instead of him. And to compound his remorse, there was the memory that he'd directed her to look after everyone else without first checking to see if *she* was injured.

It hardly mattered that the outcome for everyone in the pub had been better than anyone could have hoped with only a dislocated knee and broken wrist to add to the assorted cuts to be cleaned and sutured. That didn't excuse his negligence towards the one woman who was rapidly coming to mean the world to him.

No, much as it went against his attraction to her—and his newfound need to take care of her—it would definitely be better for Jenny if he kept his distance from her. But how could he, now that he knew about the baby she was carrying?

The baby…*his* baby… Dear God, he'd barely *begun* to take in the fact that she was pregnant, and he certainly couldn't allow himself to think about it, now, not when he was going to need every scrap of concentration to cope with a full morning's clinic, and especially if Jenny was going to be in the room with him for even part of that time.

'I remembered that it was your clinic day,' she muttered blandly, speaking softly enough not to interrupt the meeting that was just winding down around them, but his ears were so attuned to her voice that he didn't miss a word as she continued. 'I didn't want to miss out on seeing the patients I've come to know—the ones who already know me from previous visits—or seeing the new ones for the first time and finding out if there's anything you can do to help them.'

He could well understand why she would want to be there. He knew how much he looked forward to seeing how the patients were progressing, constantly delighted when progress was good and he knew he'd done his part towards bringing a healthy baby into the world. The satisfaction of such cases almost outweighed the desperate times when he was unable to work a miracle.

'You can be there *only* if you give me your word that you will tell me if you're hurting too much,' he said, torn between his concern for her and his delight that they would be working together today.

'Jenny?' Sister Rethman's voice carried easily over the buzz of conversation that followed the end of the handover. 'A word, please? Oh, and, Daniel, if you've got a minute, too?'

'I hate it when she does that,' Jenny muttered as he stepped closer to her to allow their colleagues to pass them on the way out of the door. 'It makes me feel as if I've been called to the headmistress's office to be told off for talking during assembly.'

'Did you have a lot of experience of being called to her office?' he asked, fighting to quell a grin. He could just imagine Jenny as a rebellious teenager.

'Remind me to tell you about the time I dared her to tell my parents she wanted to expel me from my mother's Alma Mater and she nearly hit me with her paperweight,' she said darkly as they approached Veronica Rethman. 'You wanted a word, Sister?' she finished brightly.

'Are you sure you should have come in today, Jenny?' her senior enquired kindly. 'By all accounts, that was a pretty nasty accident last night and you were one of the injured, to say nothing of...' She gave a meaningful glance towards Jenny's waist and once again Daniel was amazed at just how swiftly gossip could travel.

'I'm due in clinic with Dr Carterton, today,' she said, apparently calmness personified, but he could hear an edge of tension in her voice and wondered when he'd developed the facility for reading her like that. 'It's not heavy work and I've promised to let him know if I can't cope, but I would really rather keep busy than stare at four walls for a couple of days.'

'Well, you make certain that you *do* take it easy, today,' her superior said. 'Although, heaven knows we're so short of staff at the moment and there aren't many who could step in for you. Daniel, are you sure she's really fit to do it? The hospital's insurers would have a fit if anything goes wrong.'

'I'll keep an eye on her, Ronnie,' he reassured her, crazily wishing he had the right to wrap Jenny in cotton wool to protect her. 'Was that all you wanted?'

'No. Josh asked me to pass on a message that somehow got routed through his secretary. Aliyah Farouk has asked if her husband can accompany her to her appointment later this morning, if that's all right with you? Would you like me to organise things with orthopaedics and page you when she arrives?'

'If orthopaedics are happy to let Faz off the leash, I'd be delighted for him to come with her. Has he really made *that* much progress, already?' It didn't seem so long ago that the man wasn't expected to live. Was he really ready to accompany his wife to an obstetric appointment?

'Apparently so,' she said with a quick glance at the watch pinned to her uniform pocket and a grimace. 'Anyway, I've passed on the message and I'll do the organising if you want me to. Now, the two of you had better get moving or your clinic will run later than ever.'

'Do you ever feel that you should salute and click your heels when she uses that tone?' Daniel said out of the corner of his mouth as the two of them headed towards the outpatient clinic and was delighted to hear Jenny chuckle.

'All the time,' she agreed slightly breathlessly, and he slowed his steps so that it was easier for her to keep pace with him, suddenly aware that this was the first time her surprisingly long legs hadn't been able to keep up and realising with a scowl that it must be because of the horrendous bruising she'd suffered.

'She's just one of those people who was born to organise everyone and everything,' Jenny continued with the lilt of laughter in her voice that could put sunshine into the cloudiest day. 'Some of the nurses were speculating what her house must be like. Somebody suggested that she probably lines up her herbs and spices in alphabetical order, too.'

He was grateful that the light-hearted conversation lasted all the way to the waiting area outside his room so that he couldn't be tempted to turn it to more personal topics. With the gossips already having a field day at Jenny's expense, the last thing she needed was to have someone overhear them discussing her pregnancy and the events surrounding it.

'Bring the first patient in as soon as you've checked the basic details,' he suggested before he closed the door, shutting himself into the bland office space for a few moments' privacy to review the file on the top of the teetering pile and correlate the information with the computer records. He knew that he could rely on Jenny to complete the usual checks on weight, blood pressure and so on that would be completed at any pre-natal check-up.

Sure enough, it was only a few minutes before a tap on the door heralded the first patient of the day.

'Hello, Mrs Finch. Come in and make yourself comfortable. Now, how much has your doctor told you about the reason why he's referred you to see me?' Daniel asked when the scared-looking woman had settled herself on the very edge of the seat by his desk.

'Not much,' she said nervously, looking as if she could burst into tears at any moment. 'I went for my three-month scan and they told me I was having twins but then they said they'd seen something. I don't know what they called it but it's something about transfusions and they said my babies could die.'

'Was it a shock to hear that you were having twins or are there other twins in the family?' he asked as he called up the images from that first scan and bent forward to take a closer look, using his usual ploy of sidetracking a patient's attention slightly to try to lower the tension in the room a little.

'My husband was a twin but he was the only one who survived the birth,' Amy Finch said with a glance in the petrified-looking man's direction. 'His mother said she was three days in labour and the other boy was dead by the time he was born.' She reached for her husband's hand and clutched it in a white-knuckled grip. 'That's not what's going to happen to my babies, is it?'

'We'll do our very best for your babies, I promise you,' Daniel said, aware that promising anything more than that would be cruel, especially when he didn't yet know exactly how precarious the lives of her babies were. 'And Staff Nurse Sinclair can confirm that I will always tell you the truth.'

'Even when it's something you might not want to hear,' Jenny confirmed with a wry expression. 'But at least you know that you can trust him,' she added in a totally un-expected testimonial that sent a warm wash of pleasure through him.

'In that case—' Amy Finch's husband had to swallow before he could continue '—tell us, honestly, what's wrong with our babies? Why did our doctor send Amy to you in such a hurry? What did they see on the scan?'

'Well, for a start I can tell you that your twins are iden-tical, because the problem that was spotted is something that only happens with identical twins, and even then, it's very rare. It's called Twin to Twin Transfusion Syndrome and what that means is that there are problems within the placenta—that's the plumbing that connects the babies to the wall of the uterus—problems that mean that one baby isn't getting enough blood to grow properly, while the other one is having to pump so much blood that it might damage the heart.'

'S-so they're going to d-die?' Amy hiccupped, clearly fighting tears.

'There must be *something* you can do?' her husband begged desperately. '*Something* that will keep them alive until they can be born?'

'I won't know until we've done some more tests, but it might be possible to operate—'

'You can't operate! They can't be born yet!' Amy interrupted with a wail. 'It's far too soon!'

'Of course it is,' Daniel agreed, hoping the tone of his voice would help to calm the poor woman down. Out of the corner of his eye he saw Jenny hovering, ready to comfort the distraught mother-to-be if her husband's own emotions prevented him from supplying the comfort she needed. 'If the conditions permit it, this operation would be done while the babies are still inside you, using a laser to seal off the connections in the placenta that are sending too much blood to one of the babies so that the other one can get its fair share.'

He paused just long enough to be certain that they were now following his explanation rather than panicking blindly. He still had the hard part of the task to do—covering the down side to the surgery if things didn't go according to plan.

'Of course, something like this, an intrusion into the womb at such an early stage of the pregnancy, can be very dangerous to the babies because it can trigger labour. In that case, you would almost certainly lose both babies, but because there is already a marked difference in the size of the two of them—and in their hearts—it's not an operation we can afford to put off for very long or they will die, anyway.'

'So, when will you do the operation? Can you do it today?' the young woman said, suddenly almost feverishly eager to undergo the surgery.

'Mrs Finch, we don't yet know whether an operation is possible,' Daniel warned, even as he sent up a silent prayer that it would be. 'I will need to know exactly where all the blood vessels are in the placenta and which ones are supplying which baby before I will know whether it will give one or both of them a chance of developing properly and staying alive in the womb, at least long enough to survive when they're born.'

'How soon will you know? When can I have the tests?' she demanded.

Daniel wondered if she even realised that she was stroking the swell of her belly as though to soothe the babies and reassure them. He couldn't count the number of women he'd seen doing exactly the same thing and, over the years, had idly wondered if he would ever see the mother of his own child doing the same thing, but now that he knew that Jenny was pregnant…

He was sorely tempted to glance in her direction but forced himself to concentrate.

'I can understand that you want to have the tests done as soon as possible—so do I. But even if the tests show that an operation is possible, it won't happen straight away because we're going to be doing a crucial balancing act here. If we operate too soon, before the tissues surrounding the babies are tough enough to stand being punctured and pulled around, then we'll have no chance of saving the pregnancy. On the other hand, if we wait to operate only when we're absolutely certain it's safe to do so, then both of the babies could already be too damaged and too weak to survive.'

As usual, there was a slightly stunned silence while the poor parents tried to take in the sort of detail that they'd never imagined when they first realised that their first child was on the way. He wasn't surprised to see tears trickling down Amy's cheeks as she clutched her husband's hand.

'So, we'll have all the tests and then we'll just have to wait and pray that they survive until it's safe for you to do the operation,' Simon Finch said with agony in his expression and once more Daniel had to steel himself not to be overwhelmed by the situation. This was definitely the down side of dealing with problem pregnancies, seeing the parents' desperation at first hand and wanting to do everything he could to give them what they wanted, even on the occasions when such an outcome was impossible.

'For today, we'll arrange for you to have another scan and we'll take it from there,' he said as reassuringly as he could. 'Just concentrate on taking it one day at a time and, no matter how impossible it seems, try to stay calm and think positive thoughts.'

'Stay calm!' Amy's voice rose in a wail. 'My babies could be dying and you're telling me to stay calm!'

'Mrs Finch…*Amy*, listen to me!' he called sharply, knowing it was important to attract her attention before she completely fell apart. 'I'm not being insensitive when I tell you to be calm. I'm telling you for the sake of your babies because their survival may depend on it. They are even more fragile than other babies so outside influences can have a devastating effect on them.' He gestured towards her, tense and shaking and breathing far too fast. He was glad Jenny had taken her blood pressure earlier because it was probably off the scale, now.

'Look at yourself,' he said, aiming for quiet insistence. 'Surely you must realise that the more agitated you are, the more it can affect the babies.'

'But…how?' she whimpered as she clutched the handful of tissues Jenny passed her. 'I can't just pretend that I don't know what's going on in there.'

'No one expects you to, but if your heart rate goes up, so will the babies' and that will increase the strain of coping with the effects of their faulty plumbing.'

'You could try focusing on other things,' Jenny suggested, and he was delighted that she'd jumped in at that point.

'Such as housework, or television?' Amy challenged. 'That's not likely to work.'

'Probably not, but perhaps if you were to concentrate on doing something specifically for the babies, such as reading to them or singing to them to let them become accustomed to your voice. There have been lots of studies that have shown that babies respond *after* they're born to sounds they first heard while they were in the womb.'

Both Finches seemed quite intrigued by the idea and Daniel could have hugged Jenny for making the suggestion. The last thing he wanted was to short-change the couple when they'd been bombarded with such a bombshell, and his clinics rarely ran strictly to time, no matter how hard the secretarial staff tried, but he also didn't like the idea of leaving other worried parents waiting for ever for their appointment. There were only so many times they could read the various posters on the walls, and as they'd probably been referred to him knowing there was a problem with their pregnancy, it was unlikely they would be able to concentrate long enough to read one of the magazines, no matter how up-to-date they might be.

'How are they doing?' he asked, switching his tape recorder off when Jenny came back into the room a few minutes later. At least he'd had enough time to record his notes on the problems of the Finches' pregnancy before he had time to forget anything. He was never absolutely confident that his hastily jotted notes could always be deciphered accurately should another practitioner have to see his patients at some point, so preferred to tape a spoken record that would be typed as a back-up.

'All organised,' she said with a smile. 'And tonight, they're going out for a meal to celebrate the fact that the twins are identical and to start thinking of names, both girls' and boys' because they'd rather the sex of the babies is a surprise.'

'Jenny…' His heart sank at the thought that they might be celebrating too soon. There was absolutely no guarantee that either of the babies would survive.

'And don't worry that I was giving them unrealistic expectations,' she interrupted, almost as if she'd read his mind. 'I just suggested that they should celebrate the little steps—like finding out that they were identical—so that they would be making memories they could keep, no matter how things turn out.'

He should have known from the time she'd spent dealing with the most premature of the babies on the unit that she wouldn't be one to make impossible promises. But the idea of deliberately making memories that they could cherish whether the babies lived or died could be a real comfort if worse came to worst.

'So, who's next?' he asked with a smile, musing while he waited for the next couple to enter that his high-stress job was made so much easier with someone as intelligent and compassionate as Jenny to work with.

'Sharron Pickering and her husband have been referred to us after their first visit to the pre-natal clinic. She'd been attending an IVF clinic to help her to get pregnant.'

'So, why am I seeing them?' Daniel said with a frown as he flipped the appropriate folder open on the desk. 'Surely they should be attending the assisted-reproduction unit?'

'Not any more,' Jenny said dryly. 'Sharron's pregnant, but not because she had fertilised eggs returned.'

Daniel felt his frown deepen, pleating his forehead as he deciphered her cryptic meaning, then his eyebrows nearly hit his hairline. 'Tell me she wasn't stupid enough to get pregnant when her body had been stimulated to produce eggs for harvesting! They *must* have been warned what could happen.'

She nodded dourly. 'And if what I overheard in the waiting room is true, it was done deliberately.'

'*What!*' It was a real effort not to shout. 'Why on earth would they do something so stupid? Surely they were told not to have sex because it could result in dangerous multiple pregnancies?'

'Ah, but if you're already too old to qualify for IVF in your own country and have travelled abroad for treatment, believing that this is going to be your very last possibility to ever have a child, you might be foolish enough to think that the more babies you conceive, the better your chances of ending up with at least one of them surviving,' Jenny pointed out grimly.

He closed his eyes and drew in a calming breath, reminding himself that he wasn't here to take any notice of his patients' morality or intelligence, but to focus on the health of mothers and babies.

'Well, you'd better show them in, then,' he said just as his eyes focused on one particular detail in the file.

Seven babies? The stupid woman was pregnant with *seven* babies? His anger began to soar again and it took a real effort to tamp it down as the couple came into the room with smiles on their faces.

'Mrs Pickering, take a seat, please,' he said, proud that his voice sounded relatively normal. 'I understand you've been sent to see me because there's a problem with your pregnancy.'

'Not really,' she said with a cheerful shrug. 'Apparently my blood pressure's up a bit, but that's nothing to worry about, is it?'

'Actually, it definitely *is* something to worry about,' he contradicted sharply as he took in the range of results noted in her file in less than three months. 'Your blood pressure is already astronomic and you're not halfway through this pregnancy. You're in serious danger of having a heart attack or a stroke, going into heart failure or damaging your kidneys. You could even die if something isn't done soon.'

'So, prescribe some more tablets,' she suggested airily, obviously so euphoric over the fact she was finally pregnant that she was completely unconcerned about the risks she was running. 'That's what you do for blood pressure, isn't it?'

'I would be grossly negligent if I didn't make it clear that trying to carry seven babies is not what your body is designed for,' he pointed out. 'It's a strain just for your system to keep one baby healthy because it's such a drain on your body. Seven is just…' He shook his head, searching to find words to express his thoughts without causing offence. 'To try to continue with a pregnancy of seven babies is a danger to their lives and to yours, and you should seriously think about selective reduction.'

'Selective reduction?' she echoed with a frown. 'What's that?'

'That's where we would inject into the heart of some of the babies, leaving a more reasonable number for your body to cope with.'

'You mean, you'd *kill* some of the babies? No way!' she exclaimed. 'I'm not letting you do that.'

'I know for some people there would be religious or ethical reasons why they wouldn't be happy to.'

'It's got nothing to do with religion or ethics,' she interrupted fiercely. 'They're our babies, at last, and they're all alive and I couldn't possibly do anything to any of them to…' She shook her head, unable to voice the words.

'Can't you just give her something to sort her blood pressure out?' her husband said, almost hesitantly, as if he was only now starting to realise what a dangerous situation they might be in. 'I'll make sure she takes them, and keep her off the salt.'

Daniel silently counted to ten before he turned to his computer screen and tapped in the relevant prescription, hoping that before the prescription needed renewing they might have reconsidered the situation.

'If you have any headaches or your hands and feet start to swell or—' he began, only to be interrupted.

'I promise I'll read the instructions,' Sharron said eagerly, clearly still completely oblivious to the warnings he'd tried to deliver.

'I'll come out with you to make your next appointment,' Jenny said as the two of them stood to leave and Daniel couldn't help comparing his patient's already visibly swollen body with Jenny's slender one. How long would it be before there was visible evidence of the baby growing inside her? Would she be one of those who carried the baby almost invisibly until the final trimester or would she be obviously pregnant almost from the end of the first trimester?

As crazy as it seemed when he was surrounded by pregnant women throughout his working day, somehow it felt very different knowing that it would be Jenny's body he would be watching as it grew ripe and swollen with *his* baby.

His baby! Somehow the thought still hadn't sunk in properly, but that didn't mean that he couldn't reassure Jenny that he would be there for her, would support her throughout the pregnancy and beyond; would be more than willing to be by her side for the rest of their—

'I don't think I've ever felt like smacking a patient before!' Jenny exclaimed as she re-entered the room, barely closing the door behind her before she spoke. 'I understand that the biological urge to have a baby can become an absolute obsession for some women, but she must be way beyond obsessed…crazy…mad…totally deluded if she really believes she can carry seven healthy babies to term.'

'Took a bite out of a thesaurus while you were out there making their appointment?' Daniel teased and was glad to see her smile in response. Would she still be smiling when she heard that he wanted to have a permanent part in his baby's life? And when would be the best time to broach the subject with her? Tonight, or when they'd both had a chance to come to terms with the fact of the pregnancy?

At least they had eight months to make any decisions, although as far as he was concerned, the sooner the better, especially if it meant that Jenny was going to become a permanent part of his life.

'At least we've got Aliyah coming to see us later,' her voice interrupted his thoughts, reminding him of where they should be focused. 'After Mrs Pickering, it will cheer us both up to see how well she's doing.'

'And the fact that her husband's improved enough to be able to come with her,' Daniel added. 'It looks as if they're going to have the happy ending they deserve. But in the meantime, there's this whole stack to work through, so bring in the next patient, please.'

CHAPTER SEVEN

'WOULD you rather I weren't here?' Daniel said softly as the ultrasound technician prepared to perform Jenny's first scan.

'No!' She almost grabbed for his hand, desperate not to be alone for this first glimpse of the little person who had been causing her so much grief over the past few weeks. Whoever had coined the phrase 'morning sickness' deserved to be shot, because as far as Jenny was concerned it had been 'morning, noon and night sickness'.

In fact, at one point it had been so bad that she'd actually thought of asking for something...*anything*...that would stop the constant nausea and vomiting. It had been a real problem keeping enough fluids down to prevent herself becoming dehydrated, to say nothing of trying to keep her discomfort hidden as far as Daniel and the rest of her colleagues were concerned. The last thing she needed was to lose any time off work when she was going to have a baby to support in such a short time. Anyway, she hated the thought of letting people down, be they patients or fellow members of staff.

Thank goodness, at three months almost to the day the sickness had subsided and here she was waiting to catch her first glimpse of the tiny being who had completely taken over her life, one way and another.

'I'd like you to stay, if you don't mind?' she said, belatedly realising that her wandering thoughts had gone on far too long. 'I really wasn't looking forward to being here on my own, and my parents…' She shrugged, knowing that Daniel was one of the few people who wouldn't need her to finish that thought.

'Have you got any plans for this evening?' he asked, and her crazy heart gave several extra beats at the thought that he might be going to ask her to spend some time with him, which was stupid considering she was the one who had insisted that the two of them keep a decorous distance between them. Several times he'd suggested that they should talk, but she just hadn't been ready to hear him spell out the limits he wanted to place on his involvement.

'What sort of plans?' she asked distractedly, one eye on the giant tube of conductive gel coming towards her naked belly.

'A celebratory drink—a cup of tea in your case—or a meal? It's about time we talked, don't you think?' There was something in his tone and in the intent expression in his eyes that told her that this time he wasn't going to let himself be put off any longer; that this time they would be discussing, in words of one syllable, exactly how they each saw their part in this baby's future.

Her heart gave an extra kick of apprehension, then spiked again when the chilly gel was spread over her warm skin and her squeak made him chuckle richly.

'It's funny, but until I laid down on this hard bed I hadn't really noticed that I'm already starting to get quite bulgy,' she mused, her eyes flicking from the probe stroking over the surprisingly firm little bump between her hipbones to the shadowy images appearing on the nearby screen.

'As sick as you've been, I'm surprised you aren't concave rather than *bulgy*, as you call it,' Daniel said rather pointedly, letting her know that she hadn't fooled him in the least with her attempts to pretend that all was well.

'You're reasonably certain about your dates, are you?' the technician asked, frowning at the screen. 'You did say it was just under twelve weeks, didn't you?'

Guilt brought a flush to Jenny's face as she followed the glance that the woman flicked in Daniel's direction. Much as she'd wanted him here with her—felt he had an absolute *right* to be here for that first glimpse of the child he'd fathered—she really shouldn't have agreed when Daniel said he wanted to accompany her for this appointment. He was apparently oblivious to the fact that the hospital gossips would automatically presume that his presence would signal that it was *his* baby. It would certainly make it more difficult for him to deal with the legalities of his paternity in any sort of confidential way.

'The first time you catch sight of your baby is a special occasion,' he'd insisted stubbornly, apparently oblivious to the problems he would be creating. 'Even though we're the only two who really know I have a reason for wanting to be there, I don't want you to go alone because it's something you *should* be able to share.'

'Aha!' The technician straightened up with a beaming smile. 'Well, *that's* the reason why there's already a definite bulge there,' she said, pointing at the screen. 'Can you see? There and there? That's two separate heartbeats.'

'*Twins?*' Jenny squeaked in shocked disbelief. 'I'm having *twins*!' She felt her eyes widen as she focused on those two bright flickering spots on the screen, evidence that there were indeed two tiny babies developing deep inside her.

Unable to help herself, she swung her gaze up to share the magical moment with Daniel, knowing that he took delight in the miracle of new life, no matter who was the father, only there was no answering smile on Daniel's face; no smile at all as he leaned forward to focus intently on the shadowy images.

'Can you change the angle slightly?' he directed the technician tersely, suddenly very much a doctor rather than a supportive friend or a delighted father-to-be. 'I need a better view of the placenta.'

'It looks as if there *is* only one placenta. If so, it would definitely be identical twins rather than fraternal, with the twinning occurring later than the first four days after fertilisation, and the placenta *is* slightly low,' the woman murmured as she slid the probe over Jenny's belly again, an ominous pause sending a completely different shiver down her spine and stopping her breath in her throat.

Almost without realising she was doing it, she found herself reaching for Daniel's hand, desperate for the reassuring feel of his touch. For an awful fraction of a second she was sure she felt him freeze, but before she could pull her hand away, he immediately meshed his fingers with hers as naturally as if it was something they did every day.

'Well, it *is* rather low, but I wouldn't have thought it was low enough to cause placenta praevia problems,' the technician continued and Jenny dared to breathe again. At least it sounded as if that was one less thing to worry about.

'Print a shot of that view and send a complete recording of the scan to the computer in my office, please,' Daniel directed briskly, and Jenny's heart nearly stopped. That certainly hadn't sounded as though he wanted a copy just as a personal memento.

'Daniel?' she croaked, hating the quiver in her voice. It was almost impossible to speak when her mouth was as dry as the Sahara and she was certain she was going to be sick. She tightened her grip on his hand. 'What's wrong? What did you see?'

The technician held out a handful of tissues to wipe the gel off her belly and she was forced to relinquish her hold to accept them. On auto-pilot she wriggled her clothing into place as she slid off the couch onto legs that felt every bit as insubstantial as the blue jelly, and all the time she was waiting for him to speak…and all the time he was ominously silent.

'Thank you,' he said formally when the technician confirmed that the scan had been sent to his computer and handed him a printout, and only then did he meet Jenny's eyes. 'Let's go up to my office.'

'*Daniel?*' Fear had her pulse pounding loud enough for the sound to bounce off the walls. She grabbed for his elbow. 'Please. Can't you tell me what—?'

'There are other people waiting to come in for their scans, Jenny, people with full bladders,' he added with an attempt at humour that fell completely flat. The only thing it did achieve was to let her know that he wasn't going to be giving her any answers until they reached his office. But if he thought he was going to be able to put her off *then*, he had another think coming. He was going to tell her what had put that expression on his face, even if she had to lock the door and take the phone off the hook.

'Tell me,' she insisted almost before the door closed behind her, her previous desperation to find the nearest bathroom completely vanishing in the face of any threat to her baby…*babies*. 'It's something bad, isn't it? They're going to die, aren't they?' There was no point in asking the questions, really. The expression on his face as he immediately sat down behind his desk with his fingers flying over the keys to draw up the images the technician had sent was so ominous that she already knew the answer.

'Sit,' he said without taking his eyes off the screen.

'I'm not a dog!' She automatically balked at the brisk command, her response the result of far too many years of life with Douglas and Helen Sinclair as parents.

A wry twist of his mouth was probably the only apology she was going to get, especially as his focus remained on the computer.

'Sit, *please*, Jenny,' he amended distractedly, then immediately seemed to change his mind. 'Better still, come here and look at this.'

Her legs were already shaking as she made her way around the end of his desk, and when he merely leant back in his chair rather than moving away to allow her access to the screen she had to lean entirely too close to that long lean body for her senses to cope with the overload.

'Wh-what am I looking for?' she quavered, so scared that she could barely make out the flicker of the two tiny hearts that had enthralled her such a short time ago.

'The placenta,' he said shortly, pointing with one surprisingly elegant finger towards the lower edge of the image. 'As the technician pointed out, there's only one and it's attached fairly low in the uterus, but not so low that it would cause problems on its own because we both know that the uterus will stretch during the pregnancy, usually taking the placenta a safe distance away from the cervix so it won't become detached when labour starts.'

He paused the images on the screen several times to take a closer look and she'd almost reached screaming point before he began to speak again.

'It's the degree of vascularisation in the single placenta,' he murmured. 'Then there's the fact that in spite of the single placenta, the foetuses are in separate amniotic sacs and there is already a measurable difference in the size of both the sacs and of the two foetuses...' His words trailed off as he leaned closer to the screen again, his dark brows drawing together as he concentrated fiercely on detail after detail.

Jenny's sluggish brain was suddenly catapulted into frantic activity. She'd heard those exact phrases such a short time ago that it would be impossible not to recognise them or their significance.

'It's not… You *can't* be thinking it's another case of TTTS!' she exclaimed, slumping against the arm of his chair as nausea threatened and having to reach for his shoulder to brace herself against sliding ignominiously to the floor. 'It's *far* too rare to see two incidences in the same hospital within a matter of weeks of each other.' She wouldn't allow herself to think about the horrifyingly high percentage of TTTS pregnancies that ended with no live babies, or with babies so injured by their time in the womb that they could never lead a normal life.

'I couldn't be certain just from this scan,' he agreed almost absent-mindedly, his brain obviously far more concerned with picking out the first of the details that would help him to make a definitive diagnosis than choosing reassuring words to put her mind at rest, speaking to her almost as though he'd forgotten that she was the patient rather than a colleague.

'I'll need colour Doppler,' he detailed, 'to decipher exactly which way the blood is flowing in each vein and artery in the placenta to see exactly what we're dealing with…' His words tailed off momentarily then continued almost as if he was speaking to himself. 'There could be artery-to-artery, vein-to-vein *and* artery-to-vein anastomoses in there, and until we get some idea of what percentage of the blood flow is being pushed through each heart and the exact positioning of the blood vessels in the placenta, we won't know whether it will be a suitable case for surgery.'

As he'd been speaking, each detail seemed to ring a death knell for those tiny defenceless scraps. She wrapped her arms around herself, hunching forward as though curving her body around them would protect them from the disaster she could see unfolding in her mind's eye.

Her mouth was so dry that swallowing was impossible and the strange ringing sound in her ears and the difficulty she was having in focusing her eyes told her that something definitely wasn't right.

'Dan…Daniel,' she managed to stammer as a cold sweat was added to her misery, her hands trembling so much that she couldn't even raise one to touch his sleeve. 'P-please…'

'Jennywren!' she heard him exclaim as darkness overwhelmed her completely and she began to fall endlessly into space.

'Jenny?'

There was an urgent sound to the voice that was drawing her inexorably out of the darkness, and something told her that it was important not to ignore it in spite of the overwhelming feeling of dread that surrounded her.

'You're scaring me, Jenny,' said the voice that somehow didn't sound like Daniel's. 'If you don't wake up, I'm going to have to admit you to the side ward for observation and tests,' he added, then a finger that was noticeably shaking peeled back an eyelid to show her his pinched white face and reality came crashing in on her.

'Dan…Daniel?' she croaked, briefly squeezing her eyes tight shut before opening them wide to gaze up into the concern filling his expression. 'D-did I fall…hit my head?'

'Not quite,' he said gruffly, and it was only when he released his hold that she realised he'd had her hand wrapped tightly in his. 'I managed to catch you in time, before you planted your face in the floor.'

'Thank you,' she murmured and tried to use her elbows to push herself up into a sitting position only to be firmly pushed flat on the examination couch again.

'Just lie there a moment while you catch up with yourself,' he advised, hitching one hip on the edge of the couch while he watched her with eagle eyes, apparently unaware of the fact that with their thighs pressed together like that, it was the closest they'd been since *that* night.

The silence stretched uncomfortably between them, but Jenny's head was throbbing with the realisation that, no matter what turmoil they'd created in her life, she loved the two little people clinging precariously to life inside her with a fierce mother's love. The thought that either of them might not live, that they would probably only survive if she underwent a highly complex operation that even then couldn't guarantee their survival...

'I'm sorry,' Daniel said gruffly. 'That was my fault.'

His unexpected apology snapped her out of her spiralling thoughts.

'What was your fault?' She frowned her puzzlement.

'You passing out!' he snapped impatiently. 'I was yammering on about all the tests and the chances for things to go wrong and the contraindications to surgery as if you were just a member of staff rather than a patient. I should have...'

'What?' she interrupted. 'Sugar-coated the situation so I wouldn't worry?' She laughed wryly. 'Do you think, after all the details you explained about that other case of TTTS—the Finches—that I wouldn't have realised you weren't telling me everything? Do you think my memory's so bad that I could have forgotten so soon?'

'Of course not!' How had he moved so close so fast?

He'd been almost at the other end of the couch with only their thighs touching but now, there he was right beside her, reaching for her hands to take them in both of his as he leaned close enough for her to be able to draw in the delicious mixture of soap and man that was unique to Daniel Carterton. 'I know how good your memory is, Jenny, *and* the fact that once something's explained to you, you rarely forget it. But that's part of the problem.'

Those deep blue eyes seemed darker than ever when they were so close, and that reminded her all too clearly of that night when they'd been closer still. Close enough for her to have counted every sinfully long eyelash if she hadn't been far too busy exploring the rest of his delicious body to spare the time.

'Over the last few months,' he continued, apparently unaware that she was far more interested in gazing her fill than in listening to his explanation, 'I've become accustomed to talking to you…explaining things and thinking aloud as if you were another doctor. I should have remembered that too much detail wasn't appropriate this time, and put a brake on my tongue.'

'No, you shouldn't!' she objected fiercely, squeezing his hands for emphasis and loving his reassuring strength. 'I *need* to know what's going on—the good, the bad and the ugly. I know what you discovered today is about as bad as it can get, but I need to know that I can trust you to be honest with me.'

'Jenny, it might not be—'

'But most of all, Daniel,' she interrupted, 'I need you to remind me that if I hold my breath too long while I'm concentrating on what you're saying—especially when you're telling me something about me and my babies that I don't want to hear—I'm probably going to pass out.'

'You were holding your breath?' he exclaimed, clearly startled. 'What on earth for?'

'It's a habit I got into as a child.' She gave a wry smile. 'I learned that if I concentrated on holding my breath, I was less likely to argue or answer back to my parents when they were telling me off. My punishments were less, that way.'

'And you're still doing it? Deliberately?' He looked horrified.

'Of course not! I'm not stupid!' she exclaimed. 'I hadn't even realised I was holding my breath while I was looking at the scan until it was too late... I was just concentrating so hard on what you were pointing out, and what you were saying about the possibilities you could find, that—'

'Well, next time, make sure you're sitting down and concentrate a little less on the screen and a little more on breathing,' he grumbled. 'It's not good for either of us to have you passing out like that...or for the babies.'

Almost as soon as the words left his mouth, the expression on his face changed to one of dawning delight.

'It's *twins*, Jennywren!' he said softly, a wondering smile lifting the corners of his mouth and displaying the hint of dimples in both cheeks. 'We made *twins*...and identical ones, at that.'

There it was!

The sheer delight over every baby that filled this man was what had attracted her to Daniel, even more than his good looks and personality.

Just to be in the room with him at such a moment was a joy, and that was multiplied an infinite number of times now that it was her own babies—*their* babies—filling him with pleasure.

'Jenny, I think now would be a good time for the two of us to have that talk,' he said, suddenly so serious that the first thing she thought was that he had more bad news to tell her about her pregnancy.

'Talk?' she parroted blankly, wondering what else could possibly be wrong.

'About the babies and the fact that I'm their father and—'

'*No*,' she moaned, her brain and her heart already over-loaded with the events of the last hour. '*Please*, Daniel, not now. I can't possibly…not until we know how bad… Not until we can be certain that they won't…'

It was obvious that he wasn't happy about the delay, but he was a fair man and it didn't take him long to recognise that she was in too much turmoil to make any rational decisions.

'Okay,' he sighed heavily. 'We'll postpone that discussion till later, but it *is* going to happen, and sooner rather than later. Now, give me a minute and I'll organise a taxi for you,' he said, straightening up and taking several steps away from her as though only just remembering that they were in his office where such proximity would appear inappropriate should anyone walk in.

'A taxi? You certainly won't,' she countered swiftly, pushing herself up into a sitting position and swinging her legs to hang over the side of the couch. 'There's absolutely nothing wrong with me. *And* you've got a clinic that was due to start seven minutes ago.'

There must have been something in her expression that told him she wasn't going to back down, but, equally, she could tell that, once again, he wasn't happy with her decision.

'You can stay on the strict understanding that you tell me if you're not feeling well,' he said sternly, and she stifled the smile that wanted to emerge at the knowledge that he was genuinely concerned about her. The fact that it made her feel all warm and squishy inside wasn't something she should be admitting, even to herself.

'And I'll be checking the scheduling to see how soon we can start those tests,' he added, wiping out any urge to smile in an instant. 'The quicker we know what we're dealing with…'

He didn't need to finish the thought. His consultations with Amy and Simon Finch in the intervening weeks since that first appointment were very clear in her memory. She really didn't need to have the consequences spelled out for her. The fact that her babies had so little chance of surviving was something she didn't want to think about, yet, not when she needed to concentrate on a full clinic.

Luckily, as the busy session progressed she was kept fully occupied. In a couple of cases, she had to chase up test results from the labs, in others she had to provide a consoling shoulder and box of tissues when heartbreaking news had to be broken. Best of all were the cases when she was able to join in the celebration that, against all odds, a precious baby had survived to arrive strong and healthy and a new photo could be added to the array starting to take up one wall in his office.

The session was long and tiring, especially with the recent revelations about her pregnancy preying on her mind, but she silently admitted that the need to concentrate was probably the only thing that was keeping her from going mad. If she'd been at home, waiting to find out when her own tests would be done…well, she'd probably be seven different shades of demented by now, imagining the very worst diagnosis and a dire prognosis for both of her precious babies.

She could only be overwhelmingly grateful that Daniel was turning out to be such a wonderful friend; that he was willing to stand by her. Far too many men would have disappeared into the distance when they found out about the pregnancy.

Her heart ached at the thought that he could never be more than a friend, but after today's bombshell, she couldn't be more relieved that they'd preserved a little distance between them. In a way, it would be better if he'd never known that they were his babies. He already grieved for each little life lost. How much worse was it going to be for him if he couldn't save his own children?

At least with no one other than the two of them knowing that he was the babies' father, the ethics committee wouldn't feel the need to step in to prevent him being the one to operate if it became necessary. She certainly wouldn't trust anyone else to do it.

'Earth to Jenny,' Daniel called, waving a hand in front of her face when she continued to stare into the middle distance with a worried frown drawing her eyebrows together.

He'd been growing increasingly concerned about her over the past few weeks since he'd accompanied her to that first scan, and increasingly frustrated that he couldn't do anything about his concerns.

Everything in him ached to have the right to protect her; to tell her that he loved her and hear her tell him that she loved him, too; to be there in the night to comfort her when she lay there in the darkness worrying about the precious babies they'd created.

As it was, he was trying to be grateful that she was being generous with his involvement with the daily progress of the pregnancy, beyond his clinical connection, when what he really wanted to do was sit her down and thrash out some sort of…what? A formal agreement? A legal document of some sort spelling out his rights?

No, that wasn't what he wanted. What he really wanted

was his Jennywren committed to a life together, heart and soul. Just weeks ago he couldn't wait to sit down with her and thrash everything out and he'd been frustrated when she'd wanted to hold off until her emotions were back on an even keel. Now he was glad of the delay because every day that went past, he could allow himself to believe that he would eventually get what he wanted.

Luckily, there was still time for that to happen as there wasn't any immediate urgency with the TTTS situation. Her most recent scan had confirmed that, while the smaller twin was definitely growing slower than the larger one, and the greater size of the amniotic sac was evidence of the greater volume of blood the larger twin's system was having to cope with, the situation hadn't yet reached a critical point. This was a huge relief because not only was the pregnancy not far enough along for surgery to be possible, yet, neither were the babies sufficiently developed to cope with the outside world should the operation trigger delivery.

So, given the fact that there was nothing new with her own situation…

'Sorry, I just took a call from Amy Finch,' she explained obliquely.

'She's due to come in, later this week, isn't she?' The surgery had been textbook perfect and the smaller twin had shown a remarkable gain in both size and the volume of the surrounding amniotic fluid, demonstrating that the blood volume had now increased. If they saw another few weeks of similar progress, they could be reasonably certain that both babies had a good chance of survival.

'She rang to say she'd been having contractions. I told her to come straight in,' Jenny said quietly and the reason for her pensive mood suddenly became clear.

He muttered a curse under his breath. 'Have her waters broken? Did she say?'

'They hadn't when she spoke to me, but they've got at least an hour's journey to get here, so anything could happen,' she said grimly, and with her usual smile nowhere in evidence, it was all too easy to guess where her thoughts were going and the parallels she was drawing.

His heart went out to her. As if it weren't bad enough to be carrying twins afflicted with TTTS, how much worse must it be to have another mother going through the same trauma just weeks ahead of her and for that pregnancy to look as if it had run into major problems?

'Don't borrow trouble,' he said lamely, wishing there was something, *anything*, he could do to put her mind at ease. 'You know as well as I do that every pregnancy is different, and twin pregnancies are notoriously problematic with a high rate of premature delivery.'

'Her babies aren't much over twenty-six weeks, Daniel,' she hissed heatedly, obviously aware that anyone could come upon their conversation at any time. 'That's far closer to a miscarriage than a premature delivery, and twin B has still got *so* much catching up to do.'

There was the threat of tears glittering in her eyes and he would have loved to wrap her in his arms and promise her that he would be able to keep both babies safe and well, but he couldn't do either. All he could do was take each day and each case as it came and try his hardest for every one of them.

And if she would give him the slightest sign that she wanted anything more from him than his medical expertise and a slightly distant friendship...but that obviously wasn't going to happen, now, while all her energies were focused on the babies she was carrying.

'You know we'll do everything we can to delay labour— if she really is in labour—until we can get some steroids into her to give their lungs a fighting chance, but there really isn't a magic wand I can wave to—'

'I know. I know,' she interrupted hastily, fleetingly touching her hand to his arm and sending an unexpected shower of heated sparks through his body. 'I'm sorry, Daniel, I know it's not your fault and that you want those babies to arrive healthy as much as anyone does, but... Oh! It just seems so unfair! Some women have babies as easily as shelling peas while others...'

His pager bleeped before he could comment and a quick glance at the time told him what it was about.

'That'll probably be my reminder that I should be at that wretched budget meeting,' he groaned as he reached for the phone. 'I really can't afford to miss it completely if I want to put our case for increased financing for our part of the department, but let me know as soon as the Finches arrive.'

He strode off towards yet another session that would probably degenerate into the adult version of 'you got more marbles than I did' with absolutely nothing being finalised other than the date and time of the next meeting. He knew that it was going to take all his concentration not to let his thoughts wander towards the heartbreak the Finches would suffer if they were to lose their precious babies after fighting so hard to save them.

More than that, he was so conscious of the effect the situation was having on Jenny, knowing that she probably had the same circumstances to face in the near future. It had been so obvious, when he'd taken one last quick glance over his shoulder, exactly where her thoughts were centred as she stood there with one hand protectively curved over the gentle swell of her belly, and all he'd ached to do was wrap her in his arms and make the world disappear.

* * *

It took every ounce of Jenny's skill to calm Amy Finch enough to take her blood pressure. Even then, the poor woman was sobbing broken-heartedly by the time Daniel arrived in answer to her page.

'This isn't helping, Amy!' he said sternly as he strode swiftly across to her. 'The more stressed you are, the higher your blood pressure will go and the more it will affect the babies.'

Jenny wasn't surprised that both the Finches blinked at his sharp tone, but she could understand exactly why he'd spoken that way, and the fact that they were staring at him open-mouthed and silent was testament to the effectiveness of his strategy.

'That's better!' he said in his usual calming voice. 'Now, before we start running around like chickens with their heads chopped off, let's get you on an IV and get a few results in.'

'But I'm having contractions!' Amy exclaimed. 'The babies are coming and it's far too soon and...'

'And some women have spells of contractions right through their pregnancies,' Daniel interrupted, and even though Jenny knew he was stretching a point purely to comfort the woman, she was warmed by the thought that he cared enough to try to give her some measure of reassurance. 'Give us a chance to do some tests to find out if you're one of them.'

'And in the meantime, I'll set up an IV,' Jenny said.

'Why does she need an IV?' Simon demanded. 'What are you going to be giving her?'

'Just saline, initially,' Jenny soothed. 'The last thing we need is for Amy to be dehydrated. And then, if it becomes necessary to give her any medication—if, for example, it's some sort of infection causing the problem—it will be very simple to administer immediately.' And if crossing her fingers that this would have such a simple resolution would work, she'd keep them crossed for a week, but Jenny had a nasty feeling that this was going to have a very different outcome from Aliyah Farouk's problem on the day of her husband's accident.

CHAPTER EIGHT

DANIEL had to stifle a growl of frustration when he saw how much paler Jenny's face had become over the past few days.

Knowing that she was facing such a similar situation to the Finches was obviously preying on her mind. She looked as if she hadn't slept for days—since Amy Finch was admitted, in fact—and the news this morning couldn't have been worse.

'It hasn't worked, has it?' she said sadly. 'We only managed to delay labour, not stop it…and everything seemed to be going so well after the surgery at twenty-two weeks.'

'But at least we had a chance to get some steroids into her to give the babies' lungs a better chance,' he pointed out, knowing with a heavy heart that the chances of both babies surviving such an early arrival were very slim.

Had the larger twin's system recovered sufficiently from all those weeks of overload? Had the smaller twin caught up enough to have a chance of life?

Although the parents hadn't wanted to be told the sex of their babies, he knew that the very fact that Amy Finch was carrying boys was another factor against their survival after such an early delivery.

The phone rang stridently and Jenny reached for it automatically.

'Jenny Sinclair,' she announced almost absent-mindedly, then she straightened abruptly, almost as if she'd been stung. 'When? How far? Is everything going—?'

Daniel felt a grin lifting the corners of his mouth as he listened to her rapid-fire questions, a bubble of excitement giving his spirits a lift with the recognition that one of 'their' mums had obviously gone into labour. He only needed to see the smile of delight on Jenny's impish face to know that all was going well, so far.

'Who is it?' he demanded before the phone was even back in the cradle.

'Aliyah Farouk,' she said with a huge grin. 'Her labour's started early, but it's less than four weeks. Josh said to tell you that both babies have good strong heartbeats and that she's already seven centimetres dilated, and that Faz is with her in the delivery room.'

'Let me know as soon as there's any more news,' Daniel said, feeling that strange mixture of excitement and concern that always welled up in him with the news that one of 'his' patients was in labour. 'Heaven only knows what state I'll be in when it's my own children on the way,' he muttered under his breath as his eyes helplessly followed Jenny's progress away from him to return to Amy Finch, her still-slender hips moving in almost balletic counterpoint to her shoulders as she hurried to her next task, apparently energised by the latest news.

She paused by the reception desk and he watched her tuck her hair behind her ear in a familiar gesture as she concentrated on the screen and desire hit him hard and fast.

It had been that way from the first time he'd met her and had only grown stronger each time he saw her smile, met her eyes, brushed oh-so-innocently against her... Dammit, everything about the woman turned him on, and the feeling was increasing exponentially as he watched her body growing ripe and round with his babies inside her. *His* babies, and they *still* hadn't had that all-important conversation, and much though he needed to have confirmation that she was going to acknowledge his rights as their father, he really couldn't justify the likelihood that such a discussion would be too stressful for Jenny while she was so worried about the babies' survival.

Something attracted her attention but when she looked over her shoulder in his direction he knew the instant when she saw him standing there—when she met his gaze—that she recognised the likely direction his thoughts had been going. The only thing he couldn't tell was what her feelings were about that direction.

'Dr Carterton?' The male voice was almost directly behind him and from the tone of it this wasn't the first time the man had spoken. It was definitely time to get his mind on the job.

'I'm sorry, Mr Finch. I really wasn't ignoring you,' he apologised and was surprised by the wry smile on the man's face.

'With pretty scenery like Jenny Sinclair around you, it's a wonder you can keep your mind on your job at all, especially when she's just such a genuinely nice person, too.' The poor man was positively grey with fatigue, every minute of the past few days showing in the discouraged slump of his shoulders. 'She's been doing her best to keep our spirits up…but Amy's convinced that both babies are going to die. Isn't there *anything* more you can do to stop her labour?'

'We've run out of options, I'm afraid,' Daniel said, gesturing towards his office as the man obviously needed to talk and the corridor was hardly the best place.

'Tell me honestly,' Simon Finch demanded almost

before Daniel could close the door to give them some privacy. 'Is there *any* chance that either of them will live?'

'Honestly? I really couldn't tell you,' Daniel said, understanding that the man didn't need or want false hope. 'For any other twins to arrive this early, I would say they had a fair to good chance, bearing in mind the improvements we've made in the care of very premature babies.'

'But *our* babies…?' he prompted. 'Is it because of the TTTS?'

'Exactly.' Daniel sighed. This was one part of his job he loathed. 'We won't know until they arrive how well they're going to cope with the outside world. Logically, the larger twin should do well, but we have no idea exactly how much damage was caused by having to cope with so much of the overall blood volume.'

'What about the smaller one…the one that was starved of blood at the beginning?'

It was hard to see his despair. It was always hard to see that emotion in a man's eyes when his dreams of a family were being snatched away from him one by one.

'Once again, we won't know until after the delivery whether—' he only just caught himself in time '—whether the baby has caught up enough to have a fighting chance.' It took some concentration to make certain he didn't let slip the fact that the babies were boys.

'I'm sorry to take up so much of your time with questions that just don't have answers,' he apologised, then caught sight of the clock on the office wall. 'Oh, my goodness! I told Amy I was going to the bathroom. She'll be wondering where I've got to, especially as she's due in theatre in a few minutes.'

'I shouldn't worry about missing anything,' Daniel teased gently. 'They won't be starting without me, so you've got time to get back to her.'

It was probably a good thing that the poor man had been absent while the epidural was being set up. Not many husbands relished the sight of needles being poked in their wife's spine, but the couple had so badly wanted Amy to be awake while the Caesarean was performed, afraid—if the worst happened—that she might miss the few moments their babies were alive if she were placed under general anaesthesia.

'You could take yourself off to get changed, ready to go into theatre,' Daniel suggested. 'That way, Amy probably won't notice how long you've been away with nothing to show for it.'

It was only when the troubled man had hurried off to follow his suggestion that Daniel allowed himself to think far enough ahead to wonder how Jenny's pregnancy would progress.

So far, although the smaller twin was gradually lagging further and further behind his brother, things had not yet reached a critical point, which was a relief because it was far too soon for either of them to survive the invasive procedure to cut the connections between their blood supplies. Any repairs this early would be like trying to suture wet tissue. Until the pregnancy went beyond the twentieth week the amniotic sac wouldn't be tough enough to survive without catastrophic leakage, and for his peace of mind he wanted it to go as far beyond as possible.

But, as ever, it would be a juggling act, balancing the safest point at which the ablative surgery could be performed against the worsening health of the babies.

His pager bleated and a quick glance told him that it would be theatre telling him everything was ready for Amy Finch's Caesarean to proceed. That meant it was time to banish all thoughts of those precious babies developing deep inside Jenny and concentrate on the fragile beings about to be brought into the world far sooner than was safe for them.

'Boys!' breathed Simon Finch in a voice choked by tears as the second baby—looking as fragile as a tiny bird—was lifted up high enough so that they could see him over the dark green drapes hiding the Caesarean from their view. 'Look, Amy, love. They're boys. Two perfect little boys.'

Daniel's heart ached for the new parents and the agony that was to come. Their tiny sons had indeed been born and were both alive, but for how long?

Adam, the larger twin, had been extracted first and had initially looked healthy enough to survive. Unfortunately, the monitors revealed the struggle his organs were making in order to overcome the damage done in those early months.

Aidan was no better, looking so tiny and even more fragile than his bigger brother that he seemed almost transparent and totally incapable of finding the strength to draw enough breath to sustain life.

After the briefest of pauses for their parents to see them, both babies were whisked off to Jenny's old domain, under Josh Weatherby's overall supervision.

Daniel knew from what Jenny had told him about the specialist care she'd given during her time in that department, that they would each have a nurse to monitor them for every second of their time there, taking care of their every need to give them the best possible chance of survival.

As for their mother, Amy's incision was swiftly closed and, bearing in mind the fragility of the babies' condition, it wouldn't be long before she was allowed to go to the neonatal intensive-care unit to be with them.

'What do you think of their chances?' Jenny murmured as she tried to match Daniel's long-legged stride away from theatre.

'You probably know better than I do, after your time caring for those very prem babies,' he countered. 'All I can go on is the expression on Josh's face as he was looking at them, and he didn't look hopeful.'

'They've just started off with *so* many strikes against them, haven't they?' Jenny said, trying and failing to push away the dark thought that this was the situation waiting for her in the near future.

'And you know very well that every pregnancy is completely different,' he reminded her, almost as if he had tuned in to her thoughts. 'Just because your babies have the same syndrome doesn't automatically mean that the pregnancy is going to have the same outcome.'

'It's hard not to worry when, until very recently, a diagnosis of TTTS was almost the same as a death sentence,' she said, her eyes prickling at the thought of losing the precious pair she was carrying. They might not have been planned as part of a loving, committed relationship, but that didn't mean that they weren't loved. She would do anything within her power to keep them safe. Anything.

'Has there been any news about Aliyah?' he asked and she was grateful for the complete change of topics. Her rampaging hormones made her prone to burst into tears when she saw puppies in a toilet-tissue commercial. Thinking about the dangers her babies still had to face was just too much, especially when she was on duty.

Before she could answer, his pager shrilled and he reached for the phone.

'Daniel Carterton,' he announced crisply. 'You paged me?'

'Problem?' she prompted when he put the phone back down just seconds later.

'Far from it,' he said as he set off in the direction of the delivery suites, throwing a killer grin over his shoulder that doubled her pulse rate in response. 'Aliyah's first baby has already arrived and the second one is crowning. Have you got a minute or two free? If we hurry, we could be there in time for the celebrations.'

Her break was long overdue and when she hastily reported that she was going for a coffee, she received a knowing smile and a 'Going via the delivery room?' comment followed her through the door Daniel was holding for her.

If only, she thought a few minutes later when they saw Faz Farouk carefully cradling the first of his longed-for baby boys in his arms.

It would be wonderful if she could look forward to a similar scene, with her adored husband holding for the first time the children they'd made out of their love…but it wasn't to be.

Not only was there no adoring husband, but she and Daniel hadn't even properly discussed the fact that they were *his* babies she was carrying. It was true that she was the one who'd insisted on putting off any such conversation, telling him she needed time to come to terms with the abrupt change of direction her life had taken, but he certainly didn't seem to be in any hurry to initiate it.

Was that a sign that he had no intention of having anything to do with them once they were safely born? The very thought made her heart ache, even if he did seem to be keeping a watchful eye on their development and her own health. Was there any point in hanging on any longer, hoping to see a sign that he might be interested in something more than a professional relationship with her and an arm's length one with the babies? Perhaps now was the time to sit down and talk, so that she knew his intentions and could start to plan the direction of the rest of her life.

'It wasn't so long ago that I didn't believe that this day would ever come…that I would be recovered enough to even hold them,' Faz said, speaking much more slowly than she remembered, but almost perfectly clearly.

'Well, you could hardly expect Aliyah to remain pregnant for ever,' Daniel teased.

'That's what she said.' He grinned. 'I was told I had to work hard…to be well enough to hold them before they arrived…so I could take my turns with the night feeds!'

Jenny tried to remember how many weeks it had been since that dreadful day when he'd been mown down. It was almost impossible to reconcile the broken man who had actually died several times while the surgical team had tried to put him back together with the vibrant, positive man in front of them.

Yes, he still had a long way to go, but seeing him improving so rapidly left her convinced that it was a battle he was determined to fight and win.

'Have you any idea how much longer you'll be with us?' Daniel asked. 'Will you be transferring to somewhere fairly local to continue your rehabilitation?'

'I'll be going home when Aliyah and the babies are ready to leave,' he said with a satisfied smile. 'It's one time that I'm really grateful that we're from relatively wealthy families, because our new house is almost ready…*will* be ready when we leave here.'

'Will the two of you have help with the babies?' Jenny asked, concerned for Aliyah. Caring for two newborns would be exhausting enough without also taking on the care of a man recovering from a devastating accident. 'I suppose both sets of parents will be queuing up to give cuddles.'

'They can't wait!' he agreed. 'They're also providing a live-in nanny until we get the hang of it and can cope by ourselves. And a physio to take me through my paces each day, so they installed a fully equipped gym.'

He went on to explain that the man they'd chosen would be living in, too, because he would also be assisting Faz with the everyday stuff until he was able to cope on his own.

It took nothing more than the look of determination on his face for Jenny to know that day wouldn't be long in coming. Who would have ever thought, when he was first brought into A and E more dead than alive, that just months later he should have recovered so far? Was it the fact that he'd had those precious babies on the way that had spurred his brain and body to repair so fast or was it just his single-minded perseverance, day by day and hour by hour? They would probably never know, but then, what did it matter how or why as long the outcome was good?

'Mr Farouk?' a smiling nurse called from the door of the nursery. 'Your wife has been moved to her room and said to tell you to stop being selfish with her sons. She wants to get *her* hands on them again.'

That was the ideal signal for Daniel and Jenny to take their leave, while two perfect Farouk babies were settled into a crib for the journey to their mother and Faz insisted on making the journey under his own steam.

There was just time to stick their heads round Aliyah's door to congratulate her on her beautiful babies before the little retinue arrived, and Jenny had to give herself a stern lecture all the way to the staffroom and their belated cups of tea.

There was absolutely no point in feeling jealous of the perfect little family they'd just left. The fact that Faz was still in a wheelchair was stark evidence that there were always problems in everyone's lives.

In fact, the more she thought about it, most of the problems in her own life could have been avoided if she'd just had a little more backbone.

If she was honest, she could see that she'd meekly allowed herself to be bullied for most of her life. In the case of her parents, she'd told herself that she *had* to do what they said because they had been kind enough to adopt her. Unfortunately, that meant that she had been predisposed to cave in when Colin had bullied her into going to that dinner with him. She would never know exactly what he'd been planning, thank goodness, because Daniel had appeared from nowhere, like her own personal knight in shining armour, and made certain she was safe.

She smiled up at Daniel to thank him for the mug of tea he offered as a revelation suddenly burst inside her.

Daniel was the only person who had never tried to bully her.

In fact, having him at her side during that awful confrontation the night of her accident was the first time she'd openly defied either of her parents. Throughout her childhood and almost to the present day, whenever her wishes had gone contrary to theirs, she'd tried to find some way of achieving what she'd wanted by sleight of hand rather than arguing with them, even though she knew that she would once again be disappointing them.

It was all too obvious that her mother had been angry that their daughter wasn't willing to do whatever was necessary so that the family name remained unsullied, and Jenny was ashamed to admit that she'd only summoned up the courage to refuse to submit to her parents' dictates because she'd been able to feel Daniel's silent support.

It had been an absolute revelation to actually have someone angry on her behalf rather than angry with her, but she had yet to use the new confidence it had given her to tell Daniel that she was ready to sit down with him and really talk about their situation and what would happen after the babies were born.

'I've been thinking…' Daniel said a little more than a week later.

The department was only just settling down after a visit from Aliyah and Faz to show off their perfect babies before they left for their new home, and Jenny would have been lying if she said her heart hadn't ached at the perfect picture they'd made.

As per hospital regulations, each of them had been sitting in a wheelchair, but with each parent cradling a bundle swaddled in a pristine white shawl that contrasted beautifully with a thick cap of dark hair—already showing a tendency to curl—there wasn't a member of staff who hadn't stopped to coo and offer misty-eyed congratulations.

Faz's parting shot before they'd been driven away had been to joke about the hospital's infamous parking.

'In a way, it was a good job we'd caught a cab to the hospital that day,' he said with that slightly lopsided grin. 'If I'd driven here and parked in the car park, the parking charges would have bankrupted me by now.'

Jenny smiled at the memory of the burst of laughter that had followed their vehicle and the resulting lift in her spirits prompted her to tease Daniel into displaying those sexy dimples again.

'Is this a new thing?' Jenny asked, cheekily, as she

kicked her shoes off and turned in her seat to settle her feet onto the chair opposite. At his quizzical look she elaborated. 'You said that you've taken up thinking. Is that a new thing?'

'Ha!' He threw a crisp at her which she caught in midair and promptly popped into her mouth to crunch with noisy relish. 'I was actually trying to initiate a serious conversation,' he complained as he lifted her feet out of the chair so that he could sit in it then startled her by depositing both of her feet in his lap where he proceeded to press both thumbs firmly into the aching muscles and ligaments in the arch of one foot.

'Oh, yes!' she groaned with a mixture of agony and bliss. 'Forget about talking. Just keep doing that to my feet. They're starting to complain loudly about all this weight I'm putting on.'

He continued in silence for several minutes, alternating his ministrations from one foot to the other until she'd almost melted in a puddle, amazed that she'd never realised before that the soles of her feet could be an erogenous zone…in the hands of the right man.

Unfortunately, she and her hormonally overactive erogenous zones might see him as the right man, but cold hard logic told a different story.

In fact, the longer the pregnancy went on, the guiltier she felt about the situation she'd created that never-to-be-forgotten night. If she hadn't fallen apart on him, then offered herself on a plate, making it virtually impossible for a red-blooded man like Daniel to turn her down…

The fact that he'd kept a very proper professional distance between them ever since was proof enough that he had no interest in pursuing any sort of ongoing relationship with her. Well, why would he when he could have any woman he wanted, and there were plenty of high-fliers—doctors and consultants in this hospital, alone—who would have taken him up on an invitation in a flash.

As it was, if it weren't for the fact that she was pregnant, she could probably have put the events of that night to the back of her head, too. At least, one day she might, when she didn't relive them in heart-thumping detail night after night. The fact that she sometimes fooled herself into thinking that she saw desire in his eyes when she caught his gaze was nothing more than wishful thinking.

'As I said, Jenny,' Daniel began again, squeezing one foot in each hand to get her attention and dragging her thoughts out of their interminable circles, 'I've been thinking, and it seems to me that the most logical thing would be for the two of us to get married.'

Jenny stared at him in disbelief, certain she must have misheard him, or that he'd found a novel way to tease her.

Totally unable to find a single word to say, she just gazed at him. Numbly wondering if her mouth was hanging open she fought to take a breath, her heart hammering insanely as she registered the strange watchful seriousness of his gaze.

'Well?' he prompted, and if she hadn't felt the tension in the hands still gripping her feet, she might have believed that he was as relaxed and laid-back as ever.

'Well, what?' she managed, her voice sounding strangely strangled as an enormous bubble of hope started to inflate inside her chest. If the man who'd stolen her heart the first time she'd caught sight of him all those months ago was about to tell her he was in love with her, she'd leap into his arms so fast it would make both their heads swim. And the fact that her pregnancy was already making getting out of chairs cumbersome and ungainly wouldn't stop her, either.

'Don't you think it's the most logical step?' he asked, sounding so horribly matter-of-fact that deflation was almost instant.

'Why is it logical?' she managed, even as a leaden ache took the place of that short-lived bubble of ecstasy. There was nothing like being brought to earth with a bump to burst flimsy bubbles.

'Well, you know as well as I do that things can go wrong with "problem" pregnancies, and they don't come much more high-risk than TTTS.'

'And?' Her stupid heart couldn't give up if there was the slightest possibility that he might tell her that he wanted to be there for her...not just because of the pregnancy but for ever, because he lov—

'Because I want to be there for you,' he said, almost as if he'd heard an echo of the words inside her head. 'Every pregnant woman should have a partner—*someone*—at her side for support, for encouragement.'

Her spirits plunged again then dropped deeper still when he continued in a more serious tone. 'Then there's the possibility—rare though it is these days—that something might happen to you.' He hesitated a beat, as though weighing up the advisability of his next words. 'You haven't said much about your own childhood, but from what you *have* said, well, I don't think you'd really want to take a chance that your parents might end up taking responsibility for—'

'No!' she exclaimed far too loudly, trying to silence the cacophony in her head. She certainly *didn't* want her parents to take charge of her babies. If she wasn't around to show them all the love they deserved, herself, the *last* thing she wanted was for them to be brought up in the same atmosphere that she'd had to endure, always trying so hard to gain the approval that never came. It had taken far too many unhappy years before she'd finally admitted that she was never going to be the perfect child they'd wanted; the child they'd thought they were getting when they'd adopted her.

'I'll write a will,' she said into the startled silence, unable to believe her eyes when she thought she caught a glimpse of pain in his eyes. 'I'll make certain that, if anything happens to me, they'll go to a good home where they'll be wanted and loved, not just tolerated for the sake of appearances or because they're the means of perpetuating the family name for another generation.'

'And what about me?' he asked quietly, his face so expressionless that she had absolutely no idea what he wanted her to say.

'Well, obviously, the last thing I want is for you to have to take the children on. They'd be a constant reminder of… of…' She could feel the heat building in her cheeks as she tried to find an acceptable way of bringing up the fact that she'd taken advantage of his caring nature that night, falling apart on him and then seducing him. It would add insult to injury if he ended up with the burden of raising the children that were the result of her actions.

'Well,' he said quietly, his expression totally blank, 'I made the offer and I meant it. If you should change your mind…'

Jenny knew exactly why she felt so much like crying. The man she loved was offering her everything she'd dreamed of. Everything except the most important part— his love. Without that, marriage would be meaningless.

And if she felt herself weakening—felt tempted to marry him in the hope that she had enough love for both of them—all she had to do was remind herself of the most important reason why she couldn't take him up on his offer, that if he married her before the babies arrived, he wouldn't be allowed to operate, and she didn't trust anyone else to save her precious babies.

Daniel felt as if he'd been gutted like a fish, left with a huge aching hole where his heart should be.

He knew he hadn't made a very good job of suggesting that they could get married, but it was something he'd never done before. He hadn't even remembered to tell her that he was in love with her, for heaven's sake, although that might have been a bit of a stroke of luck, as it turned out. Having his marriage proposal turned down in such a way certainly hadn't been pleasant—dammit, it had hurt as badly as a knife between the ribs—but at least he hadn't had his love thrown back in his face at the same time. That would probably have been the final straw for his ego.

He'd honestly believed that the two of them had a friendly enough rapport that she would have been willing to discuss the possibility of marriage. He'd have to be blind not to recognise the electricity that sparked between them as strongly as ever, even though he was well aware that she wasn't in love with him.

He'd even been grimly prepared for the possibility that she might accept for the sake of the babies with the proviso that it would be a platonic relationship, although with his X-rated dreams that would probably have killed him. The last thing he'd been prepared for was a flat *no*, even when he'd brought up the possibility that the babies might end up with her parents. And her suggestion that the babies—*his* babies—would be better off with another couple…

'What a mess!' he groaned, raking his fingers through his hair then clenching them tight so that the sharp tug on the roots gave him something else to focus on apart from his own stupidity.

As if he didn't already feel guilty enough for taking

advantage of Jenny when she'd been in such an emotional state, but he'd been so attracted to her, right from the first moment he'd seen her walk into the department. If he was honest, he had wanted her so much that it was impossible to regret that one perfect night, in spite of the fact that it had resulted in such a high-risk pregnancy and probably derailed her career.

For weeks, now, he'd been all too aware that she'd been doing her best to keep a certain distance between them, but that hadn't stopped the sharp awareness building between them so that sometimes it felt as if there should be an audible crackle in the air.

Added to that was the fact that his concentration was deteriorating badly. It was fine when he was with a patient because his professionalism kicked in, but the rest of the time it was becoming increasingly difficult for him to think about anything other than Jenny and the precious babies she was carrying, especially as she was so obviously worrying, too.

Nothing had given him peace of mind until he'd convinced himself that she would welcome a proposal of marriage as a way of guaranteeing that there was no question about the babies' security should anything ever happen to her. The fact that by giving her that protection he would be marrying the woman he loved and desired above all others...

'So, what are you going to do about it, man?' he growled, then blinked as his words came back at him in the confines of his office, only then realising that he'd spoken aloud. At least he hadn't left the door open where anyone could have heard him as they'd passed by. *That* wouldn't have done his reputation much good.

As if he cared about his reputation when all he could think about was finding some way of persuading Jenny to change her mind. He couldn't do anything to change where he'd come from, but perhaps if he could engineer some off-duty time together, he could show her that he was something more than the boy from the wrong side of the tracks, now; that he was a man she could trust to take care of her and her babies simply because he loved them, whether she ever returned that love or not.

He certainly wasn't going to meekly accept her refusal at face value, not until he'd done everything he could to find out if there was any way he could persuade her to change her mind. He was so busy contemplating ways of bringing that about that he almost didn't hear the hesitant knock at his door.

CHAPTER NINE

'I'M SO sorry to disturb you,' Amy Finch apologised from the doorway, apparently unwilling to come right into his room even with an invitation. 'I know how busy you are and I really don't want to waste any of your time, but...'

'You're very welcome,' he said with a smile even as he catalogued her darkly shadowed eyes and her unhappy expression.

He knew her babies were still clinging precariously to life in SCBU but it was obvious that she had something on her mind.

'You're rescuing me from having to plough my way through a Mount Everest of paperwork. Would you like a cup of tea or coffee?' he offered, wondering how on earth he was going to get the poor woman to relax enough to talk.

'Oh, no!' she exclaimed hastily. 'I wouldn't want to put anyone to any trouble.'

'*Please* say you want one,' he whispered mock-confidentially. 'Then that means I can have someone bring one for me, too.'

At least that teased a half-smile out of her and she nodded and said, 'Tea, then, please,' as she perched on the very edge of the seat he'd gestured towards as he picked up the phone.

By sheer coincidence it was the very person who'd been occupying so much of his thoughts of late who answered, with a cheerful, 'Hello, this is Jenny. Can I help you?'

'I hope so,' he said, then paused to clear his throat when he heard how husky he sounded before continuing. 'Could you bring three teas, Jenny, if you've got a minute?'

'Of course I have,' she said and he wondered if it was just wishful thinking that made him hear a different note in her voice now that she knew who she was speaking to. 'I'll be there in a jiffy.'

Knowing they were going to be interrupted shortly, he kept the conversation to the mundane topics of the weather and the traffic chaos being caused by the contractors building a new block of 'high-quality apartments' not far from the hospital entrance.

Amy tried to respond but she looked fragile enough to shatter at the slightest thing and jumped visibly when Jenny's head poked around the door.

'Three teas, as requested,' she announced cheerfully, balancing the tray on the corner of his desk to deliver his cup before turning to Amy. 'Shall I give Simon a call to tell him to get it while it's hot?'

'Simon's not here at the moment…he's had to go back to work. He said he's afraid he'll lose his job if he has any more time off. He's trying to save some days for when… in case…' With a wail she dissolved into a flood of tears.

Daniel hadn't realised that the poor woman was quite so close to collapse and sent up a silent word of thanks that Jenny was here, especially when she immediately knelt beside Amy and wrapped comforting arms around her, rocking her gently while she sobbed on Jenny's slender shoulder.

'I've been visiting them every day, doing what I can for

them, or just talking to them. But all I can think of is how small they are and how sick and…and…'

Daniel expected Jenny to murmur comforting words to help the poor woman to calm down, but when she stayed silent, allowing all the agony and misery to pour out, he realised that her instincts were better. Amy needed to vent it all out of her system, rather like lancing a boil to release the trapped poison.

'And Simon…' Amy wailed afresh. 'Poor Simon…'

The man had been so excited when he'd been told they were expecting twins. Daniel could imagine only too clearly how he must be feeling knowing that he could lose one or both of them at any moment.

'You need to be strong for each other,' he heard Jenny murmur and his heart ached that she wouldn't let him be there for her while she waited and worried about the two boys going through exactly the same life-threatening circumstances inside her. 'He didn't carry the babies, but they are his babies as much as they're yours so he's just as worried as you are.'

'But that's just it!' Amy sobbed. 'I feel so guilty that I failed him—that I wasn't able to give him the strong, healthy family we wanted. And I know that if Adam and Aidan don't live, I'll never be able to bear to have him near me, to touch me. I love him desperately, but I couldn't bear it if this happened all over again.'

'Amy, that's one thing you *don't* have to worry about,' Daniel interrupted for the first time. 'We've explained to you—several times, both during your pregnancy and since—that the chances of another TTTS pregnancy are astronomically small. At the time you were probably far too overwhelmed by everything to listen and take it in, but it's time to try again, to tell you that any future pregnancies will probably be quite boringly normal, as far as pregnancy can ever be boring.'

'But…'

'I know this is hardly the moment to be talking to you about future pregnancies—when your body hasn't recovered from this one and your two little boys are still fighting to grow big enough and strong enough for you to take them home…'

'But it doesn't seem as if that's *ever* going to happen,' Amy wailed, 'and they just look so *lonely* in their separate incubators. It seems as if Adam and Aaron should be there together, the two of them together in the cot, the way they were inside me…'

'Have you suggested it to the staff in the unit?' Daniel asked.

'I didn't like to. I don't know them as well as I know the two of you, and I wouldn't want them to think that I was criticising them, or anything.'

'That *won't* be a problem,' Jenny said firmly. 'I used to work in that unit, and if a parent had a workable suggestion, Josh Weatherby and his staff are always open to new ideas. Of course, if there's a medical reason why the two of them *can't* be together, you can be certain they'll explain it to you.'

Amy's face was a mixture of sorrow and dawning hope, and Daniel almost swore aloud at the interruption when the telephone rang, until he heard the message being delivered.

'Amy, Simon's looking for you down in NICU,' he reported with a smile after a slightly cryptic conversation. 'He needs you there to celebrate.'

'Simon? In NICU? To celebrate?' Daniel completely understood the way she was having trouble stringing two thoughts together. He'd seen it happen too many times for it to surprise him any more.

'Apparently, he arrived just after you left. He came back because he'd just had an idea—he wanted to suggest that the boys should be put into the same incubator.'

'And?' Jenny prompted, knowing from Daniel's expression and the glint in those beautiful sapphire eyes that there was more.

'And, almost immediately they were settled in side by side, they reached out for each other.'

'And?' This time it was Amy asking.

'And the monitor readings are already looking better… stronger,' Daniel told her, delighted to see the dawning look of hope that spread over her tear-ravaged face.

'I must go to them,' Amy said breathlessly, then paused. 'Oh, I must look a sight!'

'Take a quick detour through the nearest washroom and splash some cold water over your face,' Jenny suggested with a smile. 'And as soon as you see Simon give him a hug—he'll probably be too busy hugging you back to notice if your nose is a bit pink, and by then you'll probably both be crying.'

'I'm so sorry for taking up so much of your time… both of you,' Amy said as she scrambled to gather up the crumpled tissues. 'I can't thank you enough for listening and for not sending me on my way with a flea in my ear—'

'We'd *never* do that!' Jenny exclaimed, clearly horrified at the idea, only just beating him to the punch.

'Any time you feel you need to have a word—either because you've got problems or because you've got good news to tell us—feel free to come over,' Daniel said and smiled as his last words followed the rapidly disappearing body hurrying towards NICU.

'You were so good with her—'

'How did you know what to say to her?' Daniel's question clashed with Jenny's compliment, and while her praise wrapped warm fingers around his heart, he didn't really feel he'd done anything special. 'How did you know that she needed to let it all out; that you should just hold her and wait?'

She was silent for a moment, her head tilted slightly while she thought. 'Sometimes it's just a case of asking myself what I would like someone to do for me in a particular situation.' She frowned briefly then grinned at him. 'Perhaps it's that infamous feminine intuition that tells me when a hug will do and when someone needs words of consolation or words of wisdom.'

'And that's what you would have wanted in the same sort of situation?' He suddenly realised that he was learning more about this complex, fascinating woman all the time.

'It's a scary thought that I might be in exactly the same situation in a few weeks,' she said, all signs of that cheeky grin vanishing as if it had never been. Now there were shadows in her eyes; shadows that he would love to be able to banish, but even if he could think of a way, Jenny probably wouldn't let him close enough to try.

Daniel remained sitting at his desk after she'd hurried off on some unnamed task, marvelling that she was every bit as energetic as ever, in spite of the fact that she was already carrying extra weight and her centre of gravity had dropped with her expanding waistline.

He marvelled that she was still just as slender from the back as ever; as lean and elegant as a ballerina. It was only when she turned that you could see the bump swelling out the front of her uniform, as often as not with her hand resting on it or stroking gently over it.

With a series of clicks he was able to access Jenny's file and bring up the images of the latest scans that showed all too clearly the worrying disparity in the sizes of the babies, worrying and increasing with each new scan, telling him that the point of no return was approaching fast.

He'd hoped that, as sometimes happened, the smaller twin would manage to develop enough—albeit at a slower rate than his bigger brother—so that they could avoid the dangers of surgery. This obviously wasn't going to be one of those times.

'So tiny,' he groaned and stared down at his clenched fists on the blotter wishing there was something he could do...*anything*...to hasten the day when it would be safe to operate. He turned his hands over and stretched them out flat, mentally comparing the length of each tiny body with the distance from fingertip to wrist. 'I could hold one of them in each hand, and the two of them together would hardly weigh the same as a bag of sugar.'

Tears burned the back of his eyes at the thought that he might never have the chance to hold them if they didn't live. They were already little people to him, from the very first second he'd caught sight of them on the ultrasound screen, and the hold their tiny starfish hands had on his heart would never go, no matter what. If anything happened to them, it wouldn't only be Jenny's heart that was broken.

Then an alternative scenario flashed into his head—the one that almost stopped his heart completely every time it tried to surface—and he knew that pushing it to the back of his mind just wasn't going to work any more. It was something that he had to confront on a regular basis, working in his specialty, even though it didn't happen very often, but because the babies she was carrying were his babies, too, he was going to have to bring it up again... What would he do if something should happen to Jenny? What would happen to those precious babies if they survived and their mother didn't?

'I *can't* leave it much longer,' he declared aloud and just hearing the words made the decision firmer. The latest scans still showed that it was going to be necessary to perform the ablative surgery, but before that happened, he was going to have to sit Jenny down and insist that they discussed their options.

Discussed their options?

'Hah!' He certainly wasn't laughing because he could just imagine how that 'discussion' would go. Jenny had far too many years of fighting her corner against domineering parents to ever meekly submit to anyone else trying to dictate what she should do with her life. He was going to have to tread very carefully along the line that separated telling her that he was in love with her and wanted to marry her with or without the babies, and pointing out that she needed to have someone with the legal right to take over the care of those babies in the event that she was unable to.

And he was a crazy fool that the mere thought that their discussion might end up with her falling into his arms and declaring she loved him too was enough to send his pulse galloping.

Jenny glanced at her watch then at the large clock on the wall, marvelling at the fact that the hands were moving so slowly when she was so jittery with nerves that it felt as if she could run a marathon at the speed of light.

He only offered to give you a lift home because it's raining, she reminded herself, cross that she'd actually tried to read anything more into the suggestion. A highly qualified consultant like Daniel Carterton certainly wouldn't be as uncertain or nervous as a teenager about offering a lowly member of staff a lift in his car when they were going to be travelling in the same direction. And the fact that he'd seemed to be watching her surreptitiously was probably nothing more than her imagination.

She certainly didn't have any reason to build his offer up into anything special; after all, despite that one unforgettable night and the fact that he was her babies' father, the two of them were nothing more than friends, now. The fact that her skin tingled and her heart took off at a gallop whenever he was near, and that she was tempted to grab hold of Daniel and hold on for all she was worth, made her feel dreadfully guilty because he deserved to fall in love with the woman he wanted to marry, not just to marry because it was 'the right thing' in such a situation.

'I couldn't do that to him,' she murmured fiercely, even though she would love to have Daniel as a permanent part of their lives. And if he should meet someone else and want a divorce…how much greater would her heartache be then?

Afraid that her tongue might give voice to the argument going on in her head—the course that she knew was right versus the one she wanted to take—she didn't dare sit in silence during the ride.

She didn't want to bring up something as depressing as the news that had been relayed to them that Sharron Pickering's gamble hadn't paid off—that she'd lost all seven of the babies she'd been carrying. Sadly, complications meant it had also been necessary for her to have a hysterectomy to save her own life, so there would be no further chance for her to have the baby for which she'd been willing to risk everything.

In a quiet corner of the staffroom a little while later, she'd come across Daniel hunched forward in one of the less comfortable chairs with a cup of cold coffee suspended between his knees, the knuckles of both hands bone-white as they clenched around the sturdy pottery.

Immediately, she'd been certain she knew what was on his mind and had paused beside him with her back to the room to minimise the chance of their conversation being overheard.

'You can't afford to let it get to you,' she'd murmured quietly. 'The Sharron Pickerings of the world just aren't worth getting upset over when there are so many other women who need and want your help enough to respect your advice and follow it.'

'That doesn't stop me from…from *grieving* for those seven babies. None of them ever had a chance to be born and draw their first breath,' he'd growled. 'Of course it's sad that a woman's obsession to have a baby nearly destroyed her own life. I'm finding it difficult to be sympathetic when it was entirely her own fault, but those babies…' He'd shaken his head and in spite of the poor light in this corner of the room, Jenny had been certain she'd seen the glitter of the threat of tears in those dark sapphire eyes before he'd looked back down into the unappetising liquid in the mug he was holding.

No, that really wasn't a topic she wanted to resurrect in the close confines of his car. There must be something else she could bring up that would break the strangely tense silence that stretched between them.

'Your patience with that last patient in the clinic certainly paid off in the end,' she said, finding a topic that would keep her out of mischief without depressing them both in the process. According to her notes, Susan Feldman had been very overweight at the time of her first appointment at the hospital, and had been very resistant to the idea that losing weight would make any difference to her chances of achieving the pregnancy she longed for. 'She was absolutely over the moon…both with her weight loss and with the fact that she'll shortly be putting some of it on again, now that she's pregnant.'

'She deserves all the credit for sticking to her diet,' he said. 'I didn't do it for her.'

'But, according to her, you were the first one to sit down and take the time to point out the probable connection between her weight and her inability to conceive, and to encourage her to do something about it without preaching and wagging your finger.'

'Sometimes I even surprise myself,' he said dryly, and the wry grin that tilted his mouth drew her gaze in the half-light and made her wish she could see it more clearly. Better still, she wished she could taste it again. One night really hadn't been enough to do more than whet her appetite for more of the same.

'I think one of the things that stuck with her was the fact I told her that very skinny woman can have similar problems, including early onset menopause.'

'Do you think it's a form of self-preservation that a significant number of women who are considerably over-weight or underweight can't get pregnant...or can't carry a baby successfully if they *do* manage to get pregnant?' Jenny asked, always eager to learn. 'Do you think that their bodies are already having a struggle to cope with day-to-day living, so they're unable to carry a baby to term?'

'There are just so many potentially awful consequences for pregnant women who aren't otherwise taking proper care of themselves. You mentioned the potential for early onset menopause for underweight women, preventing them from ever conceiving a child, but at the other end of the range there's a whole raft of other dangers...gestational diabetes, eclampsia—'

'You hardly need to list them for me,' she pointed out with a chuckle. 'When I was working in SCBU, I regularly saw babies born far too soon because their mothers weren't able to carry them any longer. And a rising number of those mums were women who were either stick thin or were already grossly overweight *before* they got pregnant.'

He sighed heavily. 'I just hate seeing innocent babies die when it's so unnecessary and so preventable. All the women have to do to prove how determined they are to have a baby is to get themselves healthy by changing their diet and taking a sensible amount of exercise. It's not rocket science, just sensible calorie counting and no cheating. And when they finally hold that baby, they'll *know* it was all worthwhile.'

'There speaks someone who's obviously never had a problem with his weight,' she teased, glad he had no idea just how often she daydreamed about the gorgeous naked body she'd explored that night; a body that was all long, lean, power-packed muscles without a trace of flab in sight anywhere. 'I can personally vouch for the fact that an un-happy, lardy, ungainly teenager with an unhealthy taste for junk food can grow up into a pretty hefty adult. It took me nearly two years to finally sort myself out, probably because I started off with a severe lack of will power and an absolute craving for anything containing monosodium glutamate.'

'Well, you certainly don't look as if you've ever had a problem,' he countered gratifyingly swiftly. 'You're slim, but without being so skinny that you look as if you could snap like a twig. Even now, at six months pregnant, you're not carrying any surplus weight. In fact, you look as slen-der as ever from the back.'

And he'd been looking? Just the thought of it had a blush heating her face at the same time as a warm glow curled around her heart. He'd noticed her body and had been admiring it in spite of the fact that she was about to start the third trimester of a twin pregnancy?

'Thank you for the compliment,' she managed, huskily. She was relieved to note that they'd reached the front of the house she currently called home and wondered how the innocuous conversation she'd started to fill the journey had ended up turning so personal. Still, they were here now and soon she'd be able to hide the volatile mixture of pleasure and embarrassment behind her front door.

So, why did she hear herself offering to make him a coffee when she should just have thanked him for the lift and hurried in out of the rain?

'You've probably had more coffee than is good for you already today,' she hastily backpedalled, but it was too late. He'd already switched the engine off and was climbing out of the car.

'Hang on. Plan B,' he said over the sound of the rain hitting the car roof as she scampered up the short path through the puddles. 'Shall I whip up to the shop at the end of the road and pick up some fish and chips? Or would you prefer Chinese, or Indian?'

'Not Indian,' she said with a shudder from the dubious shelter of the inadequate porch. 'Ordinarily, I love it, but at the moment it gives me wicked heartburn.'

'And I'm always starving an hour after I've eaten Chinese, even if I've been a glutton, so that makes it fish and chips, then,' he said with a grin. 'I'll be back in five minutes, just enough time for you to make the tea.'

Jenny wasn't quite sure how he'd demolished any trace of her determination to keep her distance from him. Probably it was the fault of that grin and the way her imagination was trying work out how much damage it would do to her heart if she had three identical grins to contend with on a daily basis.

'Oh, but I would love it if they *did* have his grin,' she whispered with a catch in her throat as she grabbed cutlery from the drawer and sandwiched a sheet of wet kitchen towel between two plates and set the microwave ready to switch on when Daniel returned so they wouldn't have to put their food on cold plates.

'And if I could be setting the table like this on a daily basis, ready for when he comes home at the end of his shift... Whoa! What am I *saying*!' she exclaimed when she realised she'd sounded as if she was ready to throw away all her hard work in building her career to stay home and play happy families. She'd had to study far too hard and had to battle against the wishes of her parents for too many years to give up her dream so easily.

'And anyway, there's no guarantee that either of the babies will survive,' she reminded herself in a tight whisper, 'and there's certainly no guarantee that Daniel would still be interested in me *without* them.'

After her stern reminders to herself, their meal was unexpectedly relaxed, their conversation ranging far and wide the way it always had in the days before *that night*.

It was only as Daniel was rinsing the plates off at the sink, having insisted that she put her feet up while she got the chance, that it became more personal again.

'How have you been feeling?' he asked casually...as if there could ever be a casual question about the babies that he'd fathered that unforgettable night. 'Are the two of them starting to kick you black and blue?'

'At least one of them is going to be a footballer, or a flamenco dancer,' she joked and rested her hand on top of what was already a pronounced bulge. 'Of course, the activity is always worse when I'm lying in bed, and any time I sit down for more than two minutes.' She paused, waiting for the next sign of activity and wondering whether it would be an elbow or a knee this time, and whether it would be right up under her ribs or on her poor battered bladder…except the activity didn't come.

'That's odd,' she said as she smoothed both palms over the tight hard curve, exploring and tracing outlines to see if the babies had managed to settle themselves in a position that would mute their activity. 'They're not usually so quiet at this time of night. They're real night owls…'

She started to feel queasy, worry making her supper feel like lead in her stomach as she tried to remember exactly when she'd last felt any movement.

'Daniel?' Something in the tone of her voice must have alerted him because he immediately whirled to face her.

'What is it, Jenny?' he demanded, dropping to his knees in front of her, his deep blue eyes darkening still further as he slid both hands between hers, his long fingers almost completely spanning the bulge of her pregnancy as he spread them wide. 'Are you in pain? You're not having contractions, are you?'

'No. Daniel, they're not moving!' She placed her hands over his and pressed them tightly against her belly. 'The babies aren't moving and I can't remember when they last kicked me. I don't know how long ago…' Panic robbed her of further words and she could hardly see the horrified expression on his face for the tears flooding her eyes.

The next hour passed in a blur.

She couldn't remember travelling to the hospital at all, and even though she tried her hardest to take note of everything going on around her—knowing how crucial a single finding could be—it was almost as if she had been isolated in a bubble with her terror so that nothing else could get through to her.

Nothing but Daniel.

All he had to do was touch her and she felt connected again, grounded and somehow protected at the same time.

She knew that it was stupid, but she'd somehow managed to convince herself that as long as Daniel was there with her, nothing bad could happen to her precious babies.

Then he crouched down in front of her and took both her hands in his, and just the seriousness of the expression on his face was enough to tell her that he was there to give her bad news.

For a crazy moment she wanted to pull her hands away and put them over her ears so he couldn't say the words that would break her heart, but she'd never been a coward. Anyway, what difference would it make if she stopped herself from hearing what he had to say? None at all.

'Tell me,' she said, the words emerging as a barely there whisper when her throat was so tight it felt as if she was shouting. 'They've died, haven't they? My babies are dead.'

CHAPTER TEN

'JENNYWREN, no!' Daniel exclaimed, then shocked her completely by wrapping his arms around her in front of a roomful of fascinated staff.

For several heartbeats she allowed herself to absorb all the strength and warmth and security that Daniel was offering before she forced herself to pull back. Briefly, he resisted, but of course he was only trying to comfort her, wasn't he? That was *her* body trembling so hard, or was he shaking, too?

'They're *alive*, Jenny. Both of them…for the moment, at least,' he added ominously even as she was trying to absorb the fact that her worst nightmare hadn't happened.

How had she managed to miss hearing the sound of their heartbeats when the ultrasound was performed? Had she so convinced herself that there would be nothing to hear that she'd totally ignored it, along with everything else around her?

A little bubble of hope began to rise inside her until she looked up into those beautiful blue eyes and saw the shadows that spoke of bad news as clearly as words.

'T-tell me,' she said, her teeth suddenly chattering so hard it was a wonder he could understand her.

'They're struggling,' he said concisely. 'It sometimes

happens like that. For no apparent reason, everything suddenly becomes critical.'

She forced her foggy brain to work, to make sense of what he was saying and what it meant for her precious boys.

'Wh-when will you operate?' she demanded, refusing to even think about the possibility that there was nothing he could do to save them.

He hesitated and a rush of panic sent her pulse rate into orbit.

'P-please, Daniel, you *have* to operate.' She was openly begging, now, and she didn't care who was listening. 'You're the only one who can do it. You're the only one who can save my babies.'

He must have made some signal to the other staff to leave the room because suddenly they were alone but for the rhythmic sounds of the monitoring equipment.

'There's a problem,' he said, sounding strangely hesitant.

Impatiently, she interrupted, 'If there wasn't a problem, I wouldn't need the surgery to save my babies' lives.'

'That's not the problem I'm talking about.' He was almost eerily calm when she just wanted to scream with frustration that something wasn't already happening to get her ready for the procedure. It was her babies' only chance of life and it should be happening *now*. Daniel shouldn't be here, talking to her, he should be scrubbing and reviewing the scans and the—

'Jenny, I think I should have you transferred to another hospital for the surgery,' he announced bluntly. 'I've held off from talking to you about this—about anything to do with the babies and you and me—because you said you weren't ready, but they're *my* babies, too, and the ethics committee will be far from happy when they hear about that. It'd be a serious breach of the rules. I could even lose my job if I were to operate on—'

'*No!*' Jenny interrupted frantically. '*Please*, Daniel, as long as no one knows, there's no reason why you can't perform the ablation. The last thing I want, the last thing the *babies* need, is for someone other than you—someone not as good a surgeon as you—to do the surgery.'

She gathered her unravelling nerves together and lowered her voice, glancing across to make sure that no one had come back into the room; that no one could be listening. 'Apart from the fact that transferring me would take time they might not have, we've been careful not to give anyone any reason to think there's any connection between you and the babies, so without DNA analysis, no one could possibly know there's a conflicting personal connection. *Please*, Daniel, I'm begging you. I want *you* to do it. I trust you. I lo...'

At the very last second she managed to swallow the forbidden admission of her feelings for him. Not only was it inappropriate at this time and in this place, but in the circumstances it was something he definitely didn't need to know, not unless there was some small possibility that he might care for her, too; that the concern he showed so readily to all his patients was for her as well as the babies she was carrying.

Once the decision was made, it wasn't long before she was being positioned with the pale mound of her belly surrounded by dark green drapes and the frightening array of technology that would enable Daniel to identify and seal off the connecting blood vessels that were causing all the problems.

Her thoughts were whirling around inside her head, prayers for the success of the surgery and the survival of her babies mixed with overwhelming gratitude that Daniel had agreed to perform the procedure. It would have been wonderful if he could have been in two places at once— sitting beside her to hold her hand as well as operating on her—but at least she was surrounded by familiar members of staff, many of whom had become almost like a family to her.

'Not long, now,' Sally Long encouraged. 'He's just scrubbing.'

Jenny managed to smile at the registrar she'd first met when she was doing a rotation in NICU. The young woman had quickly gained a reputation for her skill at being able to thread hair-fine needles into minute baby veins, the result of her love of embroidery, she claimed.

With the organised chaos going on around her, everyone focusing on their particular task to make ready as quickly as possible, she felt strangely disconnected, almost as if she was watching everything through a glass screen. There was the byplay between the anaesthetist and one of the nurses, a wink from one that put a sparkle in the eyes of the other, the serious expression on another face as instruments were tallied and laid out in readiness then the door swung open by a broad shoulder as Daniel entered the room, his hands held up out of the way of contamination as he approached her.

From the other side of the room his eyes met hers over the top of his mask and even though they were all she could see of him, their dark intensity told her everything he was feeling—his apprehension for the two little lives she carried, his determination to do his best for them, his concern for her—and suddenly, the jumble of disparate thoughts colliding inside her head arranged themselves into a strange kind of logic that seemed to make everything frighteningly clear.

She loved Daniel, loved everything about him, and had

done so ever since she'd met him. In fact, she loved him so much that even if his suggestion that they marry had only been for the sake of the babies, she was willing to accept his offer if that meant he could be a part of her life.

'Sally?' She beckoned her colleague closer. 'Can I ask you a huge favour?'

Daniel threw his cap and gown in the laundry bin and slumped back against the nearest wall, suddenly shaking so hard that he wasn't certain that his legs would hold him up.

'I did it!' he whispered and closed his eyes to send up a heartfelt prayer of thanks that his skill had been equal to the task.

It had been even more complex than he'd expected and taken nearly twice as long because, with the placenta implanted low down on the front wall of the uterus, he'd had to introduce a second trocar to be able to get the laser in the right position to seal off the last of the blood vessels. The procedure had ended with drawing off some of the excess fluid around the recipient twin, but he wouldn't know how successful the procedure had been until the amount of fluid around the smaller twin started to increase, indicating that he was finally receiving his fair share of the blood supply.

'And that is always dependent on the trauma of the surgery not triggering premature labour,' he murmured, tempted to cross his fingers, but as that was something that they couldn't be sure about for days or even weeks, keeping them crossed that long would be a practical impossibility.

For now, all he could do was celebrate the fact that the surgery had gone as well as he could have hoped, with every single blood vessel that had previously joined the two babies now permanently sealed.

He was desperate to go and check on Jenny again, needing to see with his own eyes that she'd recovered well from the strain of the procedure, but it would probably be a good idea to take the time to climb under a shower before he did. That might help him to get himself under control before he blurted out something that he shouldn't while she was in such a vulnerable state.

'Daniel?' A brief knock on the changing room door was accompanied by the sleekly elegant head of the Registrar who'd been observing the procedure, today, and his heart leapt into his mouth.

'Is there a problem, Sally?' he demanded, thrusting head and arms back into the scrub top he'd only just removed while his heart rate spiked. 'Jenny's not bleeding, is she? She hasn't started having contractions, has she?'

'No, it's not Jenny…well, it is…really, but not because of the surgery.' She stopped abruptly, muttered something under her breath and blew out a huff of laughter. 'I'm making a real mess of this, only she asked me just before the procedure was about to begin, and—'

'Sally, slow down! Take a deep breath,' Daniel advised and gestured towards the long narrow bench against the wall. 'Sit down and start at the beginning. Someone asked you to do something for them?'

'Jenny did,' she nodded as she perched gingerly on the edge of the bench. 'And she asked me to make absolutely certain that I sent you in to see her immediately after the procedure was over.'

'She *what*?' Daniel blinked. Whatever he'd been expecting, it hadn't been that. 'Did she say why?'

Sally bit her lip and couldn't seem to make herself meet his eyes. He was just about ready to break a habit of a lifetime and shout at a junior member of staff when she finally spoke.

'I don't know how much she's told you about her situation,' she began, 'and I would feel really uncomfortable breaking a confidence, but she asked me to make some arrangements for her and then said she would need to see you.' She hesitated a moment, as though unsure whether to go on, then added in an eager rush, 'I'm not certain, but I think it's got something to do with the father of her babies. I think she's going to ask you to get in contact with him for her.'

'What, exactly, did she tell you?' he managed to ask calmly, bracing his shoulders against the wall in a semblance of calm composure when there was a tornado of thoughts whirling around inside him. His own career could be on the line if the fact that he'd taken advantage of one of his staff became common knowledge, to say nothing of the fact that he'd operated on her and the babies he'd given her.

'First, she swore me to secrecy, so you have to swear that you'll never tell anyone what I'm telling you. Ever!' She looked so fierce that he knew that if he didn't promise, he wouldn't find out what was going on.

'I promise that I won't break Jenny's confidence in you,' he said and she blinked then shook her head.

'That's not the same,' she objected.

'I know,' he agreed, hoping he sounded calmer than he felt, 'but I have to leave myself some leeway to enable me to speak to Jenny, but I do promise that whatever you tell me will never go further than the three of us. Is that good enough?'

'It will have to do, I suppose,' she said grudgingly. 'But…'

'What did she tell you?' he asked before she could avoid the topic again. 'What did she want you to do?'

'She asked me to organise the delivery of a selection of balloons from the concession in the main lobby. Then she gave me the message for you, to be delivered after the ablation was finished.'

Daniel managed to force himself to stay long enough to thank Sally, but even when he left her he wasn't able to hurry to Jenny's side because an icily controlled woman accosted him in the hallway.

'Dr Carterton, it's time we spoke,' Jenny's mother said abruptly.

For just a second Daniel was ashamed to admit that his knees knocked as he was catapulted back into his eleven-year-old self, the first time he was called in front of the headmistress accused of fighting by the very bullies who had cornered him and blacked his eye.

It didn't take long to remind himself that those days were long gone. These days he could give as good as he got.

'Dr Sinclair,' he replied politely, silently reminding himself that he had every intention of putting the woman in the position of mother-in-law as soon as possible, no matter what scheme Jenny might have cooked up with Sally Long. At least she'd come to find out how her daughter's surgery had gone. 'Shall we go to my office?'

'Here will do well enough,' she snapped, clearly incensed. 'I want the name of the man who dishonoured my family by getting my daughter pregnant, and you're going to give it to me.'

Her arrogant assurance that he would do what she said just because she'd said it meant that Daniel had to bite his tongue and count to ten to keep his anger under control. The fact that he hadn't immediately complied was enough to have the colour on her cheekbones darkening with her rising anger.

'For heaven's sake, she's already noticeably pregnant!' Jenny's mother exclaimed. 'She should have the man's ring on her finger by now; should have been married months ago so people could at least have pretended they didn't notice it was only a six-month pregnancy.'

'I'm sure she could have had the ring, *if* she wanted it,' Daniel said tersely, fuming that the woman seemed to care so little about Jenny's happiness. His Jennywren was worth far more than a cobbled-together marriage of convenience purely for social appearances. That was exactly why he hadn't badgered her to accept his proposal after she'd refused him, even though he ached to make her his. 'Any man would be lucky to have her as a wife,' he added, pushing his private ache to one side. 'She's beautiful, bright, caring, dedicated—'

'Well, if you think so highly of her, why don't *you* marry her?' she demanded impatiently. 'I'd make it worth your while.'

Daniel shook his head in disbelief. 'You obviously don't know your daughter at all, and you certainly don't know anything about *me* if you think I would accept a bribe to force her into a marriage she didn't want.' He gave a brief bark of laughter that was totally devoid of any humour. 'And to think I thought you'd come here to find out how the surgery had gone!'

'Surgery? What surgery?' she demanded before a hopeful smile spread over her face. 'Did she finally see sense and decide it was better to get rid of the baby?'

'Hardly!' Daniel snapped, almost incandescent with rage that the woman should think so little of those precious scraps of humanity, only subliminally aware that Jenny apparently hadn't even bothered to inform her parents that she was carrying twins, let alone that their lives were in danger.

Well, if she hadn't wanted to tell them, he certainly wasn't going to. The only thing that really mattered to him was that Jenny had asked to see him, and her mother was delaying him for her own selfish reasons.

'I've just had to perform *in utero* surgery to save two babies' lives. Now, if you'll excuse me, I'm sure you'll understand that I need to check up on my patients,' and he had absolutely no regrets that he hadn't told her that it was her daughter and her grandchildren that he was talking about.

His heart was in his mouth and his pulse was beating at twice its normal rate by the time he tapped on Jenny's door, all the possible reasons why she might have asked Sally to pass on her message jumbled in his head.

The only thing that shone like a clear beacon was his determination to try to persuade her that he loved her enough for both of them and if she would only agree to marry him, he would spend the rest of his life taking care of her and their babies.

He knew that the next few minutes were more crucial to his future than anything that had gone before and he was terrified because this was the first challenge in his life that he couldn't overcome by hard work and persistence alone.

'Come in,' called her familiar voice and his heart gave an extra kick in response, then kicked again when he saw the smile that greeted him when she saw him at the door.

His eyes drank in the sight of her greedily, noting that she was still a little pale after such a stressful time but that one hand was gently stroking the curve of her belly as though soothing her tiny passengers.

'Daniel!' She beckoned him in with the other hand but must have seen something in his face because her smile immediately vanished. 'What's the matter? Did something go wrong during the procedure? Did you find something that—?'

'No, Jenny!' he exclaimed, silently castigating himself for worrying her. He'd thought he had a better poker face than that, but perhaps Jenny was the one person who could see beyond that; to know with nothing more than a look that he had something on his mind. 'I had my doctor's head on, checking to see that you were all right. Nothing adverse to report? Nothing worrying you?'

'Nothing,' she agreed happily, settling herself deeper into her nest of pillows. 'I feel about a ton lighter now that weight has been taken off my shoulders. How soon did you say I could go home? And how soon will you be able to tell how successful the op's been, that the bigger twin's heart has recovered from the strain of coping with so much of the circulation?'

'And how many more questions are you going to fire at me without waiting for a single answer?' he teased as he hitched one hip onto the side of her bed and took her hand in his, careful of the drip he'd had left there as a precautionary measure, using it temporarily to deliver antibiotics to ward off the possibility of a post-operative infection.

'I'm sorry!' she laughed. 'Only, for the first time since you diagnosed the TTTS I feel as if I can really look forward to these two, to start to enjoy the whole process of pregnancy and—'

'Jennywren, can I ask you a question?' he interrupted, almost hating to break into her bubbly mood, but he'd been waiting and wanting her for such a long time and he couldn't wait any longer.

'Of course you can!' she exclaimed. 'You're my own personal miracle worker so you can ask anything you like. Anything at all!'

'In that case…' With his heart in his mouth he paused just long enough to capture her hand. 'Jenny Sinclair, will you marry me…please?'

* * *

'Marry you?' Jenny managed to reply before the power of speech completely deserted her.

Of *course* she wanted to marry him! That was the whole reason why she'd sent Sally Long to give him her message, but then he'd started asking how she was, as if he was only there to check up on a post-operative patient and she'd been distracted.

The suddenly unreadable expression on his face was enough to tell her that she'd paused too long, distracted by the conflicting thoughts colliding inside her brain and that her hesitation had hurt him—the one man who had never been anything but kind to her, who had proved over and over again that he cared for her without having to say a single word.

'Daniel…' There was nothing she'd love better than to be Daniel Carterton's wife, but she couldn't accept, not until she had the answers she needed. As soon as she'd seen his handsome face her heart had done a crazy happy dance in welcome, but in spite of the fact that this was the second time he'd proposed marriage, she didn't even know if he loved her, because he'd never said so…not once…and her pride didn't like the idea that the babies might be the only reason he was with her.

Obligation and duty were not the best reasons for two people to tie the knot. In fact, the only reason she would ever marry would be for love, and that would have to be to someone who not only loved her babies—the way soft-hearted Daniel loved all babies—but loved her just as much.

'Daniel…' she began again. The muddle inside her head and her heart were almost making her dizzy, and she certainly wasn't expecting him to surge to his feet as though he was going to leave her before she could find the words to ask him why he wanted her to marry him.

Except he didn't leave; simply straightened his shoulders and drew in a deep breath before he fixed her with a stern look that stilled everything inside her while she waited for him to speak.

'Well, then, it looks as if it's time to put my cards on the table,' he said, and she wondered if he realised that she could hear the slight tremor in his voice that told her he wasn't quite as resolute as he appeared.

'I know when you were trying to persuade me to do the surgery you said that there was no personal connection for the ethics committee to object to, but we both knew that wasn't true because they're my babies and also…' He snatched another breath and met her eyes straight on before he continued.

'Jenny Sinclair, I love you, in spite of the fact that you are probably the most stubborn female on God's green earth, and even if you weren't having my babies, I would still love you. So, will you please, *please*, say you'll marry me?'

For several endless seconds she felt as if she sat there with her mouth opening and closing like a goldfish, unable to find a single word to answer him as her heart turned somersaults inside her.

'You love me?' she finally managed to echo in disbelief.

'Of course I do,' he declared fiercely, reclaiming his place on the side of her bed and capturing both of her hands in the warm strength of his. 'I've been in love with you for months, almost since the day you walked into the unit and asked what extra training you would need to join my team.' His laughter had little humour in it. 'But I assumed with your family background that you were out of my league. I can't for one moment imagine that I'm your parents' ideal candidate for son-in-law!'

'Even though I'm not their natural daughter and have

been making my own choices since I was a teenager?' she interrupted wryly, tightening her grip on his clever fingers. 'Do you really think I would allow them to influence my choice of husband?'

'When you told Colin that you were adopted and there-fore wouldn't inherit the family wealth, that was the first time that I allowed myself a glimmer of hope that some-one from so far the other side of the tracks might stand a chance with you—that you weren't hung up on position and money. But it was the fact that you were pregnant with my babies that made me determined to try to change your mind about marriage, about me.'

'Ah, well, I might have been guilty of a little misrepre-sentation about the situation of my inheritance,' she admit-ted, hoping she wasn't just about to shoot herself in the foot.

'Misrepresentation? In what way?' He frowned.

'Well, by law, once you're adopted into someone's family, you become as much a part of that family as if you were a natural-born member, with all the same rights.'

'So, does that mean that you *will* be inheriting all that stuff?' His expression was growing darker by the second but it wasn't until he drew his hands away from hers com-pletely that she started to panic.

'A house and a few fields? Yes, I could, if I wanted to,' she admitted, then deliberately took his hands back in hers. 'But that would only be after both my parents are gone and providing they hadn't got rid of it in the meantime.'

'Got rid of it?' he echoed, clearly amazed. 'Why?'

'For so many reasons.' She rolled her eyes. 'Because they're both workaholics who never spend any time there. Because it costs an absolute fortune to maintain—tens of thousands every year that can't possibly be covered by the rental that comes in from letting the fields out for grazing, or the income from letting occasional film crews use it for historic costume dramas, or as a venue for lavish weddings,' she enumerated. 'It might be different if Mum stayed at home to run everything to maximise the income—she's a brilliant organiser and would do it really well—but she'd go round the bend without her medicine.'

'So, what are they thinking of doing with it?' He was clearly intrigued, now. 'Obviously they can't just abandon such an historic place?'

'They've had several boutique hotel chains begging to be allowed to take it off their hands, but wouldn't make a decision until they saw me safely married off—perhaps, in case it spoiled my prospects? I think they were hoping I'd fall for the second son of one of the neighbouring estates, someone who wasn't in line to inherit a stately pile of his own but was accustomed to the lifestyle.'

'And as an independent woman living in London with a career you're unlikely to want to give up—'

'Except for the right incentives,' she interrupted, feeling it was past time they left the topic of her parents' hopes and wishes and got back to their own.

'And what incentives would they be?' he enquired, switching his focus every bit as quickly as she had.

She paused for a moment, as though in thought, but in truth she was taking pleasure in just looking at him, noting that the electric atmosphere between them was almost crackling with anticipation, and the extra gleam in those deep blue eyes reminded her of sunshine glinting off water.

'Well, if I were to marry, I would want it to be to someone who loved me—'

'I've already told you I do,' he interrupted, 'when I asked you to marry me.'

'He'd have to love me for *me*, not because I was carrying his children—'

'Would loving you even *more* because you're carrying my children count?' he interrupted again. 'Would loving you even more because you look more beautiful, more womanly, more sexy, more desirable with every day?' He punctuated each compliment with a kiss, the final one delivered on her parted lips.

It was several breath-stealing moments before he drew away again, just far enough to murmur in a voice roughened by emotion.

'Ah, Jennywen, don't you understand? The babies are a very welcome bonus, but the *only* reason I want to marry you is because I love you to distraction.'

He leant forward to kiss her again as though he was unable to resist and muttered under his breath when he became entangled in the strings of several balloons tied to the IV stand.

'What *is* this lot?' he demanded, trying to push them out of his way.

'What does it look like?' she asked with a chuckle and a glance up at the brightly coloured shapes bobbing silently above their heads.

The identical blue ones both bore the message 'It's a boy!' The silver one said 'Congratulations, Daddy!' The scarlet, heart-shaped one spoke for itself and the white one asked the simple handwritten question, 'Will you marry me?'

EPILOGUE

JENNY struggled to open her eyes, but she didn't need to be able to see to know whose arms were holding her so gently, yet so securely, and a tired but happy smile crept over her face.

'I'm sure you must be breaking at least a dozen hospital rules,' she managed in a voice husky with sleep.

'I don't think you'll find any rules that say a husband can't cuddle his wife to thank her after she's given him the two most beautiful sons in the world,' he said smugly, then pressed a kiss to the side of her face. 'How are you feeling?'

'As if I could sleep for a week,' she admitted. 'And as if I could run a marathon or float up to the ceiling like a balloon.'

'All at once?' he teased. 'Sounds exhausting.'

'Not as exhausting as carrying those two around that last fortnight,' she grumbled. 'Whoever said that babies are quieter the closer they get to the due date *lied*! They kick incessantly, day and night, and they never sleep, either.'

'So, how come you want to run a marathon and float round the room?' He helped her to slide up the bed just a little, knowing that the epidural wouldn't wear off for a while, yet.

'I could float because I suddenly feel as light as a

feather, *and* I can see my toes again! And I feel as if I could run a marathon because…well, I suppose it's the relief that they're finally here.'

'And relief that, after all the uncertainty, both Sam and Josh are a good weight and it looks as if we did the operation before any irreparable damage was done to Sam's heart.'

Jenny could remember all too clearly how tightly they'd clung to each other while they waited for the preliminary tests to be done on their precious newborn boys, almost unaware of the repair going on after the Caesarean that had been necessary to bring them into the world.

'How soon can I go up to the nursery to see them?' she demanded. 'I don't have to wait until I can walk, do I?'

'You know me better than that,' he chided. 'I wouldn't make you wait. I was just waiting until you were properly awake before I get some helpers in here. They're probably lined up in the corridor outside your door, hoping they'll get a chance to see our boys, too.'

Before he had a chance to do more than get his feet on the floor there was a sharp tap on the door and her father's head appeared.

'Ready for visitors?' he asked, then strode in without waiting for an answer, the very picture of health since he'd finally bowed to the inevitable several weeks ago and had the bypass surgery. Apparently, it had been his wife's accusation that he wouldn't be around to see his grandchildren that had made him see sense.

Then, during his recuperation, he'd realised that he rather loved the grand old house that had been passed down to him—and had been the venue for Jenny and Daniel's elegantly exclusive wedding—and with a bit of juggling of schedules, he could actually spend part of each week enjoying the gardens and overseeing the maintenance that would see the place in good enough repair to pass on to the next generation.

'When do we get our hands on our boys?' her mother said following close behind with a daintily wrapped parcel in her hands. 'There's a dragon in the nursery who wouldn't let us in, even though we're both consultants and we're their grandparents.'

It almost looked as if there was a hint of a blush on her cheeks as she handed the parcel over and Jenny was intrigued, quickly slipping off the elaborate blue bow and peeling back the paper covered in sleeping cherubs.

'Oh! They're beautiful!' she exclaimed when she saw the matched pair of pale blue cardigans, obviously hand-made rather than bought, and perfect in every stitch.

'I remembered that I rather enjoyed knitting for you when you were tiny,' her mother admitted, then added with a tone that was almost a challenge, 'I've decided that, since I'm cutting down on my hours in the hospital, too, I'm going to keep the babies in cardigans and jumpers. It will be up to you to tell me what they need and what colours you'd like me to use.'

Another tap at the door revealed Staff Nurse, clearly wanting the room cleared while she made Jenny's post-operative checks, and, with an unexpected hug from both of her parents and an admonishment to let them know as soon as they were allowed to visit the babies, they were gone.

'Do you want me to go, too?' Daniel asked, uncertain of the exact nursing protocols after a Caesarean now that he was on the parental side of the medical fence.

'Not at all,' Staff Nurse said with a wink. 'I thought it was probably the only way to persuade them to go so that you could take Jenny to the nursery to see the babies.'

'I can go now?' Jenny beamed. 'How am I going to get there—in a wheelchair?'

'You don't have to do a thing, just lie there and look beautiful,' Daniel said as he kicked off the brakes and began to manoeuvre the bed towards the doors that someone out in the corridor had unlatched.

It felt almost like a royal procession by the time they reached the nursery, so many people had found an excuse to be there to congratulate them, but once Daniel and Jenny had used the hand sanitiser and gone through the doors they were virtually alone, curtains enclosing them with their two precious boys, even though only the top half of her bed could fit.

'Oh, Daniel, they're so perfect,' Jenny whispered, feeling the hot press of tears welling in her eyes. She'd had only the briefest glimpse of each of them as they were delivered. This was her first chance to feast her eyes on them.

'They are amazingly alike,' Daniel said ruefully. 'I can't see how we're ever going to be able to tell them apart. They're going to run rings round us when they get bigger.'

'It's easy enough at the moment,' Jenny pointed out, reaching one hand in to stroke one downy soft cheek then another, the two of them curled up side by side. 'Samuel Peter is the bigger one; Joshua Daniel still has some catching up to do.' She inspected as much as she could see of them, glad that the room was so warm that they only required nappies. It was easy to see how perfect they both were in every detail, then she started to chuckle.

'What's funny? What have you seen?' Daniel demanded.

'I've just spotted something that will give them away every time,' Jenny said triumphantly. 'Look at Sam's hair at the front. He's got a little cowlick, where the hair grows in a little clockwise whorl.'

It was Daniel's turn to chuckle. 'Josh has got the cowlick, too, but his is anticlockwise.'

'And if we don't tell them how we know which is which, by the time they work it out for themselves, we'll know the two of them and their different characters so well that we'll never get them muddled.'

'Ah, Jennywren, you're going to be such an awesome mother,' Daniel said suddenly, his expression very serious. 'How did I ever get so lucky?'

'I'm the lucky one,' she argued. 'I fell in love with the handsomest man in the hospital and all he seemed to want was to be my big brother.'

'When *I* didn't feel in the least bit brotherly,' he butted in, 'but if it was the only way I could spend time with you…'

'Then I seduced you and got pregnant, and you had to operate to save our babies' lives, and the rest is history,' she finished with a blissful smile.

'Oh, not history,' he disagreed, wrapping a loving arm around her shoulders and holding her so close that she could hear his heart beating, strong and true. 'That would mean it was over—in the past—and our lives together certainly aren't over. This is just the beginning of our own special happy-ever-after.'

* * * * *

LET'S TALK
Romance

For exclusive extracts, competitions
and special offers, find us online:

MILLS & BOON

THE HEART OF ROMANCE

A ROMANCE FOR EVERY KIND OF READER

MODERN

Prepare to be swept off your feet by sophisticated, sexy and seductive heroes, in some of the world's most glamourous and romantic locations, where power and passion collide.
8 stories per month.

HISTORICAL

Escape with historical heroes from time gone by. Whether your passion is for wicked Regency Rakes, muscled Vikings or rugged Highlanders, awaken the romance of the past.
6 stories per month.

MEDICAL

Set your pulse racing with dedicated, delectable doctors in the high-pressure world of medicine, where emotions run high and passion, comfort and love are the best medicine.
6 stories per month.

True Love

Celebrate true love with tender stories of heartfelt romance, from the rush of falling in love to the joy a new baby can bring, and a focus on the emotional heart of a relationship.
8 stories per month.

Desire

Indulge in secrets and scandal, intense drama and plenty of sizzling hot action with powerful and passionate heroes who have it all: wealth, status, good looks…everything but the right woman.
6 stories per month.

HEROES

Experience all the excitement of a gripping thriller, with an intense romance at its heart. Resourceful, true-to-life women and strong, fearless men face danger and desire - a killer combination!
8 stories per month.

DARE

Sensual love stories featuring smart, sassy heroines you'd want as a best friend, and compelling intense heroes who are worthy of them.
4 stories per month.

To see which titles are coming soon, please visit

millsandboon.co.uk/nextmonth

JOIN US ON SOCIAL MEDIA!

Stay up to date with our latest releases, author
news and gossip, special offers and discounts, and
all the behind-the-scenes action
from Mills & Boon...

 millsandboon

 millsandboonuk

 millsandboon

It might just be true love...

MILLS & BOON
True Love
Romance from the Heart

Celebrate true love with tender stories of heartfelt romance, from the rush of falling in love to the joy a new baby can bring, and a focus on the emotional heart of a relationship.

MILLS & BOON
MODERN
Power and Passion

Prepare to be swept off your feet by sophisticated, sexy and seductive heroes, in some of the world's most glamourous and romantic locations, where power and passion collide.

Julia James

PREGNANCY SCANDAL

Jennie Lucas

SHEIKH'S ROYAL BRIDE

Kim Lawrence

A WEDDING ITALIAN'S DEMAND

Sharon Kendrick

the SHEIKH'S SECRET BABY